D0394991

Person or Persons Unknown

Also by Bruce Alexander

BLIND JUSTICE

MURDER IN GRUB STREET

WATERY GRAVE

PERSON OR PERSONS UNKNOWN

BRUCE ALEXANDER

G. P. PUTNAM'S SONS
NEW YORK

G. P. PUTNAM'S SONS
Publishers Since 1838
a member of
Penguin Putnam Inc.
200 Madison Avenue
New York, NY 10016

Published simultaneously in Canada

Library of Congress Cataloging-in-Publication Data

Alexander, Bruce, date.
Person or persons unknown / by Bruce Alexander
p. cm.
ISBN 0-399-14309-2
1. Fielding, John, Sir, 1721–1780—Fiction. 2. London (England)—History—18th century—Fiction. 3. Judges—England—London—Fiction. 4. Blind—England—London—Fiction. I. Title.
PS35530.055314P47 1997 97-5399 CIP
813'.54 — dc21

Printed in the United States of America
1 3 5 7 9 10 8 6 4 2

This book is printed on acid-free paper. ♾

Book design by Julie Duquet

For Sasha Goodman

ONE

In Which I Am
Sent on an Errand
and Encounter a Homicide

A tale was told me not long ago by a sailor with whom I passed an afternoon hour in a coffee house. No common seaman he, but second officer on an East Indiaman. I, Jeremy Proctor, had that very day represented him in my professional capacity as barrister before the King's Bench. In short, I had provided a successful defense for him against a charge of criminal assault. He had been involved in a fracas in a low dram house with three men of dubious repute who claimed he had insulted them. He had left forthwith, and they had followed, demanding an apology, and they supported their demand with drawn knives and a cudgel. They advanced upon him. He had no choice but to rely upon the only weapon he had on his person—a sword. It was not a cutlass—that is, not a proper fighting sword—but rather one of the ceremonial sort, something on the order of a rapier. Yet he knew how to use it, as was evidenced by the bloody scene when a red-waistcoated constable happened by. My client had murdered none but sliced the three up so severely that each of them urgently required the ministrations of a surgeon.

Their appearance in court, all plasters and bandages, made my work difficult. The testimony against my client by the innkeeper, who painted him as a raging, blaspheming, bilious bully, made it difficult indeed. Yet I managed to cast doubt upon all four. And in my examination of the arresting constable, I established that the "victims" were well known to him as ruffians, pimps, and procurers; one of them had served a term in Newgate for a beating he inflicted upon one of his "molls." The defendant, my client, made a superb witness in his own behalf. Only once did he falter, and that was when the judge put to him a most reasonable question: "If you were as innocent in this matter as you claim to be, what were you doing in a dram house known to be a gathering place for prostitutes, panders, and others engaged in divers criminal activities?" At that, after hesitating a few moments too long, my client replied: "M'Lord, though as you say, it was known to be such a place, its reputation had not reached me. I am not a Londoner but, as you may tell from my speech, a Welshman out of Cardiff. I have but a visitor's knowledge of your great city. Let us say I blundered into the place unawares, and I greatly rue my error." His answer, while equally reasonable, left the impression with me, and I feared with judge and jury as well, that if he had told the truth, he had not told the whole truth. Nevertheless, in my plea before the jury, I did my utmost to remove any such suspicion. I argued: . . . self-defense! . . . one against three! . . . and would not any man of you in his place have defended himself the same! Et cetera. My argument prevailed. In minutes the jury returned a not guilty finding. My client and I walked out of the courtroom together. He was so delighted, not to say surprised, by the outcome that he begged that I be his guest for a midday snack. Since I had no further appearances to make that day, and since I knew a coffee house close on Old Bailey which, in addition to that divine ambrosia to which I am addicted, served all manner of buns and sweetmeats, I gladly accepted his invitation. Also, in all candor, there was a question I wished to put to him.

As we sipped and supped in the coffee house, there was little for us to talk of but the trial just concluded, so it was in no wise difficult to bring him round to the point where I might spear him with my query.

"I had but one bad moment," said I to him, "and that was when the judge asked you what you were doing in that place."

"Well . . . I . . ."

"You hesitate," said I. "You hesitated then." I fixed him with a look as severe as any judge's. "Tell me now, what *were* you doing there? Simply looking for a night's companion on the cheap? Or did deeper matter underlie it?"

And thus his tale: "Though I am third in command of a great vessel," said he, "and have greater authority and responsibility than most men twice my age, I fear I am more ignorant in the ways of the world than any London street boy half my age. The night before the incident from whose consequences you have just rescued me, I was enjoying my first night ashore. I had attended the theatre in Drury Lane. Hoping for Shakespeare, I got him—but only after the fashion of the day: *Romeo and Juliet* cut, shaped, and 'improved' to suit the merchants and their ladies.

"Alone I had taken myself to the theatre, and alone I left, more than a little offended at what had been done to the work of a poet whom I revered. I was thus in something of a snit when, quite unexpectedly, I was caught by the sleeve and stopped by a child—a girl who could not have been more than fourteen, fifteen at most. She whispered to me urgently about needing someplace to sleep. I was struck at once by her air of innocence and, I confess, by her beauty. She seemed at the very limit of her endurance, quite desperate, you see. I asked if she were hungry. 'Oh yes, sir,' said she. 'I have not ate proper in ever so long.' That being the case, I offered to take her with me to an eating place nearby, which had been recommended to me. Her face and hands were clean, and her clothes were not shabby. They did not turn us away, though I did note we were put off in a corner, quite out of sight of the rest.

"We dined well on beef, and we talked—ah, how we talked! When she learned from me that I was an officer on an East Indiaman, she would hear everything of that land which is here so little known yet so much discussed. I told of the riches of maharajahs, of rides on elephants, and hunts for tigers. Questions she had in abundance and was so filled with wonder at my stories that her mouth quite hung open in amazement. This somehow made her all the more appealing—in a childish way, of course. Yet I confess that as we sat and talked, I fell half in love with her. I am a man of sentiment, sir, and not ashamed to admit it. Recall, too, that I had just attended a performance of *Romeo and Juliet* which, however travestied, could not have failed to affect me.

"Thus, I found myself quite at her mercy when, having inquired into her situation, I was told a most dreadful tale of woe. She said she had come to London not long before from Scarborough—a long journey, to be sure—to care for an ailing aunt. The woman soon died, leaving the girl at the hands of the aunt's creditors. They came and seized all that might have been sold to pay for a return coach to Scarborough. Fearing those vultures would then come after her and rob her of her own belongings, the girl sought lodging in a respectable house and went to look for work. Finding nothing and overstaying her ability to pay, she had been locked out of her lodgings that very morning. Her clothes and a few trinkets her aunt had given her in remembrance were there in her satchel—all that she owned. There at table she began weeping. I realized I was in a position to take advantage of her state, yet I would not be a seducer, especially not of one I judged to be so young and innocent. And so, having paid the bill for our dinners, I gave her what I had left and told her to put up in a hostelry that night, and the next evening we would meet, and I would give her all that she would need to settle what she owed at the lodging house and pay her coach fare back to Scarborough. She gave me the name of that very dram house where the trouble was to occur, and said it was near her lodging house. Kissing my hand in gratitude, she thanked me a thousand times over. I sent her away in a hackney coach.

"Next evening, she was not there, but in her place were the three you met in court. They demanded the money I had brought for her, declared they would deliver it to her. I knew them for what they are—pimps, blackguards—and called them so. Far from being insulted, they smirked at that and followed me out, demanding not an apology but the money I had promised her. I was sure at that point that they had threatened her, perhaps done her harm to force from her the reason for our meeting—and so I did punish them with my sword. But, having had time to reflect upon it, I now understand that she was an active player in the game. Whether her agents or her masters, they were acting upon information freely given by her. It was she, after all, a trollop in innocent disguise, who had named the meeting place, which was as the judge described it. Having thus brought me there meant that she had planned it all."

In one sense only did the tale told by the young merchant officer baffle me. "Why did you not tell the whole story to the judge?" I asked him. "Indeed, had you told it to the magistrate in the beginning you would never have been brought to trial."

"Early on, I sought to protect her," said he. "Then, realizing her leading role in the charade, I was ashamed that I had been gulled. I was simply too chagrined to use the whole truth in my own defense."

"Young man," said I, for I was, at forty-two, near twenty years his senior, "you must never feel embarrassment because of your own good and generous nature. Nor should you harden your heart, for next time the tale told you may be true, and the innocence you perceive may be as real as can be. So I was once advised by one wiser than me, and so I advise you now."

We parted but a short time later. I know not whether he has thought upon what I said to him since, nor whether he will much in the future. But I have thought upon it powerfully and oft, for it brought back to my memory in clearest detail one of the bloodiest and most troubling matters ever to come to the diligent attention of Sir John Fielding.

Sir John, Magistrate of the Bow Street Court and chief of the Bow Street Runners, was to me in my youth part master, part father, and something between a hero and a god. We had met when I, an orphan, had been brought before him in his court, falsely accused of thievery. Seeing through the perjured testimony of my accusers, he sent them away with a stern warning, made me a ward of the court, and eventually took me into his household. Starting at age thirteen, I lived under his protection, did whatever work Lady Fielding asked of me about our living quarters, and aided him whenever and however I could. Though blind, he required little direct assistance in his daily routine. However, in certain criminal inquiries he undertook as magistrate I was able to be of more direct help to him, or so he often assured me.

Of all such inquiries, none frustrated him more, nor caused greater panic in the Covent Garden section, which was home to us, than the one I am about to describe. That this matter also caused me some personal pain you may already have inferred.

It was then 1770, a full twenty-seven years past as I write this. Yet I recall the day it began, even now, as one on which I was kept hopping at errands and tasks of every description. Annie Oakum, who had taken Mrs. Gredge's place as cook in our household (and performed the job far better), asked me that morning to accompany her on her buying trip to Covent Garden. I was then fifteen and grown to a husky lad, but my strength was taxed on our return, for she had bought potatoes, apples, and carrots to last the month—and I was her beast of burden. No sooner back than Lady Fielding fell upon me, all excited, and bade me off to the post to pick up a letter just arrived from her son, Tom, a midshipman on duty in the Mediterranean (all fleet mail was coached up from Portsmouth). No doubt inspired by his description of the shining palaces of Constantinople, which he had but recently seen firsthand, she set me to work immediately making our own little palace shine a bit brighter. Instructing me to scrub the stairs from ground floor up to my attic eyrie, she left for the Magdalene Home for Penitent Prostitutes, whose operation she oversaw, with my assurances that the task would be completed upon her return.

It was not. A request was sent me from below that I present myself to Sir John, who had for me an urgent errand to perform. My duties to Sir John superseded all others. Yet had I been given a choice in the matter, I should just as eagerly have set bucket and brush aside and hastened to his chambers. I delighted in his eccentric nature, by turns grave and witty; I liked well his errands, for they invariably sent me out into the great world, which I was so keen to know; and finally, though I tried to keep it hid, I had come to look upon domestic work as somewhat beneath me.

In any case, I wasted no time but made straight for his door and rapped stoutly upon it. Invited inside, I found Mr. Marsden, the court clerk, at his side. A letter had just been dictated. Having folded it right sharp, Mr. Marsden was in the act of applying wax and marking it with the magistrate's seal.

"Ah, Jeremy, you, is it?" said Sir John. "Come take a seat. This will be ready for you in a moment."

"Less than a moment," said Mr. Marsden, "for it is now ready for delivery." He slipped a corner of the letter under the fingers of Sir John's right hand. Receiving Sir John's thanks, he gave me a nod as he departed.

"Sit down in any case, Jeremy," said Sir John. "I want you to know the contents of the letter so that you will better understand the special instructions I shall give you."

"Yes, Sir John." I took one of two chairs opposite his desk.

"Sir Thomas Cox has just died."

I knew the name in a vague way. It seemed to me proper to make some remark in comment, and so I did my ignorant best: "I had not known he was ill."

At that he rumbled forth a deep laugh. "He was not ill, not unless old age itself be a disease. No, he was eighty-seven years old—fourscore years and seven—long past the time most may hope for. I should applaud him for his long life had he the good grace to retire five years ago or more. He was, though neither you nor others may have known, Coroner for the City of Westminster. Indeed, there was no reason why you should have known. He had not convened a jury and held an inquest during the last five years, yet he was loath to resign his commission and what it paid him. And so he went from year to year promising to resume his official duties as soon as he was able."

"And he was never again able," said I. "Who then performed those duties?"

"Officially, no one. In effect, I did." His fingers drummed lightly upon the letter beneath his hand. "Coroner, you see, is a very old office which was created to ease man's ignorance of death. The coroner was empowered to convene a jury; he then served as a sort of judge. Together they were to return a finding on the cause of any suspicious death—accident or murder, natural causes or poisoning, and so on. Well, in any practical manner, an experienced magistrate, or even a constable, can determine that. If we find an entire household chopped to pieces—as we did not all that long ago in Grub Street—then we know, by God, that murder has been committed. The only inquiry in recent memory where some effort was made to disguise the nature of the crime was the Goodhope affair. And the exact cause of death became a matter for which medical advice was needful."

"And which Mr. Gabriel Donnelly provided."

"Precisely. And that brings me to this letter here before me. I received notification this morning of Sir Thomas's death from the Lord Chief Justice. He acknowledged that in any true sense the position of Coroner of the City of Westminster had been vacant for five years but requested me to reinstitute formal coroner's proceedings, with jury and all, until such time as a new and permanent coroner might be appointed. He means me, in other words, to perform both as coroner and as magistrate for an unspecified length of time."

"Can you do so much, Sir John?" I asked.

"Oh, I expect I can," said he. "I've had Mr. Marsden look up the procedures and read them to me, and they are simple enough. Nevertheless, I know how the Lord Chief Justice and his kith handle such appointments, and so long as a matter has been given temporary attention, they are pleased to let it run on indefinitely just so. I have no intention of allowing them to do that in this case. And so, I have set forth conditions. No need to go into them now. What you must know, however, is that these conditions are set out in this letter. Therefore I ask you, Jeremy, to put it directly into the hand of the Lord Chief Justice; if he is not there, then you must wait for him. My letter requires an immediate response—to wit, that he agrees or does not agree to my conditions. Let him write so on my letter—Mr. Marsden informs me that he left room aplenty for just such a brief reply. The point is, you must wait for that, as well. Be insistent. Be a pest, if you must. But bring back a reply."

"I shall, Sir John."

"Good lad." He held the sealed letter out to me.

And yet I hesitated as I took it. "There is but one thing," said I.

"Oh?"

"I have been scrubbing stairs up above and am not dressed proper for a visit to the Lord Chief Justice—that is, since I may have to wait for him."

"I do not quite understand."

"The Lord Chief Justice's butler will not admit me unless I am dressed in my best."

"Oh, he will not, will he? Well . . ." In this, he sounded an aggressive note. Then, after a pause, he ended in a more conciliatory manner. "Indeed, hmmm, perhaps then you had better change your clothes. Though, I confess I do not like the idea of butlers dictating dress. I do not like the idea of butlers at all. But do be quick about it. I should like this settled as swiftly as possible."

With the best of intentions, I set out a short time later for the residence of William Murray, Earl of Mansfield, the Lord Chief Justice of the King's Bench in Bloomsbury Square.

To my own mind, I looked quite the young gentleman as I turned down New Broad Court. A sudden spurt of growth in the spring had made necessary a new suit of clothes. My Lady Fielding bought quite as wisely and generously for me as she had for her son, Tom, mixing ready-made with cast-offs of good quality—even more generous, indeed, for she had purchased two pairs of ready-made breeches for me, the second of darker and more durable stuff that I might have them for quotidian wear. But as with Tom before me, my great prize was my coat—bottle-green it was, with white trim, and as the seller declared, "Barely worn by him for who it was bespoke." Who would not feel a proper London gallant in such a coat?

I had chosen this route in particular, intending to see one on whom I had lately come to dote. I knew her by her Christian name only, and that, she said, was Mariah. I doubt she knew my name at all, though I had given it her. Yet she met so many men each day, talked with them all, had more intimate congress with some—how could she be expected to remember one who would offer her neither money nor clever chit-chat in the mode of the day, but only dumb adulation and tongue-tied fascination?

It was no more than two weeks ago that I first noticed her. I had stared across a narrow street at her, quite taken by her dark beauty—yet not by that alone, for I was struck direct by the notion that I had seen her before. Oh, I might have done, of course. London was then near as large as it is today, a city of a million or so inhabitants. I knew her to be a girl of the streets, from the way she stood and sought to capture the attention of men passing by. It seemed such as she were without number on this side of the Thames, and most of them right here in and around Covent Garden. Yet the sense of recognition I felt came not, I was sure, from some passing glimpse. No, I felt as if I knew her, in a manner of speaking, from a time much earlier. What was it? When was it?

She was often in New Broad Court, and sometimes nearby in Drury Lane. I had ventured to speak to her once or twice—no, indeed it was thrice. The first time I asked her name, and she gave it readily enough. Yet when I thanked her and walked on, unable to think of another word to say, she called after me, not so much in anger as in annoyance. Hearing her name had done nothing to stir my memory. On the second occasion, I addressed her by name, told her my own, and asked in a great stammer if, perchance, I had known her from some earlier occasion. She answered right saucy that she was aware of no such occasion but that she was easily known and that such would cost me a shilling only. That stopped me short. I blurted that I had not so much, which was a lie, wished her a good day, and all but ran away.

The third occasion had been only a day past. I sought her out because I had at last had some clue of that earlier meeting, hardly more than the passing glimpse I had previously dismissed. It had come to me as in a dream, a reverie of entertainments past in Covent Garden. I would ask her but one question, and then I could be certain. Yet when I sought the opportunity and approached her at her usual place, she recognized me at a distance from my earlier attempts to converse and turned away most petulant. She walked swiftly up Drury Lane as I followed in pursuit. Then she came to a fellow of about my size, though a bit my senior in years. Whispering to him, she turned back and pointed in my direction, and then she hurried on. He, however, came straight at me, blocking my way on the walk. He accused me of "bovvering the young lady" and advised me to "shove my trunk" in the opposite direction. In order to assist me, he grabbed at my shoulders and would have pushed me back, had I allowed it. But with a swift movement of my own, I broke his hold on my shoulders with my forearms, and in the bargain, threw him off balance. He staggered back a few paces. We stood there so, each taking the measure of the other, and I looking beyond him in vain for Mariah; she had disappeared in the crowd of pedestrians on Drury Lane, or perhaps ducked into a shop along the way. Passers-by had halted, sensing the sort of acrimony in the air that might lead to pugilistic diversion. We left them unsatisfied. I must have relaxed perceptibly in disappointment when I found that Mariah was no longer in sight, because for whatever reason he turned round of a sudden and walked away. I did the same, ignoring the groans of the bystanders at their lost entertainment. Sir John had laid upon me a strict injunction against tussling in the streets, and quite right was he to do so. It would not be proper for one under his protection to disturb the peace in so blatant a manner.

And so, as I left Bow Street for Bloomsbury Square late in the afternoon in question, it is true I chose a path that might lead me near Mariah. But I had determined only to look upon her as I passed and had accordingly chosen the side of the street opposite the one on which it was her custom to take her place. She had offended me with her pettishness—running away, as she had, then siccing that bullyboy on to me. Who was he? What was he to her? If Mariah had no desire to speak to me, then I certainly had none to speak with her. Yet one last look might confirm the memory I had of a Sunday afternoon two years past, of a troupe of tumblers, a girl younger than myself, more agile and graceful than all the rest. Was it she? How was I to know if I could not view her one more time? Mariah was nowhere to be seen.

But indeed she saw me.

As I walked down one side the street scanning the other I felt a hand at my sleeve and a sudden tug. I looked round sharp, ready to defend myself and found her half hidden in a doorway.

"Mariah!" said I.

"You!" said she, quite simultaneous.

Then nothing for a moment as we regarded one another in surprise.

"You look ver' gran' today," said she.

She spoke with uncertainty, in such a way as to suggest that she spoke another language better than English. That, too, agreed with my memory.

"These are my good clothes," said I, "indeed they are my best." Then I added, hoping basely to impress her: "I am on my way to Bloomsbury Square to deliver a letter to the Lord Chief Justice of the King's Bench."

"You work for him?"

"No, Sir John Fielding is my master. He is Magistrate of the Bow Street Court."

"Ah, I have heard of him. He is a big man, yes? He send everyone to Newgate."

"No, he sends them to the Old Bailey for trial. *Then* they are sent to Newgate—or to Tyburn." Would she understand such a distinction?

"Mmmm. Tyburn!" She grabbed her throat, closed her eyes, and stuck out her tongue. "I go there once to watch them hang. Never again! It's 'orrible."

"I'm sure it is. I've never been."

Then an awkward moment. My mind went utterly blank as I looked upon her. Her hair shone lustrous black in the afternoon sun. Her eyes were near as dark. They seemed to narrow a bit. Was it suspicion, or was she merely reassessing?

"I was mean to you before. I am sorry."

She did seem sorry, it was true, though she offered no explanation for her conduct. I wanted to ask the identity of the fellow she had sent to block my way. I wanted to ask why she had done so. But I asked neither. I simply nodded, as if to say that I accepted her apology.

"There is something I wished to ask you."

She smiled most pretty. "And what you wish to ask?"

"I've had the feeling since first I set eyes upon you that I had met you before—and in a sense I believe I did. Tell me, when you were younger, did you work with a troupe of tumblers . . . acrobats?"

"*Saltimbancos? Acrobati? Si!*—yes, they were my brothers and my father. They . . . they go back to Italy."

"And they left you here?" The very idea seemed quite monstrous to me. They had, in effect, orphaned the girl, one of their own blood.

Yet as I thought these dark thoughts, her face underwent a sad and remarkable change. It seemed to crumple before my very eyes. She turned away, but I saw that she was weeping. It quite broke my heart to see her so. I dug into my pocket and found the kerchief Annie had washed for me. I pressed it into Mariah's hand. It took a minute or two of dabbing and blowing, but she managed at last to gain control of herself.

"No, not so," she said. "I was to blame. I was ver' foolish. I said I would not go to Italy. I would stay in England. They said I must do what they say—but the night before they left I ran away and hid with those I thought were my friends." Then she added most bitterly, "They prove' to be false friend."

"When was this?" I asked. "When did all this happen?"

"A month pas'."

"And you have been on the streets ever since?"

"No, first I was in a house—you understand? I escape'. Even this is better." Then, of a sudden, she pulled away and forced a smile. "But we talk about this after, yes?"

"After?"

"What a beautiful coat this is!" She fingered the material tenderly. "That Sir John, he mus' pay you well for you to have such a coat. But I tell you, because I like you and because you remember me from before, I give you a good price—two shillings only. Come. I have a place near. We go, eh?"

"No," said I firmly. "As I told you, I have a letter to deliver to the Lord Chief Justice."

"Ah, yes, the famous letter." Which was said a bit ironic. "You do that after, eh?"

"No, I must go." But, reaching deep into one of the capacious pockets of the coat, I pulled out a shilling and put it in her palm. "Take this for your time. Perhaps we can talk again?"

She took the shilling greedily and tucked it in her bodice between her dainty bubs. Ah, how I envied that shilling!

"For a shilling we talk anytime—no, I make a joke, eh? Yes, we talk. I like you. And next time you come with me, yes?"

"Goodbye."

"Goodbye, and thank you. *Grazia! Molte grazie!*"

Difficult as it was to pull myself from her, I hastened away, joining the multitude on Drury Lane, swimming against the tide of humanity, pressing on to Hart Street, which would lead me straight into Bloomsbury Square. It was not far. I had not dallied long. And I was sure I had made up for some minutes lost by my great hurry to get there.

When, however, I reached my destination, I saw that I had dallied too long, or perhaps not hurried quite fast enough, for what should I see but a coach-and-four pulling away from his door, unmistakably that of William Murray, the Earl of Mansfield, the Lord Chief Justice. I watched it go, standing there on the walk, as if wishing might bring it back. At last I saw it disappear down Great Russell Street, and I turned to the door and banged upon it with the heavy, hand-shaped knocker. It was near a minute before the butler arrived in full livery. As I had grown taller he seemed a less imposing figure. Nevertheless, his chill manner would have turned back a regiment of foot.

"I have a letter to the Lord Chief Justice from Sir John Fielding," said I, brandishing it as a constable might wave a warrant.

"He has just departed." The butler put out his hand to accept the letter.

"I have instructions to put it in his hands direct and wait for a reply."

"He may not be back for quite some time."

"Nevertheless."

"So be it then." He began to ease the door shut.

"Uh . . . may I wait inside?" I asked, damning him for a black-hearted villain, for making me beg. "Perhaps on that bench in the vestibule?"

He turned and looked at it, then looked back at me—looked very closely, in fact, scrutinizing me from top to bottom.

Then said he: "Certainly."

Stepping aside he held the door wide for me as I entered and took my place on the bench. Though it was padded, it had no back. In truth, it was not wonderfully comfortable, yet it was ever so much better than standing like some vagrant outside the door.

"Thank you," said I to the butler, ever mindful of my manners.

"Don't mention it," said he, closing the door.

Then, turning his back on me, he started away, stopped, and turned to look again.

"Young man," said he, "that is a very handsome coat."

I could scarce believe my own ears. I stammered and stuttered and barely managed to call out my thanks before he disappeared down the hall. In the two years I had been trotting between Bow Street and Bloomsbury Square I had not known the butler to unbend previously—not once, not in the slightest. This must indeed be a considerable coat to awaken admiration in one by nature so cold.

It had so raised me in Mariah's estimation that she had doubled her price. Ah yes, of course, as I sat there alone and prepared myself for a long wait, my thoughts fled swiftly back to her. I called up the image of her as we had talked but minutes before in the doorway. There was beauty in that face of hers, to be sure, but there was true emotion, life, and good humor as well. Were all Italian girls so? No, I was convinced that of all in the world she was unique. So is it when one is young.

As best I could, I summoned up a much dimmer memory of her from two years past. On a Sunday afternoon I had stood in a crowd assembled in the piazza and watched a troupe of acrobats and tumblers performing quite impossible feats. Most impressive of all was the small black-haired girl who climbed to the top of a human pyramid, posed triumphantly for a long moment as the crowd applauded, then dove headlong to the mats far below. She had tumbled, bounced to her feet, then been applauded even more enthusiastically. Pence and tuppence pieces were thrown down by the crowd in appreciation. Scrambling about, she gathered them up, and when she passed near me, I tossed her a shilling, one of three I had left in my pocket. She saw from whence it came, fixed me with her dark eyes and kissed the coin with her sweet lips. Then she called her thanks to me in a strange tongue, perhaps the very same phrase she had used some minutes ago when we had parted, the one that sounded a bit like "moldy grass." Ah, how that touched me! Even more was I moved by her gesture of blessing my gift with a kiss, and most of all by the look in her eyes; with it she recognized me, in spite of my young years, as a person of consequence. For weeks afterwards I returned to Covent Garden on Sundays, hoping to see her again and make her acquaintance—all to no avail. I later learned that such performers move constantly from fair to fair and town to town. There could be no telling where they might be.

As I sat in the vestibule, stretching my legs and twiddling my thumbs, I listened to the sounds of the Lord Chief Justice's household, as they came to me from near and far. It appeared to be empty of all but servants, yet in such a house as this, larger even than Black Jack Bilbo's, there must be an army of maids and servers and footmen about. The sounds I heard were, near as I could tell, those of cleaning. A maid called for a footman's help in moving furniture, and there were soon bumps and thumps as he complied. A ditty was hummed up above, perhaps to make the work go faster. The house, empty of its master and mistress, was fair humming with activity.

And I? I simply sat alone with my thoughts, and my thoughts were all of Mariah. There was no doubt of her situation. Alone in London, deceived into separating from her family, she had been forced to prostitute herself in order to survive. How long could she last? When first I laid eyes upon her two years past she had seemed younger than me, and now she looked a bit older. Give her some time on the street, and she would appear very much older—and not by the artifice of rouge and paint. No, if she followed the course described to me by Mr. Bilbo, the depredations of disease and gin would take their toll. While I might daydream an exchange of loving kisses with her, I would not allow myself even to imagine taking her in a more carnal embrace—though it were easily bought, and I had the price. Though I had great fear of disease, and every day had examples before me of the ravages of the pox, even more did I fear besmirching the tender affection I felt for Mariah with base brutish desires. Any man on the street could take her for two shillings—or was it just one? Only I could give her . . .

What was it I could give her? Was it love, this overflowing of attention, this constant doting upon her which seemed to have possessed me so completely? In a way I liked it not, for I seemed to have lost mastery over my own mind, and I, let me assure you, reader, had always considered myself a serious lad. Yet it was so pleasant simply to sit and wallow in thoughts of Mariah and so easy to do just that—for the little good it did.

For yet again, what could I give her? With my whole heart I wished to alter her situation, to make it possible for her to leave the streets. Yet how could I do that? I was but fifteen years of age; I had no money of my own, no regular employment. In my dependent state—I was an orphan, after all—I could do no more than wish that I could help her. Perhaps I had chosen wrong when Sir John was so eager to have me enter the printing trade; with all that I had learned from my father and my facility at setting type, I might by now have been a journeyman, able to live independent, even perhaps able to marry. But Sir John's great example blinded me to practical considerations, encouraged me to elevate my ambitions to the law, perhaps too high for such as me.

Ah, what I could do with a bit of money! It would not take a great deal, really—just enough to pay for passage for two to America. There I could start a new life for Mariah and me. There was opportunity for all in the great city of Philadelphia, or perhaps Boston or Baltimore. These were magical names to me, as they were to many young Englishmen of that time, names put on hope, symbols of optimism to stir the imagination. And indeed they stirred mine, for what else had I to do as I waited but spin fantasies of what might be for Mariah and me in the American colonies. There were adventures in the printing trade, perhaps even a career in law, speeches to be given, important documents to be signed, and in all these dreams Mariah was at my side, the very model of a wife for a personage such as myself; I would dress her in silks and laces; we would have children and a great house to keep us in. Or perhaps I should be a farmer—land was to be had for the taking out there in the wilderness; all I should need would be an axe, a plow, and some seed—and Mariah; together we would make our way, braving dangers, aiding and being aided by our Iroquois neighbors.

Thus did I pass the time, sitting alone there in the antechamber of that great house. I lost all sense of the passing minutes; whole hours slipped by (two, in fact, and the better part of a third). So deep was I in my thoughts and fantasies that I barely noticed when the butler returned, clack-clack-clacking down the long hall, until he was near upon me, illuminating my darkened corner with the candelabrum he bore. I jumped to my feet.

"He has returned," said he, placing the candelabrum on a small table.

And as he said it, I heard the rumble and clop of the coach-and-four as it came to a halt outside the door. How had the butler known? Had there been a lookout posted in the upper rooms?

He threw open the door with great authority, a "Welcome, my Lord," and a proper bow. I took a place suitably back from the entrance as the Lord Chief Justice came bustling in. Rewarding the butler with his hat and stick, the Earl of Mansfield gave me a look and grunted.

"Sir John Fielding's boy," said the butler.

"I recognize him." Then to me: "Have you a letter for me, boy?"

"I have, my Lord." And I stepped forward and handed it to him with a bow of my own.

He took it and ripped it open at the seal. He stepped over to the candelabrum to read it. "Smithers," said he to the butler, "do let us have some light in here. Lady Mansfield will be home soon, and she hates coming home to a darkened house, even more than I."

"I'll attend to it immediate, my Lord," said the butler.

And off he went as his master gave his attention to the letter.

"Oh, he makes conditions, does he? Well!"

The Lord Chief Justice continued to read, mumbling to himself to the end of the letter. Then he refolded it and offered it to me.

"You may tell Sir John that I shall do my utmost to see that his conditions are met. More I cannot promise."

I kept my hands steadfastly at my side—in effect, refusing to accept the letter.

"Sir John asked in particular that you make a reply in writing, my Lord. He said there was room at the bottom of the page."

"Oh? Indeed? Wants something he can wave under my nose sometime in the future, does he?"

"If you say so, sir."

"I just did." He sighed. "Oh, all right, come along then."

He picked up the candelabrum and led the way into the library nearby. Standing at the great desk, he took a pen, dipped it, and scrawled his message. He signed his name with a flourish and handed the letter to me; this time I took it from him with thanks.

"I wrote it down as I said—I'll do all in my power." He waved his hand at me in a dismissive gesture. "On your way, boy."

With a bow, I left him, emerging into a hall that had suddenly been transformed by the light from half a hundred candles. The butler barely noticed me as I let myself out.

It was near dark outside. The streetlamps had been lit all round Bloomsbury Square. I chose a different route, leaving by Southampton Street, then down Little Queen Street, and so on. Though it was longer so, and I was late, the way circled those streets where I might have encountered Mariah. I had no wish to see her in conversation with some young blade, and even less to catch her marching off arm in arm with one to some place of assignation.

The streets were filled, as they always were at that late time of day, with folk leaving their places of employment for their places of rest. Yet among them was one I spied who was then just on his way to work. And that was the one-armed Constable Perkins. He was just ahead when I turned upon Great Queen Street, easily recognized from the rear with his coat-sleeve pinned below the elbow. During the past year, since the time we had gone out together in search through low Thames River dives for a disappeared witness, we had become fast friends. I admired the proud way he conducted himself in spite of his affliction; he had much good sense to offer and had an attitude of hope and good cheer that no two-armed man of the Bow Street Runners could match.

"Hi, Mr. Perkins," I called, running to catch him up.

He turned, warily and swiftly—the man seemed to be always on his guard—and then, recognizing me, he relaxed and allowed himself to smile.

"Ah, Jeremy, it's you, is it? I daresay we be goin' in the same direction. Would you care to walk with me?"

"Certainly I would," said I. "And how are you this good evening?"

"No better and no worse than I was the last—which is to say in no bad fettle at all." We commenced a-pacing side by side. "And where was you so late in the day?"

"To deliver a letter for Sir John to the Lord Chief Justice, and then to wait near three hours on a reply."

"Ah, well, one must always wait on such a man as that. He must live in a grand house, he must."

"Oh, he does, grandest I've seen—in Bloomsbury Square." Having said that, an idea struck me of a sudden. "Mr. Perkins, I've a question to ask."

"Ask away, Jeremy."

"Do you think I might be made one of the Bow Street Runners?"

"You mean sometime in the future?"

"No, I mean now—soon. You and I know, as do most, that Sir John has been given authority to enlist new men in the Runners."

"True, or so I've heard."

"Why could I not be one? I know the duties. I know Westminster and the City."

"Well, you're a bit young."

"Constable Cowley was taken on when he was eighteen or nineteen, something thereabouts."

"You've twice the brains he has, and that's for certain sure. Still and all . . ."

He thought upon it, saying nothing for a space. And as he thought, he turned us onto Drury Lane, and so my plan to circle wide round Mariah had thus gone to naught.

"I thought you was for the law," said Constable Perkins at last. "That's some higher than walkin' about with a club. I, for one, would hate to see you lose such a goal in life."

"Well, I need not," said I. "I could read the law in my spare time, perhaps. It might take a bit longer, but—"

"In case you have not noticed, Jeremy, us Runners have precious little time to ourselves." He threw me a sharp glance. "And let me be honest with you in this. I'm just not sure certain you've the taste for blood. You're a plucky lad, no doubt of it, for I've seen you rise to the occasion. But on the streets at night you must be a bit angry at all times. Carry your anger and your suspicion with you, and let that be your shield. If you be challenged, you must be willing to break a head, even if the cause be slight. Only so can you win respect from the great band of blackguards who roam these precincts at night; only so can you keep it. You, I fear, would try to use reason with such." He paused, as if considering some plan, some course of action. "But . . ."

We had turned down New Broad Court at its narrowest part, exactly where I had earlier spoken with Mariah. In spite of my intentions I found myself looking for her. She was nowhere to be seen.

"But what, Mr. Perkins? What was it you would say?"

"It was this, young Jeremy, if you was to come by, I could teach you a thing or two. Whether or not you continue with this notion of joining the Runners—which I do heartily advise against—it would do good for you to know how to handle yourself better. You're sometimes called upon to go out of a night, and you ought—"

"Murder! Foul murder!"

The cry came from so close it seemed to have been shouted into our ears.

"Murder!"

Mr. Perkins and I whirled about as one, searching out the source of the alarum, but what we saw, rather, was a great swarm of people behind us pressing to get through a narrow passage. A few steps brought us to them. He led the way, throwing them right and left, pushing with his club, though not wielding it in a harmful way. While all the while he chanted: "One side, one side. I'm a constable. Make way for the law!" And for the most part, that was what they did, flattening against the rough brick of the passage, bowing to the authority of Mr. Perkins's crested club. As we came to the end of the dark way, we found that it opened up into a small space, or perhaps an alley, where doors were visible, and stairs led up to floors above. From beneath the stairs two legs projected out of petticoats and a skirt. Could it be Mariah? No, the body was too corpulent, the skirt was of another color. A small man tugged and heaved at the ankles to pull the corpus out from the stairs while his female companion grabbed at the purse tied round the waist.

"Let go that purse," snarled Mr. Perkins, "lest you take a clout from this club. And you"—to her partner—"drop her feet, or take one yourself. Both of you, stand over there, and don't think to sneak away."

They did as told, though most reluctant, as the crowd behind us murmured against them; "Vultures," they were called, "Corpus robbers," and so on.

"We was only thinkin' to put a name on her," said the woman who had been tugging at the purse. "We thought they might be a letter inside or such."

"So you say," said Mr. Perkins, "but we'll let Sir John be the judge of that."

"She could be alive," said the man, a queer-looking rat-faced fellow. "She's warm to the touch."

"Then we must disturb the body thus much. Jeremy, pull her full out from the stairs."

I leaped to the task, not in the least repelled by it so long as Constable Perkins was there watching me. I pulled hard.

"Now, which of you put out the cry of murder?" he asked.

One in the crowd, not by any means in the first rank, raised his hand. "'Twas me," he said, "I did it."

"You come over here and stand by me."

By then I had worked the body out from its resting place. It was true there was still warmth in her limbs, but there was death on her face. Her lips were pulled back in a grimace, and her eyes, open wide, stared up and saw nothing. Young she was and might, in a different circumstance, have been judged pretty. Her sallow cheeks were brightened with two large spots of rouge.

"What think you, Jeremy, alive or dead?"

"Dead, to all appearances, but I see no wound."

"Marks on the throat from strangulation?"

"None."

"Best take her wrist and feel for a heartbeat."

That confused me quite proper. "A heartbeat in her *wrist*, Mr. Perkins?"

"Never mind." He pointed his club at the ghoulish couple in a manner most threatening. "You'll stay where you are, or suffer for it."

He came over to the body, knelt and put down his club, then took the wrist in hand. "You see, Jeremy? Just here. Touch this spot with your thumb, and you can feel the blood flowing—*if* it's flowing. It ain't."

Then, throwing a wary look at the two miscreants, he returned his attention to the body. He pulled down her blouse and bodice. Her breasts, freed, flopped of their own weight. Titters and giggles arose from the watching crowd. He threw a look of disgust at those straining to see, then planted his hand over her heart. His palm came up bloody.

"There's your wound," he said, "a small one, just under the breastbone, up and into the heart. Not much blood. Death came just so." He snapped his fingers.

He grabbed up his club and jumped to his feet. Then did he address the crowd: "Now, any of you thinks you may know this poor woman, you may view her face." To me he said: "Tidy up her bubs, Jeremy. Make her decent."

I managed that as well as I might and noticed, touching her skin, that it had grown just a bit colder.

"The rest of you," continued Constable Perkins to those still crowding the passage, "I advise to leave. Sir John Fielding will be here soon, and there will be many more Runners with him. They will not take kindly to gawkers. All but those who remain for purposes of identification or to give evidence, *I order to disperse*."

Though they seemed reluctant, most began to turn away and start back down the passage.

"You've frightened them off," said I.

"And now," said Mr. Perkins, "I must send you away as well. Go fetch Sir John, Jeremy. Tell him what has happened, and when you return with him, bring some lanterns. We soon may not be able to see hereabouts without them."

I set off then, pushing through the passage, chanting something about the importance of my mission, just as Mr. Perkins had but a few minutes earlier. I squirmed past the last of them and set off down Broad Court at a run. It seemed to me that at some point along the way I caught a glimpse of Mariah, but I had neither time nor desire to make certain of that. I must to Bow Street!

TWO

In Which an Old Friend Returns and Offers His Help

Leaving in haste and in some confusion, Sir John Fielding delegated Constable Baker as messenger to inform Lady Fielding that the magistrate had been called away on urgent matters of his office.

Mr. Baker, starting away, hesitated. "Shall I give out that the matter is murder?" he asked.

"No," said his chief, "that would only upset her. Ah, but do tell her also that Jeremy is with me and will return with me. She should not, in any case, wait supper upon us." He punctuated that with a nod, and Mr. Baker hastened toward the stairs. Then, addressing the rest of us: "Now then, let us be on our way."

We were four in number. Besides Sir John and myself, Mr. Benjamin Bailey, captain of the Bow Street Runners, and young Constable Cowley accompanied us as we set off in the direction of Broad Court Street. Mr. Bailey took the lead, clearing a path for us through the pedestrians as we went; Mr. Cowley followed, and we, Sir John and I, went last of all.

Mr. Cowley turned and pointed ahead. "Here's a bit of luck, sir. There's the Raker just ahead with his wagon." I looked ahead, and there indeed he was. The Raker, a man of ill omen and ugly countenance, was the appointed collector of the indigent dead this side the river. How the citizenry did avoid him! Nor could I blame them, for with the crudely painted skull and crossbones on his wagon which was pulled by two nags quite moribund in appearance, he must have seemed the very embodiment of the death that awaits us all. Frightening tales were told of him. Even to view him was considered by some to be bad luck of the worst sort. Which explained why our side of Bow Street was so crowded and his so empty.

"Shall I tell him to wait, Sir John?" asked Mr. Cowley. "Save him a trip, it would."

"You may as well."

The young constable hied off to intercept him. By the time that he rejoined us we had started down New Broad Court and were in sight of the passage where Mr. Perkins awaited us.

"The Raker said he'd come to pick up old Josh, the beggar," said Mr. Cowley. "He keeled over dead just down from us at Russell Street."

"The old fellow with the pennywhistle?" said Sir John.

"That's the one."

"Well, you know," put in Mr. Bailey, "I can't say as I'm surprised. He ain't looked good these months past."

"That does sadden me," said Sir John. "He always had a warm greeting and made a heartfelt thank-you." Then, with a sigh: "He died swift, and that was a blessing."

We gave old Josh a respectful moment of silence as we moved on. It fell upon me to break it.

"That is it just ahead, Mr. Bailey," I called out to him. "The passage there leads back to a yard."

"Yes," said he, "I know it well enough—and from that yard back to an alley that leads to Duke's Court."

That I had not known. I avoided such dark, narrow places whenever possible.

Constable Perkins's threats to the gawking crowd had done their work. We found the passage empty, and entering the yard, we found with him but four, apart from the dead woman. He prodded two of them forward to meet Sir John. I recognized them instantly.

"Beg pardon, Sir John," said Mr. Perkins, "but I thought you might wish to dispose of these two immediate."

"Who are they?"

"Give him your names."

"Bert Talley, sir."

"Esther Jack, your Lordship. But we was just—"

"*Quiet!*" roared Mr. Perkins. "I'll tell Sir John what I saw. Only then may you speak."

"Proceed, Mr. Perkins."

"As to what I saw, that's quickly said. When Jeremy and I pushed our way through the passage, there was then a great bunch of gapers since sent off and I found these two. He was hauling the victim out from under stairs just above where she now lies. And she—she was tugging away at the purse which is tied about the victim's waist. Now, it was my opinion, and it is my opinion still, that they were caught in the act of theft; that they meant to take that purse and do a scamper down the alley. Therefore I detained them to await your judgment in the matter."

"Well presented, Mr. Perkins," said Sir John. "Now, madam, you may have your say."

"We was thinkin' only to help identify her by lookin' in her purse—a letter or somethin'."

"Was it necessary to move the corpus to do so?"

"It was, m'Lord," said the rat-faced Bert Talley. "Only her feet was sticking out from under the stairs. We heard the cry of murder, and we come running. That's how we found her. So I pulled, and by God, she was warm to the touch."

"Is that so, Mr. Perkins?"

"It is, Sir John, and so he did inform us. It was then necessary to disturb the body further to be certain the victim was not still alive."

"So they did endeavor to give some help to you in the matter?"

"In a manner of speaking, yes, sir."

"And the woman had not opened the purse?"

"No, sir, she had not, just trying to pull it free."

"Then I fear that since it is a question of intention, and that alone, we must accept their word in this. Mr. Talley and Madam Jack, you may go, but I must tell you that if either of you appear before me in the Bow Street Court, I shall remember this incident and hold it against you. Consider this fair warning."

With much nodding and hand-wringing, the two gave copious thanks and took their leave down the passage.

A conversation followed between Sir John and Constable Perkins, wherein the description of the scene, the condition of the body, and the nature of the victim's wound were discussed. Mr. Perkins gave it as his guess that the woman had not been long dead, perhaps only minutes when he and I came upon the scene of the crime.

"Is there any way to ascertain whereabouts in this yard the wound was inflicted?" asked Sir John. "She could not, I assume, have been stabbed where she was found."

"Not likely, sir. Is it important?"

"It may be. Indeed it may. Mr. Bailey? Mr. Cowley?"

The two came quickly to his side. Mr. Bailey asked Sir John's pleasure.

"Would you two examine the ground hereabouts and look for signs of a struggle? We are assuming the woman — the victim, if you will — was stabbed elsewhere. Mr. Perkins informs me she is quite corpulent, near twelve stone, so she must have been dragged to that place beneath the stairs. The yard has been tracked up a bit, I fear, but the marks of dragging a body of that size should stand out."

Mr. Cowley seemed troubled by Sir John's request. "But, sir," said he, "it's gone mighty dark. The moon's past the point where it's much help."

"Then I would advise you to use that lantern I instructed you to bring with you. I trust you did bring it along."

"Uh, yes, Sir John."

"Then light it up and get on with it. Mr. Perkins? I should like to speak with him who gave the alarum. Bring the fellow to me, would you?"

As Constable Perkins went to fetch him, Sir John leaned close to me and spoke in a low tone: "Jeremy, describe him to me, would you?"

"Certainly," said I. "He is a small man, a bit over five feet tall, though not much—less than ten stone, nearer nine—and reasonably well-dressed."

"Mmm," he grunted. "That will do. Thank you."

A moment later the man was before us. I marveled that one of his diminutive proportions could have set up such a roar.

"Tell the magistrate your name," said Mr. Perkins.

"Sebastian Tillbury, sir." He spoke up loud and clear.

"And what is your trade, Mr. Tillbury?"

"I'm an ostler, sir. I've a way with horses, if I do say so myself. And if you wish to know my place of employment, it is the Elephant and Castle on the Strand."

"Ah," said Sir John, "a very respectable inn it is indeed."

"No better address for travelers in Westminster."

"That's as may be, but tell me, Mr. Tillbury, how did you come to find the corpus of this unfortunate woman? Had you made passage through the alley from Duke's Court?"

"No, sir, that way is right dangerous near dark. I came upon her quite natural, going home, I was. I live in a room off the yard. It ain't much, but it does me. I came down the passage from Broad Court and near stumbled over her. Just her feet was sticking out from under the stairs."

"You immediately assumed murder and raised the cry. Why was that? I understand that the body was still warm."

"I thought just so because nobody would lie in such a place for a rest, no matter how drunk or tired. There is rats and all manner of vermin down under there."

"I see. Did you see or hear anyone else when you came upon her?"

"No, sir, I did not."

Then a call came from Mr. Bailey. He and Mr. Cowley had advanced in their investigation toward the perilous alley.

"What is it, Mr. Bailey?"

"We've something for you, Sir John."

"Good. Take me to them, Jeremy. And you, Mr. Tillbury, please wait a bit. We'll be through with you, directly."

At Mr. Bailey's direction we circled wide to reach them. The lantern was held high to show the way.

"What is it then, Mr. Bailey?"

"Just this, Sir John, there was no signs of dragging, and as you said, it was well trod up to those stairs where the body was found, but Constable Cowley did note that one set of footprints in the dirt was deeper than the rest."

"As would be if a man were carrying a heavy load."

"Just so, Sir John. So we tracked them back through the dirt to this spot here, which is where the alley begins and the cobblestones start. There's no following them beyond."

"I understand, but do carry on through the alley and look for any signs along the way—drops of blood, buttons, anything of the sort that might fix the exact scene of the murder."

"That we will, sir."

Together we returned, Sir John and I, to Mr. Tillbury. On our way, he did make this observation: "It sometimes happens, Jeremy, particularly in matters of arson and murder, that he who reports the crime has himself committed it. He wishes attention called to it, and believes he may push suspicion from himself by calling the alarum. I had considered this possibility with Mr. Tillbury, but I can no longer. It might just be possible for a ten-stone man to drag a twelve-stone woman, but it would be highly unlikely that so small a man could *carry* one such. I believe we may safely allow the ostler to go about his business."

He did, however, have a few last questions to offer.

"Sir," said he, touching the black silk band covering his eyes, "as you see, I have lost my power of sight. You say you have a room here. I take it that your door opens onto the yard? You have a window?"

"Yes, sir, just as you say, sir."

"How many neighbors have you?"

"Here in the yard?"

"Just so."

Mr. Tillbury thought a moment. "Well, sir, let me consider. There is the old woman lives next me. She is near blind herself, howsomever, so near-sighted is she. Then up above is a sturdy fellow named Jaggers who works as a porter at the post-coach house. I seldom sees him, though."

"Oh, why is that?"

"He works noon to midnight."

"And would consequently have been at his place of employment at the time the woman was murdered."

"I suppose he would. And then also up above, is old Joshua, the beggar—him who plays pennywhistle all round Covent Garden."

A pause then. Sir John's expression did not alter. "I regret to tell you, Mr. Tillbury, word has come to me that Joshua died today on the street. A seizure of some sort, it was."

A longer pause. "Sad I am to hear that. Him and me shared many a bottle and told many a story. But his age caught him up, I reckon. There was times of late when he could scarce struggle up the stairs." He sighed. "Perhaps it's for the best."

"Perhaps. In any case, you may go with my thanks. I would ask only that you take my young assistant here and present him to your near neighbor, the old woman, so that he might ask her a few questions. Even if she could not see, she may have heard something of importance."

"Most happy to oblige, sir."

Sir John turned to me and nodded. Then, as I started off with Tillbury, I heard the magistrate call out, "Mr. Perkins, I believe you have one more witness for me."

I should have liked to hear him question that witness, for I was always quite fascinated to listen in those situations, but I liked even better that I should be entrusted to do such work myself. It had never fallen to me thus before. I only hoped that I might extract from her some worthwhile tit-bit of information.

Tillbury led me to her door and knocked upon it.

"Some relation keeps her so, or has provided for her," said he in a low tone. "A lad from a lawyer's office comes by each month with some shillings for her—enough to pay the rent and keep her alive."

A voice came from behind the door: "Who is there?" The tone was querulous, a bit suspicious.

"'Tis Tillbury, your neighbor, Mrs. Crewton."

Something was grunted. A bolt was thrown back, and then the latch popped, and the door swung open. She stood, gaunt and wrinkled, dressed in a tattered frock once quite fashionable. Though I had no true idea of her age, had Tillbury told me she was a hundred, I should have accepted it.

"Missus," said he to her, "this young man has some questions for you."

"Is it then about the murder?"

"You knew of it, then?" I asked, trying my best to maintain a grave and severe manner in the style of Sir John.

"Of course I knew," said she. "With Tillbury here shouting it so loud, how could I not? They must have heard him clear to St. Paul's."

"Did you see anything of the crime, madam?"

"I see very little at all," said she. "I sit by the windows. Shapes pass by, mere phantasms they are. Yet what should they matter to me? I am old, you see. And at night, in the dark, I am able to see nothing at all."

"I'm . . . I'm sorry." And knowing not what else to say, I kept my silence and waited.

"Ah, but I can hear!" From her lips, that simple statement took the form of great dramatic utterance. "And often I have the power to see with my ears."

"Could you be more specific?" I asked. "What, for instance, did you hear just before Mr. Tillbury gave his cry of murder?"

"Not *just* before—let us say, not long before that I heard an argument, a most bitter disagreement it was, between a man and a woman. Her voice was shrill and strident, most disagreeable, and his, rumbling and rasping, was equally so in its way."

"And where did they come from? Were they nearby?"

"No, not nearby, yet again not so far away. Off to the right, it was, down that alley. There is an alley there, is there not, Mr. Tillbury?"

"Oh, yes, ma'am, there is. There is indeed," said he.

"And what was said between these two?" I asked.

"I did not hear words so much as voices," said she. "Him I could not understand at all. He simply rumbled on."

"And the lady?"

"She a lady? Oh, I think not, young man." She emitted a cold, mirthless laugh. "Her kind are often hereabouts for the little privacy it offers from the street. I hear them and those who give them custom doing their dirty business up against the wall."

"But what did she *say*, madam? It seems you must have heard *something*." I fear my loss of patience altered my tone somewhat. How I envied Sir John his attitude of cool persistence!

"Well, then, if you must," said she, sounding much put-upon, "there was but one phrase that I heard distinct, and it was this: 'not with the likes of you.'"

"And nothing more?"

"Nothing more that one could understand. But . . ."

"But what?"

"It was said in such a way—that is to say, her manner of speech was such . . . well, I took her to be Irish."

Having gleaned that much, I decided to leave off with my questions. I nodded to Tillbury, indicating I had done, thanked her curtly, and made to go.

"He must have been a large man," said she, muttering to herself.

"Why do you say that?" I asked.

"Simple enough. He carried her here, and tucked her under the stairs, did he not? I sat in the dark and heard all that, as well."

"Thank you again, Mrs. Crewton. You've been most helpful."

I had learned a lesson in interrogation. Thereafter I would always remember to allow the witness to have his say. She may merely have confirmed what Sir John had already concluded, yet such verification would always be welcomed by him.

I went with Mr. Tillbury the few steps to his own door and thanked him also.

Then he said: "She's a bit daft, I fear, and goes on some. But you may trust what she tells you."

As I approached Sir John, I saw to my surprise that he was alone. The woman whom he had designated his last witness was giving information to Mr. Benjamin Bailey; and he, by the light of the lantern held high by Mr. Cowley, was penciling it on a piece of paper. I wondered had she much to offer.

"Ah, Jeremy, what have you to tell? I do hope you will forgive me for sending you off to talk to that woman. It seemed to me that if she were as nearly blind as Mr. Tillbury said, I decided you would be the better interrogator. If I were to have talked to her, it would have been much like the blind leading the blind." (Thus he often joked of his affliction.)

"Sir, I welcomed the opportunity."

"Good of you to say so. But what did she say?"

I told him in far less time than Mrs. Crewton had taken to tell me the phrase she had heard from the victim's lips and her suspicion that the woman was Irish. I added that though she had been unable to see the murderer, she had heard him track by and place the body under the stairs.

"Excellent!" said Sir John. "You've done well, Jeremy, for all that you learned from her tallies with what I have heard from the woman with whom I just spoke. Her name is Maggie Pratt. She was well acquainted with the victim, whose name she gave us as Teresa O'Reilly. Thus the victim is indeed Irish, as your Mrs. Crewton guessed. The Pratt woman—she is hardly more than a girl—tells us she saw Teresa O'Reilly in conversation in Duke's Court with a soldier, a red-coated Grenadier Guard from the Tower not long before Mr. Tillbury discovered the body and gave the alarum. It could well be that the victim, pursued by the soldier, left Duke's Court and proceeded down the alley where the two had their final altercation. What was it that was heard by your witness, Jeremy? 'Not with the likes of you.' That, too, fits well, for the Irish—particularly the rural Irish—have no love for red-coated English soldiers. She, perhaps from some personal experience, may have had some special animosity against them, may have refused him, said something of the sort your Mrs. Crewton overheard. The soldier, presumably drunk, may then have stabbed her in anger. And having stabbed her, hid the body, hoping at least to delay the discovery. You see, Jeremy? It all fits right snug, does it not?"

"Indeed it does," said I.

"Maggie Pratt has consented to review the troops at the Tower on the morrow," said Sir John. "She seems to look forward to it, rather, for she says she got a good look at the fellow and would have justice done."

Having delivered the letter which I had taken in dictation from Sir John, I returned from the Tower of London in a baffled and uncertain state, unable to give absolute assurance that it would truly reach him to whom it was addressed that same night. I had certainly tried my best. Walking boldly to the gate to which I'd been directed, I had asked to be admitted that I might deliver a letter to Captain Conger, acting colonel of the regiment. The guard at the gate told me then in a most indifferent manner to come back with it next day. I had then said I would not, for the letter was from none other than Sir John

Fielding, Magistrate of the Bow Street Court. He remained unimpressed until I shouted loud as I could that a woman had been murdered, and a Grenadier Guard was suspected. That brought out the corporal of the guard who, though he would not admit me, did solemnly promise to put the letter in the hands of Captain Conger. I left then, knowing I could do no better than that, convinced also that had I worn the red waistcoat and carried the crested club of a Bow Street Runner, I should have been given direct admittance to the presence of the acting colonel.

So there was I, returned at last to Number 4 Bow Street. Though I was embarrassed by my failure to get beyond the Tower gate, I felt that Sir John would surely understand—as indeed he did. And I was quite famished, having eaten nothing but an apple or two since breakfast. Yet a surprise awaited me above which delayed my dinner further.

I waved my greeting to Mr. Baker, keeper of the strong room, as I made for the stairs.

He called to me: "Sir John has a visitor."

"Oh? Who is that?"

"You know the fellow better than I . . . a medico . . . Irish. He helped on that Goodhope matter."

"Mr. Donnelly!"

"That's the name. I sent him direct upstairs, for I remembered he was well known to the Beak."

"And to me, as well," said I exuberantly, as I jumped upon the stairs and started up them two at a time.

Indeed Gabriel Donnelly was well known to me. I had counted him a friend when first I came to London, for as I well recalled, he had taken a sincere interest in me when I was but a raw youth—no more than a boy—of thirteen. As for Sir John, he had said he would ever be grateful to Mr. Donnelly for the manner in which he eased the last days of the first Lady Fielding.

In my eagerness, I burst in upon them, for all were seated round the kitchen table. Yet at the last moment I remembered the rules of proper conduct, came to a sudden halt, and doffed my hat, easing the door closed behind me.

Mr. Donnelly responded to my rude entrance by jumping from his chair and advancing upon me with open hand outstretched. "Good God, is it you, Jeremy? You look a man already. I'd say you *are* a man—and at what age are you?"

"Fifteen, sir," said I in a modest manner, allowing my hand to be pumped most vigorously.

"Well, you look older and most particularly in that fine coat—quite the young gentleman!"

"Do sit down, Jeremy," said Lady Fielding. "Mr. Donnelly has kept us royally entertained with his tales of the Ribble Valley."

"Indeed he has," seconded Sir John with a deep chuckle.

I brought over a chair and took a place next Annie, our cook. I could tell she and all the rest were in a merry mood. Their faces were flushed from laughter; all wore smiles. Annie passed me a wink as I sat down.

"Ah, but I feel I've been unfair to folk there," said Mr. Donnelly, resuming his recital. "They are good, simple country people, no more nor less. And if their country ways and their speech—oh, God, their speech!"—rolling his eyes most expressively, provoking more laughter—"if they seem strange to us, you may be sure that London ways and speech would seem even more strange to them."

"No doubt, no doubt," said Sir John. "Who are we to set the mark?"

Yet when he resumed, Mr. Donnelly seemed distinctly more serious in style and mien: "No, they are not fools. I would venture to say that of any and all, I was the bigger fool ever to have gone there in the pursuit of that reluctant widow." He sighed a bitter sigh yet kept a smile upon his face. "You see before you that figure of comedy, a rejected suitor. It were not enough that I followed Lady Goodhope into deepest Lancashire where I attempted to begin a medical practice among folk so poor they could only offer to pay me with hens, piglets, and promises to whitewash my cottage; nor that I felt great pity for her in her widow's state and tenderness for her even in those fits of foolish haughtiness to which she was often given; nor that I gave her ignorant son the only glimpses of education he had had in all his nine years. No, none of that were enough. As I finally discovered, it was also necessary that I have a great personal fortune with which to finance the boy's education and his return to London to take his father's place in the House of Lords. What had I to offer her? A few hens, a piglet or two and one last offer of help from my father amounting to five hundred pounds. It wasn't sufficient. She chose, rather, to sell herself to a Lancashire coal merchant of the town of Wigan, a man of such remarkable ignorance that he supposed that all that was needed for him to become Lord Goodhope was to marry Lady Goodhope. Even though he was disappointed to learn otherwise, he showed himself willing so that he might live in her house, which I myself heard him praise as 't'grandest in t'valley, or mos' Lanc'shire.' No doubt she feels comfortable with him, for she herself comes of that class, though she is better educated. In any case, her choice is final. The banns have been posted. There was no reason for me to stay longer, and so . . . here I am."

As he finished, he sat silent for a moment with his eyes downcast. Each of the listening women let out an "aah," which sounded in chorus as an expression of great disappointment and sympathy.

For his part, Sir John leaned forward, clasping his hands upon the table. "True enough," said he, "here you are. What are your plans, Mr. Donnelly?"

"Why, to begin again. My father has made a small portion of that five hundred pounds available to me that I might open and equip a surgery in a section of Westminster. If I cannot thus establish myself here in London in . . . oh, say a year, then there is always the Navy for me. I cannot go on forever taking money from my father—not at my age."

"Have you a place now?"

"I have," said he, "though it is not yet set up proper."

"I see," said Sir John, musing then for a long moment. "It is not mere curiosity prompts these questions of mine. There is a particularly troubling matter of homicide which has taken place today within shouting distance of this very address."

With that, Lady Fielding shot to her feet. "I do believe that it has come time for we of the weaker sex to retire."

Annie, who had listened with wide-eyed fascination to Sir John's news (for the murder in the alley had in no wise been earlier discussed) rose most reluctantly, clearly consternated that she might not hear the details of this awful event.

As the rest of us stood to our feet, Sir John then said, "Yes, perhaps it is best that you leave us. Good night to you, my dear—and to you, Annie."

Mr. Donnelly thanked Lady Fielding for her hospitality, and Annie whispered in my ear that there was a meat pie waiting for me in the oven.

A moment later they were gone, and we three resumed our seats at the table.

"Tell me of it, please," said Mr. Donnelly. "I am ever interested in those matters in which medicine may aid in criminal investigations."

"Homicide in particular," put in Sir John.

"Yes, the body of the victim is often the most eloquent witness."

"Well said, sir, but let me give you a few details of this case. . . ."

And that Sir John proceeded to do, summarizing skillfully, giving particular attention to what was said by Maggie Pratt and the witness I had questioned, Mrs. Crewton.

He concluded: "We take this mention of the soldier sufficiently seriously that I have written to the acting colonel of the Guards regiment, demanding that all under his command given leave this day be put on review so that Miss Pratt may look upon them and pick out the fellow with whom the victim was speaking. Jeremy delivered the letter. Were you able to put it in Captain Conger's hand, lad?"

"I fear I was not, sir," said I. "I was not allowed within the walls of the Tower. But the corporal of the guard took it and promised to put it in the captain's hands."

"Did you tell him the content of the letter?"

"Loud and clear, Sir John."

"Then I rest assured he kept his promise." The magistrate fell silent for a moment and drummed his fingers upon the table in agitation for a moment or two. When he stopped, he seemed to have come to some sort of decision. "Mr. Donnelly," said he, "I wonder, is your surgery sufficiently set up that you might now have a look at the body of this woman?"

"A complete autopsy?"

"I know not what that entails. Let me tell you what I wish to know. The wound that killed the woman was of a very peculiar sort. It was, as described to me, a small one that produced little bleeding, and it was inflicted directly below the breastbone."

"One thrust only?" asked the medico.

"That was my understanding."

"That is most unusual."

"Oh? What I wish to know, however, is whether or not this narrow wound might have been caused by a military bayonet. Can you measure a wound as to width and depth with that sort of precision?"

"Oh yes, my surgery is certainly equipped for that."

"And of course anything else you might find of interest would be welcome."

"Of course. I understand."

"And I assure you," said Sir John, "that my office has funds to pay for your professional services—just as before."

"Then my first patient is to be a corpse."

"As you say, Mr. Donnelly. Oh, just one more thing. The woman in question—that is to say, the victim—is Irish. Teresa O'Reilly is—or was—her name."

"That presents no particular difficulties. It has been my experience, sir, that inside we are all alike."

And so it happened that late that evening Mr. Donnelly and I rode with Constable Cowley in a wagon to the Raker's little farm near the banks of the river. Though the Raker planted often, nothing ever grew in the field surrounding his cottage. There were weeds and a few wildflowers barely visible to us as we pulled up next the surrounding fence, but the dark Thames soil of that field presented itself as an expanse of black before us like some great moat that must be crossed ere we reached the barn where a dim light burned.

"There is a gate just ahead," said I to Constable Cowley. "Drive on, and I'll open it."

Mr. Cowley urged the horses forward, and I jumped down and ran to the gate. I wrestled it open long enough for the wagon to pass through, then I hopped back upon the wagon.

"What a strange and sinister place this is," said Mr. Donnelly.

"I hate it, outside and in," said the young constable. "It's ha'nted."

"It is as you said, Jeremy, quite like a little farm, especially here in the moonlight. Why, it could indeed be a cotter's place in Lancashire."

"This field is where he buries the poor. It's said he layers them one atop the other, so that the last are laid in quite shallow."

"They get no Christian burial, of course," said Mr. Donnelly.

"Perhaps some do. I'm not sure."

The narrow road led round the little cottage where the Raker and his sister lived. I had glimpsed her a few times and talked to her but once. She was quite as odd as he and looked to be his ugly twin. The cottage was dark, its shutters closed tight. The dimly lit barn loomed just ahead.

"Sir John once told me," said I, "that the Raker came by his job through his family. Some ancestor of his—grandfather or great-grandfather perhaps—performed great service to the cities of London and Westminster during the great plague of the last century. They carried out the dead when none would dare touch them."

"And now he continues in this century performing the same service."

"Just so, sir."

"And for his trouble he is no doubt regarded as something of a pariah."

Then did Constable Cowley speak up right sharply: "I ain't sure what you mean by that, sir. But I can tell you that there's some horrible tales told of him."

"Tales of what sort?" asked Mr. Donnelly.

"Well, it's said that him and his sister never want for meat—if you get my meaning."

"Has anything ever been—"

Mr. Donnelly's query was cut short by a sudden commotion in the yard surrounding the barn. The two skeletal, spavined nags that pulled the Raker's wagon, usually so utterly still, were thrown into disorder by our approach; they whinnied and clopped awkwardly about, throwing their narrow heads this way and that. Our livery team also went a bit restive, but Constable Cowley stood high on the wagon box and held them down, urging them ahead.

Just then a figure appeared, outlined dimly in the open barn door. It was the square, squat form of the Raker. In his hands was something long, yet too thick to be a broom; he held it most menacingly.

"Who is out there?" he called. "Halt where you are, or you'll get what's in this fowling piece."

Mr. Cowley reined in the horses. All was silent for a moment. I realized it fell to me to identify us and make known our purpose.

"'Tis I, Jeremy Proctor," I called out to him. "We've come with an order from Sir John."

"Well, come ahead then, but leave that wagon and team where it's at. My horses ain't fond of their kind about this place at night."

We had no choice but to do as he directed. Mr. Cowley remained with the wagon as Mr. Donnelly and I climbed down and started toward the barn. The Raker remained at his station, the fowling piece now held a bit less menacingly tucked under his arm.

"Is it always so with him?" asked Mr. Donnelly in a tone not much more than a whisper.

"I've never come at night before," said I, "never wanted to."

Then called the Raker to us: "I must ask you to climb the fence. In the state they're in, my horses would be out in a trice, if you was to open the gate."

Mr. Donnelly grunted his assent and scrambled over without much difficulty, and I did so with my customary step-step-hop. The two horses shied from us and moved at a clumsy trot to the far end of the yard. Once there, they settled into their usual pose, necks bent and heads low, altogether stationary.

"Watch where you step. I ain't cleaned up around here in a while, I ain't."

There was still moon enough to see us safe across the yard. Yet as we approached, the Raker left his post and retreated from the door into the interior of the barn. We followed him in, and I found myself wondering just what Mr. Gabriel Donnelly would make of this place.

The Raker's barn served London as the mortuary for the poor, the unclaimed, and the unknown. I had visited it far oftener than I would have liked during the past two years, yet the place never really changed. In summer it smelled far worse than it did the rest of the year, but summer or winter the dead had their places, men on the right and women on the left, a piece of canvas thrown over each. Right and left, too, were piles of clothing removed from the dead. It was said he made a pretty penny selling off these garments to those who made a pretty penny selling them to the living.

The medico surveyed the scene with a dark frown of disapproval, and the Raker, for his part, had a frown for him, too. The single lantern that lit the place did little to cheer it. I sensed an immediate strong antipathy between them both.

"And what might you want?" asked the Raker. It was more than a question, it was a challenge. He took a step or two towards Mr. Donnelly and studied him close. Though his eyes were not well mated (the left being distinctly smaller than the right), he saw well enough from both. He had no need to come so close; it seemed likely he hoped to intimidate.

Mr. Donnelly, however, was not intimidated. "I have an order here"—he produced the letter from his pocket—"from Sir John Fielding, who is known to you as Magistrate of the Bow Street Court, empowering me to remove the body of one Teresa O'Reilly for purposes of medical examination."

The Raker broke the seal and opened the letter. His eyes roamed indifferently over the page. I was certain he could not read. He handed it back to Mr. Donnelly.

"Who's she?" He growled it out in a most hostile manner.

"She it was you hauled off earlier on this evening from New Broad Court," said I.

He threw me a look that seemed to treat the information I had supplied as an irrelevant interruption. Then he turned back to Mr. Donnelly.

"And who're you?"

"I am the surgeon who will perform the medical examination."

"So I thought. And I suppose you'll be doing your examination in front of a whole troupe of medico students, and you'll be makin' jokes as you cut open the body and put the innards on display. I don't like my ladies or gents used for such purposes. Seems every week or near it some saw-your-bones comes by tryin' to buy one of these good people. These people ain't for buyin'."

"I understand. I assure you, sir, I have no students. I have no apprentices. The medical examination will be conducted in the privacy of my surgery."

Having had his say, the Raker relaxed a bit, in fact took a step back and cast his eyes down as if giving the matter consideration.

"Well," said he at last, "it's as you say then, and Sir John hisself has given the order." Then to me: "There be no arguin' with Sir John, ain't that right, boy?"

"I fear so," said I in sober agreement.

With a wheezing sigh, he turned, beckoning us to follow, and led the way on his short, bandy legs to the farthest mound of canvas on the left. He bent down and in a single motion ripped the cover from the body. Then he walked away, folding the sheet of canvas as he went.

"Go ahead," said he, "take her."

Mr. Donnelly and I managed as best we could. I ran after the Raker and begged from him some clothes to cover her. He found those she had come in at the top of the great pile and tossed them to me. The stiffness of death had begun to set her limbs and trunk. This made her more difficult to dress, which we managed only after a fashion, but easier to carry once we had done. The only help given us by the Raker was to walk with us to the fence and light our way with his lantern. He remained as Mr. Cowley brought the wagon forward. I cast a glance over my shoulder at the two horses at the back of the yard; there was not a move from them. They seemed soundly asleep. With Mr. Cowley's help we loaded the corpus into the wagon. The Raker remained, saying not a word until the job was done. He then turned and walked back to the barn.

We three remained silent until we were past the cottage and had crossed the field. When Mr. Cowley reined in at the gate, I jumped down and bounded over to open it. And then—why particularly then I cannot say—Mr. Donnelly suddenly exploded forth with a torrent of verbal abuse directed at none other than the Raker. By the time I climbed back into the wagon and took my place next Teresa O'Reilly, the good doctor was fairly shouting his complaints out to the darkness.

"By Jesus and by all the saints, I do believe that man is mad! He presides there in that barn as if he thought he were king and it were his kingdom. Calls them 'his people,' he does, as if those poor forgotten cadavers were his subjects. And that charnel house of a barn! The next great plague of London will start there. Mark my words! Such filth, the place alive with all manner of vermin, the floor littered with horse shite and who knows what else! Never in Dublin, no place in Europe, have I seen such . . . such . . ."

And so he continued for minutes more.

THREE

In Which Sir John
Plays the Role
of Coroner

It was evident that Sir John's letter for Captain Conger had been received. I cannot attest that the corporal of the guard was as good as his word and put it direct in the captain's hands; it may have passed through others. Yet there could be no doubt it had reached him to whom it was addressed, for he was there at the gate to meet our little party.

Captain Conger was a man of some six feet in height, long-faced, sharp-featured, and unsmiling; he looked to be one who seldom smiled. Or so he seemed to me as we made our crossing of the moat on the narrow bridge near the Thames shore. He was easily recognized from the excess of braid upon his coat and the epaulettes upon his shoulders. We had been passed without question at the outer gate. He now waited at the Byward Tower Gate just beyond the moat bridge. Only as we approached near did he bestir himself and come forward a few steps. I touched Sir John's arm at the elbow that he might stop and receive the captain's greeting.

"Sir John, may I present myself? I am Captain George Conger, acting colonel of our regiment in the absence of Sir Cecil Dalenoy."

"Who is doubtless off in some woody corner of the realm depleting the game population." Sir John extended his hand, and the captain took it in a warm clasp. "Very pleased to meet you, Captain, though I think it regretful that it should be under these sad circumstances."

"No more than I." He then looked beyond the magistrate at me and at the third member of our group. "If you will be so good as to follow me, I have done as you requested and formed a parade of those of the regiment who were granted leave the day past."

To me the captain gave a sharp nod, turned round, and set off at a good pace. We two had no difficulty keeping up, yet Mistress Maggie Pratt, small and short-legged, was somewhat pressed to hold tempo.

Captain Conger had looked at her a bit askance, as if dubious of her qualifications as witness. She had described herself to Sir John as an "unemployed seamstress." Yet I suspected, as I was sure he did, that her acquaintance with the victim, Teresa O'Reilly, a confirmed woman of the streets, was of a professional nature.

It had been arranged that she would wait for us that morning at the point where Drury Lane meets Angel Court. But when our hackney arrived at the meeting place, she was nowhere to be seen. And so Sir John, cautioning me to be careful, sent me into Angel Court to seek her out. Angel Court was, and to some extent still is, a most disreputable little street. ("Street" is, in truth, too grand a name for it, even "lane" was more than it deserved, for while it led in, it did not lead out.) It was what was called at that time a "rookery," a dark, narrow passage in which low lodging houses, some no more than common dormitories, were crammed together with no space between. There was no telling how many lived there—or perhaps better put, slept there of a given night. How was I to find Maggie Pratt? How was I to find anyone in such a place? I determined that the best way was to go through it calling her name. As I walked into Angel Court, squinting into the dim light of the early cloud-cast morning, I heard a door slam nearby, a flurry of footsteps, and a young man appeared before me and hurried past. There was something most familiar about him. Then that same door slammed again, and I heard a most horrendous stream of invective, well-laced with obscenity and profanity, hurled out into the air—presumably in pursuit of the young man who had just hurried by me. The voice was feminine, though the language certainly was not. It came, as I heard, from a porch just above. There Maggie Pratt leaned out, perhaps hoping to catch sight of him who had just departed. When she had exhausted herself, I called up to her that Sir John awaited her in a hackney coach and would she please hurry. That she did, for she could not have taken more than a minute to find her coat and lock her door. She ran down the stairs then, bladdering her apologies but offering not a word to account for the scene I had just witnessed. It was not until we were all three settled in the coach and well on our way to the Tower that it occurred to me that the familiar-looking young man who had bustled by me so quickly in

Angel Court was the same who had blocked my way when I went up Drury Lane in pursuit of Mariah.

"Captain Conger," I called boldly ahead, "our witness is having a bit of trouble keeping to the pace you've set."

"And alas, I, too," lied Sir John in a gallant manner. (I knew it as fact that he could make me hop to keep up when he'd a need to hurry.)

"Forgive me," said the captain, stopping, waiting, looking left and right in an effort to disguise his impatience. "An old campaigner such as myself finds it difficult to adjust."

Once we had caught him up, he proceeded in company with us at a near-funereal gait, though silently, looking sternly ahead.

We walked along with the moat to our right and the Thames just visible over the wall. Then, moving along a passage to our left, we emerged into a great open space, in the middle of which stood the grand White Tower, the castle which all these fortifications did protect. I had never seen it so close, though I had often glimpsed it from a distance when on bright days it seemed to glitter in the sunlight; this murky morning, however, it appeared more gray than white, yet most impressive in its size and shape. Our destination was beyond the castle to a narrow field whereon soldiers did drill. And even beyond them, where a lesser group of soldiers were lined in two ranks in one corner of the field.

I chanced a look at Maggie Pratt. While before she smiled, cheered by this adventurous outing after her encounter with the bully-boy in Angel Court, she was now solemn-faced and uncertain. It appeared that the grave purpose of our visit had at last begun to weigh upon her.

Upon our approach the sergeant in command called the two ranks to attention. Captain Conger stepped forward and had a few words with the sergeant. He returned to us and spoke direct to Sir John.

"You may have your witness pass through the ranks and examine the faces of these men one by one," said he. "All who were on leave are present here. She may take as long as she likes, of course. It would not do to be hasty on such a matter as this."

"I quite agree, Captain." Then did Sir John turn in the direction of the witness. "Mistress Pratt? You heard the captain?"

"Yes, sir, I did."

"Then proceed as he described."

"Yes, sir."

These last several words, the first she had uttered since we had departed the hackney, were spoken in a tone so low they were little more than whispered. She walked purposefully to the first rank where the sergeant awaited her. A small woman at best, perhaps a girl not yet full grown, she seemed to shrink further in size as she took her place among the Grenadier Guards. The shortest of them was my size—and I was then exactly as I am now, a man of medium height; they ranged up from there, and one or two seemed taller than the captain. Yet she moved along from one to the next quite slowly, looking each full in the face, scrutinizing each most carefully. Thus she went, and when she had finished with the first rank, the sergeant took her through the second, examining that with the same searching thoroughness she had shown the first. For their part, the men submitted to the inspection, showing no outward signs of emotion; from their reaction, or its lack, they would as lief be looked at by their colonel, or by King George himself. There were, in all, twenty—as I myself had counted.

Once she had done, she returned to us. Yet she had made no accusation, pointed no finger, so that I—perhaps with all the rest—supposed she had not seen him for whom she searched. Sir John brought us back to a point quite distant from the two ranks so that we should be out of earshot. Captain Conger trailed along.

"Did you recognize the man you saw talking to the victim among those assembled here?" asked Sir John.

She hesitated, then said at last: "This is most confusin', sir."

"Why? What do you mean?"

"I saw two who looked like him."

Sir John said nothing for a long moment. "Two, is it?" He sighed. It was at that point evident she was not near so good a witness as he had hoped. "All right, which are they?"

"The fifth one from the left in the first row, and the third from the right in the second."

"I'll talk to both. Captain, are you here?"

"I am, sir."

"You heard her choices?"

"I did."

"Have those two men isolated from their fellows and from each other. And if you can provide a room in which I may question them separately, I should be greatly obliged to you."

"All that will be done. But, Sir John?"

"Yes, Captain Conger?"

"Do not think ill of your witness. She has a better eye than I would have expected. The two she picked out are brothers. They bear a strong family resemblance one to the other."

Once the two soldiers had been tucked away separately, Sir John asked the sergeant if he would search the personal effects of both to see if either had a narrow-bladed knife. "Something on the order of a stiletto," was how he described it. Then he directed that one of the two brothers be sent in to him.

"Which one will you have, sir?" asked the sergeant.

"Oh, I don't know, the elder I suppose."

And so it was that only moments after the sergeant had left, a knock came on the door to the captain's office, where we two had been settled. Sir John bade the knocker enter, and in marched the first of the two brothers. He was also the taller and had been, I assumed, in the second rank. I had not so good a look at him because of that, but he did indeed resemble him who was fifth from the left in the first rank.

He stood at rigid attention before us.

"Your name, sir?" asked Sir John.

"Sperling, Otis, Corporal, *sah!*"

"You may sit down, Corporal. I have a few questions for you. I am, if you have not been told, Sir John Fielding, and I am Magistrate of the Bow Street Court."

"Prefer to stand, *sah!*"

"Well, suit yourself. The questions I have are directed at you as a witness. No accusation has been made. I should like us both to be at our ease, and I cannot be at mine if you shout '*sah!*' at me each time you address me. Now, please relax."

Corporal Sperling made an effort to do so, shifting to a less strenuous military posture. He managed also to say "As you will, sir" in a normal tone of voice as he ventured a glance at me.

"You were given leave yesterday, I believe."

"I was, sir, though not the whole day."

"Tell me about it, if you would—what you did, who you saw, that sort of thing. Start with the time you left the Tower."

Corporal Sperling gave a good, brief accounting of his time after he had left the gate three o'clock in the afternoon in the company of his brother, Richard, and one Corporal Tigger, both of this regiment of Grenadier Guards. His plan, said he, was to take the five o'clock coach to Hammersmith with Richard, so that the two might dine with their parents; their father was a wheelwright in that community. They had separated early on, Richard agreeing to meet them at the coach house, and the two corporals going off together to enjoy themselves as they would.

"And how did you two propose to do that?" asked Sir John.

"Oh, as soldiers usually do, sir—by drinking and yarning and offering complaints on the conduct of the regiment." Then he added, "I will say, sir, that we was just passing the time together, and at no time did we take strong drink, just beer and ale, sir."

"I see. And where did you pass your time in this manner?"

"Well, there was two places. The first was a place near the end of Fleet Street, which makes no objections to serving soldiers so long as they're well behaved—the Cheshire Cheese."

"I know the place well and have drunk and dined there myself," said Sir John. "And what was the second place?"

"That would have been the Coach House Inn, where I was to meet my brother."

"And did Corporal Tigger remain with you there?"

"Yes, sir, until Richard come and we left on the coach."

"And at no time were you direct in the area of Covent Garden, the two of you—or you alone?"

"No, sir, I had no business there."

"I quite understand." Sir John paused at that point, then gave in summary: "So you were in the company of Corporal Tigger from the time you left the Tower at three o'clock until you left with your brother, Richard, on the five o'clock coach to Hammersmith. Is it then so?"

"To that I would have to say yes and no, sir."

"Oh? Explain yourself, please."

"Yes, I was with Tigger the whole time, but no, Richard and I did not leave on the five o'clock coach."

"How was that?"

"Richard was late. I was quite cross with him, for there was not another coach until half past six. This was meant to be a party—a celebration, so to say, and we was late to it."

"And what were you celebrating?'

"My promotion, sir."

"To corporal?"

"Yes sir."

"Hmmph," Sir John grunted, then fell silent for a long moment. "Corporal Sperling," said he, "you say your brother arrived too late for you to leave on the five o'clock coach. When did he arrive?"

"That I cannot say exact, for I did not then own a timepiece, though I do now. My father presented me one last night, sir."

"He must be very proud of you."

The corporal flushed with embarrassment, looked left and right and shuffled his feet. "As you say, sir."

"Give it to me approximate, then."

"Sir?" said he, frowning. Surely he had understood.

"The time of your brother's arrival."

"Oh, well, he wasn't terrible late—less than half an hour, I'd say."

"A quarter of an hour, would you give it that?"

"About that, not much more." The corporal glanced my way again.

"Very good," said Sir John. "What excuse did your brother give? What business did he have that kept him so late?"

"That you would have to ask him, sir."

"Are you reluctant to say?"

"No, sir, he never told—just that it was a personal matter. Then, when he was late, he said he couldn't help it."

"And that was all he gave by way of explanation?"

"He keeps his counsel. You must understand, sir, that things is not always so easy between brothers, even those in the same regiment."

"Perhaps especially not then."

"As you say, sir."

"We are nearly done," said Sir John. "I do want to ask you though, Corporal, when was it that your brother, Richard, left you and the other corporal? You said that you left the Tower with him—you three together."

"Yes, sir. Richard stayed with us until we reached the Cheshire Cheese. He left us there."

"At approximately what time?"

"Again, I must reckon, but it seems likely it would have taken about a quarter of an hour to walk there."

"So that you did not see your brother from about a quarter past the hour of three until a quarter past the hour of five. Correct?"

"Correct, sir."

With that, Sir John dismissed Corporal Otis Sperling, but instructed him to return to the room where he had awaited our call. When he had gone, Sir John sat back in his chair and touched fingertip to fingertip. He thought for some time.

"Well, what thought you of that?" asked Sir John of me.

"It would seem," said I, "that Richard Sperling is our man."

"So it would seem indeed. There is some discrepancy on the matter of time. But tell me, Jeremy, how did the corporal seem when I asked him to be specific on the lateness of his brother? He answered readily enough."

"Yes, but he seemed to grow a bit uneasy. He frowned, he delayed, he looked about. By the end of the interrogation, a bit of perspiration stood on his brow."

"There is an open window behind me. This room is quite cool."

"Exactly," said I.

"It could well be," said Sir John, "that having let slip that his brother had failed to arrive in time for them to leave together on the five o'clock coach, he realized from my subsequent questions that the matter of time was essential. And so, he began perhaps to minimize his brother's tardiness. It could well be that Richard arrived at the Coach House an hour or more late. Perhaps he barely made the six-thirty coach to Hammersmith."

"Which would put it within the limits of time set by Maggie Pratt's sighting and the discovery of the body."

"Then still warm," put in Sir John.

He seemed about to add something to that when a knock came upon the door. Invited to enter, the sergeant came through the door appearing quite pleased.

"I'm happy to report," said he, "that I found no knives of any description among the personal property of Sperling, Otis, or Sperling, Richard. And a good thing, too, for possession of such would indeed be a court-martial offense."

"Well, Sergeant," said Sir John, "if you are happy, then I am happy."

"Both have good records, sir—though Sperling, Richard, has been in the regiment only a bit over a year."

"How old is he?"

"Just nineteen, sir."

"So young! Well, be that as it may, we must have him at Bow Street to continue our inquiry."

"That will be a matter for you to take up with Captain Conger, sir."

"I thought as much," said Sir John, rising from his chair. "Would you take us to him, please?"

Once the sergeant had led us to the captain, out in the drill yard, Sir John had a little difficulty convincing him of the necessity of removing Richard Sperling to Bow Street.

"Is he accused?" asked the captain.

"By no means," said Sir John. "I do believe, however, that he would be responsive in a more formal setting."

"The full weight of the law, is that it?"

"Something of the sort, I suppose. In any case, will you grant him permission to appear as witness?"

"I will, of course, if I may have him back."

"Beg pardon? I do not understand, Captain. If there is no need to bind him for trial, of course you may have him back."

"And if there is such need, we shall also want him back so that we may convene a military court-martial. Military justice is swift, sure, and impartial, Sir John."

"Well, I am convinced that it is swift, in any case. But see here, Captain, it is entirely too early to argue about matters of jurisdiction. A coroner's court must be convened in order to establish formally that the matter at hand is murder."

"Is there any doubt of it?"

"No, but a surgeon has examined the body and will give testimony. A good deal may be established by him in favor of your Private Sperling."

"Or against him."

"Indeed. Yet it is an open inquiry that draws no conclusion on guilt or probable guilt."

"I see," said the captain. "And who is the coroner?"

"Uh, well," Sir John hesitated, "I am acting in that capacity *pro tem.*"

Captain Conger looked at him in a manner most skeptical. He considered. At last he said, "Sir John Fielding, I bow to your reputation, for it is a good one. Nevertheless, I shall not allow you simply to whisk him off as you seem to suggest. Private Sperling will go with an armed guard to Bow Street. If any attempt is made to hold him, or bind him over for criminal trial, they will be under my orders to bring him back to the Tower, and if necessary, to use force."

Though apparently vexed, Sir John nodded his acceptance, but then said he: "Then, I, too, have stipulations. They are these: First of all, Private Sperling is not to be brought in chains, for he is a witness and does not stand accused of any crime."

"Agreed."

"Second, that Corporal Tigger be a member of the guard party, and that he himself be allowed to testify."

Though the frown on the captain's face indicated he had no real understanding of the implications of this proviso, he offered no objection.

"Agreed," said he.

"And finally, that at least one other of equal or superior rank be in the party to ensure that Corporal Tigger and Private Sperling do not discuss in any way the crime or their activities of the day past."

"Agreed."

"Then if you are satisfied, Captain, I am," said Sir John, smiling pleasantly. "And I offer you my hand upon it."

Which indeed he did, wherewith the two shook hands.

"By the bye, Captain Conger, I wonder, is Lieutenant Churchill about? I encountered him last year. I think it only proper that I look in on him while visiting the Tower."

"Sir John, he is off shooting in, as you put it earlier, 'some woody corner of the realm,' as is near every officer in the regiment but me. Note, sir, that I am putting my trust in you in this matter. If you go against me in it, I shall be sore embarrassed and will no doubt suffer evil consequences. Good day to you, sir."

With that, he turned on his heel and walked away at his brisk campaigner's pace.

"The hearing is at eleven this morning," Sir John called after him. (Though the captain gave no sign, I was sure he heard.) And to me Sir John said: "The man drives a damned hard bargain." Then, remembering, he called out again loud and clear: "And, Captain! Do see that Private Sperling brings his bayonet along."

To which the captain gave out the reply: "It shall be done, Sir John."

"Gentlemen, this is a solemn proceeding under law to determine the nature of the death of one Teresa O'Reilly. To that end, we have assembled witnesses to give testimony that may or may not be pertinent when and if a magistrate's hearing be called on this matter. I, as magistrate, am acting *pro tempore* as coroner. And so as I conduct this coroner's inquest, I shall be attending to all that is said with my magistrate's ear."

Sir John was addressing a group of twelve men lured off the street by Mr. Marsden with the promise of a shilling. They were seated six and six in the first two rows of the small courtroom on the ground floor of Number 4 Bow Street. The witnesses sat to one side—Maggie Pratt, Gabriel Donnelly, and Private Sperling, who sat between a corporal, whom I took to be Tigger, and the unnamed sergeant who had assisted us at the Tower. Mr. Marsden sat beside Sir John. As it happened, I was the only one present who did not take some part in the proceeding.

"First," said Sir John, continuing to speak direct to the coroner's jury, "let me acquaint you with the facts. The deceased was found in a yard off New Broad Court which leads direct into an alley that connects to Duke's Court. You may know this territory well, for the site is quite near to where we now have gathered. She was found, feet protruding from under a stairway at a bit after six by a resident of the yard, a Mr. Sebastian Tillbury, who immediately gave the alarum. Constable Perkins was passing and came swift to the call. He read his timepiece and fixed his arrival at eight minutes past six. Note the time, please, for it may prove quite important. The body was still warm to the touch."

Here he paused, muttered soft in the ear of Mr. Marsden, and waited till he had his response. Then he continued:

"At this point I should like to call the first witness, Mr. Gabriel Donnelly, a surgeon. He has performed a post-mortem examination upon the deceased. I call him before me now to give testimony upon the cause of death."

Mr. Donnelly rose from the chair whereon he had been seated and walked heavily to a place before Sir John. He appeared quite exhausted, poor man, for I knew it to be so that he had been up most the night performing the autopsy upon the victim. However, in the exchange with Sir John that follows, his voice was strong and confident.

"Mr. Donnelly, could you tell us briefly your experience as a surgeon?"

"Gladly. I had seven years' service in His Majesty's Navy, ending in 1768, at which time I practiced briefly in London and subsequently for two years in Lancashire. I have lately returned to London to resume my practice here."

"And have you, in that time, performed other post-mortem examinations?"

"Many. Particularly in the Navy did I have occasion to do so. I should say that the number would stand at something over twoscore—fifty, give or take."

"Very good. Would you now tell us what you determined to be the cause of Teresa O'Reilly's death?"

"I will, sir." Yet before beginning, he took a deep breath and let it out in a long sigh. "She met her death by a single stab wound to the heart. It was administered at a point only slightly below the sternum—that is to say, the breastbone. The instrument that caused her death, a sharp, narrow blade, was directed at a moderate upward angle into and through the great cardiac vein and held in place, probably until the victim stopped struggling. As a result of this sort of wound, there was a good deal of internal bleeding but little at the point of entry."

(At this point I ought to say that Mr. Donnelly's testimony, far from confusing the members of the jury, seemed to interest them greatly. This motley collection of men, most of them ill-educated, if educated at all, leaned forward as one as the anatomical details of Teresa O'Reilly's death were presented. I noticed not one but two of the twelve grope on their dirty shirts to find the sternum, then the precise spot below it where the wound was inflicted.)

"Was there anything unusual about all this?" asked Sir John.

"Why, yes, sir," said Mr. Donnelly. "What was unusual was the precision of the wound. The fact that it was perfectly placed, that only one upward thrust was made, sets it apart, in my experience, from the common death by stabbing, which is usually characterized by many wounds and much external bleeding. The heart, you see, is well protected by the body. It is surrounded by a cage of ribs and lies behind the sternum, a very strong, flat bone, which serves as its shield. Most do not know this, and as a result would continue to inflict wounds in the thorax and abdomen of the victim until a mortal one is struck. Death from a single thrust is, I would say, quite unusual."

"And what," asked Sir John, "do you infer from all this?"

"Simply that he who caused the death of Teresa O'Reilly knew something, perhaps a great deal, about human anatomy. He knew the location of the heart and the most direct route to it."

"Though I intend to call you back, I now have one last question for you, Mr. Donnelly. It is this: In my summary, you heard me say that Constable Perkins arrived at the place the body was found at eight minutes past the hour of six, at which time it was still warm to the touch. Could you, from that, give some opinion on the time of the woman's death?"

"Not a very exact one, I fear. It could have been any time from half an hour before to only minutes before her discovery in that yard."

"Thank you, Mr. Donnelly. That will be all for the present."

Thus dismissed, the surgeon returned to his place. The coroner's jury, released from the thrall in which they had been held by his testimony, came suddenly alive with murmurs and whispers. It was necessary for Sir John to call them to order.

"I remind you, gentlemen," said he, "this is a solemn proceeding. Any discussion or comment among yourselves at this point is out of order and quite improper."

Having spoken in so severe a manner, he then lightened only a little in summoning Maggie Pratt to witness. So it was that when she came forward, it was with trepidation and uncertainty.

"Will you give us your full name, Mistress Pratt, for the record which Mr. Marsden is keeping?"

"Margaret Anne Pratt," said she in a small voice, cowering a little.

"Did you get that?" he asked Mr. Marsden, who grunted affirmatively in response. "I must ask you in your further replies to speak up louder. But now, again for the record, you earlier gave your occupation to me as 'seamstress, currently unemployed.' Do you wish it to stand so?"

"Uh, yes, sir."

"Your age?"

"Near as I know, twenty-two."

"You identified the corpus of Teresa O'Reilly to Constable Perkins, did you not?"

"Yes, sir."

"Could you explain your relationship to the deceased?"

"Sir?"

"Were you friend or acquaintance? Did you know her well?"

"I knew her well enough, I reckon. We shared a room in Angel Court."

"Then you must have known her very well indeed."

"Not so well as that. She had it in the daytime, and I had it at night."

"A curious arrangement," commented Sir John dryly, "but no doubt practical in certain circumstances. Tell us what you know of her."

"Well, I know she was Irish, and she come here about two years past of a place she was forever speakin' of called Waterford. She was about my age, give or take a bit, and, uh, that is surely all I do know of her."

"And that is surely not a great deal."

"No, sir."

"Perhaps I can help you remember more. How did she earn her way?"

"Well, sir, I cannot be sure, for the room was hers in the daytime, and I was certainly not one to poke my nose in where it was not wanted, but I believe she had gentleman friends. They give her money."

"How many such friends did she have?"

"Oh, many, sir. She was a real worker, that one, and bold as brass."

"So what you are telling me is that she was a woman of the streets, a common prostitute."

"You might say so, sir—though I am not one to pass judgment on another."

"I dare say not," said Sir John, "for I doubt you are in a position to do so."

At that, one or two in the jury who had caught the implication of his remark burst out in sniggers and giggles. Again, Sir John called them to order, though in a somewhat more indulgent manner than before.

"Were there any of these 'gentleman friends,' as you call them, who visited her often?" he asked. "Any whom she mentioned by name to you?"

She opened her mouth right quick, and the thought came to me that she would give the name of him who had passed me in Angel Court. But then, perhaps thinking better of it, she shut her mouth tight, saying not a word and giving no name. I saw this, as did those in the jury—though Sir John, in his blindness, did not.

"You hesitate," said he.

"I'm trying to remember," said she. "But no, sir, I can think of none. Teresa just took who come along, and she feared none. Big as most men, she was—twice my size—and she could handle herself, if it come to it."

"She would not easily wilt to a threat then?"

"Oh no, sir."

"Nor would she hesitate to defend herself if she felt in danger?"

"Not her."

"All right, Mistress Pratt, enough of that. Let us to the information you gave me when we talked last night in the yard off New Broad Court. What did you tell me then?"

She looked at him suspiciously, almost in disbelief. "Don't you remember?"

Her response, delivered in innocent ignorance, sent the entire room into great thundering laughter. Taken quite by surprise, Sir John himself joined in. And having done so, he could deal with neither jury nor witness as harshly as he might otherwise have done. In truth, all he could do was wait until the laughter had subsided, his own with the rest, and bang upon the desk before him with the carpenter's mallet he seemed always to have at hand. He pled with one and all to be silent as Maggie Pratt stood, looking about her, pouting as a child might, finding itself a laughingstock for adults. I noted that she was the only woman in the room and wondered did not that have something to do with their derisive hilarity. I found myself moved to pity for her.

"No, my dear Mistress Pratt," said Sir John, having brought the room to order and gained control of himself, "I remember quite well what you told me. It is necessary, however, for you to repeat it for the benefit of the jury and for the record."

"I see," said she, rather coldly. "Well, in that case, I'm willing to oblige." Then did she take a deep breath and commence: "I was walkin' about, just after a bite and a brew at Tompkins Ale House, and I found myself in Duke's Court, and there do I see a big blowen in talk with a soldier."

"You're sure it was a soldier, are you?" asked Sir John.

"Ain't I? No mistakin' that red coat."

"I suppose not. Continue, please."

"Well, she turns half about, and I see it is Teresa for certain. So I goes to her, for I had somethin' to ask of her."

"And what was that?"

"Something personal, it was," said she and waited, testing the effect of that. When she realized that such an evasion would avail her nothing, she resumed: "It had to do with one of her gentleman friends kept coming around to the room asking for her at all hours."

"What was his name? He must have given it."

"I cannot remember, sir."

"Yet you remembered it right enough when you went to Teresa O'Reilly after spying her in Duke's Court."

"P'rhaps. But I believe I meant to describe him only."

"Then describe him to us."

She sighed. "Well, he was younger than me, but not all that much. In size and shape he's like that young sir who come with us to the Tower, him that's sittin' over there"—she pointed at me. "But I don't mean it's your young helper—just like him is all."

"I am relieved," said Sir John. (And so, reader, was I.)

"He wears his hair cropped short like an Irishman, though he ain't one so far as I can tell from his talk. And his nose is bent a bit. That's all I can tell you, sir."

She had given a fair description of him whom I had dubbed the "bully-boy" and had met twice—in Drury Lane and Angel Court. I was sure that she must also know his name.

"Well enough, thank you," said Sir John. "Now, you approached Teresa O'Reilly in Duke's Court to complain about this fellow. And what did she say to you?"

"Not a thing, sir. As I come close, she winked her eye and nicked her head at me, as if to say, 'Move along. Can't talk now.' And so that's what I done. But as I was there, real close to them both, the soldier turned round and looked at me, and I at him."

"Would you recognize him again?"

"I would, sir."

"Would you say that Teresa O'Reilly and the soldier were in an acrimonious state?"

"Sir?"

"Were they arguing? Quarrelling?"

"Oh no, sir. I would say Teresa had found herself another gentleman friend."

"And tell us what happened after your meeting in Duke's Court. What, to put it direct, did you do then?"

"Why, I just wandered round a bit more. And then, when I was in New Broad Court, I heard the cry of 'Murder!' and a terrible commotion that followed. I went down the passage to see what was about, and when they pulled her out from under the stairs, I seen it was Teresa. I knowed it would be her, though I can't say why."

"What length of time passed between your meeting with Teresa O'Reilly and the soldier, and the moment you came down the passage and saw her dead?" Sir John asked this in a most severe manner, emphasizing the seriousness of the question.

"I can't rightly say, sir. Such as me don't have no timepiece."

"But when we first talked, Mistress Pratt, you said you had seen the deceased 'just before' with a soldier who looked to be a Grenadier Guard."

"That's right."

"Well, how long was it? A short time? Did you go direct from Duke's Court to New Broad Court and then hear the alarum, or did you stop someplace along the way?"

"Oh, I stopped. I popped into Shakespeare's Head, which is a right respectable place. I make ever so many friends there." Then she added in a reassuring way: "But I didn't stay long."

"I can see we have a difficulty on time," said Sir John to the jury. "But we must get on with this." Then to Mistress Pratt, who stood yet before him: "Do you see the man who was in the company of the deceased in this room? If so, please point him out."

She turned and pointed at Private Sperling. "That's him, at least I think it is. There was two soldiers, as you know, sir."

"Indeed I do. That will be all, Mistress Pratt." He conferred a moment with Mr. Marsden, then said he: "Let the record show that Mistress Pratt has pointed out Private Richard Sperling, Grenadier Guards."

As she walked back to take her place beside Mr. Donnelly, Sir John turned back to the twelve seated on the front benches.

"This matter of two soldiers is easily explained," said he to them. "In fact, when Mistress Pratt went to the Tower with me early this morning, she did pick out not one but two soldiers as possible candidates. This does not, however, impugn her as a witness, for the two are brothers, and I was told they bear a strong resemblance each to the other. I talked with one of them and satisfied myself for the time being. However, I shall take the opportunity now to confirm the story that I heard earlier from Corporal Otis Sperling with a Corporal Tigger."

Corporal Tigger rose and stood ready to take his place before Sir John.

"Hold your place, Corporal. Sergeant? Are you here? Give your name, please."

"I am here, sir," said he, standing. "Silas Tupper, Sergeant, Grenadier Guards."

"You may remain where you are, for I have but a question or two for you. Tell me this: Were you charged by Captain Conger to see that Corporal Tigger would say nothing of the matters before this coroner's court to Private Sperling? That there would be no discussion of it between them at all?"

"I was, sir."

"And did you carry out that charge?"

"I did. There was absolutely no talk of it at all, the entire time they were together."

"Good, Sergeant. Thank you. You may be seated. And now, Corporal Tigger, please take your place before me."

The cutlass he wore rattled a bit in its scabbard as he walked. That and the brace of pistols strapped at his waist made him a most impressive figure. He stated his name as John Tigger, Corporal, Grenadier Guards. Then, at Sir John's request, he told essentially the same story we had heard from Corporal Sperling. The only difference I perceived was that he was able to be more specific as to the private's tardy arrival. He said that he had looked at his own timepiece as Corporal Sperling went to meet and scold his brother there at the Coach House Inn, and it placed the younger Sperling's coming at a quarter past the hour of five. He had remained with the two in the Coach House Inn until they boarded the coach and left for Hammersmith at half past six.

After dismissing Corporal Tigger, Sir John summoned Richard Sperling as witness. The young private slumped pathetically as he walked up to take his place and looked quite like he had already been convicted and condemned. He managed, however, to pull himself erect in more soldierly fashion once he had arrived. He stated his name and rank and gave his age as nineteen.

"Private Sperling," said Sir John, "I fear you must tell us how you spent the two hours, perhaps a little less, between leaving your brother and Corporal Tigger at the Cheshire Cheese and rejoining them at the Coach House Inn."

"Yes, sir," said he, his voice so strained that it was barely audible.

"Speak up, young man. Proceed."

"Yes, sir, I shall." He cleared his throat.

The members of the jury had now assumed those same attitudes of intense concentration they had adopted earlier in listening to Mr. Donnelly's testimony.

"I left them there, as you say, and hied off swift to the streets surrounding Covent Garden," said he. "Once there I did but wander, searching, putting myself in the way of temptation."

"And what were you searching for?" put in Sir John. "How did you wish to be tempted?"

"I wished the temptation of the flesh. I was searching for a woman."

"Well, there are a plenty of them hereabouts and a good many available for the purpose you seemed to have in mind."

"I know that, sir, and that was the why of my coming here." He looked down, but his voice held steady as he continued: "I . . . I had never been with a woman in that way, and I had come to be ashamed of it, thinking myself less than a man. I had made up my mind to change that, and I thought the time I had before the coach left would be enough to do what needed to be done. Yet once here in these streets, seeing the worn, hard look of those women who made themselves available; thinking of the possibility of disease, probability p'rhaps; remembering my Christian childhood—I found it hard to proceed with my plan. I went into a place and had an ale to steady myself."

"What was the place?" asked Sir John.

"I do not remember, sir, I truly don't, though perhaps I could find it if—"

"Never mind. Continue."

"Very well. But upon leaving the ale house, I was engaged in conversation by a woman. It may have been in Duke's Court. If that woman there says so, I will accept that. In any case, she gave her name as Teresa, and . . . I liked her. She was a big woman, Irish, and she seemed to understand my problem. There was something motherly about her—not like *my* mother, you understand, but . . ."

"I do understand. Continue."

"I . . . consented to go with her, and she took me to a place in Angel Court, right enough, a filthy place—a straw mattress, a chair, nothing more. My time there was short. I . . ." He hesitated, looking for the right words. "I failed in what I set out to do. She was understanding, though she would not give back my money."

There and only then a few of the men on the jury began to snigger. They were hushed by their fellows. Sir John felt no need to call for order.

"And so I left. I left quickly, thinking I must be late—and of course I was. We had to catch the next coach to Hammersmith, which made us more than an hour late to the party for my brother. I'm sorry for that. I'm sorry I went with that woman. But please believe me, sir, for I swear by the Almighty and all that is holy, *I did not kill her.*"

He was near panting with emotion. His eyes glistened with tears.

"I have but one question for you—or perhaps two," said Sir John. "Are you a surgeon's helper in the Grenadier Guards?"

"No, sir, a simple foot soldier."

"Were you ever apprenticed to a surgeon?"

"No, sir."

"Well and good. You may return to your seat."

And that he did, moving swifter and more confident than before, having now made his confession.

"Sergeant Tupper? If you will again stand and keep your place?"

The sergeant shot up to his feet, allowing his scabbard to clang against the chair. And, taken by surprise, he sang out the military "*Sah!*"

"I sent you on an errand earlier today to search through the personal effects of both brothers Sperling to see if either owned a knife. What did you find?"

"Nothing of the kind for either of them, sir."

"I also asked that Private Sperling's bayonet be taken along in evidence. Did you bring it?"

"I did, sir, and handed it over to the surgeon, as you asked."

"Very good. You may sit down. Mr. Donnelly?"

He rose in a more leisurely manner. "Yes, Sir John?"

"You have had opportunity to examine Private Sperling's bayonet?"

"I have, sir."

"Were there any traces of blood upon it?"

"None, sir. It was glistening clean, as one might expect from a Grenadier Guard."

"Well and good. In the absence of any sort of knife, could the bayonet have inflicted the wound you described in Teresa O'Reilly?"

"No, sir, it could not. Had it been pushed to the depth to do the damage I described, it would have left a wider, slightly crescent-shaped wound, and that was not the wound I found in her body. From what I found, the wound came from a long, flat, narrow blade—what might be described as a stiletto."

"Thank you. That, I'm sure, will be all I need from you. But you, Mistress Pratt, will you stand at your place, please?"

She did, somewhat reluctantly, looking a bit put-upon.

"Sir?"

"You have, if you listened closely, become aware of the difficulty regarding time to which I referred. You said you saw the soldier, whom Private Sperling admits to have been himself, with the deceased 'just before' the body was found. And Mr. Donnelly, the surgeon, has told us that if the body was still warm at a bit after six, the earliest that Teresa O'Reilly might have been killed was half an hour before, let us place it at five thirty, at the very earliest. But even so, according to Corporal Tigger, Private Sperling arrived at the post-coach house at a quarter past five and thus could not have inflicted the mortal wound. And so, I must say to you I think you a good witness as to identification, for you have proved that. But I think you a poor witness as to time. Do you still insist you saw Private Sperling but a short time before the body was found?"

"I do," she said most emphatic. "It were not far from that yard, if you go by the alley, which they was near. I saw him there plain, right in the daylight."

"Did you say 'in the daylight'?"

"I did, sir."

Sir John leaned over and held a brief conference with Mr. Marsden, at the end of which he nodded and returned his attention to Mistress Pratt.

"In that case," said he, "I must reject your testimony, for Mr. Marsden informs me that clear daylight lasts this time of year a bit past five. That from that time on it is well into the dusking hour. I can therefore only judge that you spent far longer in Shakespeare's Head than you realized. You may be seated, Mistress Pratt."

"But I—"

"Be seated, please."

Even more reluctantly than she had risen, did she sink back down in her chair.

"And now, you men of the jury," said Sir John, turning and facing in their general direction, "will the one of your number who has been appointed foreman please identify himself?"

Then rose a tall man, a bit older than the rest. "Yes, sir," said he to Sir John, "that would be me."

"I fear you and your eleven fellows may be disappointed in your part in this, for I must now direct a verdict to you. There can be no doubt that murder was committed. Teresa O'Reilly did not die of natural causes—that much is obvious. Nor could she have committed suicide, removed the knife from her heart, disposed of it, then hidden herself where she was found. It was proved, even by the testimony of Mistress Pratt herself, that Private Sperling, whom she had seen in conversation with the deceased, could not have been involved in her demise. He accounted for his time. Corporal Tigger confirmed the hour and minute of his arrival at the Coach House Inn.

"Therefore, I direct you, in the matter of the death of Teresa O'Reilly, to a finding of 'willful murder by person or persons unknown.' You must concur in this by an acclamation of 'aye.' Do you so concur?"

A ragged "aye" went up from the twelve.

"Then it shall stand. The verdict is 'willful murder by person or persons unknown.'" He banged solidly once with his mallet upon the table. "The jury is dismissed with thanks."

I, who was sitting quite close to the men in the front benches, heard one remark to another: "'Twas the easiest shilling I ever come by!"

"That's as may be," replied the second juror, "but it was enlightenin', very enlightenin'."

FOUR

In Which Another Victim
Is Discovered and
Identified

The passing days brought Sir John no closer to solving the puzzle. Who was this person, who were these persons unknown, who had taken the life of Teresa O'Reilly? And for what purpose? There had been, in fact, eight shillings found in that purse about her waist which the larcenous couple were eager to make off with. Murders have been committed, and are committed still, for far less; theft was clearly not the motive. Revenge? Who could say? None but Maggie Pratt had come forward to tell us details of the Irishwoman's life. Bills had been posted round Covent Garden announcing the murder and asking for information—yet to no avail. Had she been killed in a fit of rage by a rejected client? What Mrs. Crewton had told seemed to support that, yet the well-calculated placement of that single thrust to the heart seemed to deny it. Could there be murder without motive?

I had my own, rather baseless, suspicions in the matter. They were focused upon him I had dubbed the "bully-boy." True enough, I had seen him leave Maggie Pratt's place—the room she had shared day by night with Teresa O'Reilly. There could be no doubt he was known to Mistress Pratt, for she had indeed addressed him in crudely familiar terms; that did not mean, however, that he had been equally well known to O'Reilly. For that matter, if he had murdered the woman, could he have carried her to that spot beneath the stairs where she had been so crudely hidden away? To myself, I admitted that was doubtful. At twelve-stone or more, she had been a proper load for the two of us, Mr. Donnelly and myself, when we had hauled her body from the Raker's barn. I, who was about the same size and strength as the fellow in question, could not have managed her alone—or only with great difficulty; I doubted that he could have done much better. Still and all, I did not like him, and it is easiest to attribute black deeds to those whom we dislike. If anyone of my acquaintance were to hang for the murder of Teresa O'Reilly, I should like it to be him. I decided to learn more about him.

On my daily errands about the district surrounding Covent Garden I looked for my "bully-boy," thinking I might have time to follow him at a distance and unobserved, and thus discover something of his haunts and walks. Yet look as I might, I found him not. Had he suddenly disappeared? Left London altogether? No, I decided, his sort would be more likely to be about at night.

By chance, however, I happened to meet Maggie Pratt one morning in Covent Garden whilst I was doing the day's buying. She recognized me right enough but looked at me with distrust as she attempted to push past.

"Please, Mistress Pratt," said I, "might I have a word with you?"

"What manner of word would you have?"

"A few questions—just a few questions."

"It seems to me I gave all the answers I have to your master."

"These are a bit different from his. Perhaps we could move over there, a bit out of the crowd's way."

Merely to stop there in the piazza was to risk being bumped and buffeted by the milling crowd. She consented to be led off to one side and out of the flow of humantide.

"Awright now, what is it?" she challenged me, eager to be off.

"When I came to fetch you in Angel Court, you recall that a young man left your place there and you called after him most angrily."

She looked at me sharply. "I remembers well enough."

"Who was he?"

"That's my affair and none of yours."

"Was he the same as came often asking after Teresa O'Reilly? You said he was something of my size and shape."

"But I said it plain it weren't you."

"Indeed you did. But that is not the question. Was that the same fellow I saw in Angel Court?"

"If he was or wasn't has got nothin' to do with Teresa. Now, if you'll step aside, I'll be on my way."

"But what was his name?"

Lips pursed, she made to push me aside. I had no authority to detain her, and so I stepped back and let her pass. As she bustled on her way, she threw one look back at me over her shoulder—not so much a look of fear, as I somehow expected, but one of annoyance. With a sigh, I turned back and resumed my way to the stall of Mr. Tolliver, the butcher.

There was, obviously, one other who knew something of the fellow in question. Yet I blush to tell that I was reluctant to question Mariah about him for fear of angering her. There was also no little difficulty, I had found, in managing to talk with her at all. She was less dependably to be found at her regular post in New Broad Court. Where she wandered and how far I could not say, for I seldom had time to go searching for her as I dashed about bearing letters and requests for Sir John to all parts of Westminster and the City. On those few occasions on which I did spy her, she was in conversation with one or another, and I had no wish to wait about until the discussion ended and she were free—or else had marched off arm in arm (as I once witnessed) with her companion in conversation.

I did at last find her alone towards the latter part of one afternoon, and I determined to put a few discreet questions to her. I greeted her politely and with a smile, and offered her a shilling.

She smiled sweetly and said to me, "Ah no, young sir, I see how rich you dress! Is not possible to come to me in your old coat and *pantaloni* and make a bargain to me. I say two shillings before. That is my price. I go no more for one shilling."

"I want only to talk to you," said I. "For that I would pay a shilling."

"Like before?" She laughed quite merrily at that. "You pay me. We talk."

I placed a shilling in her hand. Again she dropped it down her blouse to her bodice; again I felt that twinge of envy. Yet I was not so taken with her on this occasion that I would be swayed from my purpose and talk mere pleasantries to her. Nor would I try to win her with my fantasies of escape.

"Do you recall," said I, "that earlier, when I was dressed as I am now and thought to talk with you, you became annoyed and fled down Drury Lane without speaking to me?"

"But you pardon me, yes? I was not gentle that time. I tell you before I am sorry."

"Oh, I accepted your apology then, and I bear no ill feelings toward you now. But you sent a young man to speak to me, to send me away. I was wondering, what is his relation to you?"

"Relation?" She sounded the word out carefully; there seemed a hint of suspicion in her tone.

"Yes, what I mean to say, is he your friend? How do you know him?"

She set her face, considering, and found it quite impossible to lie: "He is not my friend, no. I owe him money. I must pay."

I had in no wise expected such an answer. How could she owe him money? How much could it be?

"I don't understand," said I. "Did you sign a contract of some sort? Is this why you work as you do?"

"I think you go now. We talk another time. Perhaps."

"But . . ." I felt quite baffled, knowing not what to say or do. "At least tell me his name?"

"Why you want to know?"

"Well . . . I have seen him since. I would like to know . . . so I may greet him by name should I see him on the street again."

"Ha! You learn to lie better, or you tell the truth. Here . . ."

And with that, she dove her hand down into her bosom and found my shilling, or one just like it.

"Take this," she resumed. "No more talk. Don' come back unless you pay two shillings and come with me. Now *go!*"

Indeed I went, but I left her holding the shilling. I could not take it from her, of course. In my fantasies, at least, I was her rescuer. How could one who pretended to such a role take back money freely given?

I stumbled on, attempting to master what I had just learned, forgetting for a bit that I had a specific destination—yet perhaps not forgetting entirely, for somehow I made the proper turn up Drury Lane and continued along the route I had been given by Constable Perkins to reach his place of lodging.

Mr. Perkins lived atop one of the stables in the stable yard at the foot of Little Russell Street, just behind Bloomsbury Square. He held it to be a favorable location for a man such as he, who lived alone. He had told me he had two rooms there, good and spacious, and did not mind the smell of the horses, for he grew up among them on a farm in Kent. ("They're cleaner than us," he had once confided.) Best of all he liked the space afforded him by the stable yard for the pursuit of his favorite pastime, which he declared to be "keepin' fit." He was most regular at it, devoting an hour each day to the maintenance of his astonishing strength. (I myself had seen him use his only arm to lift a man of ten stone or more off the floor.) His hour for "keepin' fit" was the one directly preceding his departure for duty as a member of Sir John's Bow Street constabulary. He had invited me to come by that I might begin a course of instruction in methods of defense, for he thought me ill-prepared to traverse certain low precincts of London, "where they'd as soon cut you as not." It so happened that that very day was the one appointed for my first lesson. I knew not what to expect from it and was therefore in some manner uneasy.

Though not tardy, I found him already hard at work, perspiring freely, banging away with his fist at a great bag of sailcloth about the size of a man's trunk which swung free from a tree in one corner of the yard. It seemed to be filled with sand or dirt, for its weight was substantial.

He happened to turn as I crossed the stable yard, which was empty but for two grooms lounging indifferently about. I was glad he spied me coming, for it seemed a risky matter to tap him on the shoulder when he was so engaged.

"Ah, Jeremy," said he, "glad I am to see you. I took an early start, seeing I'll be doing more teaching than working. I do like to get up a sweat each day, you see. Seem better for it, somehow."

"I'll remember that," said I.

"Aye, you'd do well to keep it in mind."

He was panting a bit. I wondered if he had not already put in a full hour.

"Now," he continued, "where might we start? First of all, doff that hat and pull off your coat. Though it's a bit cool today, you'll soon warm up."

I did as he told me, then rolled up my sleeves as well, as he had also done.

For a good five minutes he put me through a most strenuous series of stretches and pushes which quite exhausted me. But then I learned that all of it was mere preparation for what was to follow. And that was a period of hard work beating upon that heavy bag which hung from the tree. I could not make it swing freely as he had, yet that did not trouble him. Mr. Perkins was far more particular that I delivered my blows in the correct manner, leaning forward with each one, or as he put it, "throwing the body behind it." When I got the knack of that, I was able to make the bag swing a bit, and very proud I was. Yet just as I began to enjoy myself a bit (in spite of the rawness in my hands), he stopped me, saying that would do for now.

"But we're not through for the day," said he. "Ah no. For you must understand there's more to defendin' yourself than fisticuffs. As a matter of pure fact, you'll meet with few troublemakers willing to stand up and meet you man to man. If they're bigger than you, they'll try to wrestle you down and gouge out an eye or throttle you dead. If they're your size or smaller, then you must watch out for a knife."

"What then?" said I.

"Then, well . . . Take a look at me, Jeremy. If we were of the same strength and had the same skill with our fists, you'd have an advantage, now wouldn't you?"

"I suppose I would."

"Because you have two hands, and I have but one, ain't that so?"

"Yes, sir."

"But look sharp now." He stood close. "I have a knee to cause you great pain in your privates." And with that he pumped his leg so that his knee touched my groin yet without the force of a blow. "And I have a head to butt with." He grabbed my shirt and pulled me even closer, and then he touched my forehead with his own.

"Now," he continued, "some of your blackguards are quite adept at kneein' and buttin', but few of them—I've yet to meet one—who could manage this or defend proper against it."

He left me and went to the big bag hanging from the tree and put on a remarkable demonstration. He whirled about the bag, delivering kicks at it from one side and then another. He would feint with one foot, then hit with another—and then perhaps a double feint before striking. He kept constantly in motion, moving with the grace and speed of a dancer. But the kicks were delivered sharply and from every angle; some of them, it seemed, were sent home with deadly force. I had never seen, nor even imagined, the like.

Then, of a sudden, he stopped, turned, and walked to me. Again he panted slightly, yet he was nowhere near exhausted, as it seemed to me he should have been.

"Your kick is your best weapon," said he with a wink. "And that is because your legs are stronger than your arms. You can deliver it from your arse and break a bone. At the shin is good, for even if you don't break a leg, you can cause great pain. At the knee is better, for the kneecap is not well set, and if you dislodge it or crack it, you've crippled him absolutely. Best of all is the kick in the ribs, for if you break one of them—and they're not terrible strong—you may damage his inwards."

"But Mr. Perkins," said I, "is it fair to fight so?"

"Are you daft, Jeremy? You're no bully. You'll not go out looking for trouble. But trouble may find you just any day or night. When some villain seeks you out, you must defend yourself. He will not fight fair. You shouldn't neither."

"Yes, sir, I understand."

"Now let me see some kicks from you. You needn't keep moving as I did—not for now—just give me a few."

I let fly two, shifted my position, then hit the heavy bag twice more.

"Good," said he, "but put more snap into it. Snap it from the knee."

I went at it hard, trying to do as he had instructed.

"Better," said he, "but hit higher. Aim for the ribs."

More kicks, then:

"Put your arse into it. This time I want you to kick with the left, and feint with the right. The only defense he has is to grab your foot and set you hopping. If he shows you he intends that, then you let him have a fist in the face. His guard will be down most certain. So let's see a kick, a feint, and a blow to the face. Go on, Jeremy, you're doin' fine. You're a right good scholar, you are."

The second victim was found twenty-eight days after the first. Here, as I understand them, were the circumstances of the discovery: Constable Clarence Brede, a man of taciturn nature not well known to me personally, had been making a tour of those streets and lanes beyond Covent Garden as far as St. Martin's Lane. Circling back on Bedford Court to Bedford Street, where the stews and dives were well filled even at that hour of four o'clock in the morning, he found his way to that narrow alley which led to the churchyard of St. Paul's. It occurred to him he had not checked it first time round, and so he set off towards the locked gate of the churchyard. There was apparently no one about. A setting moon was low over the church. It provided sufficient light for him to see a large bundle or object up against the spiked bars of the churchyard fence. He hastened towards it, and coming near he saw that it was a body, the clothed body of a woman. She was, for the most part, supine, yet her shoulders were propped up against the fence, and her head lolled forward upon her chest. Any thought he may have had that the woman might simply have fallen there in a drunken stupor was quickly dispelled when he made to slap her cheek lightly to waken her. The cheek was cold. Her head flopped to one side. By the light of the moon he then saw that her chin and jowls had obscured a mortal wound circling her throat.

Immediately he pulled his tinder box from his pocket and lit the lantern he carried with him. Lifting her chin slightly he examined the wound more closely and saw that at its center there had been a good deal of bleeding which was not immediately apparent, for the blood had run down to the collar and bust of her frock, which was of a shade of dark blue called indigo, and been absorbed. It was half-dried and tacky to the touch. Constable Brede left the body where it lay and, with his lantern held high, made a general search of the area. By the time he had satisfied himself that his first impression was correct, that there was indeed no one about, he had returned to Bedford Street. Seizing upon the first nearly sober fellow to happen along, he asked his name and where he lived, then instructed him to proceed in haste to Number 4 Bow Street and inform the first-constable met there that there was a murdered woman at the gates to St. Paul's churchyard, just off Bedford Street. Constable Brede added that if the fellow were to fail to deliver the message, he would be guilty of hindering a constable in the discharge of his duties and would be dealt with severely by Sir John Fielding, Magistrate of the Bow Street Court. The messenger set off at a tipsy jog-trot, and the constable retired to the gates to stand guard over the corpus.

Thus it came about that I, called from my bed by Annie Oakum, accompanied Sir John and Benjamin Bailey to the site of the second homicide. It was well on to five o'clock, perhaps a bit after, by the time that we reached our destination, and there were in the east gray hints of dawn approaching. If Constable Brede's messenger had faithfully fulfilled his mission to Bow Street, he must also have told quite a few others along the way about the murder at the churchyard gates, for upon our arrival, we found that a considerable crowd had gathered. There must have been twenty or thirty there, and among them, five or six women. They had congregated at the far end of the narrow alley near the gates, inspired by nothing more than rowdy curiosity. Most were inebriated; a few seemed to have difficulty keeping their feet. They seemed to be pressing in on the constable. But for his part, he held firm, keeping them at bay a good eight or ten feet from the prone figure which he guarded.

"Follow me," said Benjamin Bailey.

And that we did—Sir John last of all with his hand upon my shoulder—proceeding close in the wake of that giant of a man who had long served as captain of the Bow Street Runners. Mr.

Bailey simply pushed through the assemblage, his club held before him in two hands, spilling them right and left as he led the way to Mr. Brede.

"Ah," said the beleaguered constable, "glad I am to see you. I've had to whack a couple, though I've broken no heads."

"Well, you and Mr. Bailey must clear them out. You have my permission to break a few if you must," said Sir John. "But first I shall give them warning."

He stepped forward so that he was near nose-to-nose with the front rank.

"I am Sir John Fielding, Magistrate of the Bow Street Court," he announced. There were grumbles in response. "I order you to disperse," he continued. "Any who think they may know the identity of the victim of this attack or have information to offer, I would have you wait in Bedford Street. The rest of you are to return to your dwelling places that we may be free to conduct our inquiry without interruption or bother. I shall give you a minute to clear the area, then I shall bid my constables to drive you out. Any who resist will be subject to arrest, fine, and imprisonment for not less than thirty days."

Sir John took two steps back and waited. About half the crowd, including all the women in their number, immediately turned about and started for the street beyond. The rest remained for but a moment, exchanging sullen glances, then began backing away, some slowly, most at a quick-step.

"Mr. Bailey, when you and Mr. Brede have seen them to Bedford Street, I would like you to remain there to see that they do not return. You might also interrogate those who may have information to see if any are worth my bother. Mr. Brede, when you have reached the street, please return to me and give your report." He gave a moment's pause. "You may proceed, gentlemen."

The two constables set out with some wide distance between them. Each held his crested club before him in two hands. What was left of the crowd scattered before them. One of the most drunken, however, permitted his legs to become entangled one with the other and fell sprawling before Mr. Brede. Unable to rise, even with the assistance of a whack on the backside administered by the constable, the poor fellow simply scrabbled with his elbows and knees quite without result. Mr. Brede bent down and said something that was lost to me in the clatter of feet on the cobblestones, then he moved on and left him lying. It took but a minute more to clear the alley.

"Have you noticed, Jeremy," said Sir John, "that there seems to be an increase in riotous behavior, unruly crowds, and the like?"

"Now that you mention it, sir, yes, I have."

"There was a terrible disturbance in St. Martin's Lane but a month past and another in Drury Lane two weeks ago near as bad." He paused, then added, "I do fear the rule of King Mob."

Constable Brede came back at a jog-trot, pausing only to have a word with him who had fallen. Then, a moment more, and he was with us.

"Mr. Brede?"

"Yes, Sir John, I am here."

"Then give your report, sir."

That he did, using far fewer words than I have in describing his discovery of the woman's body. He was, as I have said, a taciturn man, reserved in nature, one who kept himself a bit apart from the other constables. Not unfriendly was he—simply a bit stiff in his manner—an uncomfortable man who seemed to make others uncomfortable, too.

"Do you believe the attack took place where you found the body?" asked Sir John.

"Yes, sir, I do."

"Well . . . why, Constable? What did you find to support your belief?"

"It's what I didn't find."

"Yes?"

"After I saw she was dead, I lit my lantern and went searching in case the killer was still about—though I thought that unlikely. I also kept an eye open for blood spots. They wasn't any to be found—nowhere in the alley. There was something else, as well."

"And what, pray tell, was that?"

"Well, sir, if you wouldn't mind stepping over here to where she's lyin'." I guided Sir John for the three necessary steps. "When I come back, and before the crowd started to come, I took a closer look at her with the lantern, and I saw her dress was unbuttoned and just pushed together, like. So I ventured a look—I know we're not supposed to disturb things but I thought it might be important. May I now, sir?"

"Yes, of course."

Except for a cursory glance upon our arrival, I had not looked at the victim lying against the gates. The ugly wound at her throat was quite visible as Mr. Brede held up his lantern for us to see. Then he knelt beside her and pulled open her frock. Though certainly not experienced at viewing the dead and having little knowledge of the sort of damage possible to the human body by a determined assassin wielding a knife, I was not then, nor have I ever been, what one might call squeamish. Nevertheless, I was so shocked at what I saw that my stomach took a sudden, nasty turn. I turned away in disgust.

"I know you can't see, sir, so you must take my word she's quite bad cut-up in her body."

"Jeremy, can you be more specific?"

"Yes, sir, I'll try." I took a deep breath to begin and was suddenly aware of a bad odor compounded of blood and bodily organs, a slaughterhouse smell. "There's a big long cut from between her breasts to as far down as I can see. Then there are cuts under the breasts and the skin has been pulled back and sort of tucked to her sides so her inwards are exposed. There's a deal of blood, and some stuff like thick, bloody rope has been pulled out of her."

"That would be the intestines," said Sir John. "You've told me enough, Jeremy. Cover her up, Mr. Brede. Come, let us get away from the smell."

It was done, and we retired some several steps back. Yet once released, the odor seemed to follow us, pervading the air all round.

"When I saw how bad she was cut up, I looked beneath her and found there was blood had soaked through her dress onto the stones. So it does seem to me her throat was cut from behind, as is usual, then she was turned round, so to speak, and dropped down as she is now and all that cuttin' of her middle was done." He paused, then added: "I blame myself in this, Sir John."

"How is that, Mr. Brede?"

"Well, I came by here after midnight and took a look down the alley from Bedford Street. The moon was higher then, and I could see fairly well, and all seemed well, so I went on to St. Martin's Lane, where most of the trouble is. Perhaps if I'd come and taken a look, I might have caught the villain who done this deed, might even have prevented it."

"Not likely, Constable. There is an element of chance in these matters. You should put it out of your mind, for you have conducted yourself well, particularly in handling that crowd of rowdies before we came. I commend you."

Then did Sir John turn in my direction. "Jeremy, I must send you and Mr. Brede for Mr. Donnelly. You have visited his new surgery. Can you find it?"

"I'm sure I can, sir."

"Then you and Mr. Brede must find a stable open at this hour, get a wagon, and rouse Mr. Donnelly. This poor woman is not for the Raker."

"I know just such a place on Half Moon Street," volunteered Mr. Brede.

"Then go, both of you. I shall remain with Mr. Bailey. Send Bailey back to me with any potential witnesses he may deem worthy of interrogation."

"We'll be back as soon as ever we can," said I.

Mr. Brede said nothing and would continue saying nothing until we reached the stable. He did, however, point his club threateningly at the drunken man, as we passed him by, as if to say, Remain exactly where you are. The unfortunate man, whom I took to be under arrest, was sitting where he had fallen. He stared back at us, blank and befuddled.

The next time that I saw the fellow was in Sir John's courtroom at Number 4 Bow Street. He had been taken in by Mr. Bailey, as I understood, after they had finished a canvass of buildings and houses nearby which had yielded nothing; none who slept near the gates had been awakened by cries; the woman, whose true name was yet unknown, had been murdered in silence.

Sir John had fared better. Four of the women brought to him by Mr. Bailey had information to give—yet all gave similar information. Each was allowed separately to view the victim's face (though not the horrible wounds on her trunk); each identified her only as "Polly" though one said the woman was known in St. Martin's Lane as "Tuppence Poll," for having sold herself for so little when she was greatly in need. All but one had heard of her fierce argument with a "foreigner"; only one had actually been witness to it, and her name was Sarah Linney. Two said that he was a Jew named Yossel and described him as a "high-ripper"—the sort of thief who robbed prostitutes of their earnings, often at knife-point. They were greatly incensed and certain he had murdered their sister, Polly; all said they feared for their own lives.

As for myself, after assisting in the delivery of the corpus to Mr. Donnelly's surgery, I returned with Sir John to Bow Street. There, to my disappointment, I was sent up by him to perform my usual household duties. It was then but seven in the morning, and Annie Oakum and Lady Fielding were sitting at breakfast in the kitchen when I entered. They jumped from the table eager to know all about the matter that had taken Sir John and me away before dawn. Their questions put me in an awkward state. He had cautioned me to say nothing of what I had seen or heard. "Not even to Lady Fielding?" I had asked him. "Perhaps especially not to her," he had replied. So what was I to say when they came asking to know details of every sort? I allowed only that Sir John had been called to begin a homicide inquiry. (It seemed safe to say that, for nothing short of such a homicide would have brought him out at such an hour.) They were, of course, not satisfied with that and continued to question most vigorously. At last, I threw up my hands and told Lady Fielding and Annie that they must ask Sir John if they wanted to know more, for he had instructed me to say nothing. They took it as a challenge. Lady Fielding told Annie to do the buying in Covent Garden that day and find out all she could on the street; whilst she would make inquiries at the Magdalene Home for Penitent Prostitutes—news from the outside always seemed to find its way there. For me—I took it as a form of punishment for my silence—there was more scrubbing to be done. Since I had recently given a shine to the stairs, I was condemned to do the same to the floors of the kitchen, our little-used dining room, and the sitting room as well.

After breakfast, which I quite devoured so hungry was I, I went quickly to my task. Lady Fielding left. Annie went out and returned (pleasing me with her report that she had learned little but that the victim was a woman). All the while I worked with great enterprise. Whilst I was in no wise fond of scrubbing and such like, I was well practiced at it and knew that if I pleased myself with the job I did, I should certainly please Lady Fielding. Thus I managed to finish not long after noon, at which time I made straight for the stairs and, descending to Sir John's courtroom, I went to wait until I might learn more of the progress of the inquiry.

I opened the door quietly and just as quietly found a seat near the door. As I settled myself, I found Sir John concluding with a case of disputation between a Covent Garden merchant and a builder. From the little I heard, I concluded that the builder had erected a permanent stall, of which there were an increasing number in the Garden, that the stall had subsequently collapsed in the first heavy rainstorm, ruining not only the structure but a full day's supply of fruits and vegetables, as well.

I quote Sir John's judgment, for I have it still very well in my mind. May he forgive me if I have a word or two wrong:

"While the defendant has argued for himself ingeniously indeed, I cannot but believe that there is something specious in his argument that since no other buildings collapsed during the storm in question, the collapse of the stall constitutes an Act of God. He has even gone so far as to suggest that this calamity was visited upon the plaintiff as a punishment for his sins. There, Mr. Beaton, I believe you overstep yourself, for it is not up to us to judge the sins of others, unless they be so flagrant as to be considered criminal in nature—and then, only unless we be jurymen at trial. And just as you go too far there, you go not far enough in your understanding of what constitutes an Act of God. Under the law, this term of divine agency refers to an event that occurs without human intervention or participation—a great flood or a great wind, or the like. Since there was no flood and the wind that blew was of no particular consequence, we cannot attribute the collapse of the stall to such natural causes; and since I would not presume to be privy to the plaintiff's relation to his Creator, then we are left with your own faulty workmanship as the only possible cause for the collapse of the stall. That is how I rule—in favor of the plaintiff. Therefore, I obligate you, Mr. Beaton, to build a new stall for Mr. Grimes, one to his satisfaction that will stand a minimum of, let us say, five years—barring an Act of God, of course. You must also pay him the sum of five pounds for his loss of stock and custom. If you fail in carrying out this court's directives—well, sir, that is worth a stay in Newgate. Am I understood? Yea or nay?"

Mr. Beaton was beaten. He hung his head and answered with a docile, "Yes, sir, understood."

"So be it." Sir John clapped down his mallet, which did him for a gavel, and called forth, "Next case."

(Reader, I quote thus at length as an example of the lessons I learned in Sir John Fielding's Bow Street Court long before I began formally to read the law with him. In this instance, of course, I was never to forget what it was that legally constituted an Act of God.)

"Thaddeus Millhouse, come forward," bellowed Mr. Marsden in full voice.

Then Sir John conferred a moment with his clerk, listened attentively, then nodded. As he did so, a small man rose in a manner most diffident and measured off the five or six paces which brought him before the magistrate. I recognized him as the drunken man who had fallen before Constable Brede.

"Thaddeus Millhouse, you have been detained for disobeying my order to leave the alley which leads from St. Paul's churchyard to Bedford Street. Since I gave the order, and Constable Brede who put you under arrest had a long, hard night of it, I have dispensed with his presence. I am well enough acquainted with the circumstances of this matter. So you must tell me, Mr. Millhouse, what have you to say in your defense?"

"Well, sir," said he, in a voice so small I felt it necessary to strain forward to listen. "I had every intention of doing what you said, but I could not."

"And why was that?"

"I was drunk, sir."

"A little louder, please."

"*I was drunk!*" It came from him as a loud wail of despair.

His shout brought forth a great roar of laughter from those assembled in the courtroom. They came to be entertained and sought every least occasion for merriment. Sir John hammered them to silence.

"Mr. Millhouse, you were not the only drunk in that alley last night. Others managed to stagger out to Bedford Street, why not you?"

"Alas, Sir John, I was so lamentably besotted that I tripped over my own feet and could not then for the life of me rise up."

"I regret to inform you, sir, that the penalty for public drunkenness is the same as that with which I threatened that unruly crowd last night—fine and imprisonment for not less than thirty days. Have you nothing more to say in your defense?"

"In truth, I have not."

"Then I have but little choice—"

"May I speak for him, sir?" It was a woman's voice that rang out in the small courtroom. And it was a woman in the first row who stood up, a babe in her arms, and took her place beside Thaddeus Millhouse.

"And who might you be, madam?" asked Sir John.

"I am his wife," said she. "My name is Lucinda Millhouse. And though you cannot see him, he may make himself heard to you," said she, "and so I mention that I have in my arms our son, Edward Millhouse."

Far from inciting laughter from the courtroom crowd, the sudden and dramatic interruption by Mrs. Millhouse hushed all present immediately. Even Mr. Marsden could but stare wide-eyed at the two of them together—or perhaps three, better put. I know not if anything such as this had ever happened in his memory; I know it had not in mine. All present simply waited to see what would happen next. Would Sir John countenance such an interruption? Or would he simply instruct Mr. Fuller to eject her from the room?

"What would you say, then, Mrs. Millhouse?" asked the magistrate.

"I would say, sir, that if he is fined, we cannot pay, and if he is imprisoned, Edward and I shall starve. This is no defense, to be sure, but a plea for mercy. Thaddeus has just been given employment. Do, please, let him work."

There was a great murmur among the courtroom crowd, yet for once Sir John made no move to silence it. He sat quiet for near a minute.

"Mr. Millhouse, tell me, what sort of work do you do?"

"I am a scholar and a poet."

"Oh, dear God!" gasped Sir John. It was a cry of exasperation.

"Formerly a schoolteacher," added Mr. Millhouse.

"And no doubt you gave up that position to come to London where you would seek fame and fortune as a poet."

"Yes, sir." He hung his head. "That was some six months past."

"And you have not yet found it."

"No, sir, only mere occasional work in Grub Street."

"But now, according to your wife, you have been granted steady employment, presumably of a long term nature. Is that correct?"

"Yes, sir, I have been employed by Mr. John Hoole to assist him in the translation of Lodovico Ariosto's *Orlando Furioso* and to perform general secretarial duties for him. He is incapacitated with a broken knee. I . . . I was to begin Monday next. I went out last night with friends to celebrate our good fortune."

"Friends who allowed you to drink far past your capacity."

"I cannot blame them, sir. I fear that when I start drinking, I cannot stop."

"Well, it would seem, Mr. Millhouse, that you would then be wisest never to start."

"That would indeed seem to be the answer, sir."

Again, Sir John fell silent. He clasped his hands before him and gave thought to the matter.

"This court is not in the business of starving mothers and babies," said he at last. "Nevertheless, you, Mr. Millhouse, have admitted you culpability. You have declared that it was your intention to obey my order, but you could not because of your drunken state. Either way, sir, you are liable for punishment. What shall your punishment be?" He left us all in suspense for a moment. "I am willing to waive the jail term of thirty days in answer to your wife's plea. However, I shall fine you one shilling to be paid each month for a time not exceeding one year from today. Can you manage that?"

Both Mr. and Mrs. Millhouse cried out at the same time, he offering his heartfelt thanks, and she blessing him in God's name.

Sir John waved them quiet and continued: "However, Mr. Millhouse, if in that year you appear before me again for public drunkenness, you may expect little mercy from me. Is that understood?"

"Oh yes, sir, indeed it is. But, sir," he added, "there is but one thing more."

"And what is that?"

"That woman, out in the alley, the victim of the murder . . ."

"Yes, what about her?"

"I gathered from what I heard this morning as I waited to go before you that you have had difficulty fixing her identity."

"That is correct."

"I believe I know who she is."

Mrs. Millhouse turned to her husband in surprise.

"Of course, it was dark there in the alley. The moon was near down by the time I arrived to look. And it's been established I was in a drunken state . . ."

"Yes, man, out with it."

"Nevertheless, I believe her to be one Priscilla Tarkin who lives in our court in Half Moon Street."

"Oh, Tad," wailed his wife. "Polly? Say it is not so."

He could offer her little hope, for in spite of his reservations, having now spoken, he seemed quite sure.

"And why did you not come forward with this at the time?"

"I would have," said he, "but I fear that when I tripped and fell, my mind went completely blank. I can recall nothing of that period afterwards."

"Well and good," said Sir John. "I must, however, ask you to remain, for the law requires a more formal identification than you have just made."

Mrs. Millhouse insisted on accompanying us to Mr. Donnelly's surgery on Tavistock Street. As I led the way, for I was the only one of our company who knew its exact location, she had poured out to

Sir John all she knew of poor Polly Tarkin. Though I had no way of knowing, the story she told was one characteristic of many older women forced into prostitution—a husband who died leaving her in debt, a son who had disappeared into the American colonies, desperation, no way of earning her keep except by selling herself. She was neither young nor pretty, and so she frequently went hungry. The Millhouse family had often shared their little with her. By way of repayment, she would care for Edward when Mrs. Millhouse left on errands about the town.

"Had she no trade? no craft? no means of employment?" asked Sir John.

"She said not," said Mrs. Millhouse. "The poor woman felt only shame for what she did. We had not the heart to turn our backs on her."

Through it all, Thaddeus Millhouse had listened to his wife's dreary tale as it was told across streets and down lanes. At the end of it, he commented only thus: "What she did or did not do is all the same now. We all feel shame before God." He said it queerly, and in such a way that ended the discussion. Only young Edward Millhouse, who looked to be some months shy of a year in age, had much to say after that. He began carrying on rather fretfully, and by the time we reached the entrance to Mr. Donnelly's building, he was in full cry.

"Teething," explained his mother, as she bounced the babe in her arms.

Whatever it was that vexed Edward served to announce us to Mr. Donnelly, for by the time we reached his door, the surgeon had it open, so eager was he to welcome patients to his new office.

"Ah, it is you, Sir John." To his credit he seemed not the least disappointed. "Come in, come in, all of you."

Sir John introduced the visitors and explained the nature of our visit. I noticed Mr. Donnelly cast a dubious glance at Mrs. Millhouse.

"I'm afraid, madam, I cannot allow you to view the body."

"But why?" said she. "I knew her best."

"You might not know her at all as she is now." He went to the door to the next room. "Give me but a moment, and I shall prepare the corpus for viewing, Mr. Millhouse."

When Mr. Donnelly called out to come ahead, Sir John signaled that I was to remain as he followed Thaddeus Millhouse through the door. Fumbling a bit, he managed to close it after him.

We waited—Lucinda Millhouse, Edward, and I—as voices muttered low from beyond. Mr. Donnelly's was a humble surgery. There were but two rooms. This one provided him with living space and would also do for him as a place where patients might wait for his attention—if patients ever came. They might sit upon the couch where I sat, a couch which also served him as a bed. For minutes Mrs. Millhouse paced the floor with Edward, who continued his fussing. Then, of a sudden, she seated herself on one of the simple chairs which had been pulled away from the deal table in one corner of the room. She began dandling the young fellow on her knee.

"He is not always so," said she to me in the nature of an apology. "Edward is usually the sweetest-tempered of lads. It's his teeth coming in, you see. It distresses all babes."

I assured her that his cries did certainly not distress me.

"It will be good for Tad—Mr. Millhouse, that is—to get away from our room in his new employment. It has been most difficult for him to work, day or night, with all of us cooped together."

"No doubt," said I in a sympathetic manner.

The door to the next room opened, and the subject of her concern swiftly emerged. His eyes were red, and though he had wiped them dry with the kerchief clutched in his hand, it was evident he had been weeping.

"Come, Lucy, let's away," said he.

Yet as she rose, Mr. Donnelly came out, a small container in his hand. "But a moment," said he. "I have a salve here for the baby's gums. Just rub the tiniest bit where the tooth is coming in, and it will give him relief."

Mrs. Millhouse accepted it rather reluctantly. "What is in it?" she asked.

"It is a very mild mix of opium. Don't worry. It was used often on babies in Lancashire with no bad result."

"We . . . we cannot pay."

"Take it with my good wishes. But remember—only the tiniest bit."

"Thank you ever so much. I—"

"*Lucy!*" Mr. Millhouse stood at the door to the hallway, hurrying their departure. "Please, let us be off."

She nodded to us all and scurried after him, pulling the door shut with a loud bang. We listened to the descending footsteps. And only then did Sir John emerge from the examination room.

"Why did you do that?" Mr. Donnelly asked him. "There was really no need to display those horrible wounds in the abdomen. A look at her face would have done, surely."

"I wanted to get a reaction from him," said Sir John calmly.

"Well, you certainly got one! I thought for a moment I should have to apply some oil of turpentine to his nose in order to revive him. And dear God, the tears! Why, I thought he would 'drown the stage with tears.'"

"It was rather a surplus of reaction, wouldn't you say so?"

"Well, he had spoken of her as one might speak of a family friend. Imagine living on such terms with a prostitute."

"And the fellow does claim to be a poet."

"Well, with a poet such a surfeit of emotion is always possible, even likely."

"Nevertheless," said Sir John, "it does make one curious. That is why I invited him to come in and talk to me tomorrow morning."

"But you said you wanted only to discuss certain details of the victim's life—friends, frequent visitors, and so on."

"I would not put him on his guard, Mr. Donnelly. But enough of that, what have you to tell me of the wounds of Priscilla Tarkin?"

"Ah, the victim, of course. Well, I've written out a report, as you requested, for the record. Shall I read it to you?"

"No, tell it. That way I shall retain the essentials."

"Oh, very well. Let me see now." He paused but a moment to collect himself. "She was almost certainly attacked from the rear. There were bruises left and right on her cheeks, which I should say indicated that a large hand had been clamped over her mouth. A single cut was made across her throat from the left. Her gullet and windpipe had been severed right down to the spinal cord. Thus we have the cause of death. The mutilation of her abdomen and interior parts was done afterwards. That consisted of a cut made from sternum to pubic bone and lateral cuts made below the ribs and approximately two inches below the navel. They were deep, long, dragging cuts and did considerable damage to the organs beneath—stomach and intestines were badly lacerated. The skin of her abdomen had been flapped back, perhaps to get at her womb, which had been stabbed through—or perhaps merely out of curiosity at what lay beneath. The intestines had been displaced, perhaps again to get at the womb."

"In other words, he knew where to look for that female organ," put in Sir John, "and it was important to him to find it."

"You might say so, yes."

"This would then be consistent with your speculation with regard to the first victim that the assailant had some knowledge of anatomy."

"Well . . . yes." It was reluctant agreement at best. Then added the surgeon: "There are differences here, though, that make me a little less certain about that. The hacking and slashing nature of these wounds makes me think they were done swiftly and with a practiced hand. Also, their nature suggests to me that they were done in anger—an absolute rage."

"And what about the size of the woman? I had not asked that earlier. I should have."

"She was not small, about nine stone, I should say. Nothing like the Amazon he first took on. In any case, he had no trouble controlling her. For that matter, he had no trouble with either woman."

"Indeed," said Sir John, and grew thoughtful for a space. Then: "May I ask a very basic question?"

"Of course, Sir John. They are often the most important."

"Would it be possible to inflict the wounds you have described without spattering yourself with the victim's blood?"

"The mutilation, perhaps, although it was done in haste—and whatever is done in haste is sure to be messy. But that long cut across the throat also severed both the major carotid artery and the major jugular vein. Blood would have gushed, perhaps spurted. His hand, wrist, and forearm would almost certainly have been spattered with blood."

"Jeremy? Are you here?"

"Yes, of course, Sir John."

"Have we overlooked the obvious? Was Mr. Millhouse's coat-sleeve or cuff bloodstained?"

I thought upon it but a moment. "No, sir," said I, "and his coat was of such a color that it would show most plain."

"I will second that," said Mr. Donnelly.

"And what would you judge his size to be?"

Before either of us could answer, a sturdy rap came upon the door. Mr. Donnelly looked at me and shrugged, then stepped over and threw open the door. There stood Dr. Amos Carr, the former Army surgeon who had upon occasion and in Mr. Donnelly's absence, served Sir John and the Bow Street Runners. It was he who had amputated Mr. Perkins's arm when Mr. Perkins thought it might be saved. Sir John did not hold him in high esteem.

"Well, Mr. Donnelly," he boomed forth, "I had heard you were returned to London and set up your surgery here. Though we have met but twice or thrice previous, I thought to come by like a good colleague and give you a warm welcome."

For a moment or more, Mr. Donnelly was quite struck dumb. But he recovered himself and bade his visitor enter.

"Ah, Sir John!" exclaimed Dr. Carr, spying us both. "Working again with Mr. Donnelly, are you? I had heard he gave you help on that nasty homicide behind New Broad Court."

"And now there is a second," said Mr. Donnelly.

I noted Sir John's lips purse at that. I could tell he felt that Mr. Donnelly had spoken out of turn.

"You don't mean it?" said the former army surgeon. "Who was it?"

"A prostitute, like the first," said Mr. Donnelly.

"Ah, those poor women. I daresay they are the least safe of all on the street."

"Unfortunately so," agreed Sir John.

"You know," said Dr. Carr, "when I heard of your service to Sir John, it was days after the event, and the victim was already underground, I'm sure. But if there is indeed a second victim, you may be able to put this bit of advice to work for you."

"What advice have you, Dr. Carr?" said Sir John. "I am most eager to know."

"Mr. Donnelly, I seem to recall that formerly your surgery was equipped with a—what do they call them? micro . . . ?"

"A microscope, sir."

"Ah yes, most up-to-date and scientific you are. I trust that you still have it somewhere about?"

"Oh indeed I do. I find it aids me in a multitude of ways."

"Now, what I tell you may sound a bit outlandish, but I assure you that it is proven fact. I myself have observed it after a fashion, as I shall explain." With the attention of both men, he seemed to expand visibly, wishing to extend his lecture and thereby hold them even longer. He paused to build a sense of anticipation. At last he resumed: "Now, in several instances while in the Army I had the occasion to examine the eyes of the dead, and I can tell you that it is true that in their pupils you may see the last image imprinted upon the living eye. There was indeed *something* there! The difficulty is, of course, that it cannot be perceived even with a magnifying glass. I know that, for I tried on those several occasions with just such an instrument.

"But you, Mr. Donnelly, with your microscope, would fare much better. My advice is this: Simply remove the eyeballs of the second victim and place them in such a way that the pupils may be minutely examined. I know the power of those micro . . . uh . . . scopes. They are quite amazing. Once you have a clear picture of the pupil before you, increased many tens of times over, you will also have a picture of the murderer. Is that not quite logical?"

"Oh . . . very . . . I suppose," stammered Mr. Donnelly.

"Would you like me to assist in the operation?"

"That will, unfortunately, not be possible," said Sir John, "for Mr. Donnelly has concluded his examination, and the victim has been sent off to the Raker."

"Perhaps the body could be returned," suggested Dr. Carr.

"Why, perhaps it could! Come along, Jeremy, let us go and look into that possibility. Goodbye, all."

And faster than we entered, we left that modest surgery, Sir John pulling me by the arm, and the deserted Mr. Donnelly staring after us unhappily. The magistrate said not a word until we reached the street, and even then he kept his voice to just above a whisper.

"Jeremy," said he, "I always thought that man Carr was a fool, but I was wrong. I see now that he is quite mad."

FIVE

In Which the Search for Yossel Begins and Ends

That evening, having returned with Constable Perkins from another of his exhausting lessons in self-defense, I happened to be about below when Sir John summoned the full complement of Bow Street Runners to his chambers. Curious as always, I trailed in among them. Though I had not been invited, I had not been told specifically to stay away. I chose for myself an inconspicuous spot in one corner. None in that group of red-vested worthies questioned my right to be present; none so much as looked at me askance. When all had come together, and Sir John had been so informed by Mr. Benjamin Bailey, he stood up before them and addressed them as follows:

"Gentlemen," said he, "you have all been made aware by now of the two homicides perpetrated within our precinct during the last days. The unfortunate victims were both women of the streets. Our inquiries have so far yielded naught save a single name which I shall give to you presently. We have no proper motive. Each of the women was left with money, however little, on her person. The second, whose body was discovered last night by Constable Brede, was horribly mutilated. I can only speculate that the murderer, whoever he may be, took some perverse pleasure in the insult to her corpus.

"Now, there is little, perhaps, that can be done to prevent these attacks, for they are accomplished in secret and in dark places. What can be done, however, is to make the probable victims of them aware of their danger. That for whatever vicious reason the murderer has made women his particular victims seems obvious. The nature of the mutilation of the second victim confirms it. I should hazard that prostitutes have been chosen because of their availability and their willingness to accompany the murderer into dark corners. What you must do tonight and each night until this man be caught, is to warn these women, all of them you may come across—and that will of course be a great many—of the threat to them. If they have not heard that there has been a second victim, then inform them.

"And while you are about it, give them the name 'Yossel,' and ask them, do they know him, and have they seen him. This name was given me by four women, all of whom knew last night's victim by sight and one of whom had seen him and the victim quarreling earlier last night. He was described by two as a 'foreigner,' and by two others specifically as a 'Jew'—though he has no beard, and his garments are not such as a Jew might wear. All four agreed he is the sort who robs prostitutes of their earnings. That was likely the basis of his quarrel with the victim, whose name, by the bye, was Priscilla Tarkin, better known as 'Poll.'"

At this point, Sir John paused. Then said he: "It comes to me that at least some of you may know this fellow Yossel by reputation and by sight. Would you give me an 'aye' if you do?"

The men exchanged glances, as if seeking permission each from the other to speak out. As a result, the response was delayed somewhat but came as a resounding affirmative when at last it was heard.

"Ah!" said Sir John. "It appears Yossel is well known to most of you. Then by all means, bring him in if you see him. Detain him for questioning. In all truth, I cannot yet call him a suspect, yet his name was given me, and it is at present the only one that we have. He is said to go armed with a knife, so treat him with the proper degree of caution—though I doubt not that each of you is capable of handling him."

Again he paused—but just long enough to offer a nod in dismissal. "That will be all, gentlemen," said he. "I thank you for your time, and I do put my faith in you."

With that, he resumed his seat behind his desk, folded his hands before him, and waited thus until we had all filed from his chambers. I ascended the stairs to our kitchen, secure in my belief that when next I came down again, the villainous Yossel would be apprehended, locked up in the strong room, and awaiting Sir John's pleasure as to when and where to interrogate him.

Alas, however, it was not so. For when, next morning, I answered Sir John's summons and returned, I found the strong room empty and

Mr. Millhouse arrived, pacing up and down, looking left and right. He recognized me immediately and came to me forthwith.

"Ah," said he, "young Mr. Proctor, is it not?"

I agreed that it was.

"Perhaps I've come too early for my appointment with Sir John. He asked only that I come by in the morning. I sent in word by that gentleman there"—he ducked his head in Mr. Marsden's direction—"that I'd arrived. But I was told simply to wait. If this is an inconvenient hour, I should be happy to return later. I wonder," said he, hesitating, "could you possibly tell him that for me?"

"I should be happy to do so," said I, bobbing at the waist in a tight little bow, "*if* he will admit me to deliver your message. He does sometimes prefer to sit alone and consider those matters that weigh upon him."

"I quite understand," said he, returning my bow most gracefully.

"If you will excuse me," said I.

Turning, I left him where he stood and made straight for the door to Sir John's chambers. Contrary to what I had said to Mr. Millhouse, I was quite confident that I should be invited in—and I was. Closing the door quietly behind me, I made swiftly across the room to the desk. Sir John leaned across it in a conspiratorial manner.

"He's here now," whispered Sir John. "Millhouse, I mean."

"I know," said I. "He spoke with me out in the corridor."

"We must think of something for you to do, some work for you here whilst I put questions to him."

"Those boxes in the corner," said I. "They're filled with papers. I'll go through them and divide them in piles."

"Perfect," said Sir John, quiet as he could. "Call him in now."

I opened the door and did so, then swiftly did I retreat to the biggest of the boxes, threw it open, and scattered papers about. Let Mr. Millhouse make what he will of it, said I to myself.

This subterfuge, though perhaps not absolutely necessary, was occasioned by Sir John's desire to have an observer present during those interrogations he deemed to be of potential importance. Sir John believed that one who told lies must needs always give some indication of it. If not in his voice, then in his eyes, his manner of breathing, even in the posture he assumes on a chair. "A man might even tell the truth," he had said, "and betray worry over his answer—even worry over the question. When I know what worries a man, I shall know better how to direct my interrogations."

And so it was that when Mr. Millhouse entered, he found me in a corner, worrying over a great stack of papers. That corner afforded me an angle from which I might view his face as he would converse with Sir John.

"Come in, come in, sir," said the magistrate. "Sit down, please. Perhaps you can tell me a bit more of poor Poll's background, her visitors, and so on."

"Perhaps I can," said Mr. Millhouse. He looked round him then. His glance seemed to linger upon me. At last he eased down into a chair which stood directly opposite Sir John; only the desk separated them.

"Oh . . . I hope the presence of Jeremy will not disturb you greatly. I have given him a task of sorting through past records of the Bow Street Court. The Lord Chief Justice has demanded a survey of us, and it must be done."

"No, no, that's quite all right."

"Very good. Now, Mr. Millhouse, your wife was quite forthcoming regarding Priscilla Tarkin's unfortunate circumstances and sterling character, and so on, and while I'm sure what she said was quite accurate, so far as it went, it was not the sort of information likely to help our inquiry into the death of the poor woman. I was hoping that you, as a man and as Polly's neighbor, might have been more observant of her habits, her commerce, and so on."

"Well, I'll tell you what I can, of course."

"How long were you acquainted with her?"

"The entire six months we have been here in London."

"And how was it that you became aware of her—what shall we call it?—her line of work? Surely she herself didn't inform you immediately?"

"No, certainly not. I would say that our knowledge came only gradually."

He seemed to grow more tense. His hands, which he had rested on his knees, no longer rested; they twitched a bit as his fingers examined the seams of his breeches. "Not long after our arrival, perhaps a month, we were wakened quite late at night by an awful row next door. The wall between her place and our own seems quite thin. In any case, there were cries and shouts, and one of the voices distinctly male. An accusation of theft was made and denied. My wife urged me to go next door to see what I could do to settle the matter, or at least calm them down. I was just pulling on my clothes when suddenly we heard the door slam and loud footsteps departing. Well, one naturally wonders at a male guest well after midnight, or perhaps one assumes the obvious; I know I did. My wife was unwilling to do so, and so next day she approached Poll in a manner most sympathetic and heard from her the story she gave you yesternoon. She had already formed an affection for the woman; her pity for her now deepened it."

"But you said you came upon this gradually," said Sir John. "There must have been hints earlier."

"Well, there were. First of all, she was a widow, living alone, and had no means of support that I could tell. She slept late in the morning. And I had already spied her out on the street in the evening, loitering about in such a way as to make herself available to conversation with strangers."

"I see. Now, if I may take you back to that occasion when you and your wife were wakened by the row, let me ask you this: Was the accusation of theft which you mentioned made in her voice? I know that women of the streets are often preyed upon by thieves of every sort. We are now searching for one who made a practice of robbing prostitutes of their earnings. He was seen quarreling with her earlier on the night she was murdered. Did the male voice you heard give indication of a foreign accent?"

"Oh no, nothing of the kind," said he. "First of all, it would have been difficult to say that the man in question spoke, as you describe, with an accent that might be described as foreign. I only heard him say quite clearly, 'You got it, ain't you, you thieving bitch.' Pardon the language. You see, *he* it was who accused *her.* And her response was all in denial."

"Oh? Interesting. Did you see men entering her room in her company?"

"No, never, which seems curious, since our rooms were adjoining. On a number of occasions, however, we heard male voices."

"In accusation?"

"Not that we could tell. There were no more rows, in any case."

It is worth noting at this point that gradually Mr. Millhouse had relaxed during the last questions put to him by Sir John. However, during the next few he tensed as never before. His body seemed to coil. He shifted his position in his chair so restlessly that I should have thought him sitting on a cushion of thorns had I not often sat in it myself.

"You mentioned having seen her on the street before the night of the row. Did you see her afterwards upon occasion as you have described—loitering, on the lookout, as it might be?"

"Yes, on a number of occasions."

"Was she sometimes in conversation with men?"

"Sometimes, yes."

"Well, did you take note of them, sir? What did they look like? Did you see her more than once with the same man?"

"No, no, no, really, Sir John, I took no notice of them at all." Mr. Millhouse sounded near as agitated as he appeared. "It was most embarrassing to meet her in such situations. I looked away and hurried past. I had no wish to scrutinize those she sought to tempt."

"When you met her on the street just so," said Sir John, "did she speak in greeting? Did she give some sign of recognition? Did she smile or perhaps nod her head?"

"No . . . well, yes, perhaps. I don't know. Why do you ask such a question? Well, all right, I suppose I must answer. On a few occasions she did greet me."

"I take it these were occasions when there was no man about."

"Of course!"

"And how did she greet you, Mr. Millhouse? Did she seem to look upon you as a potential client?"

"No!"

"How can you be sure?"

"Because she gave an ordinary greeting as one might give a neighbor—'Good day, Mr. Millhouse,' or some such."

"And what was your response to her neighborly greeting?"

"I told you! I hurried by. Oh, I may have given her a hello in return, but I certainly did not stop to pass the time of day!"

"And why not, sir? From your description, I would say that you snubbed her. Why did you do that?"

"Because I did not wish to be seen as one of those men who passes his time idly talking to whores! I cannot make it more plain than that!"

Sir John allowed Mr. Millhouse to calm himself a bit. Indeed he did need calming. His face had reddened. For a time I thought that he kept himself seated by pure force of will. His legs twitched. He seemed to wish to leap to his feet and run from the place. But at last Sir John resumed:

"But a moment ago you asked me why I should ask you such a question. Let me tell you, I ask you such questions as these so that I may know your relation to the victim. Your wife made hers plain. Yet I have yet to understand fully your own feelings towards Priscilla Tarkin—and, for that matter, hers towards you."

At that moment Mr. Millhouse threw a rather desperate look in my direction. He caught me staring. I had given up all pretense of separating the ancient court records into piles, so fascinated was I by the progress of Sir John's interrogation. Mr. Millhouse turned back to Sir John then, yet for a moment he seemed quite unable to respond.

"Well, I . . . ," he began uncertainly. "I pitied her, of course, but I . . ."

We waited. But having begun, he seemed quite unable to proceed. Nothing was forthcoming. He sat dumbly for near a minute.

"Let us put that aside for a moment," said Sir John. "Another question for you—one that should be easy to answer. And that question is this: Did you see Priscilla Tarkin alive on the night she died?"

He sighed. "Yes, she made an appearance in the Dog and Duck on Bedford Street where I was drinking with my friends. She walked through the place, seeking custom."

"Did she speak to you?"

"She said hello."

"Did you speak to her?"

"No."

"Who were those with whom you drank that night?"

"Mr. Oliver Goldsmith, poet, historian, romancer, and once, as I understand, physician, as well."

"That is one. Were there others?"

"Mr. Thomas Davies, actor, author, and editor, and briefly, a Mr. Ephraim Butts, a friend of Mr. Davies, of whom I know little, having first met him only on that occasion."

"Very good. Now, I have something here." Sir John opened the drawer in his desk and felt about in it for a moment. He brought out a key and placed it before him on his desk. "Yes," he continued, "this key. Do you recognize it, Mr. Millhouse?"

"Why, it looks quite like the key to our room."

"No doubt it does. It is, I take it, the key to Polly Tarkin's room, for it was found in her pocket by Mr. Donnelly, together with a shilling and a few pence. Jeremy?" He turned in my direction. "I hear papers shuffle from time to time, so I assume you are still with us."

"I am, sir," said I.

"Would you go now and fetch your hat and coat to accompany Mr.

Millhouse to Half Moon Street that he may point out to you her room. I wish you to search it, Jeremy. Learn what you can of her, those she may have known, and anything else that may be helpful to the inquiry. Feel free to bring back to Bow Street anything you deem of particular interest."

I jumped up quickly from the station I had taken in the corner. "I should be happy to do so, sir." And I made to go. Mr. Millhouse gaped.

"Close the door after you," Sir John called after me, "and wait in the hall."

This was, for me, quite an unexpected turn. First to be given the opportunity to put questions to a witness, as I had done with Mrs. Crewton, and now to be asked to search for clues in the domicile of the victim—it was clear that Sir John was offering me greater responsibilities in the conduct of his inquiries. The prospect excited me as no other since I had been accepted as a member of his household.

My hand fairly shook with anticipation as I attempted to insert key to lock. Yet with an effort, I took hold of myself and rammed the thing home. At that point, before turning the key, I faced Mr. Millhouse, who had been hovering over me there on the narrow porch.

"Sir," said I to him, "I must now ask you to go about your business."

"What? Why, see here, you young—"

I interrupted him firmly: "You heard, as well as I, that Sir John Fielding assigned this task to me and to no other. If you insist on accompanying me, I shall have to return tonight with one of the constables, who will assist me. I hope I have made myself clear."

It seemed that I had. Mr. Millhouse drew himself up as if about to unleash an harangue, then stood baffled, quite unable to speak. I waited a decent space. Then, with a firm nod and a "good day," I turned the key, swung the door open, and stepped inside. Then I removed the key, and closed the door firmly behind me.

The place was quite dark. I went to the windows and threw back the heavy curtains. The sudden light revealed a room of medium size, certainly larger than my own at Number 4 Bow Street, one with a small fireplace, complete with a small cookstove, at the far end. It was altogether better furnished than I had expected. The bed was good-sized and laid-over neatly with a comforter. There was a chest three drawers high, a writing table with a straight chair, a wardrobe, and two comfortable chairs for sitting, even a small rug upon the floor. All these bespoke an earlier life of some comfort. It was indeed far from the squalor of the room described by Private Sperling to which he had been taken by Teresa O'Reilly. How had "Tuppence Poll" managed to live in such a manner as this? I set about in my search to discover the answer to that question.

The wardrobe yielded nothing but clothes. There were a great many of them, more by far than I would have expected. Some were obviously old and threadbare, some were not. Of a sudden I recalled the frock she wore at her death. It was of good, heavy wool stuff which, with the shawl she wore, would have kept her warm even at the late hour at which she was found. Surely that was new, was it not? How had she managed?

Through the chest I searched, but the drawers I ransacked contained naught but undergarments and stockings and keepsakes of various kinds. These last I examined closely. There were a great many—ribbons in abundance of every color, combs which were crested and plain, rings. I examined them closely; a few appeared to be of gold; others, not of gold, were of intricate design; and there were two in which were set stones of some worth. Most striking of all were two cameos, which I guessed to be of considerable worth. This, it seemed to me, was too grand a store for any single woman, much less one who pretended to great poverty.

I found something of great interest in the single drawer of the writing table. It was an account book or ledger—I was not sure how to call it, for I had then no experience of commerce—but I saw that it was a dated list of transactions which went back some three years into the past. There must have been some twenty pages filled, with thirty entries to the page. Though the items sold were in some manner of code, as were the listed buyers, the amounts were given plainly in shillings and pence. This must certainly go back with me to Number 4 Bow Street. If she were so active in selling as it appeared, then she must have had a treasure trove hidden away in some secret place. I looked around me. It was not a large room. Surely I could find it. And so I began my search in earnest. I pulled out the drawers and looked behind each of them and found—nothing. There were a few incidental discoveries: when I threw the bed apart, I found a dagger tucked in easy reach beneath the mattress, and under the bed was a loaded pistol. Had she them with her the night she was murdered, she might be alive in this very room today.

Remembering my efforts in the Goodhope residence two years past, I took out my tinder box and lit a candle. Thus readied, I carefully examined each and every brick in the fireplace. It took me near an hour to do so. Yet none had been loosed. All were firmly set. Not a single brick rang hollow.

By the time I finished, I was soot-stained to my wrists; my clothes were also streaked; and I was so vexed at my failure that I retreated to the middle of the room and stamped my feet in a little dance of frustration.

Thus did I find what I was looking for.

Though there was a rug covering that part of the floor, I distinctly felt a board give beneath my right foot. I threw back the rug and went down on my hands and knees—knocking, pressing, searching to find with my hands what my foot had but a moment before found quite without design or intention. In the end, I was forced to jump up and go stomping about once more with my heels in search of the place. Then, having rediscovered it, I grabbed the dagger off the bed and proceeded to dig away at a board in the floor of about the width of my hand, or perhaps a little larger. I did then manage to pry it from its place and look below.

The space beneath was filled fair to overflowing with all manner of items that might easily be napped from gentlemen. There were three or four silk kerchiefs, washed and folded neatly; there were three timepieces, one of them in a case that looked to be of gold; there were even two pairs of eyeglasses in the square style that was then most popular. This was a store of goods waiting to be sold. But where . . . perhaps . . . yes!

What I sought was beneath the pile of kerchiefs. Call it a wallet, or a purse, but it was of good leather and bound with thongs. I undid them carefully and peeked inside. It was fat with gold sovereigns and guineas, the harvest of three years dedicated to criminal pursuits.

Quite unable to help myself, I let out a yelp of triumph. Then, remembering that only a thin wall separated me from Mr. Millhouse, I quietened immediately; yet I could not resist muttering quietly, "Polly Tarkin, I have you to rights! You, my good woman, were a great thief!"

Barely had I time to present Sir John with the purse and account book (which he dropped in his desk drawer) when I was whisked off by him in the direction of Tavistock Street. I naturally assumed that we were on our way to visit Mr. Donnelly; this, however, was not to be the case.

As we went, I told him in detail of the search I had conducted. I was altogether bursting with pride at what I had accomplished. So it was that when I began to sense a certain lack of satisfaction at what I reported, I hastened to the end of my tale and asked a bit petulantly if there were anything wrong.

"Oh no, no, of course not. You've done well, Jeremy," said he, "but I had hoped you might find letters, notations of one sort or another—in short, *names*. There were none, I take it?"

"No, sir." Then, thinking further, I offered: "But, Sir John, there must be names aplenty in her account books. They are in code, but could the code be broken—"

"Mr. Marsden has a talent for such games. I'm sure he will have no difficulty with the Widow Tarkin's attempts to disguise the buyers of her wares. But, you see, these are mere fences, dealers in stolen goods. It may be that an arrest or two will result—and that is all to the good. But as for the homicide, I fear that having fixed the victim as a thief only makes the task of discovering her murderer that much harder."

"Oh? How is that?"

"Why, don't you see, anyone from whom she stole might seek her out and take revenge. And that, as you have proven, could be one of a great number."

"I understand," said I, feeling somewhat chastened.

It was about that time we passed the building which housed Mr. Donnelly's surgery. Yet when we continued on, crossing Southampton Street and proceeded down Maiden Lane, I had a better idea of our destination.

"I have some interest in Mr. Millhouse," said Sir John. "The fact that he was there at the scene says something, surely. He seems at a loss to explain his relation to the victim. When you went off to fetch your hat and coat, he confessed that he sensed something evil about her and disliked his wife's charitable attention to her. When I pressed him further, he told me he thought the woman was attempting to seduce him, that she might hold it over him to extort tribute for silence, or some such. That seems a bit far-fetched—unless, of course, something of the sort were already underway. Tell me, what had he to say on your journey to Half Moon Street?"

"Almost nothing at all. He seemed quite lost in thought. Yet he did expect to enter the Widow Tarkin's apartment with me. I had to threaten to return with a constable to persuade him to give up that notion."

Sir John gave a great deep chuckle. "Good boy, Jeremy," said he. Then: "I believe we are quite close to our destination. Are we near the synagogue?"

"It is just ahead." I had been right—on my second guess, at least.

"I had thought to seek Rabbi Gershon's help in finding this fellow, Yossel, who seems to have quite disappeared."

I held Sir John at the door to the synagogue. It was a new building of brick, put up in short order by the congregation of Beth El on the site of the old one of wood, which had burned under mysterious circumstances two years past. They had made a proper job of it. It looked to be the solidest and most durable of any structure on the street.

"Should I knock?" I asked.

"Try the door," said Sir John.

It was unlocked. I swung the door open and eased him up the single step and inside. We stood in the hall and listened. There seemed to be no one about.

"*Halloo!*" he called. "Anyone here?"

There was indeed someone there. At the far end of the hall, a face appeared—bearded yet still peculiarly youthful. "Ah!" said the face, and out popped the body, black-clad and rotund. Rabbi Gershon hurried to greet us, his short legs propelling him forward with a rolling gait, the toddling walk of a very young child. "Sir John Fielding! Jeremiah! Welcome!"

I could tell from the smile spreading over Sir John's face that he did indeed feel truly welcome. Yet he did not reply until the rabbi was upon us. Then did he grope forward with his right hand for the hand of the other. He grasped it firmly and shook it.

"Good day to you, Rabbi Gershon," said he. "I trust we are not intruding?"

"Not at all," said he. "I was studying Talmud, and that I can do, Baruch HaShem, every day of my life."

Then did Rabbi Gershon shake my hand, as well, murmuring my name as he did.

"Now," said he to Sir John, "to what do I owe your visit? I am always happy to see you here, but I sense this is some special mission. How can I help you?"

"Well, you are right that this is a special mission. And right, too, that we seek your help."

"So . . . explain."

And, briefly, Sir John did just that. He told of the two murders, twenty-eight days apart, and dwelt upon the brutality of the second. Putting emphasis on the difficulty he had encountered so far in his inquiry—the lack of clues, the absence of witnesses—he concluded by saying that there was one whom he wanted for questioning that had so far eluded them completely. "I had hoped," he concluded, "that you might help us find him."

"Then he must be a Jew."

"Well, er . . . yes, so it is said."

"And what is his name?"

"I have been given a first name only—or perhaps just a nickname, one in any case, with which I was heretofore unfamiliar . . ."

"Sir John, please, what is his name?"

"Yossel." Though not difficult, the name seemed to come ill to his tongue in this instance.

"Ah, Yossel! Yossel Davidovich!—the very one who came to mind!"

"Would you think him capable of such acts?"

Rabbi Gershon considered this for a good, long moment, then he shook his head. "In my opinion, no," said he. "He is, in the Christian phrase, a 'lost sheep.' He has turned his back on his family, his heritage, his religion. Yossel has, as I have heard, even denied he is a Jew. He goes about clean-shaven and dressed as any other who might be seen in the street."

He paused and looked unhappily first at Sir John and then at me. "But no, I would not say he could do the things that you describe, Sir John Fielding. Let me tell you a story. In the town I lived in as a boy, there was a man who owned a dog. He was a hateful man, and his dog was vicious. He called him his Jew-killer, thinking that a great joke, and he let him roam free, so that every time we set off for *shul* it seemed that the dog would block our way. He would growl and bark at us wildly, like a monster, and come at us. He put fear into our hearts, for we were but children, and we would run from him and go another way to the synagogue which took us near a *verst* out of our way. Finally, as we grew older and our *bar mitzvah* approached, we began to take heart, thinking ourselves near manhood. One of our number declared that he would not again be stopped by that dog, no matter what his name and no matter how loud he barked. And so, the next time we took that same path, that same dog appeared. He growled—oh, how he growled!—and he barked like thunder and showed his teeth. Yet the brave one among us, who was neither the largest nor the strongest, would not turn round and run. He walked forward directly at the dog, slowly, staring him in the eyes. When they were close, the dog stopped, but the boy kept on. The dog could only attack or retreat. He retreated, barking at first, giving ground. But as the boy continued to come at him, he began to whine and trot, looking back at his tormentor. Finally, he ran away. The rest of us cheered at that, and from that day, whenever the dog saw us he went slinking off, never bothering any one of us again."

A moment passed in silence. I took it that Sir John was waiting to be sure that the rabbi had concluded.

Then, having satisfied himself, he spoke: "Are you suggesting that Yossel's bark is worse than his bite?"

"Is that how it is said here? It is different in Russian." Rabbi Gershon nodded. "Perhaps I am saying that. But perhaps Yossel Davidovich has no bite at all."

"It was reported to me that he stole from prostitutes, sometimes threatening them with a knife."

"To threaten is one thing; to use, another. I think Yossel is a coward who would appear dangerous."

"That's as may be, but he was seen quarreling with the second victim by four witnesses—a woman, by the bye, who it now seems was herself a thief. In all truth, Rabbi, I wish only to put questions to him. He is not yet a suspect. Yet it counts against him that he is nowhere to be found."

"I will find him," said Rabbi Gershon. "I will try."

"Thank you," said Sir John. "I hoped that you would do this for me."

"In all truth, Sir John, I do it also for my people, my congregation. Matters such as this often have a way of turning out for the worse for Jews."

As if to justify the rabbi's apprehensions, upon our return to Number 4 Bow Street Mr. Marsden handed me a broadsheet with a frown and a shake of his head.

"Just see what they're hawking in Covent Garden," said he quietly. "You'd best read it to Sir John."

"Read what?" demanded Sir John, whose keen ears had picked up Mr. Marsden's muttering with no difficulty whatever. "What have you there?"

"A broadsheet, sir," said the clerk. "It's all about the murder of that woman two nights back. I don't think you'll like it, not one word of it."

No, he did not. I have not kept a copy of that inflammatory document, so I shall not attempt to quote verbatim. The important points were these: It had been a bloody murder (the writer had no idea *how* bloody, for he mentioned only the wound at her throat). The victim, one Priscilla Tarkin, known commonly as Polly, frequented the streets and inns surrounding Covent Garden. Those who knew her well had seen her that very night in great contention with a villain known as Yossel. Said Yossel was certain to be Polly's murderer, her friends agreed, for he was known as a "high-ripper," one who robbed women such as her of their meagre earnings at knife-point, threatening to disfigure or otherwise wound them. Yossel was known to one and all as a Jew, and the mortal wound he inflicted was of the ceremonial sort, well known in parts of Europe where Jews kidnap Christian children and bleed them dry in heathen ceremonies.

And so on. Each of these main points was developed at some length, particularly the last, which repeated many of the calumnies commonly laid upon the Israelites. It was noteworthy, however, that the anonymous author made no effort to tie the most recent murder to the one which had been discovered twenty-eight days before. It made me wonder if it was known to him.

Anonymous author, indeed! I was near certain that I knew him who had written this by his past works and even by name! Could Sir John be as certain as I? If so, then judging by all outward signs manifested by the magistrate, Ormond Neville, poet and journalist, was in for a rough go of it.

I had never before actually known Sir John to gnash his teeth. Yet as I sat in that chair which Thaddeus Millhouse had earlier occupied and read to the magistrate from that scandalous broadsheet, I became aware of a most disconcerting sound of grinding which came to me from across the desk. I looked up and saw that Sir John's mouth was shut tight, his chin perhaps thrust forward a bit, but that his jaws were moving perceptibly from side to side. This reaction from him was intermittent and came at those moments when he was trying hardest to suppress his rage at what I read. Yet throughout my reading—in any case, each time I glanced up—I saw his hands on the desktop fixed tight in fists. At last, I concluded.

"That is all? There is no more to it?"

"That is all, sir."

"It is quite enough." He sat, inhaling deeply, saying not a word, until: "Never, and I repeat, *never,* have I known such a vicious and unprincipled piece of ordure to be printed and given general distribution in this city. Not only does it interfere with and impede my inquiry and thereby the judicial process, it also goes so far as to irresponsibly slander an entire people. Do you realize, Jeremy, that there are those who can read who truly believe that if even the grossest fabrication appears in print, then it must, for that reason, be true?"

Being myself at that age somewhat overawed by whatever I might happen to read, I had not given the matter sufficient thought. And so, under the circumstances, the best I could manage was a rather lukewarm agreement.

"I suppose that is so, Sir John."

"Indeed it is! And perhaps the more lasting damage has been done the Jews. Who knows, when such an evil seed is planted, what may grow from it in years to come? I will *not* have such filth circulated in my precincts! I will *not* allow Londoners to behave in the manner of denizens of some benighted province of Eastern Europe."

He punctuated this by beating with both fists upon the desktop. I had not seen him before quite so overwrought.

"I foresee a bad night ahead," said he. "I shall have to post two men at three-hour intervals at Rabbi Gershon's synagogue. I'll not see it put to the torch again. And then let us—" He broke off of a sudden and leaned across the desk towards me. "Jeremy," said he then, "I know you to spend a good deal of time in Grub Street. You must have the acquaintance of one or two there?"

"I do, sir, yes."

"Could you go asking about there and discover the author of this . . . this . . ."

So seldom was he at a loss for words that I relieved him of the task of putting a name to it. "There is no need, Sir John."

"Why? What do you mean?"

"I believe it to be the work of one Ormond Neville. You recall that he was author of the broadsheet which demanded the swift trial and execution of John Clayton, the poet?"

"I do indeed."

"There have been others, not near as inflammatory, which have appeared since then which have caused you some distress. You recall the dissertation in support of public hanging?"

"I do, yes. It called for executions to be moved from Tyburn to Covent Garden. That was his?"

"Of that I'm sure, for we happened to meet at the shop of his printer, Boyer, and Mr. Neville claimed it proudly. He asked impudently what you thought of it."

"He did, did he? Well, I shall be happy to tell him my opinion of this, his latest work. Do you know where this fellow lives?"

"No, but I know where he is likely to be found."

"Excellent. After you have finished your hour with Constable Perkins . . ."

I looked at him questioningly. "But . . . ," I offered, having no idea what I might say beyond that.

"Ah," said he, "you may have thought I knew nothing of his course of instruction, yet I do. And while I do not wholly approve, he has nevertheless made me see the sense of it. Go then, and when you two have done, I would like you both to go a bit out of your way to Grub Street, if that be where you would seek him, and bring Mr. Ormond Neville to me, that we might have a chat."

Neither finding Mr. Neville, nor persuading him to come along with us, provided much difficulty. I led the way straight to the Goose and Gander across from Boyer's on that street of booksellers, publishers, and the hacks who served them. It was an ordinary inn and eating place, much like the many situated round us in Covent Garden—dark, close, and at that hour of the day, quite crowded and noisy. Men stood round the bar and spilled out to the tables where they sprawled in circles and clusters, yelling out loudly at one another. There were very few women to be seen, perhaps two besides the barmaid, and they seemed as hacks rather than whores. Supposing that Ormond Neville would have been there at the Goose and Gander for most of the afternoon, I ignored the crowd at the bar and sought him at the tables. And there it was that I found him, surrounded by his fellows, the broadsheet in question spread out before him. There must have been five or six round him there, and the mood at the table was one of celebration—tankards were raised, tributes were voiced in rollicking tones, while above them all, Mr. Neville shouted out the text of the broadsheet, which he read by the candle on the table. One of them, however, seemed not so jolly as the rest.

"Is that him?" asked Constable Perkins.

"Indeed it is," said I.

"Well, he's havin' a proper good time of it, ain't he? Shame to spoil his party—but spoil it we must. Come along, Jeremy."

He led the way. I noted that he had pulled out his crested club and held it up where it might be seen; that and his red waistcoat identified him unmistakably as one of Sir John's force of Bow Street Runners.

As we pushed through the throng and between the tables, I shouted loud into Mr. Perkins's ear, "There are a great many at the table. I'll give you all the help I can."

"That lot?" he shouted back. "They'll give us no trouble."

Though I was ready and felt myself capable of giving aid to Mr. Perkins, I was nevertheless relieved when he proved right. He announced our presence by slamming down his club on the broadsheet which lay upon the table. An immediate silence fell upon those ringed round Mr. Neville and spread swiftly to those seated nearby. Mr. Perkins had their attention.

"Mr. Ormond Neville?" said he.

In response, Mr. Neville simply nodded; his eyes bore a look, not so much of fear but of consternation.

"Are you the author of that broadsheet from which you was readin'?"

He looked about him. Having accepted the congratulations of his colleagues, he could hardly deny it. "I am," said he.

I looked about the group at the table for signs of aggressive resistance—but saw none. What I did see, however, quite took me by surprise: one whose back had been turned as we approached now faced me. Our eyes met. I recognized him immediately as Thaddeus Millhouse, as he indeed must have recognized me, for he swiftly averted his face and raised a hand to shield it from my sight.

"I must ask you to accompany us to Number 4 Bow Street, sir," said Constable Perkins to Mr. Neville. "Sir John Fielding would have some words with you."

"Am I arrested then?"

"Only if you resist."

"Then I have no choice?"

"None that I can see, sir."

With that, Ormond Neville rose slowly, turning left and right to his fellows at the table. Seeing no help from them, he nodded his compliance.

"Why not take along your copy of the broadsheet, sir," suggested Mr. Perkins, "since that is the matter to be discussed."

Mr. Neville scooped it up, folded it roughly, and stuffed it into his coat pocket. He lifted his chin.

Then said he in a manner most dramatic: "I am ready."

Yet as we began to depart, one of those at the table took heart at last. It was him who was a bit sour-faced when the toast was drunk to Mr. Neville. Though careful to keep his seat and not rise to challenge the constable, he nevertheless spoke forth loudly and truculently. He had the look of an Irishman.

"See here," said he, "what right have you to take him away in such style? Neville is no criminal but a poor scribbler, as are all of us here. Is it a crime to work by the pen? Is Britain not a free land?"

Constable Perkins stopped and fixed him with a cold stare.

"Perhaps you'd like to come with us and present your views to Sir John?"

"Nooo," said the fellow, "I fear I have urgent business elsewhere. I was just about to leave."

"Then we wish you a good evening," said Mr. Perkins. "Come along, Mr. Neville."

And that he did, in a most docile manner.

As soon as we emerged from the Goose and Gander into the evening darkness and began our march to Bow Street, Ormond Neville fastened upon me and made to discuss the matter of the broadsheet, whilst the constable coolly ignored him.

"Here, young sir, we two are well-acquainted," said he to me, shining up to me a bit. "We've had words on a number of occasions. Perhaps you could tell me, what part of the broadsheet displeases him?"

"I believe it would be fair to say that it displeases him in its entirety."

"The *whole* of it?"

"Yes, sir."

"Oh."

As I recall, he had nothing more to say during the entire journey. We three simply marched on, side by side. When it became necessary to go single file, Mr. Perkins led the way, and I took the rear.

For my part, I turned over and over again in my mind the unexpected meeting I had had with Mr. Millhouse. Seeing him there at that table with Ormond Neville had surprised me, of course. What seemed far stranger to me, however, was his reaction. Why had he turned from me and attempted to hide his face? I should not have expected him to jump from his chair, shake my hand, and give me a great thump on the back in greeting. Still, to pretend somehow that he was not there seemed rather outlandish. It was as if he had been found out—that I had caught him doing what he ought not to have done. He had every right to be there, after all. Though drinking, he was not drunk. Was it his association with Mr. Neville that caused him embarrassment? It seemed very likely, seeing them together, that Mr. Millhouse had given the author of the broadsheet the name of the victim, since it was he himself who had identified her. Yet if that were so, why had he not also told him of the mutilation of her torso? I wanted to ask Mr. Neville about this, wanted to ask him what, in general, he knew of Thaddeus Millhouse, but, following Constable Perkins's example, I said nothing at all.

Upon our arrival, we found Number 4 Bow Street quite alive with comings and goings. Sir John and Mr. Bailey were in the center of it all, assigning shifts of guards for the synagogue, revising the streets to be covered by other constables to compensate for a force reduced by two every three hours. It was quite complicated and, it seemed to me, somewhat confused, as well. Into all this we ventured, with Mr. Neville between us. He seemed quite properly intimidated by the helter-skelter; he looked as if he wished himself to be anywhere but where he was. (And he would wish that even more sincerely by the time his ordeal was done.)

"But where are constables Langford and Brede?" shouted Mr. Bailey above the hubbub. "Has anyone seen them?"

Apparently no one had. There were a few replies, but all were in the negative.

Mr. Perkins marched Mr. Neville forward through the milling group to Sir John; I followed along.

"Here's your man Neville," said Perkins. "Jeremy found him, and we brought him in."

"Oh," said Sir John, a bit owlish, "so we have our author, do we? You are the writer of that broadsheet which appeared today, are you not?"

"I am, sir," mumbled Mr. Neville.

"Well, speak up, speak up, sir. I hear a good deal about the pride of authorship. Surely you feel a bit of it. Anyone who can cause *all this confusion* must be a very powerful writer indeed. What have you to say for yourself?"

He said nothing.

"Not a word? Well, I have many words for you—you may depend

upon it—but just at the moment all the trouble you have caused me prevents me from speaking them, so I must detain you until such time as I am free to do so, and that may not be until tomorrow. And so, sir—what is his name again, Jeremy?"

"Ormond Neville," said I.

"Thank you. And so, Ormond Neville, I arrest you for interfering with a criminal inquiry and inciting to riot. I shall hear your case in my court at noon."

"Riot?" cried Mr. Neville. "What riot?"

"Mr. Baker," yelled Sir John, "lock him up in the strong room."

The words that Ormond Neville lacked a moment before rushed of a sudden from his lips as he was dragged away. He protested the unfairness of it all, the injustice, the—

Just at that moment there was a great commotion down the hall. The door to Bow Street flew open. There were footsteps, a few shadowy forms, and a great rush of noise from beyond.

"Bar the door! Bar the door!" came the cry.

"What is it?" called Sir John. "What has happened?"

I started down the long, dark hall with two or three others and nearly bumped into Rabbi Gershon. He was pulling along a dark man about twenty years of age who was sniveling and wailing with fear. This, it seemed, was the notorious Yossel.

"There is a mob out there," panted the rabbi. "They chased us, would have killed us, except for Sir John's men." He pointed back at the two missing constables—Alfred Langford and Clarence Brede—as he pushed past.

I turned about in confusion and saw the rabbi had already reached Sir John. He must already have told him all about the situation. I saw his prisoner backing away. I grabbed him stoutly by the arm and pulled him forward.

"Cutlasses and clubs!" shouted Sir John. "Cutlasses and clubs!"

The Runners grabbed up swords and pulled loose their clubs. They poured into the hall, filling it.

"Sir John," said I, "here is the prisoner."

"Yossel Davidovich," put in the rabbi.

"You were as good as your word, Rabbi Gershon," said Sir John. "Mr. Baker! If you are about, take the fellow with the rabbi and put him in the strong room with our author. That should give them both something to think about."

Down the hall I heard the voice of Benjamin Bailey, the captain of the Runners. It was in such skirmishes as these that he proved himself a leader of men.

"Now, when the door goes open, we shall fly at them like the very devils we are. Clubs first, and if they don't give way, use the flat of the blade. Just follow me!"

A pause. Then: "*Open the door!*"

SIX

In Which the Third Victim Is Found By Mr. Tolliver

The anticipated battle did not, in fact, take place. The Runners swarmed out the door of Number 4 Bow Street with a grand hurrah and hollo, only to find no mob to oppose them. The few stragglers still hanging about took to their heels, scattering in all directions. Whether from surprise or in genuine amusement, the band of constables looked one at the other and let out a sudden great roar of laughter, all in concert.

"What is it, Jeremy?" demanded Sir John. "What is it strikes them as so damnably funny?"

We stood together in the doorway. The Runners were ranged out in an arc, still looking about them, and still chuckling as the laughter gradually died down.

"Why, I don't know, sir," said I, "unless it be that they came out looking for a fight, and there was none to be had. The mob has dispersed."

"Well, they may yet have their wish." Then he shouted out: "Hi, you fellows! Get yourselves off to the Jewish church on Maiden Lane, and be quick. The mob may have formed up again there. And, Mr. Bailey?"

The captain of the Runners came up swiftly at a jog-trot as the others started off.

"Aye, Sir John?"

"If there be no great crowd at the synagogue, leave two men there, as we agreed, and send the others out on the routes as you altered them."

"As you say, sir."

Then the captain went off at a run to catch the rest up.

"Now, Jeremy, I have a man-sized job for you. I would not ask you to perform the task, but as you can tell, we are at this moment a bit shorthanded."

"Whatever it be," said I.

"I want you to convey the rabbi back to the synagogue. But use good sense. When you come into Maiden Lane, be sure there is no disturbance there before proceeding." He hesitated. "Reluctantly, I think it perhaps best that you wear a brace of pistols. They should be loaded, but think of them only for purposes of display. If you discharge one of them, you had better have good reason—and let it be into the air. Now go, fetch the rabbi and get properly outfitted by Mr. Baker."

We must have looked a queer sight as we made our way down Tavistock Street—Rabbi Gershon in his flowing black robes and dark beard; and I a mere stripling, a raw youth wearing two great pistols, pretending to manhood. We did not hurry but went watchfully at first, listening as well for sounds of disturbance. Yet none who passed seemed notably hostile; if they stared a bit, it was in the spirit of curiosity, or perhaps mild amusement.

Still and all, we talked, for the man quite fascinated me, and whenever I had him to myself (which was not often) I had questions for him. On this occasion, they had to do with matters close at hand. I recall asking him if he had had difficulty in finding the fellow Yossel.

"Oh no," said he. "I knew where to look."

"And where was that, sir?—if you don't mind my asking."

"Jeremiah," said he—for that was what he called me—"I shall tell you something about Jews. When one of them gets in trouble—let us say he has turned his back on his people and on HaShem, let us suppose he is a miscreant, a terrible villain—nevertheless, when such a one gets into trouble, he goes straight to his people, begging to be taken in, asking forgiveness. And his family takes him in—for who could turn his back on one of his own blood?"

"And so that was where you found him?"

"Yes, with his family, who are good, pious people, all of them together praying for Yossel's deliverance. But—" He halted, frowning with concentration. "Listen! What is that?"

It was the raucous noise of shouting voices—nor was it indeed so distant. But then I noted that just ahead of us was Shakespeare's

Head, a place for eating and drinking which attracted a rather rough crowd.

"There," said I, pointing just ahead at Shakespeare's Head. "It comes from there, I think."

"Then let us hurry past," said he.

And that we did, spurting forward at a sudden brisk pace. It was not until we were a good distance beyond that he resumed his speech to me.

"Where was I? Ah yes, now I recall. I had but entered their home and found them at prayer, Yossel with the rest. I told them that perhaps I had come with the deliverance they sought for Yossel. I also told them of Sir John and praised him as a just man. They listened unconvinced, Yossel most skeptical of all. And then his brother came forward and pushed into my hand that terrible sheet with all the old lies about the people of Israel, and he said, 'Here, read, there will be a pogrom—not just Yossel, all of us will be murdered!' So I argued with them. Yossel denied that he himself had murdered any—*threatened* murder maybe, *threatened* to cut off a nose or an ear. I said to him, 'See what your threats brought to your family. Just think what they could do to all the Jews in London!' Oh, I soon had him crying, begging our forgiveness, and finally he agreed to go with me. We thought it wise, though, to wait until after dark. And so we waited an hour, and you know, Jeremiah, what happened then. We were halfway to Bow Street when one of the women on the street, one he had threatened with that knife of his, she sees him, and she shouts, 'There's Yossel. That's him! There he goes!' And then he did something foolish—he started to run. That brought forth a great multitude. If he had not run straight into the arms of two of your constables, I believe we would both have been torn apart by the mob. Oh, they were good, those two men of Sir John's—they faced them, they drove them back, they—"

"Uh, Rabbi Gershon?"

"Yes, Jeremiah?"

"We're here, sir."

So consumed was he by the telling of his story that somewhere between Tavistock and Maiden Lane he had quite lost the sense of his surroundings. The synagogue lay just ahead on the quiet street. The red-waistcoated Runners hung about the place, arguing over the new routes handed out them by Mr. Bailey (thus does the human animal abhor changes to his set routine). The rabbi looked around him and, greatly reassured by this concentration of constables at his front door, he turned to me with a hesitant smile.

"So many?" he asked.

"I believe there will be but two through the night," said I. "The others must now go off on their rounds."

"Well, two is a great number. I shall always remember how we were saved by two from our pursuers." He threw me a wave at the door. "Goodnight to you then, Jeremiah."

I called a goodbye and gave him a wave as he hopped up the two steps to his door. Mr. Bailey snapped a salute in his direction. The rabbi produced a large key, which he used to enter. There were squeals of children, the voice of a wife, as the door shut; he was home and safe.

Walking over to Mr. Bailey, I presented myself to him in hopes of some further assignment. His men were leaving now, going off singly and in pairs.

"Well, look at you, young Jeremy—a brace of pistols by your side and ready for a fight, you are. All you lack is a red waistcoat, or you'd be one of us."

Was he serious? My hope that he might be, rekindled my fanciful desire to become a Bow Street Runner at age fifteen.

"You accompanied the Jewish priest home, did you?"

"I did, Mr. Bailey. It was Sir John's idea that I wear the pistols. He quite surprised me in that."

"Are they loaded?"

"Yes, sir."

"No sense carrying a gun about if it ain't loaded. Have any trouble on the way over?"

"No, none, just a few curious looks."

"People will stare, won't they? But listen, Jeremy, my lad, if there's no great demands upon your time, I wonder would you care to take a stroll with me round Covent Garden just to be sure they ain't no great mob of them skulking about, biding their time, looking for their chance. That is sometimes the way with mobs—they go off and hide for a bit."

I eagerly agreed to his proposal. He took but a moment to give final instructions to constables Langford and Cowley, who would stand the first watch before the synagogue, then beckoned me to follow as he started off in the direction of Bedford Street.

Going at an easy pace, we turned right as we reached it, and at that same easy pace we came upon Henrietta Street, one of those that entered direct into Covent Garden. We were at that point not at all far from the alley off Bedford where Constable Brede had found the mutilated body of Priscilla Tarkin's body against the churchyard fence. But here at the corner of Henrietta Street, Mr. Bailey paused to listen. What could he hear more than the rowdy noise issuing from the stews and dives on Bedford? They were not yet as noisy as they would later be, nor were the streets yet as crowded. The day-people had by then left the Garden; the vast night population had not yet come out in full force.

Mr. Bailey nodded in the direction of Henrietta Street, and we started off at that same easy pace. Since he had been listening so keenly but a moment before, I was a bit surprised when he spoke up in jaunty style once we were underway.

"You and me, Jeremy," said he, "we make quite an army between us—you with your pistols and me with this great sword in its scabbard."

"It's true," said I. "We've no cause to fear man nor mob."

"Nevertheless, I can't wait until we get back to Bow Street and get shed of this cutlass. It's an annoyance having it rattling against my left leg."

It did rattle a bit. To me, however, it seemed a reassuring sound. The street was dark; streetlamps were few, and few windows along the way were lit. There were no pedestrians ahead or behind us, and there was no horse traffic, so that the entire scene had a rather deserted, sinister aspect. Of a sudden, it came to me that I should not like to be walking this street alone, nor even less should I like walking down even darker, narrower, emptier streets at night with only a club to protect me. Perhaps I was not as ready as I had supposed to join the Bow Street Runners.

As if to confirm that conclusion, a call came from the far side of the street.

"Hi, you two! Are you Beak Runners? Over here!"

We looked, but we could not see. There was but a dark passage between two buildings. The cry could have had no other source. Then, as we started across the street, I dimly perceived a crouched figure in the shadows of the passage. The figure waved, then stood and stepped forward, beckoning us towards him.

"Careful, Jeremy," said Mr. Bailey. "It could be bait for a trap. Keep your hands on those pistols."

I did as he told me until we came quite close to him who had hailed us, for by the dim light of a streetlamp then I recognized him as none other than Mr. Tolliver.

"It's all right," said I to Mr. Bailey. "It's our butcher."

"Your butcher, is it? You're sure of that?"

For his part, Mr. Tolliver seemed sure: "Jeremy! How lucky you should come along with one of the Runners—though I'm not sure I want you to see what lies back here in the passage."

"What is it then, sir?" asked Mr. Bailey. The two tall men were now face to face. Mr. Bailey's eyes shifted from Mr. Tolliver to the dark space behind him. There was something or someone lay crumpled on the ground about six to eight feet from the narrow walkway where we stood.

"Why, it's a woman. She's dead, rightly enough, though I swear she's still warm to the touch. Come see for yourself."

Mr. Bailey gave him a curt nod. "I will, sir, and I thank you."

He moved round the butcher, who stepped aside in such a way as to block my path. I attempted to follow Mr. Bailey.

"Jeremy," said Mr. Tolliver, "there's no need, surely, for you to see, too."

"Oh, I'm sure I've seen worse."

Reluctantly, he gave ground, and I scrambled after Mr. Bailey.

Indeed I had seen worse. This woman—or girl, for her age could hardly have been greater than mine—was situated against the wall at one side of the passage, almost in a sitting position, sagging a bit forward in such a way that her chin rested upon her chest in much the same way that Priscilla Tarkin's had.

"She's dead, all right," said Mr. Bailey to the butcher, "and still warm she is." He stared down at her. "I wonder what killed her." He was not by nature a detector.

"Pull back her head," I offered, remembering the Widow Tarkin, "and see if her throat's been cut."

At my suggestion, he did just that. There was no wound to be seen, and no marks on her throat from strangulation, but her unbuttoned frock invited examination.

"Is she cut open?" I asked. "The last one was."

"Well, let's see about that."

Kneeling down beside her, Mr. Bailey threw open her frock, exposing the girl's small breasts—but no jagged belly wound.

"Here now," said Mr. Tolliver, "that ain't proper. It ain't decent." He seemed unduly disturbed by a process I had come to accept as quite routine.

"But, sir, she's dead." Did that explain it? Someone—I couldn't then remember who—had said that the dead don't care, a crude philosophy at best. I ought to explain myself better to Mr. Tolliver: "You see, if she died by foul means, there must be an autopsy. If she died fair, then she will be taken away for burial in the city plot—unless someone claims the body, of course."

"I see. Well, then, I suppose it must be done."

Mr. Bailey had looked from one to the other of us during this discussion, as if not quite understanding the sense of it. It then occurred to me that perhaps this unfortunate had been killed as Teresa O'Reilly had.

"Check just below the breastbone," said I to him. "See if there is a small wound there."

He did as I directed, then held his fingers up to the light. "By God, there it is, Jeremy, just as you said. There's so little blood come out of it I missed it altogether when first I looked. She's been stabbed by a very narrow blade—one thrust. That's what done her in!"

I glanced at Mr. Tolliver. He was leaning forward to stare, fascinated in spite of himself.

Mr. Bailey covered her as best he could, stood up, and came back to the entrance of the passage.

"It's murder, right enough," said he. "Now, Mr.—what is your name again, sir?"

"Tolliver."

"Now, Mr. Tolliver, if you could tell me, how did you happen to notice the body of this poor girl here?"

He thought about that a moment. "Why, I don't know, exactly. I finished late tonight at the stall, washing up and so forth. I locked up and started home down this street, as I always do. Come to think of it, I always take a look down this passage when I walk this way after dark—so as not to be surprised by some villain."

"And that was when you saw her?"

"That was when I saw *something*. It could've been a drunk collapsed from too much gin—common enough in this district. But I stopped and stared, and whether it was the head hung so low, or whatever it was, I thought it best to look. I felt her pulse—there was no pulse—but she was still warm, as you yourself discovered. Then I looked about for help and spied you two passing by. You had the look of authority, and so I hailed you."

"And that is all? You saw nobody down the passage?"

"No. The light is poor, as you can see, but as near as I could tell, there was no one."

"And you didn't hear anything?"

"No, not in the passage."

"No footsteps, nothing?"

"Not then—only your own as you came down the street."

"Where does this passage lead, do you know?" He knew that, I was sure. I wondered why he asked.

"I think it must lead to St. Paul's churchyard. I've heard that it does, though I've never had cause to go down it."

That registered sharply. Polly Tarkin had been found against St. Paul's churchyard fence in the alley that led from Bedford Street. Perhaps it had been the assailant's intention to take this body to the fence and carve it up as he had Tarkin's. If that were so, then it would mean he was still about—down this dark passage, or in one of the houses crowded along the way.

"If you will pardon my asking, sir," said Mr. Bailey to Mr. Tolliver, "what is in that leather packet you have tucked under your arm?"

I myself had noticed it but thought so little of it I did not wonder what it contained.

"Why, my knives are inside. I carry them home every night," said Mr. Tolliver.

"Knives, is it?"

"Yes, knives. I'm a butcher. They are the tools of my trade."

"Ah yes, so Jeremy said. Would you mind, sir, opening it up so I might have a look at them?"

"Well, I . . . "

Clearly, he did mind, yet to show that he had nothing to hide, he brought the packet from under his arm, untied it, and carefully opened it. On the chamois leather, eight knives of diverse sizes and shapes were displayed, each in its separate pocket. Even in dim light they glinted as Mr. Bailey removed them, one by one, for inspection. Each was clean of blood, and not one had a blade narrow enough to have inflicted the sort of wound I had seen on Teresa O'Reilly's body and the one described by Mr. Bailey on the nameless girl in the passage. Indeed Mr. Bailey must have realized that, for when he had concluded, he nodded and thanked Mr. Tolliver kindly for his cooperation.

Then, waiting until the packet of knives was safely wrapped (even offering his hand in tying the leather thongs that secured it), Mr. Bailey told the butcher that much as he regretted it, he must detain him for a bit until such time as Sir John had arrived, for the magistrate would surely have questions for him.

Then to me he turned and directed me to fetch Sir John. "But, Jeremy, I want you to go back the way we came. Stop at the Jewish church, and if all's quiet there, tell Constable Cowley to come here to Henrietta Street. Tell him to see can he borrow a lantern from the priest there. Then I want you to go on to Tavistock Street, and if the surgeon's about, the Irishman . . . "

"Mr. Donnelly," I put in.

"That's him. Ask him to come here, too. Then, of course, on to Bow Street to fetch Sir John. Offer my apologies for breaking into his evening, but due to the circumstances, he'll want to be here. Got all that, have you?"

"Certainly, Mr. Bailey."

"Oh, and have Mr. Baker give you a lantern, too. We need light here." He nodded, dismissing me. "Off you go."

And indeed I went.

There was no problem at the synagogue. Maiden Lane was even quieter than Henrietta Street. Constable Cowley seemed near half-asleep on his feet.

"Go on, take him, send him away," said Constable Langford. "If a great mob did attack us, I do believe he would sleep right through it."

"I need to be moving around," said Cowley.

"You need to be sleeping in the daylight hours instead of playing in bed with that would-be wife of yours."

"We'll be married soon. You'll see."

"Why buy the cow when you're getting your milk free?" Constable Langford must have thought he had made a great joke, for he laughed most heartily at it.

I rapped hard upon the door. A minute later, shutters opened above and Rabbi Gershon's head popped out.

"You, Jeremiah! Is something wrong?"

"Oh no, I was just wondering, sir, if you might have a lantern we could borrow."

"Certainly! Of course! I'll be right down with it."

I liked not the notion of leaving Mr. Langford alone, if only for an hour, and so I offered him one of the two pistols I carried. "If you shoot into the air, we'll hear and come at quick-time. We're just a street away."

He accepted it and tucked it into his belt.

Then the door to the synagogue opened, and Rabbi Gershon handed out the lantern. I thanked him and promised its return, but said nothing about why it was needed. It would have upset him greatly to know that another woman had died.

I gave over the lighted lantern to Constable Cowley and urged him on his way. Then on to Tavistock Street and Mr. Donnelly.

Having no idea just how the doctor spent his evenings, I feared I might find him away. Yet light shone beneath the door to his two-room surgery as I arrived, somewhat out of breath. I took a moment to regain it, then knocked upon his door.

After a moment's pause, I heard footsteps and then his voice from the other side.

"Yes? Who is there?"

"'Tis I, Jeremy Proctor from Bow Street."

He slipped the bolt and threw open the door. "What a fine surprise," said he. "Come in, come in."

"I cannot, much as I would like. I've been sent to summon you to Henrietta Street. There's been another woman found dead."

"Ah, sweet Jesus, when will it end? Was she cut up all horrible like the last?"

"No, sir, she was not. It was done quite like the first—a small wound just below the sternum—an upward thrust through the cardiac vein."

In spite of himself, he laughed. "Why, Jeremy, I do believe you're quoting me. You were present at the inquest, weren't you?"

"Yes, sir, I was," said I, blushing.

"All right then, I'll fetch my bag and be with you in a moment."

"I'm sorry, sir, but I cannot accompany you, for I must be off to alert Sir John. It was Mr. Bailey and I who were called to the scene by him who discovered the body." I then gave him the exact location of the passage on Henrietta Street and advised him to go round by Maiden Lane and Bedford Street. "Cutting through the Garden can be right risky at night."

"I'll do as you say."

"And bring a lantern, if you have one," said I, backing away, "for it is dark in that passage in spite of the full moon."

"Go then, Jeremy, but come back and visit when you've more time to spend."

"I will, sir! Goodbye, sir!"

Then I turned and flew down the stairs.

It was difficult running with the pistol and empty holster at my waist, and so I soon slowed to a fast walk. Mr. Bailey had not bade me run, had in fact sent me first to the synagogue and to Mr. Donnelly. If

I were in a great rush, it was not at his direction but out of consideration to Mr. Tolliver. He must indeed feel badly repaid for the kindness he showed in stopping to see what ailed that poor girl in the passage. How long would they detain him? Surely Mr. Bailey could not suppose that Mr. Tolliver could be guilty of such a vile crime. If he but knew the many kindnesses that he had shown me—and to Lady Fielding before she became Lady Fielding—he would simply have ascertained the pertinent facts and sent him on his way with thanks. Instead, he had insisted upon looking at Mr. Tolliver's collection of knives as if he were suspect in the crime. Why, of course a butcher would have knives! Any fool would see that plain. Benjamin Bailey was no fool, but there were times when he showed a certain lack of . . . of —

Thinking thus, I was perhaps not near as observant as I ought to have been. I had just crossed Russell Street when, from an entry, a hand reached out and grabbed me firmly by the left arm and jerked me to a halt. I turned about sharply, throwing off the grasp as I grabbed for the pistol with my own right hand.

"Here, chum, leave that barking iron be. You and me, we got things to discuss."

He stepped from the shadows into the dim light given by the streetlamp at the corner. In that instant I recognized him as Mariah's "protector"—him whom I had dubbed the bully-boy. He was the last person in London I expected—or wanted—to see at that moment. Yet as I stood there staring, within me duty contended with curiosity—and curiosity won.

"What would I have to discuss with you?" I asked in a manner much colder than I felt just then. I seethed inside.

"Well, first off, I hear you been asking about me. I want to know what for."

"I can tell you that. I wanted to learn your relation to Mariah, the Italian girl."

I could not have expected his reaction to that—for he laughed, yet not as any ordinary fellow might; his was a whinnying, high-pitched, almost girlish giggle.

"My relation is it?"—still snickering—"Well, I ain't her father, and I ain't her brother. I ain't even her cuz, so I guess that ain't the kind of relation you mean. Am I right?"

I said nothing; but the distaste I felt for him must have been evident as I began to pull away. I turned and started to walk off.

"Awright, awright, I'll give it you straight," he shouted after me. "I *owns* her."

Stopping in midstep, I asked myself if I had heard correct. I came back to him.

"What did you say?"

"I says I owns her—much to m'sorrow. Now hear me out." He talked earnestly, as one who wished to do business. "When her people went back to where they're from, I got her to stay. We dorsed together, got all lovey-dovey; I turned her out proper. Then I took her to Mrs. Gould—best house in the Garden—right around the corner on Russell Street. There's girls on the street who'd give anything to get inside—but not her, not our Mariah. The long and short of it is, Mrs. Gould pays me ten ned for her, which is quite generous, not knowing how she'll perform, like. And she didn't perform worth a damn. She sulked, she spat, she scratched, and screamed. Mrs. Gould called me to her and demanded her money returned and said I could have the little blowen back. Well, by God, you don't argue with Mrs. Gould, she got some real villains at her call, so I up with the full wack, ten ned, and I took Mariah back. I'd no choice but to put her out on the street myself, but to do that I had to take a flogger to her and buy her some proper duds. So I spent a bit on her and I keep her fed. She brings in a few shillings a day, but she ain't a real worker, if you get my meaning. So the long and short of it is, if you want her, you can have her, for you've an interest in her. All I want is my ten ned back. I call that a square bargain."

Reader, as you might suppose, if I seethed before, I was now at my boiling point. It was all I could do at that moment to control my anger. My hands trembled; I clasped them behind me so that he might not see. The very idea of offering another human being, a woman, for sale would have made me shudder uncontrollably under different circumstances, yet I would not show to him such a sign of revulsion, for he would sure take it as proof of weakness. Striving for the same control over my voice, I attempted a reply to his huckster's pitch.

"And what would I do with her then?"

"That's up to you, chum. Keep her out on the street, if you like. Dorse with her in your own little love nest. Marry her, if that's your mind."

"I will say this: I have not ten guineas to my name, nor anything like it. Yet if I did, I should pay it quite immediate, if only to get her away from you and that terrible life you have forced her into."

"Nothing would suit me better, chum, believe me." Then he stepped close and whispered: "You say you ain't got the wack, and I believe you, but listen to me. You're in a good position to get it. There's a good lot of bit flows into Bow Street—fines, swag lifted from scamps, and that. It's not like the Beak would miss it if you helped yourself, maybe a little at a time. It'd be"—and then he let loose that hideous giggle again—"it'd be like stealin' money from a blind man."

That was when I left him where he stood. I'd heard enough. In fact, reader, I'd heard far too much.

Sir John had insisted upon cutting across Covent Garden, even though he had often warned me against venturing there at night. When I had reminded him of this, he had then said, "You've a brace of pistols by your side, have you not?" It was then I told him I had but one, for I had given the second to Constable Langford that he might use it to summon help. After a grunt and a long silence, he had muttered, "Very sensible."

After taking him from the dinner table—he had but just finished his meal—I had waited while Annie fetched his hat and coat. During this brief space of time, it was Lady Fielding—and not Sir John—who had directed a great volley of questions at me. Was it truly Mr. Tolliver who had found the girl's body? she asked. Why was he being detained? Does Constable Bailey suspect him? How could he? And so on.

Sir John, who had stood aside in silence during the interrogation, then stepped forward and waved his hand to end further questioning.

"Enough, Kate, please. Mr. Bailey was acting in a reasonable way when he held him for my arrival. He knew that I would want to question him myself."

"But, Jack, Mr. Tolliver is such a good man! He would never . . ."

"And a wonderful butcher, as well, as I can attest. And of course he would never—but he *found the body,* and I must ask him about that."

Somewhat mollified, she waited until Annie had him properly tucked into his coat. Then did Lady Fielding step forward, squared his hat upon his head, and planted a kiss on his cheek.

"I'm sure you'll do what's right, Jack."

With that, we left, going by way of Russell Street—I hoping to catch no glimpse of the evil fellow who had laid that evil proposition before me, and mercifully having my hope fulfilled. As we tramped along Russell, I found myself looking among the imposing structures for the one which housed Mrs. Gould's notorious bagnio. I had been there once to deliver a letter. I remember thinking it a great joke to be among all the ladies walking about in their shifts. I no longer thought it so funny. What might I have thought then had I heard Mariah's screams resounding through the place? All that I knew now of her life in London burdened me greatly.

Entering Covent Garden, I urged him to the left that we might walk its perimeter, rather than attempt to traverse it. There was a bit of light from the windows in the surrounding buildings, and the moon was out. Nevertheless, I was glad to have the lantern Mr. Baker had given me. I held it high with one hand, and the other I had fixed round the butt of the pistol on my hip.

Sir John moved with me, step for step, his left hand upon my right shoulder. He had little to say, which surprised me somewhat. I thought perhaps to volunteer my views on the matter of this latest homicide, yet decided against burdening him with them, for he seemed deep in thought. At one point, after we had turned right in the direction of Henrietta Street, I heard the murmur of voices from the stalls. Sir John must have felt me tense in response, for he spoke to ease my apprehension.

"Women and men together," said he. "I doubt there's much to fear from them."

"As you say, sir."

"How many will be there when we arrive?"

I named them all, including Mr. Tolliver.

"You've neglected one," said he.

"Oh? Who is that, Sir John?"

"The corpus. Let us hope she has a thing or two to tell us."

Thus we came to Henrietta Street with the passage now well within sight. There I saw an unmistakably familiar wagon and team.

"There's a surprise," said I.

"What do you mean, Jeremy?"

"Just ahead on Henrietta, by the passage—the Raker's arrived. I see his wagon."

"No doubt he was called to some house nearby," said Sir John. "He's rather an unfortunate creature, is he not?"

I considered that a moment. "I suppose that he is. Yet he seems to like his work, repulsive though it may seem to us. He has his own little kingdom there in that barn of his," said I, again echoing Mr. Donnelly. "He rules his house of the dead."

"Would you not call such a one an unfortunate creature?"

"I see your point, sir."

All except Mr. Cowley were gathered at the entrance to the passage. He, I learned, had been sent up the passage with his lantern to search for the murder weapon. There was a great quarrel in progress between the Raker and Mr. Donnelly as we approached. Remembering their previous meeting, I was not in the least surprised.

"Ah, there you are, Sir John," called out Mr. Donnelly. "Perhaps you will settle this for us."

"I will if you gentlemen will let me."

"Aye, you're the man to do it, sir. I was tellin' this gent here, this phy-si-cian, that the way it was always done before was, you'd look at a body, say it was murder or wasn't, and I'd haul it away. They ain't no need for him to grab this one, take her away, and go messin' up her inwards. That's insultin' to the body. It don't show respect."

"You are correct as to your account of how things were done in the past," said Sir John. "But you will recall that up to five or six years ago, Sir Thomas Cox would convene his coroner's inquests and often required you to deliver a corpus to one medico or another that he might give testimony at the inquest."

"Aye, so it was."

"Well, we are back once again to that."

"And who is the new coroner?"

"I am—until a proper one be appointed."

"So this here phy-si-cian gets the body?"

"I fear that is the case, sir."

"Well, then, if that be so, I reckon I'll just be on my way with the old party I collected up Half Moon Passage—no marks on him, and his landlord said he was at his bedside when he passed."

"But that is what we argued about!" said Mr. Donnelly. "He said he would wait about only so long as it took you to decide who had claim to the body. He now refuses to wait the few minutes more it will take me to communicate my preliminary findings to you. He has a wagon standing by that is near empty. If he takes it away, we shall have to rent a wagon and team from a stable, or Jeremy and I must carry her body through the streets to my surgery."

"Now, that does not seem reasonable, does it, sir?" said Sir John to the Raker.

"Well, it's like I said, Sir John," said the Raker, sulking. "Cutting them open and poking round inside don't seem right to me—shows a lack of respect, it does. It's not the sort of thing I wants to be part of."

"Come now, sir, have I not heard you say on more than one occasion that the dead don't care?"

"Well . . . yes, but that was different times—not the same thing."

"I'll not argue the point with you. You and I have worked together satisfactorily in the past. Let it be done as a favor to me."

"When you puts it so, sir, I can't hardly say no."

"Good. Mr. Donnelly and I will conclude our business quickly, and then you may be on your way."

With that, the group shifted a bit. The Raker went off to grumble to his gray, ghostlike nags. Mr. Donnelly took Sir John to one side that he might discuss with him, and I—in no wise barred from their talk—followed close with Sir John. Mr. Tolliver, who had waited through the wrangle with the Raker, showing signs of growing impatience, was pulled farther away by Mr. Bailey so that he might have no chance of overhearing what was said between surgeon and magistrate.

Mr. Donnelly's report was brief and concise. He told Sir John that the dead girl seemed to be no more than fifteen or sixteen. She was killed in the same manner as the first victim, Teresa O'Reilly, and apparently with the same weapon. He had examined the butcher's knives at Mr. Bailey's urging, but none was of a size to inflict such a small wound. The body had been warm when it had been found, and still warm when first examined by Mr. Bailey. Since Mr. Bailey had checked his timepiece when summoned at half-past seven, that would place the time of death at not much earlier than a quarter past. In his opinion, the girl had been killed where she had been found, though the young constable who had gone off to search the passage at Mr. Bailey's direction might possibly discover evidence to indicate otherwise.

"That is all you have for me?"

"At the moment, yes. The autopsy may yield something more."

"Well, that little you have given me is sufficient to shift suspicion from our friend, Yossel—who is, by the bye, our overnight guest at Number 4 Bow Street. He seemed rather glad to accept our hospitality, seeing that there was a mob in hot pursuit of him."

"That hideous broadsheet?"

"Exactly. As I see it, because of the matter of time, Yossel could not have murdered this young girl, for at the time of her death he was in our custody and under lock and key. Since the weapon which killed her was almost certainly the one that was used to kill the first victim—the Irishwoman, O'Reilly—that probably eliminates him also as suspect in that homicide. Which leaves us only with the second in the series, the one for which he was brought to our attention—and we may find him alibi for that one. Sir John paused but a moment, then cocked his head curiously. "Tell me, Mr. Donnelly, could this knife with the narrow blade—I believe it was described to me as a 'stiletto'—could such a knife have been used to cut the throat of the Tarkin woman?"

The surgeon hesitated. "Well, I would have to consult my notes on her autopsy, but I would say possibly so—but quite unlikely. The mutilation was accomplished with a serrated blade; I'm almost certain the same knife was used on her throat."

"Well, it seems then that we have a killer who uses two weapons."

"For two methods of murder. But there is another possibility, of course."

"I think I know what you are about to suggest."

"That there are two murderers abroad in Covent Garden."

"I must reject that for the moment," said Sir John, "as too dreadful a prospect even to contemplate." He sighed and offered his hand to Mr. Donnelly, who shook it warmly. "I thank you, sir, for coming, yet I need not ask you to do your work on her this night. I shall hold an inquest at nine tomorrow on the Tarkin woman. We need to know more about this latest victim before convening a jury—her name, at least."

"I'll be there in the morning with my notes."

"I'm sure you will. The Raker should give you no more difficulty. Let me know if he does."

I hoped Sir John would prove correct. Mr. Donnelly left us to find him.

Then did Mr. Bailey bring Mr. Tolliver to the magistrate and introduce him as "the one who found the body and hailed us as we was passing by."

"Well, Mr. Tolliver," said Sir John, "you come with a very fine character from Lady Fielding. Jeremy, too, has spoken highly of you, and I myself have supped on your meats with great pleasure. In the light of all this, I can only offer my apologies to you for having detained you so long. You may have heard my efforts to play Solomon in the dispute between the medico and the corpus collector—the Raker, they call him; I know not his proper name."

"I did hear, yes," said Mr. Tolliver. He sounded a bit grudging, a bit hurt.

"It delayed me, took time that I no doubt owed to you as the first upon the scene of this lamentable crime. This one is, by the bye, the third such homicide in a short period of time. We are quite concerned, as you may suppose."

"I heard of the earlier two, of course. A butcher in Covent Garden hears it all."

"I'm sure you do, sir. Perhaps you had heard, too, that the manner in which this unfortunate met her death was quite like that of the first."

"That I had not until Jeremy here asked the constable to look for the wound especial. I had always thought the boy showed good sense."

He threw a glance at me. I lowered my eyes modestly.

"Indeed," said Sir John. "But, please, sir, tell me your story—how you happened upon the corpus, what you may have seen or heard at the time, et cetera. Leave out no details, please, for it is by the details that villains identify themselves and are apprehended. I will no doubt have some questions when you have concluded."

Then did Sir John take a step back and bow his head in an attitude of listening; he leaned lightly upon his stick and touched his chin, massaging the day's growth of whiskers there.

The tale told by Mr. Tolliver was the same one he had told earlier to Mr. Bailey, and the words he used to tell it were virtually identical. I forgave him this, instructing myself to remember that a man may make an excellent butcher, yet be altogether deficient in imagination and have no skill at all in the verbal arts. But given thus, it was given swift; and given twice, there was no reason to doubt it.

Sir John remained silent during a long moment afterwards. Then, hearing nothing more, he launched into his interrogation.

"Mr. Tolliver, you have made it clear that you neither saw nor heard anything in the passage at the time you stepped inside to investigate the condition of the body you had spied there. But tell me, what was the condition of the street?"

"Sir?" It was clear he had no idea of what was meant.

"I mean, just before you left it to look at the body—were there many people there? Were there hackneys? Wagons?"

The butcher seemed no little nonplussed by the question. He screwed up his face as he made a painful effort to remember. "I would say, sir, that there were very few people walking on the street, which is not unusual at such an hour. It may well be that all who were there with me on Henrietta were the constable and Jeremy here, and they would have been farther down and across the street. I may have gotten a glimpse of them under a streetlamp, though, for I was not surprised when they come walking along. I heard their footsteps."

"And vehicles? Riders?"

"Well, none passed by, but I saw one behind me, which surprised me, as I had seen none before when I passed that way."

"*Behind* you? What caused you to look?"

"It was the footsteps *before* I came to the passage. I turned round and looked, for after dark on these streets you should always keep an eye out. But I saw nothing, no one, except the wagon, and I saw it but part—halted in the Garden."

"Could you have failed to notice it before?"

He thought. "Yes, I s'pose I could. After all, a wagon—how many does a man see in a day?"

"Hmmm, well . . . yes. But, sir, you might very well have heard the fleeing footsteps of the murderer. Has that not occurred to you?"

"No, sir, I can't say that it did."

"What about the wagon? Was there anything unusual about it—what you saw of it, that is?"

"No, sir, it was just a wagon. I didn't see it well, just the shape of it. The light is none too good there"—he pointed—"as you can see yourself." Then, realizing his embarrassing error: "Oh, but you *can't* see, can you? Sorry, sir. I forgot."

"Many do," said Sir John, with perhaps a modicum of irony. "But tell me, sir, how long did it take you from the time you ducked into the passage to realize the girl was dead and call for help from Constable Bailey and Jeremy?"

"Not long, a minute or two, not much more."

Sir John turned to me. "Would that be about the length of time it took to walk from Bedford Street—or just this side?"

"That would be about right, sir."

"In that length of time, say, when you were called by Mr. Tolliver, did you see any part of that wagon?"

"No, sir, I did not." Of that I was sure.

"So in that brief space of time the murderer could have made his escape. Isn't that likely?"

"Well . . . it might be so, sir."

"It might indeed." Sir John gave a firm nod. "I have but one last question for you, Mr. Tolliver, and it is this: Did you know the girl you found dead?"

"Know her in what way?"

"In any way, sir."

"I saw her on a few occasions in the Garden. She bought from me two or three times in the past months."

"You knew her by name?"

"Oh no. I never asked it, and she never gave it."

"Was she a girl of the streets? A prostitute?"

"I don't know—p'rhaps, probably. So many are hereabouts. I saw her once in conversation with a man beneath a streetlamp in such a way."

"Was that, by any chance, here on Henrietta Street?"

He thought about that a moment. "Why, so it was—right at the corner of Bedford."

"Very well then, Mr. Tolliver. There will no doubt be an inquest into this death sometime in the future. I cannot yet fix the date, but I would like you to come and repeat what you've told me."

He frowned and nodded. "I understand."

"But you are now free to go."

Mr. Tolliver wasted no time on speeches. "Thank you, sir. And goodbye to you, Jeremy."

He turned and stalked off down Henrietta Street.

"Mr. Bailey?" Sir John called out to his captain. "You have that man's address?"

"Aye, sir—and of course he's at his stall in the Garden every day but Sunday."

"Good. I shall want to talk to him again, sometime soon. There's something not quite right there. Either that, or he is the worst witness I have come across in quite some time. Both—or either—are possible."

"Here's the Raker back with Mr. Donnelly," said the constable. "And I see Cowley's lamp swingin' this way in the passage."

"In a few minutes more then, we'll be able to leave. Jeremy," he added to me in a low voice, "I almost wish that I'd not come out at all."

SEVEN

In Which Yossel Is Sent Away and A Fourth Homicide Is Discovered

As it happened, I missed the better part of Sir John's inquest into the death of Priscilla Tarkin, for I had been appointed to write and deliver an advert describing the girl discovered in the passage by Mr. Tolliver the night before. It was an appeal to any and all who might know her to come and identify her body. Because of the conditions under which I viewed her, I found it difficult to write a description of any sort. She had not a distinctive face, so far as I could remember, and the bad light had made it most difficult to retain a clear impression of it. And so, knowing not what else to do, I set off for Mr. Donnelly's surgery that I might have a better look at her.

Arriving a bit before eight, I knocked upon his door. When it opened, again he expressed his surprise at seeing me there, but in no wise did he make me feel unwelcome. He bade me enter, and I explained my mission. All was well, but he reminded me, checking his timepiece, that he would have to leave in an hour's time to attend Sir John's inquest. Then he brought me into his examination room, where the body of the unknown girl lay upon a long, narrow table beneath a sheet.

"I have not cut into her as yet," said he. "She is as she was when you saw her last night, though she has gone stiff during the hours since then."

"How should I begin a description?" I asked.

"Why, with height and weight, I suppose. I have measured her at five feet tall, and I reckon her weight at not much more than seven stone. Though not a starveling, I would say she was not well fed for some time—perhaps had never been."

I noted height and weight down with my pencil on the paper I had brought, and I began to study her face.

"Her hair is plain brown," he continued, "and her face long and oval. She has three missing teeth in back, two on the left side and one on the right. There were no scars I could detect, except one on her left cheek—half-moon shaped, as a ring might have left an impression from a blow to the face. The two missing teeth are directly below the scar. As for her age, I'd give it as fifteen or sixteen."

All this, as well, I duly noted down.

"These women," said I, thinking of Mariah, "these girls—they lead hard lives, don't they, sir?"

"They do indeed, and for that it is men must take the blame."

"I . . . I see what you mean, sir." I continued studying her face, hoping for some inspiration; none came. "How do you describe a face?" I asked.

"Ah, that is a question, is it not?" said Mr. Donnelly. "What is it makes one different from another? Aside from it being long and oval-shaped, what is there about hers that makes it different from all others in London? It is a great mystery to me that God has endowed each of us with a physiognomy quite unlike any other. I have heard it said that each of us has, somewhere in the world, a double—a twin born of a different father and mother. Yet I have traveled some in this world, and I have seen no evidence to support that. In short, Jeremy, I fear I cannot help you much. I have neither the wit nor the art to describe a face properly."

During all this he had stood opposite me, looking down upon her as I did. But then, of a sudden, he glanced up at me, declaring, "I must prepare for my session with Sir John. If you will excuse me?"

"Of course," said I, "and if you will permit me, I'll go to the writing table in the next room and see can I compose an advert that might satisfy us both."

Thus I took leave of him, sat where I said I would, and sought to write what must be writ. I wasted sheet after sheet in the effort. In the next room I heard the surgeon splashing and humming as he readied himself for the day. At last he came forth, clean-shaven and properly dressed, and I held out to him the latest (though not necessarily the final) version of the advert.

Here is what I had put down:

Sir John Fielding, Magistrate of the Bow Street Court, seeks the identity of a young woman, 15 or 16 years of age, a homicide victim, whose body was discovered in the passage off Henrietta Street two nights past at half-past seven. She is five feet tall and no more than seven stone in weight. Her hair is a dark brown color, and her eyes also. There is a small scar upon her left cheek in the shape of a half moon; two teeth are missing that side, and another on the right side of her mouth. Her face, oblong and meagre, has upon it a long straight nose and a mouth of some width. When found, she was clothed in a frock of homespun, blue in color.

Any who believe they may know who she is may view her remains at the surgery of Mr. Gabriel Donnelly, 12 Tavistock Street, City of Westminster.

Having read through it twice, Mr. Donnelly offered a judicious nod.

"That should do quite well," said he. "'Oblong and meagre'—a nice phrase that."

"Thank you, sir. I had tried to scatter other, more decorous phrases throughout—but they seemed inappropriate."

"Best keep to the facts in such circumstances." He took a second peek at his timepiece. "Shall we go?"

And indeed we departed together, descending the narrow stairs, he leading the way. When we had reached the bottom and exited to the street, he offered me his hand, just as he might to any gentleman. I gave it a good and thorough pumping.

"I'm glad to see my surgery mentioned in print, even in such a matter as this," said he. "Who knows? It may bring me a live patient or two. The dear Lord knows I could use them. So far, all my patients have been dead—not that I'm ungrateful to Sir John for the work he has given me."

I bade him goodbye, knowing full well that I might see him again soon at the inquest. Then was I off in a great hurry to the offices of the *Public Advertiser,* located some distance away in Fleet Street.

Had I but known the difficulty I would encounter at the newspaper's offices, I might have supposed it impossible to return to Bow Street in time for any part of the inquest into the death of Priscilla Tarkin. The clerk who had taken my advert had been reluctant to agree to my demand that it be placed prominently on the front page of the next day's broadsheets. We went round and round about it, more times than was needful—or so it seemed to me. At last, I demanded to see the man in charge—editor, publisher, whoever he may be. When Mr. Humphrey Collier appeared, he turned out to be both editor and publisher, and he settled the matter swiftly: "Why, of course," said he, "if this has to do with Sir John's investigations, you can be sure it will be displayed most prominently. We'll put it in big type at the top of the page with a black band about it. None will miss it. Please tell him so for me."

Thus relieved of that onerous responsibility, I set out at a gallop for the court. Shank's mare served me well, for I discovered upon my arrival that the proceeding was not near as far along as I had expected. (I later learned that Mr. Marsden had had a little difficulty in assembling a jury; the word had gotten round that a shilling would be paid, so naturally two shillings were asked.) As I entered the little courtroom, taking care to be quiet, I saw that Mr. Donnelly had just completed his testimony and was returning to his place in the bank of chairs to one side reserved for witnesses; there were others seated there, some of whom I recognized and some whom I did not.

One of the former was called, Mr. Thaddeus Millhouse, but he appeared only briefly before the court of inquest. Sir John wanted from him the victim's identity, which was given as Priscilla Tarkin, commonly known as "Polly."

"And what was her work, Mr. Millhouse?"

"Her work, sir?"

"Her occupation. How did she earn her bread?"

"As a prostitute, sir. She made no secret of it."

"She also, it seems, supplemented her earnings in that line by thievery. Or perhaps, unknown to you, sir, theft was her chief occupation. We have proof of this from a search of her quarters. This complicates our investigation of her death somewhat."

The witness seemed quite startled by this information.

"You may step down, Mr. Millhouse."

And so he did, leaving Mr. Marsden space to rise and call the next witness, one unknown to me, a Mistress Sarah Linney. As soon as she had placed herself before Sir John, he began to question her.

"Mistress Linney, you were acquainted with the woman, now deceased, known as Priscilla Tarkin, were you not?"

"I was, y'r Lordship, but I—"

"Let me interrupt you and assure you I am not so august a personage as to deserve the title you have just conferred upon me. I would be pleased to be addressed simply as 'sir.'"

"Yes, sir," said she. "Well, as I was sayin', *sir,* I knowed her but only by the name of Polly. In our game we don't much go by our right names."

"And what is your game, if I may ask?"

"Polly and me and half the women in Covent Garden, we was strumpets together. But I must say it come on me as a surprise to hear she thieved."

"Ah," said Sir John, "you introduce a Biblical term, 'strumpet,' yet I understand you well and accept the word. But now I ask you, when did you last see Priscilla Tarkin, known to you as Polly?"

"That would be the darkey she croked."

"Would you repeat that in plain English, please? While the court accepts words to be found in the Bible, it will not recognize such flash cant."

"Yes, sir, that was the night she died."

"Give me the circumstances, if you will. Tell me the whole story, as you remember it."

"Well, there ain't much to tell, but it was on Bedford Street outside the Dog and Duck, just round the corner from that alley where she croked—uh, died. It ain't a place where I go, the Dog and Duck, so I was just passin' by, like. But I hear this bloody roue—a quarrel, sir, a turrible quarrel it was. And I looks over, and I see it's old Poll havin' it out with *him!*" She pointed at Yossel, who was seated next Mr. Donnelly.

"I take it, Mistress Linney, that you have just pointed to someone in this room. Do not point. Name the party if you know him by name."

"Yes, sir. Poll was havin' it out with him that's known as Yossel."

"Do you know him by any other name?"

"No, sir."

"Then that will do."

"Anyways, I went right over to her, and I asked her did she need help, and she said no. Then he—Yossel—raises his hand to me to strike me, like, then he thinks better of it, turns and walks away down Bedford, toward the Strand. Then I turn back to Poll, and I find she left me, too, headed into the Dog and Duck. Like I said, it ain't a place I go to, so I just shrugged and walked on down Bedford, telling myself it was none of my affair."

"So you never really discovered the reason for their quarrel?"

"No, sir, but I had a good notion seeing that fellow Yossel, who had bothered us poor girls in the past, tryin' to rob us of our earnings, like."

"Had he ever tried that with you?"

"Aye, he tried."

"Without success?"

"No, sir, no success."

"Mistress Linney, you were very specific about the altercation between Priscilla Tarkin and this fellow Yossel, yet one thing you have not made clear is just when this took place."

"Well, that's a bit hard to say, sir. Y'see, when you're out on the game, prowling about all night, well, a body loses track of time. Also, I had some to drink that night, as I must admit, and gin does no good keeping things in order in your head."

"You must be more definite than that," insisted Sir John. "Was it early or late?"

"Something in the middle, I'd say. I'd put it between my second gent and my third."

"Mr. Millhouse!" spoke Sir John, loudly summoning the last witness, "if you will stand where you are, perhaps you can clear up this matter for us. I recall that you declared in your interview with me that you saw Priscilla Tarkin in the Dog and Duck before her death on that night. Was it only once she was there?"

"So far as I know, sir," said Millhouse, who had risen from his chair as instructed. "I, at least, saw her only one time whilst I was there—and I was sitting in view of the door."

"We shall assume, then, for our purposes, that it was her only visit to the Dog and Duck that night. I recall, too, that you said she simply walked through the place and left. Is that correct?"

"Yes, sir."

"Can you place the time of her visit?"

"Yes, I can, for shortly after she came and went, Mr. Goldsmith, who was one of our party at the table, pulled out his timepiece and said that it was just past one o'clock and that he must be getting on, for he had work to do that night. He then generously settled for our drinks and advised us all to follow his example and return home. Would that I had taken his advice!"

"Indeed! You may sit, Mr. Millhouse. Now, Mistress Linney, will you accept that estimate of the time? You saw Polly enter the Dog and Duck. Mr. Millhouse places that visit at one o'clock, give or take a bit."

"If you says so, sir."

"I say so. You may step down, Mistress Linney." He gave her a moment or two to scuffle back to her chair. Then did he resume: "And so, as far as we know, Priscilla Tarkin was not seen nor heard from further until her body was discovered nearby by Constable Brede at four o'clock. She had been dead for some time. The blood from her wounds had begun to dry. You have heard Mr. Donnelly say that that fact would suggest she had been dead about an hour. So between one o'clock and, roughly, three o'clock, we know not where she might have been. Yet she was found quite near the Dog and Duck, where she was last seen. Is this a mystery, or simply a discrepancy? Let us proceed. Mr. Marsden?"

The twelve ordinary-looking men who sat together at Sir John's right took uncommon interest in the next witness called by Mr. Marsden, for it was Josef Davidovich, whom I recognized immediate as the man brought in by Rabbi Gershon the night before. There was a murmur of discussion from the jury. Sir John silenced it at once, calling for order.

"You are Josef Davidovich, commonly known as Yossel?" he asked the man who had taken his place before him.

"I am, sir, that's me, yes," said he.

"Did you encounter Priscilla Tarkin, commonly known as Polly, on the night of her death?"

"I did, yes, I did, sir." He had an eager, quick way of speaking—as if he wished to assure his cooperation by the readiness of his replies.

The fellow was somewhat the worse for the night he had spent in the strong room. Yet in spite of the two-day growth of beard and his unkempt hair, there remained something crudely handsome about him. I wagered with myself that he had charmed more money from women than he had taken by threat. Here and now, however, he made no attempt to charm Sir John, which would have been quite useless in any case. He stood before him, nervously crushing his hat in his hands.

"You were seen to be quarreling with her," said Sir John. "What, pray tell, was the reason for your quarrel?"

Yossel hesitated. "Well, sir, I may be stickin' my head in a noose, like, but it won't be for no murder. I knowed Polly as a thief, and a skilled one at that. And while I didn't do no thievin' myself, I had given her a tip, so to speak, where she might put her skill to work—a partic'lar place, a partic'lar house. Now, for that, I was entitled to a share—not a big one, not a halver or any such. Now, I awready knowed she had visited this house in a manner I thought of special, and she had taken certain objects of value, so I wanted my full wack, I did, like we'd agreed. So I sees her on Bedford Street, and I approached her and demanded what was comin' to me, for truth to tell, I had to share my share with one who worked in that partic'lar house. And so, seein' Polly, I—"

Sir John interrupted: "Would you care to be more specific as to the house and its residents?"

"Uh, no, sir, I would not. But mind you, I did no thievin' myself. I just pointed her in the right direction, so to speak."

"So this is not to be taken as a confession of guilt in the matter?"

"Oh no, sir, not if I can help it."

"And if you can't?"

"Surely, sir, you would not hold this against me?"

"Proceed with your story, Yossel."

"Well, in for a penny, in for a pound, I always say." He looked about him with a nervous smile upon his face. And, having made his choice, he pressed on with his story: "And so I seen Polly on Bedford Street, and prob'ly about one o'clock in the early morning would be right, then I went right up to her, and I said I wanted my wack, and she said she ain't got it, that she ain't visited that house as yet, which I knowed to be a lie. So we started at one another, callin' each other terrible names, cursing something awful. Then along comes Biddy, as she is known to me—that woman Linney, you just spoke to—and she asks Polly does she need some help, and Polly says no. Even so, Biddy whips out her razor, and she comes at me—like, in a very threatening way. Then didn't I shove my trunk down Bedford Street! I stopped just once to look back, and I seen Polly headin' into the Dog and Duck and Biddy all alone, with her razor in her hand."

He stopped at this point, apparently hopeful that what he had said thus far would suffice. It seemed for a moment that it might, for Sir John deviated then from his line of questioning and turned in the direction of the jury.

"You twelve gentlemen may be shocked to hear of the sudden appearance of a razor in the hand of our last witness, Mistress Linney, but I fear that appearance is all too credible. You heard her say on two occasions that she did not frequent the Dog and Duck. The truth is, as Constable Brede found out after making inquiries, that the innkeeper of said establishment had barred her from entering the place some months before, because during an altercation she had produced just such a razor. *Is that not so, Mistress Linney?*"

There was a grunt and a mumble from her as she slid down deep in her chair, as if hoping thus to make herself invisible.

"Speak up, please!"

"Yes, *sir!*"

"Thank you." He returned to the witness: "Now, Mr. Davidovich—Yossel, if you will—I understand you carry a knife with you. In fact, one was taken from you by Constable Baker when he locked you up in the Bow Street strong room. When Mistress Linney approached you with that razor, why did you not simply produce the knife and have it out with her right there on Bedford Street?"

"I would not do such a thing, sir."

"Oh?"

"No, truly I would not. I gave up that rough practice a few months past, I did. Besides, I never cut nobody. By me, it was always threats. You may ask about, sir, you'll find it's so."

Just at that moment, Mistress Linney bounded up from her chair, determined to be heard.

"If he give it up," she screamed, "it's 'cause I sliced him good on the arm! Ooh, didn't he bleed!"

She ended her boast with a cackle which was heard by few, for the jury exploded suddenly in a great uproar of laughter. Sir John slammed down his open hand upon the table before him, then went feeling about for the mallet which served him for a gavel. Finding it, he beat down hard enough to put dents in the hardwood surface.

"Mr. Fuller!" he shouted after the constable. "Is Mr. Fuller here?"

He was. "At your service, sir."

"Expel that woman from this proceeding."

"That I will, sir."

She offered no resistance; in fact, she continued to laugh most merrily as Mr. Fuller ushered her roughly to the door—and through it. He did not immediately return. Swiftly, the courtroom settled to silence.

"We shall leave it, then," said Sir John to Yossel, "that you had good reason to leave when that woman came at you. The question now is this: Where did you go then? You have heard it given that Priscilla Tarkin was slain at about three o'clock in the morning, give or take a bit. Where did you spend the time between one and three?"

"I spent them with a lady, sir." He answered quick and sure.

"Have you proof of this? Will she stand witness for you?"

"She is here. You may ask her yourself."

Murmurs swept through the jury once again. Sir John silenced them with a scowl.

"You may step down, Mr. Davidovich. Mr. Marsden, call the witness."

"Lady Hermione Cox." Mr. Marsden quite bellowed it forth in a voice far louder than he had earlier used to summon previous witnesses. The reason for this became apparent when a side door to the courtroom opened, and the figure of a woman appeared. She was dressed in black, in widow's weeds, and wore over her face a black veil that obscured, but did not completely hide her features. From her walk, which was graceful enough but a bit stiff, I judged her to be nearer seventy than sixty.

The effect of her entrance upon members of the jury seemed noteworthy to me. While before, when surprised, they had been given to whisperings and mutterings, and on one occasion to laughter, in this instance they simply sat hushed and expectant, eager to hear the next development in this matter.

She took her place before Sir John, leaning slightly upon a cane which she had used as no more than a walking stick, swinging it freely in her approach to the bench.

"You are Hermione Cox, lately made widow to the late Sir Thomas Cox?"

"As you well know," said she, her strong voice denying any weakness due to age.

"And you have come to testify on behalf of Mr. Davidovich?"

"Yossel, you mean? Of course I have. Why else should I be here? I wish to prove him alibi, John Fielding—I believe that is the phrase, is it not?"

"It is indeed. And how do you propose to do that without causing yourself considerable embarrassment?"

"I propose to do that by telling the truth and giving no thought to the consequences. To be frank, I am too old to give any thought to embarrassment."

"As you say then, Lady Cox. Tell your story, please."

"That I can do quite briefly. Mr. Davidovich—was that what you called him?—called at my residence at Duke's Court, St. Martin's Lane, between the hour of one and a quarter past. I can be certain of the time, for I had been looking forward to his visit and was slightly piqued that he had come so late. I heard the hall clock strike one, yet it was not so much after that when he arrived. I myself admitted him.

I had sent the servants below stairs for the night. He stayed through most of the rest of the night. I should say it must have been a bit after four when he left."

"I hope, dear lady, that you tell me this in earnest and not as some high-minded jest by which you hope to divert all suspicion from this fellow."

"I'll not change it in the slightest, for it is true," she declared, and to prove it so she struck the floor once with her cane.

"You may bring shame upon your children."

"I have no children."

"Then on your late husband."

"My late husband outlived his usefulness in any sense of the word by at least ten years. He was, for most of his life, a boring man. Toward the end of it, he was not only boring, but ill, as well. In any case, he could not discharge his duties as Coroner of the City of Westminster, yet he had not the good grace to resign the office, which all knew he should have done. He left me with a house and enough money with which to run it, an income, and a terrible case of insomnia. Yossel provided relief from my sleeplessness. He never failed to amuse me, and that is a good deal more than I can say for the late Sir Thomas. I have always been able to sleep when Yossel left me."

Perhaps I was the only one to notice when Constable Fuller reentered the courtroom, for all eyes but mine were on Lady Cox as she made the above speech, which was to be repeated oft in drawing rooms and eating houses all over London; it entertained society for near a month, until they found the next tit-bit for their tittle-tattle. I happened to note Mr. Fuller's entry, because he wished it so. He waved to me until he had my attention, then beckoned me to him. I got up from my place on the back bench and tiptoed over to the door where he stood next.

"Jeremy," he whispered, "I want you to tell Sir John that there has been another homicide—a woman in the house which is located at Number 6 King Street. He will want to go, as will the doctor, for by description, it is the horriblest yet. I must go ahead of all, for there is said to be a great crowd there gawking at the body and taking souvenirs."

"But he will be *furious!*"

"That's as I know, and so I'm going ahead to put things in order if I can. You go tell him about it right now, for I must be off."

Mr. Fuller, whose daytime duties consisted of little more than serving as jailer for the Bow Street Court, had little opportunity to prove himself a proper constable. He wore his red waistcoat proudly, yet the most demanding duties he was called upon to perform were the handling of rowdy or recalcitrant prisoners and their transportation to gaol. Using stout rope and hand-irons, he could handle a whole company of malefactors.

And so he had done when we three—Sir John, Mr. Donnelly, and myself—arrived at Number 6 King Street. There must have been a great number at that address, for it was posted over a passage which led back into a court, dirty, cluttered and crowded, a true "rookery," as one might then have called it.

We trudged down the passage, I in the lead, with Sir John's hand upon my shoulder and Mr. Donnelly bringing up the rear. As we emerged into the court, we were greeted by a great murmur of voices. The entire muttering population of the place seemed to be scattered about, seated on the steps and leaning in the doorways—all except one group of five, which stood silent and sullen in the yard outside a ground-floor door. Each of them had a noose of rope twisted round his neck—a noose of the same rope, for each was thus tied to the next; the first and last were in hand-irons. Mr. Fuller held the ends of the rope in one of his big hands. With the other he waved us over to him.

"I sense a great many people here," said Sir John to me.

"They are ranged round us, looking on," said I. "Mr. Fuller has arrested five and has them trussed up and ready to march off."

"Well and good," said Sir John. "Take me to him."

(I had done as Mr. Fuller urged in the courtroom and gone straight to Sir John, surprising Mr. Marsden and greatly annoying Lady Cox, who seemed to enjoy giving scandal to all assembled. I had whispered in his ear just what I had been told, and in response received a solemn nod. Working as swiftly as he could, Sir John was forced to take near a quarter of an hour to bring the proceeding to a close by discharging Yossel Davidovich and directing a verdict from the jury of "murder by person or persons unknown." Then he collected Mr. Donnelly, and we all set off together, leaving Mr. Marsden to put the loose ends together. Thus had Mr. Fuller no more than a quarter-hour, and probably something less, to deal with the situation he found at Number 6 King Street.)

He presented himself to us in full gear. He wore a brace of pistols and had also on his left side a cutlass in its scabbard. In the hand with which he beckoned us, he held a club, his weapon of choice; from the look of his prisoners, he had used it liberally upon two of them at least.

"I never saw the like," said he in greeting.

"You mean all these gawkers I sense around me at this moment?"

"No, sir, I mean what was goin' on here when I come."

"Explain yourself, Mr. Fuller."

"With your permission, sir, I'd like these I've detained to do my talking for me, for I'm curious to see, can they justify themselves to you any better than they done to me."

Then did the constable seize the best-dressed of the five men by the back of the neck and thrust him forward to Sir John; I noted that he was one of the two who wore hand-irons. At the same time did Mr. Donnelly step round them all and make for the door which stood open. Was it my fancy, or did he stir more whispers from the onlookers when he entered?

"Go ahead," said the constable to the unlucky prisoner. "Tell Sir John who you are and what you done."

"My name," said he, attempting to recover what little he could of his lost dignity, "is Albert Palgrave, and I am a man of property—this property, in fact. I own the building, the entire court, for that matter."

He spoke perhaps a bit too loud, for in his effort to impress Sir John he had been heard by all those assembled round the courtyard. His opening remarks were met by catcalls, whistles, and hoots.

"If that be so," said Sir John, "you are not popular with your tenants."

"What landlord is? These riff-raff expect to live here for naught. It is a constant effort to collect from them the rents to which I am entitled. If truth be known, half those hanging about and staring at us now are behind in their rents."

"Get on with your story, man, and be swift."

"Yes, sir. Well . . . I was on just such an errand, collecting back rents, when I came to that door—you see? behind me there?—oh, I'm sorry, you can't—"

"*Get on with it!*" Sir John did not seem merely exasperated. He was plainly angry.

"Oh . . . well, indeed. So I went to that door there, a Mistress Tribble—behind seven shillings on her rent, she was, and by God, I would have it, or have her out of there. I knocked on her door, and there was no answer—but I suspected her of shamming, and so I peeked through the window, which was so dirty I could get no clear picture. I could see, however, that she was there on the bed, so I let myself into the room. Naturally, as landlord, I had the key. I took one look—I daresay she is a rather horrible sight—and raised the cry of murder, which perhaps I should not have done. Out they came—the whole court, echoing the cry. I thought it wise to lock the door, lest they invade it as a mob. Yet they wanted in. They wanted to see. People are quite naturally curious about such spectacles, but I lectured them to return to their domiciles, until one fellow whom I recognized as Mistress Tribble's, uh . . . factor said he would pay a shilling to be let in. It occurred to me that that would be one shilling less what she owed me. Others said they would pay the same. Now, as owner of the premises I had every right to allow in whom I liked. If they wished to pay for the privilege, I had every right to take their money. But I could not get that first fellow out of there. He simply—"

"*Silence!*" shouted Sir John. "I have heard enough."

"Your fellow arrested me," persisted the landlord. "I have the right of property! When I told him that, he clamped me in hand-irons, would not tell me the charge, simply trussed me. There was no reasoning with him."

"Sir," said Sir John, "had I been present, I would have ordered him to do precisely the same. Have no doubt. The charge will be made plain to you in my magistrate's court."

A great *huzzah* went up from the listening crowd.

"Mr. Fuller, you've made your point well. I've never known the like, neither. Now who have you to talk to me? I hope it is him whom the landlord Palgrave named as her factor."

Mr. Fuller jerked another from the group of five, this one by the noose double-wrapped about his neck. He was young, only three or four years older than I. His face was twisted in a scowl with which he seemed to wish to express disdain. He had a bruise upon his face, and he, too, wore hand-irons.

"Not having the landlord's command of language," said Mr. Fuller, "I would call this fellow a pimp. That's how he was named to me by those who live hereabouts. They said he beat the poor woman regular."

"Course I beat her," snarled the pimp. "She was my whore."

"Speak when you're spoken to," said Mr. Fuller, and cuffed him roughly on the bruised cheek. Then said he: "You may tell Sir John your name."

"Edward Tribble."

"You were married to the woman?" asked Sir John, much in surprise.

"After a fashion, I s'pose. 'Twas a Fleet marriage. I ain't sure it was legal, but I let her use my name. We dorsed different places, howsomever."

"A Fleet marriage? And what unlucky parson performed the ceremony?"

"No idea. I disremembers his name."

"Tell Sir John what you were up to in there."

"I was selling souvenirs of the occasion."

Sir John was silent for a moment. Then he shook his head. "I . . . I do not understand."

Then said Mr. Fuller, in the deepest and darkest of tones, "Sir, he was sellin' her off piecemeal. You ain't been in there yet, ain't had her condition described to you, but she's all cut up, and her inwards have been emptied out and scattered about the room. He was offerin' her organs and such for sale to those who come in—and there was buyers—these other three among them. I know not how many more."

What I saw then I had never seen before, nor would I ever afterwards. Sir John raised his walking stick, and in his blindness struck out at Edward Tribble. He thrashed away at him for a minute or more until, his anger exhausted, he gave it up at last. His blows were remarkably well placed, considering they were delivered in what must have been, for him, total darkness. All Tribble could do was cower and cover his head until they ceased.

When they had, he was unwise enough to speak up in his own defense. "You'd no cause to do that," said he, whining. "She was my wife *and* my whore."

"And so you, too, claim the right of property? She was a human being, you little turd!"

So saying, Sir John whipped one last blow across Tribble's upright form, doing little hurt but perhaps easing his own sense of outrage. I noted that throughout Sir John's thrashing of Mr. Tribble there were no huzzahs and no applause from that great crowd of witnesses. They stood and sat most quiet, impressed by what they saw. Their silence gave approval, for only when it was done did the murmuring begin.

Then did Mr. Albert Palgrave wail forth, "I did not sanction it. I tried to get him out of there. I urged him to leave."

Yet he had fallen back out of range of Sir John's punishing stick. The magistrate stepped back in disgust.

"Mr. Fuller," said he, "take them away. I have heard enough, quite enough. I will meet them again at my noon session."

"It will be my pleasure," said the constable, and, having in his hand the rope to which their necks were all attached, gave a great tug to it and set them on their way, an awkward ten-legged beast.

Yet before they had traveled far, Sir John called after them, "Mr. Fuller, halt just a moment, if you will. You seem to have the situation well in hand, so could you leave off a weapon or two for Jeremy? He may be put to guard, and he will need something to keep the curious at bay, I fear."

"Come here then, Jeremy," Mr. Fuller called back to me, "and take the pistols."

I jog-trotted up and relieved him of the brace on the belt round his waist.

"They're loaded, make no mistake," said he.

"I'll be careful."

"See that you are. Here we go, chums!"

And then he gave another tug upon the rope, and willy-nilly his prisoners followed. I, in my turn, made my way back to Sir John, buckling on the pistols, strutting a bit for the benefit of the crowd.

"Jeremy," said Sir John, "take me to the room in question. I believe there are two stairs and a small porch." He was, of course, correct. "I would address those who have looked on at our tawdry show. They are still out and gawking, are they not?"

"They are, sir."

I led him up the stairs and onto the porch, where he turned and spoke forth as he might have in court:

"To all you assembled here, I now address a plea. If you have any information to impart which might lead to the apprehension of him who committed the murder of this unfortunate woman who was your neighbor, then I ask you to report it to this young man here. If you saw a visitor come to her last night, please describe him. If you know her habits, please describe them. Even if what you have are only suspicions, unburden yourselves. Tell him all or anything that might help us. We are quite desperate to find this most vicious killer."

Then, having made his address, he slapped the floor of the porch with his walking stick as a sort of final punctuation, turned, and carefully entered the room, taking only two steps inside. As I took his place upon the porch, I caught a glimpse over Sir John's shoulder of that something on the bed. It could hardly be called a corpus, much less a woman. It resembled far more the sides of beef and hog carcasses I had seen on display in Smithfield Market—ribs exposed, the white of other bones protruding through great gashes, and a gaping red hole where the belly should have been. I turned away, not wishing to see more.

Turning to face the court, I folded my arms so that the fingers of each hand rested upon the butt of a pistol. I pulled a stern face, thinking I ought to look formidable; then remembering that I was to be available to any who wished to give evidence, I adjusted my expression to suit that purpose—benign and approachable. Yet from the look of the sitters and the layabouts, there would not be many to come to me; one by one, two by two, they began to depart—some from the court, and others into their rooms and behind their doors; their morning's entertainment was done.

And so, the while I stood, I had naught to do but listen to the earnest conversation of Sir John and Mr. Donnelly.

Having made his careful entry into the room, Sir John had remained quiet for a time. Then: "Is it as bad as Constable Fuller described?"

"I know not what the constable said, but it is a horror, sir, an absolute horror. In all my days as a surgeon, I have not seen a human body so completely destroyed. The monster who did this must have spent well over an hour at his work."

"I smell blood and all manner of unholy odors."

"There is blood quite everywhere one looks. It is here on the wall above her head where it spurted and ran when her throat was cut—that was the immediate cause of death, by the bye—it is here on the bed, bled out from this huge wound in her middle, and it is on the floor, dripped from the organs he removed from her body. All of it is well on its way to drying."

"That means, of course, that she is some hours dead."

"Oh yes, I would say she is a good six hours dead, at least, likely longer. Rigor mortis has stiffened her in the carnal posture, naked, of course. She was no doubt murdered late, late at night, at three or so."

"Given an hour to do his cutting and hacking, he would have left at four—still pitch dark this time of year. Yet, from what you've told me, he would have been bloodied from head to toe."

"A greatcoat could have covered all. Or, another possibility, he himself may have been naked through it all. There is bloody water in a wash basin and traces of scarlet on a dress on the floor nearby. He may have used it to wash and dry himself."

"A grotesque thought," said Sir John. "May I come forward a bit without tracking the floor in blood?"

"Oh, no need to worry. Blood has been tracked all about the room. You're standing in a bit of it now."

I noted some movement in the room behind me. Silence followed.

"What organs are missing?" Sir John asked after a minute or more.

"That," replied the surgeon, "is difficult to say at the moment. I shall have to have her brought to my surgery and attempt to put her back together, as it were. There will, in any case, be some missing parts, I suspect."

"Due, no doubt, to her pimp's trafficking. I had never heard of such a thing before, could not conceive of it."

"Perhaps not only to him. The murderer made a fire in the fireplace—or it could be that she lit it to keep them warm during their . . . their transaction. In any case, I found in the ashes in the grate remains of what appears to be her tongue, which was cut from her mouth. Her eyes, too, were dug out of her head. They would have melted swiftly in an open flame."

"Good God, what did he leave her?"

"Not much, I fear. Heart was gone and is in the grate complete. It's a great piece of muscle and not easily burnt. Liver, pancreas, and womb all are gone. Stomach and intestines are intact, and that is lucky, for the digestive process is often helpful in fixing the time of death more exact."

"I hardly know what to say. Perhaps only that in this instance I am relieved that I need not look upon what you describe to me. It is, as you named it, Mr. Donnelly, a horror."

There was a long, somber space in which neither man said a word. Then did Mr. Donnelly at last speak up:

"Sir John," said he, "I believe you must give serious consideration to what I suggested to you last night. You recall, of course?"

"Yes, and I recall that I said it was too dreadful a prospect even to contemplate."

"Will you now contemplate it?"

"I fear I must."

"What we see in these four homicides is two very different, even opposed methods of murder. The first and third were done in such a way as to inflict as little outward damage to the victim as possible. This one and the second were done in a fury of slashing and hacking. I believe that very likely the murderer of the second victim was interrupted, or feared he might be. What we have before us here is what he is capable of when left with time and opportunity to follow his devilish design to its end. It amazes me that what was done in a mad fury could be so long sustained through these horrible mutilations. In short, this murderer—shall we call him the second?—wished to cause the most grievous possible damage to the body of his victims."

"All right," said Sir John, "let us suppose that there are two murderers. How would you characterize each of them?"

There was the first sign of hesitation from Mr. Gabriel Donnelly who, from the moment he had reopened this question to Sir John, had been speaking rapidly and most persuasively. It was not merely that he paused a good, long moment before replying, but that when he did, he also repeated himself and even stammered a bit.

"How would I characterize each? Yes, well, that is . . . If I were to say . . . Let us take the first—him who murders with the narrow blade."

"Indeed, let us. What do we know of him?"

"First of all, we know that he uses a stiletto, and that is a gentleman's blade."

"You think him a gentleman then?"

Mr. Donnelly ignored Sir John's conclusion. "And we know that he uses it with the knowledge and skill of a surgeon. Those thrusts are simply too well placed to have been made by one ignorant of human anatomy and too sure to have been made by an unpracticed hand."

"I suppose I must accept what you say. You, after all, are a medico. But what of his strength? Remember that he held and murdered a twelve-stone woman and then picked her up and walked with her some distance to hide her away."

"Ah yes, that's true, isn't it?"

"And so we must find a gentleman surgeon with the size and strength of an ape. The parts make a strange whole, do they not?"

"I see what you mean."

"But what about the one you have named the second murderer?" asked Sir John. "How would you describe him?"

"As a madman."

"We know him thus by his work," said Sir John with some assurance. "But even in his madness, he may show some logic. You argued convincingly last night that the same knife could not have been used in all the murders—that there was what you call the stiletto used in the first and third of the homicides and a sawtooth weapon in the second. I take it that the rougher, thick-bladed knife was used in this murder, as well?"

"Oh yes, I'd swear to it."

"Perhaps he used the ugly weapon to do ugly things to those victims who had displeased him in some way. Perhaps Polly Tarkin had attempted to rob him, to pick his pocket—for we know now that she was a thief. Perhaps this poor woman, Tribble, had said something to offend him. Then, rather than simply killing, he mutilated, as well. He punished them."

"You're suggesting then that I'm wrong—that there could, after all, be a single murderer."

"Yes, I've given it some thought, but I'm far from certain of it. You could indeed be right and I wrong. But consider this: Are we not, all of us, in our interior portions, so very different from beef, hogs, and sheep?"

"Well, of course there are differences, but in general, I suppose that, yes, that is true."

"And so you will grant that a man could become familiar with human anatomy by analogy, so to speak, if he had come to know the interior anatomy of lesser animals quite well through years of experience?"

"I begin to see what you are aiming at."

"Who is it works most commonly with sawtooth-bladed knives?"

"Why, a butcher, of course."

"And who, of those you have recently seen, would be big enough and strong enough to throw a woman of twelve-stone over his shoulder and march away with her?"

"Again, the butcher—last night, of course. He's as large as your Constable Bailey and no doubt as strong, throwing sides of beef about daily. But you do recall, Sir John, that I examined his knives, and not one of them had a blade narrow enough to inflict the wound on that girl in the passage."

"Yes, certainly, but Mr. Bailey failed to frisk him, as he admitted to me afterwards. He is not always as thorough as he ought to be. And even if he had, the stiletto might well have been secreted away somewhere in the passage. A night search by lantern light would not likely turn up much. I believe I shall send Jeremy to look again this afternoon and perhaps also to drop in at the butcher's stall and extend my invitation for an evening conversation."

Ah, dear reader, you may suppose just how little I would welcome such a task. If I could have but talked to Sir John at some length, perhaps I could have persuaded him of Mr. Tolliver's innocence. Yet he was such an intimidating presence that it was difficult for me to approach him in such a way. At such times as this I felt my youth as a terrible burden.

"By the bye, Mr. Donnelly, you have a timepiece, have you not? Could you tell me the hour?"

After a moment: "It is nigh on noon."

"Then Jeremy and I must be off, for I have my session to attend to, and it should prove an interesting one. The key is in the door. I take it you will have further business here?"

"For some time to come."

"I shall have a mortuary wagon sent for. They will bring a coffin. It would not do to carry her out in such a state."

"I quite agree."

EIGHT

In Which Sir John Dispenses Justice, Swift and Rough

Of all that has been said of Sir John Fielding in these years since he has passed on, that which has been said oftenest is also truest: He was a just man.

In the field of law, that is a quality, alas, far rarer than one might suppose. Upon Sir John, as magistrate, fell the duty of charging the wrong-doer. This was sometimes no easy matter, for it might happen that a deed has been done that is plainly a punishable offense, yet for which no precise law, neither felony nor misdemeanor, may exist. In such circumstances, and in the interest of justice, the magistrate must show ingenuity in fitting a proper law to the particular wrong that has been done. At meting out such rough justice, none did ever excel Sir John.

I know of no better example to put before you than his handling of those prisoners taken by Mr. Fuller at Number 6 King Street. Clearly, each had committed an offense of greater or lesser gravity, but was there anything in English Common Law to fit their crimes? I knew of nothing—but then, I was just a boy who hung about the court to learn what he might. Yet now I am no longer that boy but a barrister, and I would still say that I know of no laws that would have fit them exact.

That their actions had been most scandalous and shocking was evidenced by the reaction of the courtroom crowd when, at Sir John's bidding, Mr. Fuller gave forth his discoveries upon reaching the premises of the murdered woman, Mistress Tribble. There were murmurs among the listeners, and again and again that sound of breath sharply taken in which is the commonest expression of horrified astonishment. Towards the end of his story, when he told of the actions of the victim's putative husband, there were groans and shouts of anger from the assemblage. For once, Sir John withheld the gavel. I daresay he wished the prisoners to sense the outrage of all against them.

When the constable had concluded, Sir John banged down his gavel at last and called the court to order.

"Mr. Fuller," said he, "remain where you are, if you will, for I expect I shall have some questions as I consider the matter of each of the prisoners you have brought me." A pause, then: "Prisoners, stand before me."

The five rose raggedly, and no doubt with some discomfort, for they were still attached at the neck, each to the other, with Mr. Fuller's double-length of stout rope; the first and fifth of them wore hand-irons.

"First of all, you must identify yourselves for Mr. Marsden's record of these proceedings."

That they did—as Albert Palgrave, Ezekiel Satterthwait, Thomas Coburn, Lemuel Tinker, and Edward Tribble. Mr. Marsden had a bit of difficulty with the second name; he asked Mr. Satterthwait to spell it, which the prisoner could not. The court clerk made do.

"Now, each of you," said Sir John, "has behaved shamefully. There can be no doubt of that. Or would any one of you care to take serious issue with the account you have just heard from Constable Fuller? This is your opportunity to speak in your own behalf, if indeed anything can be said. I advise you to speak now."

There was the briefest silence. Then did all five men begin talking at once.

Sir John gaveled them to silence.

"And so you all have something to say? Well enough, I shall hear you one at a time—Mr. Palgrave first. Sir?"

"Well, I fail to see why I am here at all," said he. "I was not even informed of the charge against me when I was brought here so rude. It's true I discovered the body of that trollop, but—"

"And did you then send word of your discovery to Bow Street?"

"Nooo, but—"

"No, you did not. Mr. Fuller has informed me that word was brought him by a boy of the court who knew the deceased and had come on his own. So there, sir, if you want a charge, by failing to report the murder of your tenant, you impeded the inquiry into her death. But that, I would say, was only the beginning of your sins. Did you, or did you not, charge a shilling each to all those who wished to view her corpus?"

Mr. Palgrave's response was drowned in the shouts of the four who stood beside him. They made vigorous assurances to Sir John that indeed Palgrave had admitted them for payment of a shilling. "There was some in before us," shouted one of the prisoners, perhaps Satterthwait. "He made a pretty penny off her."

"Is that so?" said Sir John. "How many paid to look upon the corpus? How many shillings did you earn from this bizarre enterprise?"

"Not a great many—well, ten altogether. But as I told you earlier, this whore, Tribble, was behind on her rent to the amount of seven shillings. I felt it was my right, as landlord, to recompense myself as I saw fit. And since I was owner of the dwelling—of the entire court—I had the right to admit whomever I pleased."

"Mr. Palgrave, something interests me. You have referred to Mistress—or perhaps Mrs.—Tribble by epithets indicating you thought her to be engaged in prostitution. Or perhaps you meant them loosely, only to indicate that she was a woman of loose morals, a woman of low degree?"

"No, by God, she was a proper whore!"

"You're certain of that?"

"Course I am! I saw her bring her men in her room all hours of the day and night. I spied on them a few times, too. Once I even saw money changing hands. If that doesn't say she's a whore, I don't know what does! Everyone knew what she was."

"And yet you allowed her to continue paying rent and occupy a room in the court?"

"What of it?" said Mr. Palgrave defensively. "A man's got to get income from his property. It wasn't till later she fell behind in her rent. She was quite regular the first year."

"Why then," declared Sir John, "we have another charge against you, sir. You were running a bawdy house, knowingly giving over your premises for the purpose of prostitution and sharing in the proceeds. But let us go on. Tell me, when you first looked upon the body of that woman this morning, how did you find her? In what condition?"

"Why, dead, of course."

"You miss my point. Was she sitting or lying? Clothed or unclothed?"

"Well, then, her body was on the bed, and she was unclothed, though at first look, what I thought to be a covering of some sort turned out to be a great hole dug in her middle."

"And you took a shilling each from these men and others so that they might view this sight?"

"Yes."

"Since you admit to that, I now charge you with offering to the public a lewd and obscene show and taking money for admission to said show."

Albert Palgrave sputtered for a moment, trying to find words suitable for a denial. "It was no show," said he, having recovered himself. "It was more of an exhibition—like—scientifical and not for entertainment."

"She was naked, was she not? And obscenely hacked open? No, Mr. Palgrave, I reject your argument. The charge stands, and I find you guilty on it and sentence you to ninety days in the Fleet Prison."

"The Fleet? I am no debtor, no bankrupt!"

"You may be by the time you emerge, for I am not done with you yet. I further find you guilty of knowingly running a bawdy house and receiving the proceeds of prostitution, and for that I sentence you to sixty days in the Fleet, and finally, in the matter of impeding an inquiry into the death of Mistress Tribble, I also find you guilty and sentence you to thirty days in the Fleet. Sentences to run consecutively—six months in all. And if you wish to add to your sentence, you will continue to argue against me, so I may find you guilty of contempt."

Mr. Palgrave, shocked into silence, bit his tongue. And Sir John, satisfied that he had dealt his last with him, slammed down his gavel, indicating that the matter was done.

"And now, let us deal with Edward Tribble. We have heard Constable Fuller declare that this man, who claims to be the victim's husband, was offering parts of her body for sale, as 'souvenirs.' Mr. Fuller, how came you by this information? What was seen and what was heard by you?"

The constable stroked his chin in thought. "Well, sir," said he after a bit, "when I come into the murder room, there was three men between me and that fellow Tribble, so I was not recognized as a constable right off. I said nothing for a spell, so shocked was I by the condition of the victim I could scarce believe my eyes. Yet I become aware there was dealing going on between Tribble and that one, I believe he gave his name as Lemuel Tinker. They seemed to me to be haggling over the price of something. I, bein' taller than the rest, got myself into a spot where I might have a better view of what was goin' on. And I saw Tribble holding out to him something smallish and all covered with blood. Tinker asks him, 'What part of her is it?' and Tribble replies, 'I know naught of inwards, but for three shillings, what does it matter?' 'If I'm to buy it,' says the other, 'then I should know what to call it.' At that moment, realizing what they were about, I drew sword and pistol and arrested the lot of them."

"So you did not actually see the purchase made, the money change hands, or the body part given over, even for inspection?"

"No, sir, I did not. I'd never seen the like, or even heard of such a thing, and I wished to put an end to it at that moment."

Sir John nodded approvingly. "I'm sure," said he, "that I, in your place, would have done the same. But now, Mr. Tribble, it is time for you to speak. Do you accept the constable's account?"

"Not a bit, I don't," said Tribble most impudent. "I knows a deal of how the law works. You got to prove it against me. So I denies it all!"

Those in the courtroom did not like this, indeed did not like Tribble. A resentful rumble went round the benches. Had he, at that moment, been turned over to those assembled, I do not think he would have survived longer than a few minutes' time.

"I should think," said Sir John, "that we were well on our way to proving it with Mr. Fuller's account. It was reasonable. He did not claim to have seen or heard more than he did. But perhaps another witness. The logical choice would be Mr. Lemuel Tinker. So speak up, Mr. Tinker, was the constable's account of what passed between you and Mr. Tribble an accurate one? Would you care to enlarge upon it?"

"It was remarkable accurate, sir," said he, a small weasel-faced fellow, "right down to the very words was used. What went before was this fellow was in the room when us three come in after payin' a shilling each to the landlord. He says to us, 'This is a great crime has been committed here. It will be historical. This poor darlin' was my wife, and much as it pains me to do it, I shall offer to sell these parts of her that was cut out by him who committed this foul murder upon her. I do this for to raise money to give her a proper Christian burial.' He made it seem like we'd be doin' charity if we bought something of her. I swear to God he did, sir. Her heart he put a great price on, asking a ned for it, the liver ten shillings, and the smaller part he offered me five shillings. I talked him down to three. I was the only one of us with money to spare. And the rest of what was said went just like the constable told it."

Then said Sir John, "There is but one of you three who were found inside with Tribble whom we have not heard from, and that is Thomas Coburn. So let me direct this question to you, Mr. Coburn. Did you see evidence that Tribble had sold any of the organs before you entered the room?"

Thomas Coburn spoke low and rather reluctantly—or so it seemed to me. He began once, and then again when Sir John ordered him to speak louder. "Sir," said he, "I am very ashamed to be here, and even more ashamed to have gone into that place of horror. I wish I had not, sir. But I will do me best to answer your question." He came then to a complete halt, took a deep breath, then continued: "Us three stood in line, held back by the landlord till others cleared out of the room. Two came out. One of them, sir, was a great large fellow, near as wide as he was tall, with a patch over one eye. He held up for all to see a bloody gobbet of something, then made as if to eat it, making a great joke of it, he was. Some laughed, and some did not. Having seen that, I should not have gone inside, and I would not if I had not paid my shilling."

Sir John nodded, satisfied. "All three of you have been quite forthcoming as witnesses. I note this and am grateful, but just to calm my nagging doubts about you, will Satterthwait, Coburn, and Tinker raise your hands, palms out? Now, Mr. Fuller, will you inspect those hands and tell me if you see any traces of dried blood on them?"

The constable did as his chief directed and took the task most seriously. He went to each one and looked closely at each hand, front and back. Then, having concluded, he made a sharp turn and went front and center before the bench.

"Make your report, Mr. Fuller."

"Well, sir, ain't one of them got what I'd call clean hands, but I don't see no blood on any of them."

"Very well. Now satisfy me further and inspect Mr. Tribble's hands, if you will."

That was done as well, though the constable was forced to handle him rather rough to get a proper look.

"Quite soiled with crimson they are, sir—both hands. Even got it caked under his fingernails, he has."

"Thank you, Mr. Fuller," said Sir John. "Now, as to you three—Satterthwait, Coburn, and Tinker—I accept that your actions within that room were just as you presented them. You were there to gape and gawk, chiefly. Mr. Tinker was tempted to buy one of the unholy relics offered to him for sale by Tribble. Lucky for him he did not. His punishment would have been greater had he done so. And yes, there will be punishment, for if Mr. Palgrave offered a lewd and obscene show for personal gain, you three paid your money and attended that show. And for your attendance at it, I sentence you to thirty days each in the Fleet Prison. It is also true that by your very presence in that room you impeded the inquiry into the death of the victim of that ghastly murder. And so I thus charge you further and find you three guilty. That sentence, too, like the first, is thirty days in the Fleet Prison, but it shall run concurrently with the first. In other words, at the same time. One of you has already expressed sorrow and shame at his actions. I would advise the other two to use the month ahead to meditate upon the moral wrong you have done."

With that, Sir John slammed down his gavel, indicating that matter was concluded.

"Now to you, Mr. Edward Tribble," said the magistrate. "Yours is by far the gravest offense, as I'm sure all those in this room would agree. When I first was told what you had done, my wits balked at what my ears heard. I thought surely I had misunderstood. Thus does the mind boggle at the nature of your crime. When you come before the judge, I advise you to use as your defense that bit of humbug you tried upon these three misguided men. Tell *him* that you were selling her parts that you might give the rest of her a decent Christian burial. Who knows? He may accept that. The jury may believe you. I, for one, do not. That, however, matters little, for in this instance, my only duty is to charge you and bind you over for trial."

"Wot?" screeched the prisoner. "You mean I ain't goin' to the Fleet with the rest?"

"No, you are not. You are to be sent to Newgate where you will await trial at the Old Bailey."

"On what charge?"

"Disturbing the dead."

There was an immediate hush in the courtroom.

"But . . ." Tribble sought words, unable for a moment to find them. "But that's like grave-robbing, ain't it? I never done that. She weren't in the ground."

"No," said Sir John, "you did not even wait until she was beneath the ground until you insulted her corpus. To my mind, what you did was at least as bad and probably worse."

"Disturbing the dead—that's a hanging offense!"

"It is, but I offer you this hope. If you cooperate with my constables in the recovery of the organs you sold—and I believe you know the buyers—then I shall recommend transportation. Judges at the Old Bailey accept my recommendations in sentencing—nearly always."

Edward Tribble looked about him wildly, yet uttered not a word.

"Mr. Fuller," said Sir John, "take these five to the strong room and bring forth him who is inside. While that is attended to, I declare this court in recess and give permission to talk and walk about. And I summon to the bench Mr. Oliver Goldsmith and Master Jeremy Proctor."

This was a right rare occurrence. I had never before been called before him in court except at our first meeting when I, a boy of thirteen, had been falsely accused of theft. And now, to be summoned in the company of one so well known as Oliver Goldsmith was a sign of how my estate had risen in the past two years. Nevertheless, I had no notion of what we two might have in common.

When, however, I reached Sir John, delayed somewhat by the milling crowd, I recognized the man who was leaning over in deep conversation with the magistrate. Was this then Oliver Goldsmith? It was the same man who had spoken out in defense of Ormond Neville when Constable Perkins had arrested that poet *cum* journalist at the Goose and Gander. If this indeed be Goldsmith, he was about my same size, near bald on his head (which he made no effort to disguise with a wig), and most Irish in appearance.

The man in question glimpsed my arrival and said to Sir John, "Would this be the lad, sir?"

"Jeremy, is that you?"

"Indeed it is, Sir John."

"Ah, well and good. I knew not for certain that you were in the courtroom when I called you forth. Mr. Goldsmith and I have need of that scurrilous broadsheet authored by that fellow, Neville—you remember him, of course."

Before I could say yea or nay, Mr. Goldsmith nodded at me sharply.

"I'm sure he must remember him," said he. "He was with the constable when Neville was taken in."

"Ah, so he was!" Sir John agreed. "But, Jeremy, would you now go and fetch my copy of that broadsheet? It is in the drawer of the desk in my chamber. You should have no difficulty finding it."

"Certainly. I'll be back in a trice," said I.

Leaving them without another word, I made swiftly for the side door of the courtroom, through which Mr. Fuller had just tugged his five charges. That door, of course, led to that part of the ground floor given over to the backstage business of the court—the strong room, the constabulary armory, Mr. Marsden's alcove and record bins, and Sir John's sanctum. I knew it, by then, as well as any part of Number 4 Bow Street.

There was Mr. Fuller, herding his prisoners into the strong room, once more the court jailer. Yet when called upon, he proved himself a proper Beak Runner. None could have improved his morning's performance. When would I be called upon, as he was, to prove myself? Oh, if the need arose, I might be assigned to guard a door, or to accompany one like the rabbi home through streets that might be dangerous in the potential. Nevertheless, I had not truly been put to the test. What was I but Sir John's errand boy, sent to fetch this or that, deliver a letter, or summon a witness?

And here I was once again, sent off to fetch that vile broadsheet from Sir John's chamber. Could he not have sent Mr. Marsden? No, such an errand would have been beneath the court clerk. Better to send Jeremy; he will do any and all that is asked of him.

(Boys not yet men do often thus experience such attacks of dissatisfaction, overestimating their powers and underestimating the blessings bestowed upon them by fortune.)

I stormed through the open door and into the room kept by Sir John for private and informal interrogations, meetings with the constables, and the like. I knew precisely the location of that for which I had been sent. There was but one drawer in the desk, which in truth was more in the nature of a table, but one drawer did him well enough. He had no need to store papers; for that he relied on Mr. Marsden. I jerked it open and pulled out the broadsheet, folded over on account of its large size.

Just as I was about to shut the drawer I stopped, for my eye had glimpsed something familiar inside. It was the leather purse I had found under the floorboard in Polly Tarkin's room. Unable quite to help myself, I tugged it open and satisfied myself that the same heap of guineas and sovereigns was intact, just as it was when I had brought it in to Sir John. Nor had I any doubt that they had gone uncounted. It was true. The magistrate was careless about money that flowed into the court. In my mind echoed the words of the bully-boy from the night before: "It's not like the Beak would miss it if you helped yourself, maybe a little at a time."

I dipped my hand into the purse and let the treasure run through my fingers. It would not be necessary to take a little at a time. Ten guineas would never be missed from such a store. And had I not found the purse? In that sense, was it not as much mine as Sir John's? Had I kept it, none would have been the wiser, yet I had handed it over to him, thinking it would have importance to the inquiry—yet it had none. He simply tossed it indifferently into the drawer. Yet how could I be indifferent to that bag of money when just a fraction of its contents would buy Mariah's freedom from that despicable, giggling wretch?

All this, reader, passed through my brain in the merest part of a minute. Yet what then came to mind were the jeering words of that pimp, those which were his last to me: "It'd be like stealing money from a blind man." And with that, in my mind's eye formed the gentle, generous visage of Sir John Fielding—he who had taken me in, clothed me, and fed me—and I knew then that I could take not a single guinea from that bag. Putting behind me all sophistry and self-deceit, I pulled closed the purse by its thongs and slammed shut the drawer. Grabbing up the broadsheet, I ran from the room and made straight for the court.

The hum of conversation told me, as I opened the door, that the session was still in recess—and yes, I saw that they were still up and milling about. Sir John was still in conference with Oliver Goldsmith at the bench, and he spoke most heatedly.

"—if need be, yes, Mr. Goldsmith, for it must be made clear that that petty criminal Yossel has been dismissed for good and sufficient reason. You need not be specific. Say only that his time that night was accounted for. We need not bladder about who accounted for it and how. That story will be all about London swiftly enough."

"I daresay," agreed Mr. Goldsmith. "Uh . . . the lad is back, sir."

"Ah, Jeremy, good. Have you the damned thing with you? Give it me. I shall need it for brandishing purposes."

He groped for it, and I put it in his hand.

Mr. Fuller appeared with Ormond Neville in tow. "The prisoner's present," said he.

"Then we may start. Mr. Goldsmith, do not sit too far to the rear. I shall ask you to come forward. And again, sir, I thank you for what you have offered."

"Glad to be of service, sir."

And then did Sir John beat mightily with his gavel upon the table before him.

"The Bow Street Court is back in session," cried Mr. Marsden, rising to his feet. "All take your places, and be silent, for Sir John Fielding, magistrate, will now hear the final case of the day."

It took bare a minute for the crowd to disperse to the benches and chairs provided. I noted with interest that when Oliver Goldsmith returned to his place, which indeed was near the front, he seated himself next Mr. Millhouse, the neighbor of the second victim, Polly Tarkin. I, for my part, scrambled to find a better place than I had had earlier, and found one off to the side behind Mr. Fuller and his charge, Ormond Neville.

"Order, order now," said Sir John, and the room fell silent. "Mr. Marsden, call the prisoner forward." And then did the clerk summon him by name. As Mr. Neville took his place before the bench, the magistrate called forth: "I summon also Mr. Benjamin Nicholson."

Was I not then amazed, reader, to see the younger partner of the publisher William Boyer rise from a place much in the rear of the courtroom and come forward with his head hung low. He was a man of reputation in Grub Street, so highly esteemed by his elder partner that the name of the firm had recently been altered from Boyer's to Boyer and Nicholson. Yet there was little pride in the man as he shambled up to take his place beside the prisoner.

"Mr. Neville," said Sir John, picking up the broadsheet and waving it before him, "are you the author of this scandalous concoction of surmises, suspicions, fabrications, and ancient lies?"

"Ah, well, yes, I suppose I am. Yes."

"Such hesitation. Where is that pride of authorship? And you, Mr. Nicholson, did you not publish it?"

"Well, we printed it."

"You seem to be making what I would call a false distinction. Did you not pay Mr. Neville for his work? Did you not cover the cost of printing right in the Boyer and Nicholson shop? Did you not then engage a company of hawkers to take the broadsheet through the streets of London and sell it for the price you set? Did you not, finally, claim the profits from this little enterprise for the firm?"

Mr. Nicholson sighed a great sigh. "Yes, Sir John," said he.

"Does the process I have described not constitute publication, as it is generally understood? So I put it to you again, sir—did you not publish it?"

Another sigh. "Yes, Sir John."

"Now tell me, either one of you, whose idea was it to create this"—Sir John hesitated—"this tissue of hasty conclusions and outright calumny?"

The two men then spoke in chorus: "It was his." And so saying, each pointed at the other.

"Well," said the magistrate, "I see that there is some difference of opinion here. Let me ask the questions and weigh your responses. Mr. Neville, how is it you say Mr. Nicholson initiated the enterprise?"

"Why, sir, because he called me to his office and suggested I make a journalistic inquiry into the murder of Polly Tarkin, which I had then not even heard about. He believed there to be material for a broadsheet in it."

"Very well," said Sir John, "and how was it you came to hear of the murder, Mr. Nicholson?"

"From Giles Ponder, vicar of St. Paul's Covent Garden, who has a book in preparation with us. He said that he was wakened by a commotion—voices, lanterns, and such—at the back gate of the churchyard. He went down to investigate and heard from a constable that a woman had been found murdered just there. The constable and a lad were just then in the act of moving her body."

I was that lad, of course. And I recalled a visit from a half-dressed churchman, his nightshirt hanging down over his pantaloons, who demanded to know what we were about. (Sir John was off at that moment talking with Mistress Linney and her colleagues.) Constable Brede, tight-lipped as ever, had told him simply that—a woman had been murdered—and wished him a good night. Or a good morning, for by then dawn was breaking.

"And on that information you summoned Mr. Neville, did you?"

"I did, yes, sir."

"And you, Mr. Neville, set out to discover what you could about this grisly affair?"

"Yes, sir," said Ormond Neville.

"And how came you by the information you wrote?"

"Well, I found to my surprise and good luck that one of my circle of acquaintance was a neighbor of the victim, that he lived literally next door to her. He gave me her name, informed me of her occupation and where I might look for those among her scarlet sisters who could tell me more. I went to Bedford Street, bought a few glasses of gin for them, and soon had much of what was needed."

"Let me detain you, sir," said Sir John. "That member of your circle must have been Mr. Thaddeus Millhouse, a poet by his own description. He was that morning in the strong room here at the Bow Street Court awaiting his time in court for refusing to obey my order to clear the alley where the murder had taken place. Did you talk to him there?"

My attention had been drawn immediately to Thaddeus Millhouse at the mention by Ormond Neville of "one of my circle of acquaintances." I fear I stared. Whether out of shame or guilt, he shrank down in his place next to Mr. Goldsmith, and when his name was mentioned, he actually sought to hide his face. And to what purpose? Only five or six in the courtroom would have recognized him and one of them was blind. But of course no man would wish to hear his name in open court in such circumstances. Still, it did seem strange.

Mr. Neville surprised me with his response to Sir John's question.

"Yes, I did. Mr. Millhouse's wife had heard of his misfortune and asked me to bring him a clean shirt that he might look more presentable for his appearance in court. That I did, and your jailer allowed me in for that purpose. I had a brief conversation with Mr. Millhouse at that time, in which I mentioned the matter of my investigation for the purpose of the broadsheet."

"Hmmm," said Sir John, "most interesting. And then to women of the streets that you might learn more. It was from them that you learned of Yossel Davidovich and his altercation with the victim."

"Yes, sir."

"Had any of those you talked to actually witnessed the altercation? I can near answer that myself, for I think it highly unlikely, unless you talked with Sarah Linney, for she was the only witness."

"Well, I did not take their names. There were but two."

"*Did* either of these women claim to have witnessed the altercation?"

"Not in so many words, no, but they said this Yossel fellow *was seen* in such a situation with the victim. They did not like him at all; one swore she'd been robbed by him, that he'd produced a knife and threatened to cut off her nose. He seemed to have been a very nasty individual."

"Yet as concerned the quarrel between Yossel and the victim, you accepted hearsay."

"Well, I could not search further for witnesses and such. The broadsheet had to be written that very day!"

"And due to that press of time, you were willing to accuse him of murder with no more to support the accusation than a surmise that he *could* have returned to that spot, taken her down the alley, and murdered her. And that surmise, further, was based on nothing more than hearsay. Mr. Neville, *that will not do.*" That he said most solemnly. Yet the next moment Sir John seemed to be suppressing a smile. "You said, sir, that from what you were told, Yossel Davidovich seemed a very nasty individual. But tell me, what was your impression of him?"

"*My* impression? Why, how would I—"

"You passed the night in his company."

"Do you mean, sir, that that sniveling little wretch in the strong room was he? He shivered half the night in fear because 'they' were after him—never said who 'they' were, actually. Said he'd never be able to walk the streets of London again. So *that* was Yossel! You don't say so!"

"Ah, but I do, sir. And in fact, he had reason to fear, for 'they' were indeed after him. He and the rabbi who persuaded him to obey my summons to come in for questioning were chased and harried all the way to Bow Street by a citizenry enraged by your inflammatory broadsheet. If two of my constables had not interceded to protect them, bodily harm might have been done to both men—the one because you had erroneously defamed him and the other because he was manifestly a Jew. And so the charges against you are proven. You did interfere with and impede my inquiry into the death of Polly Tarkin by wrongly yet with great certitude identifying Yossel Davidovich as her murderer. It was established in the course of this morning's inquest that he could not have done the deed by a witness who accounted for his time. And as for inciting to riot, that charge is also proven, as what might have been a riot was averted by a swift show of force by the Bow Street Runners. And so, Ormond Neville, you are found guilty on both charges. But to me, sir, perhaps more flagrant and damaging than the charges were the ancient calumnies against the Jews which you repeated in the broadsheet. Whatever possessed you to do so?"

"Uh . . . well . . . sir, you must understand that it takes a great many words to fill a broadsheet, and I thought to fill it out with a bit of history."

"*History,* is it? And how came you by this 'history'? Was it taught you in school? Was it read in a book?"

"No, but for a period I served as secretary to the British consul, Sir Anthony Allman, in the city of St. Petersburg in Russia. I had many conversations with Russians at that time regarding the Jews, and they seemed very certain of the facts regarding the secret practices of the Israelites. Let us say, I had the information on good authority."

"I question that authority," said Sir John, "just as I deny your so-called facts. Did you find these Russians to be otherwise well informed? Did they exhibit great wisdom in other matters?"

"They seemed to me very cultured," said Neville, "for they all spoke French."

"And is that your standard? *Bah,* I say, and bah again. The Russians are a benighted people who would say the world was flat if they did not own so much of it. I reject your 'history,' sir, and if there were a law against slandering a people, I should charge you on that count as well, for you are clearly guilty of slandering the Jews." With that, Sir John paused, as if to catch his breath. "But there is no such law, and so we must turn now to Mr. Benjamin Nicholson. Mr. Nicholson, tell me, when Mr. Neville brought to you what he had written, did you read it through?"

"Why, yes, of course."

"You did not also show it to Mr. William Boyer, your partner?"

"No, his interest is in books and their sale, to the exclusion of all else. I handle all production of said books, as well as the occasional broadsheets, adverts, and the like."

"I see. And when you read it through, you found nothing objectionable in it? Nothing inflammatory?"

"Ah, well, Sir John, I am no lawyer, nor for that matter is Mr. Neville. It seemed to me that there was information in it to which the public had a right. He named a malefactor, perhaps a bit too certainly, but then the public likes certainty. It will have nothing of the law's niceties."

"How well I know that," said Sir John. "But had you no misgivings about the heinous practices attributed to the Jews—the murder of Christian infants and the like?"

"On that I have no expertise whatever. Let me say I have nothing against them, except that which we are given in Holy Scripture. My personal advisor in financial matters is a Jew, and I count him a friend. However, if there is one principle to which we hold at Boyer and Nicholson, it is the author's right to have his say. We do not dictate to the writer."

"You mean to say he will have the right to say whatever he will, and you will simply publish it as written?"

"Well, there are limits, of course."

"And Mr. Neville's—what shall we call it? essay?—it did not exceed those limits?"

"No, I suppose it didn't."

"Indeed it did not, for you published it. And so, as a consequence, I hold you equally guilty with Ormond Neville of the charges put against him—to wit, interfering with and impeding a criminal inquiry; and inciting to riot."

"But—"

"There will be no 'but's,' sir. He transgressed in writing what he did, and you in publishing it. But now comes the most difficult task, and that is meting out proper punishment to the two of you. By rights, you should both be made to serve a sentence in gaol—I should say a minimum of thirty days. But when I arrived here at Bow Street to preside over this day's session, I found waiting for me a letter from Mr. William Boyer. It was, in effect, a plea for leniency for Mr. Nicholson, couched in the most practical terms. He said in it that he had grown a bit too old and was out of touch with the printing and production aspects of their enterprise. And that if Mr. Nicholson were unavailable for any extended period of time, he would have to close down all but the bookstore in front. Printers and binders would be unemployed for the length of his absence. I know Mr. Boyer. He has been of service to the court in the past, and I have no reason to doubt the truth of the situation as he describes it. Having no wish to put honest men out of work, I therefore refrain from imposing a gaol sentence upon Mr. Nicholson. Yet since I have found the two equally guilty in this matter, I cannot then impose a sentence upon Mr. Neville. Nor can I allow their wrong to go unrighted."

Sir John paused and leaned back a moment as if in thought. He stayed thus for near a minute. And then said he, as if still giving consideration to the matter:

"I am especially desirous that no profit should be made from this criminal act in which you two collaborated. Tell me, Mr. Neville, what were you paid for writing the broadsheet?"

"Two guineas, sir."

"That shall be your fine. And you, Mr. Nicholson, what did the firm profit from its sale across the city?"

"That's difficult to say exact, sir, but it should come to about twenty-five guineas, give or take a bit."

"Ah, there is a lesson for authors in that disparity, is there not? But that is neither here nor there. Twenty-five guineas shall be your fine, Mr. Nicholson."

"But, Sir John, that is the firm's money, and not my own."

"You are a partner in the firm, are you not? Work it out with Mr. Boyer. Yet still the wrong has not been righted, and considering this dilemma, I was quite at a loss until Mr. Oliver Goldsmith stepped forward and made a most generous offer. Mr. Goldsmith, will you come now and repeat it?"

Come forward Oliver Goldsmith did, at the bouncing pace of one who was accustomed to moving through London by foot; the man had a leg, or rather two of them, and he used them to good advantage. He took his place next Ormond Neville.

"I understand, sir," said Sir John to him, "that you have certain scruples that you wish first to make clear?"

"I do, sir, yes. In general, I am in agreement with the position voiced by Mr. Nicholson—that an author should be free to have his say, and that if he is in error, his errors will be corrected by others writing against him. That is the very nature of controversy, and controversy is the very heart of intelligent life. Nevertheless, when I read Mr. Neville's broadsheet, I strongly objected to certain passages in it, in particular those which dealt in general with the Jews, their history, and criminal practices. I, like you, impugned his sources, and we had been in argument at table in the Goose and Gander before your constable arrived to take him away."

"And what then do you suggest, Mr. Goldsmith?" asked Sir John.

"The only proper answer to such a broadsheet is another broadsheet pointing out—as you described them—Mr. Neville's surmises, fabrications, and ancient calumnies—and correcting them. My offer is to write just such a broadsheet, that it may appear as soon as possible and do the fullest good."

"Your generous offer is accepted, sir, and Mr. Nicholson, I assure you, will be pleased to publish it, terms to be settled between you."

From Covent Garden I returned most dejected and worried. I had been sent there by the magistrate on that errand that I had so dreaded. The butchery of the murder in King Street had returned Sir John's suspicions to the butcher, Mr. Tolliver. In the end, when given the task of inviting Mr. Tolliver to come by to talk a bit more about these matters, I did manage to blurt out a few words in his defense. He was, I told Sir John, "a fine man who would do naught to harm a soul. He—" And then had Sir John cut me off sharply, saying, "It is not harm to souls we are concerned with here, Jeremy, but rather grievous attacks upon corporeal bodies. Go and find him; invite him to come to me; I wish to talk with him."

(Sir John was seldom so short with me—indeed I rarely gave him cause. Yet in his defense, should he need one, it ought to be said that he had complained only moments before that he had never had a more exhausting day in court. He seemed, and even looked, much diminished by it.)

And so I had gone to Covent Garden to deliver the invitation to Mr. Tolliver, finding my way through the afternoon crowd, looking not far ahead, thinking perhaps too much of my own discomfort at having been given this task. Thus was I quite amazed when I arrived at his stall and found it closed.

I looked about me. Could I have mistaken its location? No, of course not. I had been to it too often, buying meat for the household. But here I was, where I had always gone, and there was no Mr. Tolliver, no meat hanging, waiting to be carved, nothing at all but a shuttered stall secured by a great, large padlock. Where could he have gone? No doubt he had closed up early that day. But why?

I stepped up to the greengrocer stall next his. The woman behind the table there was busying herself rearranging her stock of carrots, potatoes, and such. I stood, waiting for her attention, but it was slow in coming. At last she raised her eyes to me and grunted.

"I was wondering, ma'am," said I, "if you could tell me where Mr. Tolliver has got to."

"No idea." She returned then to her work of shifting her stock about.

"Well, when did he leave?"

"He never come," said she, without looking up.

"Did he leave no word as to where he was going, or where he was off to?"

"Not a word. Him and me, we have little to say one to t'other. Just 'cause he's the only butcher in the Garden, he thinks he's right special. He don't belong here, and he ought to know it. It's the Garden for greens and Smithfield for meat, as all well know." Then did she look up at me once again—nay, glared. "Now, if you ain't goin' to buy nothin', I'll thank you to move on and make room for those who will."

Indignant but still baffled, I said no more but did as she advised. Indeed, I thought, were I Mr. Tolliver I should have little to say myself to such a rude sort of woman. I sought information from him who ran the next stall down from hers. Though farther removed from Mr. Tolliver's end stall, he might well have been on better terms with the butcher. But while far more polite—he recognized me as an occasional buyer—he was no more helpful than the shrew in the place next his. So far as he knew, Mr. Tolliver had made no appearance that whole day; his stall had remained just as it was now—padlocked tight. And though they sometimes spoke in greeting or goodbye, there was seldom anything more between them, certainly nothing to explain why the butcher might have chosen this day to absent himself.

Deciding it would be useless to ask further, I set off across Covent Garden for Number 4 Bow Street. Had I known Mr. Tolliver's dwelling place I would have gone there and looked for him. No doubt, I told myself, the man was ill; yet if he were so, it would be the first time in my memory—and he seemed right enough the night before. Thus I fretted as I went, worried that his absence would weigh heavily against him in Sir John's mind. Surely he could be found at home, or barring that, he would show himself in a day or two.

I found Sir John ensconced in his chamber, a bottle of beer on his desk which Mr. Marsden would have fetched for him from across the street. He bade me sit down and give my report, and that I did. He listened, giving little outward sign of his response. In truth, he seemed listless and a bit distracted, as if his mind were on other matters. And as it happened, that was so.

"Jeremy," said he, "I fear I gave you a bad example today."

I was a bit surprised to hear that. Though he had complained that his day in court had exhausted him, I had thought him most specially shrewd and ingenious on the bench.

"In what way, sir?"

"In my treatment of that young villain, Tribble." He sighed. "First of all, I should not have thrashed him. Had Constable Fuller done that—or Mr. Bailey, or Perkins, or any of them—they would have received a stern reproof from me. But, dear God, did you hear what he said? 'She was my wife and my whore'—as if that gave him the right to do whatever he liked with her, alive or dead."

"I heard that, yes, sir."

"All the way back to Bow Street, I labored hard to think of some suitable charge for what he had done, and none came to me but the one I used against him. Yes, disturbing the dead *is* a hanging offense meant to discourage grave robbing—but it should not be. Murder should be, I suppose—though even in willfully causing the death of another there are more mitigating circumstances than the court generally allows. What is done to a body after death is not near so serious as killing. Perhaps in that depraved mind of his, he truly did have some vague intention of giving her a proper burial from the proceeds of his sales, a revolting idea but practical, I daresay. Who can reckon such matters?" A pause, a shrug, and then: "Well, a judge and jury must. They will be shocked, no doubt, and as horrified as I—and they may be all for hanging him. But he should not hang—not for that which he did. It would be unjust. Tomorrow morning, Jeremy, we shall compose a letter to the Lord Chief Justice, giving the facts of the case, but also giving some emphasis to his burial plan. I shall plead for leniency in sentencing, suggest transportation for a period of years. Perhaps they can work some of the nastiness out of him in the colonies."

"You had already said you would do that if he helped recover the . . . missing organs."

"Oh, he has already done so—gave two names and even an address. There was no end to his helpfulness. I'll send two constables to bring them in tonight."

"I could go to Mr. Tolliver's tonight and offer your invitation. I believe Mr. Bailey has the location."

"No, I'll have one of the constables attend to it—and it will be, as I promised you, just an invitation to come in and talk—tomorrow sometime."

I rose from my chair. "Is there anything else I can help you with?"

"No. Why not go on to Mr. Perkins? He tells me you're quite an apt pupil, that you grow more dangerous by the day."

I laughed in embarrassment. "Hardly that, sir."

"But, Jeremy," said he, "never be a bully."

The mention of that word reminded me in a flash of my experience earlier that day in that very room.

"Oh, Sir John, there was a matter I thought I ought mention to you. When you sent me earlier to fetch that broadsheet from your desk drawer, I noticed that in the drawer you had left that bag of booty I brought from Polly Tarkin's room. I thought perhaps you'd forgotten it was there. I have no idea how much is inside, but it seemed a goodly amount."

"You're right. I had forgotten. I'll hand it over to Mr. Marsden for the strong box until we decide what's to be done with it. And . . ."

"Yes, Sir John?"

"Thank you for reminding me."

NINE

In Which Sir John Looks Forward To All Hallows Eve

Mr. Tolliver had quite disappeared. Constable Langford returned that night from the butcher's place of dwelling on Long Acre with this dismaying revelation as the four of us—Sir John and Lady Fielding, Annie Oakum and I—sat at table. We had just completed our evening's meal when his footsteps sounded on the stairs and his knock came on the door. I jumped to open it, and the red-waistcoated constable asked permission to enter. Sir John bade him come ahead, and Mr. Langford doffed his hat, stepped inside, and blurted it out. And those were his very words: " . . . disappeared he has, sir. There is nor hide nor hair of him to be seen."

In my surprise, I looked at Lady Fielding. Her eyes were wide, as indeed my own must have been. Surely Mr. Tolliver could not have fled as some fugitive might. I could not, I would not believe that.

The constable continued his report: "I banged on his door right hard and failed to raise him. Now of course that meant nothing; he could've been out to sup or wet his whistle or both. So I started through the house to get some word of him from his neighbors, and that way I happened upon his landlord, who dwells at the same address right below this Tolliver fellow. He tells me he was out last night and as he was coming in, he run into his tenant hauling a portmanteau and in a great hurry. 'Where are you off to?' says he to him. 'That's my own affair, ain't it?' says Tolliver, who, says the landlord, is often inclined to be rather short. He noticed that he turned off in the direction of Covent Garden. Now, the landlord—his name is Coker, got it all down in my book—he was right puzzled, for he says all the years this Tolliver lived there, he never knew him to go off like this on a trip, and the way that portmanteau was stuffed, he meant to stay a while.

"Well, Sir John, I asked this man Coker if he had a key to Mr. Tolliver's place, and I convinced him this was a matter of some importance to you—'a court matter,' I told him—"

"And quite right you were to do so, Mr. Langford," said Sir John.

"He opened the place to me," said the constable, proceeding, "and accompanied me inside, which was quite proper, as I reckon. I was quite taken with the size of it, I was. There was two large chambers—one for sittin' and one for sleepin', and a smaller, separate place for cookin'. The thing that struck me, sir, was that sittin' room and—what would you call it?—the kitchen were clean and neat as a pin. Don't often see that when a man lives by hisself. But the bedroomnow that was a different matter. The bed was made, right enough, but there was clothes thrown atop it, all helter-skelter. I looked inside the wardrobe, and in a chest at the foot of the bed, and I saw he'd quite emptied them, he had, and just grabbed up the clothes he wished to pack and left the others lie. I says to the landlord, 'It looks like your tenant left in a great hurry.' And he says to me, 'It does indeed.'"

"Did you happen to notice a packet of knives about?" asked Sir John. "They would have been wrapped in . . . How were they wrapped, Jeremy?"

"In soft chamois," said I, feeling quite the traitor.

"No, sir, I never seen such, but then, I didn't do a proper search of the place because, for one, I hadn't been told to, and for another, I'd no idea for what to look. Anyway, that's what happened, for I left then, and telling the landlord he might be hearing from you later on."

"Indeed he might," said Sir John, and except for thanking Constable Langford, praising his initiative, and bidding him a good night, that was all Sir John said. Which, to make clear the matter, might be better said, he refused to talk about it with us further.

As soon as the sound of the constable's footsteps on the stairs had died, Lady Fielding attempted to open up the matter for discussion, beginning most sweetly, "Jack, I'm sure there is a very sound explanation for Mr. Tolliver's sudden departure."

But Sir John would have none of it. He, having resumed his place at the table, simply shook his head and said, "Please, Kate."

No more was said of it that night, nor to me, for some time to come.

Next day there were letters to write, including that to the Lord Chief Justice on Edward Tribble's behalf. More and more, Sir John depended upon me to take his dictation, thus leaving Mr. Marsden free to attend to his many other duties as court clerk. Often, when letters of no great gravity were to go out, the magistrate would simply tell me in summary what he wished them to say and would depend upon me to put them into his words. After hearing them read to him, he would then sign them. In spite of his blindness, once the quill was put in his hand and placed upon the paper, he proved quite adept with it. His may have been, as some said, a scrawl, but it was an impressive scrawl, far more legible than that of some other men who had the power of sight.

Thus it was that we two often sat opposite one another at that same large table which served him as a desk—I, scrivening away, and he, lost in cogitation. And perhaps, from time to time, he would rise and pace silently about the room, whose dimensions and plan he knew by heart.

So were we that morning when a tap came at the open door and Mr. Marsden announced Mr. Oliver Goldsmith. Sir John, caught in one of his rambles about his chambers, invited the author in and hastened to his usual place behind his desk. I, in turn, moved to one side that Mr. Goldsmith might have the place opposite the magistrate. After taking the hand offered by Sir John and giving it a manly squeeze, Mr. Goldsmith took from his coat a sheaf of papers and seated himself.

"Well, sir," said the magistrate, "have you come to me to gather more facts about that rascal, Yossel Davidovich?"

"No, Sir John, your clerk, Mr. Marsden, was more than helpful in that regard. He gave me the gist of the inquest from his notes. I have written the broadsheet."

"Already?" Sir John asked in some surprise.

"Indeed, sir. I am a night worker. I thought it best to get it out of the way, so to speak, that I might get on with matters that concern me more. Since you were quite insistent that my broadsheet should not only carry the news that this Yossel had been released but explain how and why this came about, I thought to read it you to make sure I had in it observed the proper formalities and legalities."

"Why, by all means," said Sir John, most pleased. "Proceed, proceed."

Mr. Goldsmith produced a pair of spectacles and fitted them over his ears. As he did so, he resumed his address to Sir John: "By the bye, I was most favorably impressed by the testimony of the surgeon, Mr. Donnelly. Being myself a physician—"

"I had only lately heard that, Mr. Goldsmith."

"Ah yes, Trinity College, Dublin—though I have not practiced that art in London."

"You are indeed a man of parts."

"But as regards Mr. Donnelly. Since I assume he is Irish as I am, I should like to make his acquaintance."

"As I am sure he would like to make yours. That can certainly be arranged. But, please, sir, proceed with the reading."

"Ah yes."

And so Oliver Goldsmith directed his attention to the sheaf of papers in his hand and began reading. There was a sentence in preamble in which it was announced that what followed was "both an answer and a correction to mistakes, misconceptions, and misrepresentations put forth in a broadsheet in reference to the Jews, and one in particular, which was distributed earlier in the week. As regards the particular Jew, one Josef Davidovich, commonly known as Yossel . . ." Then did Mr. Goldsmith present a concise and cogent account of the inquest into the death of Priscilla Tarkin of Half Moon Passage. The witnesses were named, with one exception, and their testimony was summarized in a few graceful sentences. Particular emphasis was put upon Mr. Donnelly's fixing of the time of death "with remarkable precision." And finally did he come to the unnamed witness, Lady Hermione Cox, whom he referred to as "a lady of considerable courage and unimpeachable word." Her testimony, wrote Mr. Goldsmith, "made it certain that Josef Davidovich was in her company during the space of time in which the murder was accomplished. And so he was rightly released, and the coroner's jury voted a directed verdict of 'murder by an unknown assailant.'"

There the author stopped, laid down the sheaf of papers, of which he had only read the first, and waited.

"Excellent, excellent," said Sir John. "I have but a single correction, and that at the very end. The phrase used, Mr. Goldsmith, is 'willful murder by person or persons unknown.'"

"Ah, thank you. That will give that dash of authenticity which I seek." And he whipped out a pencil and bent to the task of correcting his text on the table top.

"But pray continue," said the magistrate. "I should like to hear the whole of it."

Having made the change, Mr. Goldsmith folded the papers and dropped them in his pocket. Then said he firmly, "No, Sir John."

"No? You refuse to read the rest?"

"I regret that I must disappoint you, but on principle I must decline your request."

"I . . . I do not understand. On what principle do you decline?"

"On the right of authorship. Were I to continue and read it to you entire, you might call for further changes of a more material sort. Out of respect to you, I should probably feel obliged to make them. But since Mr. Nicholson has stipulated that my name is to appear on the broadsheet as author, it is I and I alone who must stand as guarantor of its contents. It would not do to call it, 'A Truthful Way with the Jews,' which is the title I have chosen, by Oliver Goldsmith and Sir John Fielding—now would it?"

"But you did not hesitate to seek my advice on the portion you read."

"There I sought only your legal opinion. I was not present at the inquest. I wanted to be sure the facts were right. I might assure you, by the bye, that I followed your recommendation and sought information from Rabbi Gershon of the synagogue on Maiden Lane, a remarkable man by my measure. He was most forthcoming and helpful, and he gave to me so much information that I might indeed have extended this from a broadsheet to a pamphlet. Yet he did not ask to read what I would write. He put his trust in me. I ask you to do the same. I came here seeking your help in a limited way. I did not come seeking your imprimatur."

Sir John Fielding found himself for once at a loss for words. I saw him twice form answers on his lips until at last one came.

"I fear you have misconstrued my interest, Mr. Goldsmith. I had no intention of censoring what you might have written. I myself wished to hear the remainder because I was aware that it was in it your true attachment to this enterprise lay. I wanted only to hear what you had done with it."

"That's good to hear, Sir John, and I promise you shall have a copy of the broadsheet as soon as it be in print." He sighed. "I confess, however, that I fear you would be altogether happier if there were no journalists about to get in the way of your inquiries."

"It's true, my experience of journalism has not been a happy one. But then, few of its practitioners are so careful of their facts as you have been, consulting first with Mr. Marsden and then with Rabbi Gershon. As for the ideal you stated in court—the duel of ideas and opinions leading ultimately to truth—"

"Controversy, yes."

"Such an ideal is possible only in an ideal society of intelligent men and not one, like our own, ruled by ignorance and riot. It is I, as magistrate, who must deal with the consequences of careless journalism."

"Sir John," said Oliver Goldsmith, rising from his chair, "I appreciate your position, as you seem to appreciate mine. Let us say that this is a matter upon which reasonable men may differ, and leave it at that."

Also rising, Sir John extended his hand to his visitor. They clasped warmly.

"For the time being, we shall, but I am sure we shall speak of it again in our future discussions."

"I look forward to them, sir. But for now, goodbye."

So saying, Mr. Goldsmith turned and walked swiftly from the room.

Once settled again in his chair, Sir John inclined his head in my direction.

"Jeremy? You're still here, I take it."

"Still here, sir."

"What thought you of that talk we had?"

"Very stimulating, sir—though I felt you certainly got the better of him." In truth, I was not near so certain of it as I sounded.

"Perhaps. By God, these Irish can be near as contentious as the Scots. I believe I shall ask Kate to put together a dinner for Goldsmith and Mr. Donnelly—should prove an interesting evening, don't you think?"

It should not surprise you to learn, reader, that when, later in the day, a copy of "A Truthful Way with the Jews" was delivered to Sir John from Boyer and Nicholson, Sir John Fielding was near as pleased with it as he might have been had he written it himself. Nay, more, for he did tend to be rather critical of his own efforts at composition which he gave to me in dictation; and as heartily as he did endorse the contents of Mr. Goldsmith's brief history of the Jews, he did as much marvel at its style. "Can you imagine," said he to me, "writing so many such surpassingly beautiful sentences all of a single night?"

Those sentences described both the history of the Jews and their practices of worship. The lie was put firmly to the horrendous tales of human sacrifice repeated by Mr. Ormond Neville. These Mr. Goldsmith dismissed as "notorious fabrications of Eastern European origin." He concluded:

> Some will tell you that the Jews have no right to be here, and that, in a strict sense is true, for Edward I expelled them in 1290, and that ancient Medieval ban has to this day never been lifted. Yet if their presence here is illegal, so also, in a similar sense, is that of the Irish Catholics who are with us in far greater number, though they may not here legally practice their religion. I put it to the English public and their representatives in Parliament that it is time that outdated primitive laws directed against whole peoples were repealed in order to conform with present reality.

"Well said," declared Sir John as I ended my reading of the broadsheet, "very well said. It is the laws—and the draconian punishments prescribed—that are at fault and not the judges and magistrates to whom it falls to enforce them."

And so, well satisfied, he dictated invitations next day to Mr. Goldsmith and Mr. Donnelly, to dinner one week hence. I myself delivered them.

Thus did the days pass. The month was October. It was yet near dark as I rose each morning to kindle the cooking fire in the kitchen, and daylight went so swiftly in the late afternoon that it seemed no time at all until the day was done. Yet each day was counted by Sir John Fielding both a defeat and a victory: a defeat since he was no nearer to discovering the identity of him who had murdered four women; a victory because a fifth had not joined the list of victims.

In his capacity as acting coroner, Sir John conducted inquests into the deaths of the third and fourth women to die in less than a month. Nell Darby, the young woman (hardly more than a girl) whose body Mr. Tolliver had discovered, was identified through the advert I had written; she was a runaway from service in the household of a Kentish farmer, had not been in London long, and as Mr. Tolliver had guessed, probably kept herself alive by prostitution. Elizabeth Tribble, commonly known as Libby, was she whose body was so horribly mutilated by the murderer. There had been two organs sold off by her husband (if that he was in truth); they were recovered, so that she was made whole, after a fashion, by Mr. Donnelly—except for her eyes, which he had assumed were burned in the fireplace. A great crowd turned out for the Tribble proceeding, most of them women of the streets who so loudly hissed Edward Tribble when he appeared to testify that Sir John was forced to eject a dozen of the loudest from the courtroom. This was our last look at Mr. Tribble, who was far more docile than earlier; next day he went in irons to a ship bound for the town of Savannah in the colony of Georgia, where he would work seven years in servitude. But neither of the two inquests turned up matters in testimony that might be of use in Sir John's inquiries. And in both cases he was forced to direct the jury to verdicts of "willful murder by person or persons unknown."

There was no sign of Mr. Tolliver, which gave me both a feeling of chagrin and a sense of sustained relief. I was sure that there was a good explanation for his absence, and Sir John admitted he had not greatly emphasized that he remain for the inquest—who would have thought it necessary? It was clear, however, that in Sir John's mind the butcher's absence counted greatly against him. He gave me the task of checking Mr. Tolliver's stall in Covent Garden from time to time. And sometime each evening Mr. Langford was detailed to stop by the apartment on Long Acre to see if there was any sign of him. Those constables who knew the butcher by sight were urged to keep a sharp eye out for him. Yet as time passed, he remained disappeared.

The four murders, particularly that of the unfortunate Libby Tribble, had a dampening effect upon the commerce in flesh in the Covent Garden area. For nights after the inquest into her death had made public the awful mutilations of her body, there were no, or perhaps few, prostitutes to be seen on the streets. They remained in the dives and dram shops, drinking away the little money they might have, skeptically assessing the men who came to them as customers, rejecting all except those who were earlier known to them.

Lady Fielding mentioned to me in passing that the number of those seeking admittance to the Magdalene Home for Penitent Prostitutes, which she oversaw, had risen so sharply that they were near full-up. "I know not," said she to me, "if these are true penitents, or whether they merely seek temporary shelter until this terror passes. Of some I am downright suspicious."

She named it terror, and terror it was—yet one of silent and sullen nature, perhaps closer to dread. When a night passed with no news of a murder, there was no feeling of relief among the inhabitants of Covent Garden, but rather a sense of growing fear for what the next night might bring. None doubted that the murderer was still among us; none suggested he may have hopped aboard a ship for the colonies and gone off to inflict his horrors upon the whores of Boston or Philadelphia. No, he was with us still, and it was only a matter of days until he would strike again. The Bow Street Runners were aware of this, and their chief, Sir John, most keenly of all. He had instructed them to go out each night in full gear—cutlass and pistols—and to be most specially watchful, to explore the passages and the dark courts. To aid them in their searches, each also was obliged to carry an oil lantern, which became a cause of irritation to them. Some said it reduced them to the level of the old night watchman; others said it made easy targets of them should the murderer be armed with a pistol; and all seemed to agree that with sword and pistols, it was all just too damned much to carry about. Thus with each night that passed did the constables grow more tight-lipped and snappish.

As for Sir John, he did not outwardly exhibit such signs of unease. He simply went silent for days at a time. Oh, of course he did say all that needed be said: he sat his court each day, gave those instructions to Mr. Marsden and to Mr. Bailey and the Runners which needed be given, and in short did all that needed be done. Yet those times before and after his daily court session during which he often wandered backstage, as it were, discussing all manner of doings and topics—such times he now spent in his chambers with the door shut. And at table morning and night where talk did ever flow from him so generously, we found the source now dammed, leaving us to wonder what, in that vast reservoir which he held back, might pertain to the Covent Garden murders and what, individually, to us. He had grown unusually distant, having retreated within himself. To one who knew him not so well, he may even have seemed somewhat lethargic.

I, with the rest of the household, looked forward to the dinner to which Mr. Donnelly and Mr. Goldsmith had been invited, for it was supposed by us that surely those two garrulous gentlemen would bring forth the magistrate and restore him to his old self. In the meantime, there was little for me to do to aid Sir John in his official duties. My time was open to Lady Fielding, and she did heap upon me those tasks of the domestic sort which I had come to despise as beneath me. Yet I did not complain, and to the utmost of my ability I scrubbed the floors, beat the rugs, and polished the dining table and the silver. Eventually she ran out of such duties, and I was left with time of my own to fill.

Whenever given such an opportunity, I was off to visit Constable Perkins for another in those lessons in self-defense which he taught right rigorously. He seemed quite pleased with my progress, both in the matter of my knowledge and in the way my muscles were hardening as his lessons were learned. My duration had also greatly improved. In the beginning, I could go not much more than a few minutes at a time at his big dirt-filled bag ere I was quite wasted in sweaty exhaustion. Now, after a month of instruction, I had easily trebled and perhaps quadrupled that time; nor was I afterwards near so depleted of my powers. Mr. Perkins usually ended my fantastical bouts whilst I was still ready for more.

I had told my old chum, Jimmie Bunkins, of my sessions with the constable, and he was most keen to accompany me so as to learn more of them. "I always counted on me heaters to get me out of a roue when I was on the scamp," he said to me. "But I ain't a kid no more, and there's times a joe's got to scrap it out with his daddles or take a flogging."

(Which, for those readers unfamiliar with the street language of "flash," I may translate thusly: "I always counted upon my feet to get me out of trouble when I was engaged in thievery. But I'm no longer a child, and there are times when a fellow must fight with his fists or take a beating.")

And so, there came a day when, having completed the tasks given me by Lady Fielding by early afternoon, and she having departed for the Magdalene Home for Penitent Prostitutes, I was left free to fill the rest of the day as I saw fit; and I did then set my heaters in the direction of St. James Street where my pal, Jimmie Bunkins, lived in relative splendor as joe to his cove, Black Jack Bilbo.

Now, let it be said in passing that Black Jack Bilbo was proprietor of what was, in those days, London's grandest gaming house. He wore a fearsome black beard from which his nickname came, and he was credited (if that be quite the word) with a past near as dark, for it was said of him that he had made the fortune with which he began his lucrative enterprise from years as a pirate in the Caribbean and the waters off the North American colonies. Such was his reputation, yet the man himself was not near as fierce as the tale told of him might imply. Sir John Fielding counted him a friend, as did I, and to Jimmie Bunkins he was no less than savior, for he had taken him off the streets, offered him an education, and treated him, in his own rough way, as his ward.

I arrived at the grand house in St. James Street, which had previously belonged to Lord Goodhope, with much of the afternoon left before me. I knocked at the great double-door and waited, then knocked again. Who should open it but the cove of the ken himself. Black Jack kept only a small serving staff and had little use for butlers; the rule of his house was that he who heard a knock upon the door was obliged to answer it.

"Well, it's you, Jeremy, is it? Come in, boy, come in. You know you're always welcome in this house."

"I thought to invite Bunkins for a ramble," said I, "if he be willing and able."

He let the great door slam behind me and stood scratching his bald head in perplexity.

"Now, that I cannot say. Willing he does seem always. Able is not for him to decide but rather his tutor, Mr. Burnham. Of a sudden he's started doing right well in his lessons. Sums were always easy for him. Any good thief can do plus and minus. But plain reading always escaped him—until this fellow Burnham came along. He brought with him a primer, such as we all learned from, and Bunkins got the hang of it right away. The other tutors I had for him thought to teach him Latin and Greek at the same time. It was too much for the lad. Now he's got him reading from the *Public Advertiser* and such like. Soon, says he, he'll be starting Bunkins on proper books."

"He has no need of Latin," said I, "and Greek is a mystery to me."

"So I told Mr. Burnham. I'm so well pleased with him that I gave him a room of his own upstairs. He dorses here, and I give him bub and grub, as well."

Just then did the door open to that room off the front hall which I knew to be used as the schoolroom. Bunkins emerged, smiling, with him I took to be his new tutor. Mr. Burnham was a young man of about twenty years, tall and gentle of manner. He was, I noted, of mixed African and white blood, and I wondered at his history.

We were introduced by Jimmie Bunkins and shook hands. Accepting a nod from Mr. Bilbo as permission to put my request, I asked if Bunkins might be spared from his studies for the rest of the afternoon.

"That is up to young Mr. Bunkins," said he without a moment's hesitation, "for we have finished for the day." Then to Mr. Bilbo: "Best to end when there is still pleasure in the lesson."

Mr. Burnham spoke a good and proper English with a bit of a lilt such as a Welshman might give it. (Such I have come to recognize as the accent of the Caribbean islands.)

"Will that be right with you then, sir?" Bunkins asked Black Jack Bilbo.

"On your way, lad," said he with a wink and a nod.

"I'll just get me hat," Bunkins called to me, already off at a run for the stairs.

"He does well under your tutelage," said Black Jack to Mr. Burnham. "His manners have even improved. He did not earlier 'sir' me so regular."

"Ah, well, I insist upon that."

"As well you should, sir."

Then was Bunkins back, hat in hand, far sooner than I could have expected, stopping only to give a quick bow to both men in goodbye, then grabbing me by the wrist and pulling me to the door. I had only the chance to wave before I was out in the street with Bunkins.

"He's a rum joe, ain' he?"

"Certainly seems to be," said I.

We set off in the direction I had come, towards Covent Garden. All London was ours, and we'd a good hour to kill before reporting to Mr. Perkins.

"He's from Jamaica. He showed it me on one of the cove's maps."

"How did he come here?"

"Oh, ain't that a story!"

"Is it? Well, give it me then."

And as we made our way, he told Mr. Burnham's tale as it had been told to him.

Robert Burnham, of mixed blood, grew up on a plantation some distance outside Kingston. His father, the youngest son of a Shropshire squire, was the owner of the plantation and was then a bachelor; his mother was the plantation house cook. Though she was a slave she was held in great regard by her master; he accepted her son as his own and set about early to educate the boy, Robert, himself. He had a considerable library, though no texts in Latin or Greek, and so the boy learned only to read English and to write a good hand and as much of practical mathematics as his father could teach him. Yet what the boy learned, he learned well; he read his way through his father's library, and his father appointed him to serve as his secretary and also to teach the younger children, black and mixed blood, how to read and write. When his father brought a widow with three young children over from England and married her, Robert taught her children, as well. Ultimately, the time came when the master had to return to England for reasons of business—family matters and others pertaining to the coffee trade—and Robert accompanied him as his secretary. It so happened that while the two were in London, Robert happened upon an advert placed by Mr. Bilbo in the *Public Advertiser* seeking a new tutor for Jimmie Bunkins—the fifth in two years had just been discharged. Unknown to his master, he answered the advert, convinced Mr. Bilbo of his qualifications, and was hired. Young Robert Burnham, who knew the law well, returned to his master and claimed his freedom, for while slavery was permitted in the colonies, it had been banned in all Britain for centuries. His master was somewhat affronted, hurt to learn that Robert valued his freedom more than he did his favored life in Jamaica, yet there was little he would do to prevent him from remaining in London. Nor would he have been likely to prevent him though it be in his power to do so, for after all, master and slave were also father and son. And at their parting, it was as a father that he gave to Robert sufficient money to see him through in London for months to come; and it was as father and son that together they wept.

So did Robert Burnham come into Black Jack Bilbo's employ as Jimmie Bunkins's schoolmaster. I shall not pretend, reader, that all that I have revealed above I gleaned from Bunkins's first telling of the tale, which was at best patchy. Yet I would come to know the young gentleman from Jamaica better and learn far more about him than I have given here.

Let it be said merely of Bunkins's recital that it ended very nearly as it had begun—with Bunkins proclaiming his tutor "a rum joe" and adding that Mr. Burnham was the only teacher from whom he had ever learned a thing.

"Oh?" said I, "what about that French lady who taught you in her language? You learned nothing from her?"

"Madame Bertrand? What I learnt from her in Frenchy-talk was just to parrot what she said—though she taught me a few other things worth keepin' in me napper. She was a rum blowen, she was, but she wasn't no real teacher, wasn't meant to be such."

"How is Mr. Burnham different from the rest of them?"

"Well, first of all, he talks to you like you was a joe and not some eejit. And I remember one time, he takes me out for a walk, and he shows me there's writing all round London—names of streets, shops and such, adverts and bills posted on walls, things I'd never bothered with. He showed me what I'd been missin', he did. And he showed me, too, I could read some of them right off. It wasn't just what was in the book. So I been practicin'—like each time I goes out on tasks for Mr. Bilbo."

By that time, Bunkins having told the long story of Mr. Burnham's arrival in London, we had reached Chandos Street, where shops abounded of all purposes and descriptions. I thought to put him to the test and asked him to demonstrate his new-found skill. He quailed not at my challenge but stopped at the next shop and gave thoughtful study to the sign hung in front.

"Well," said he, "from lookin' inside, I know what sort of shop it be, but that ain't what the sign says. It says 'a-po-the-ca-ry'"—sounding it out carefully just so—"which, putting it all together, would be apothecary. And that must be some fancy name for a chemist's shop, for that is what it is. There now, ain't I right, chum?"

I was indeed most favorably impressed. "Right as can be, Mister Jimmie B.," said I, saluting him in rhyme.

At which he stuck his tongue out at me. "Me tollibon's out to you," said he, seeking to match me in rhyme, "for daring to doubt me so."

"That's no proper rhyme," said I.

"'Tis," said he.

"'Tisn't," said I.

And, laughing, we repeated our claims for near half the length of the street. Then, thinking to play a trick upon him, I stopped quite sudden before the dressmaker shop of Mary Deemey.

"There," said I, "read me that." And I pointed at the daintily printed sign in Mary Deemey's window.

He had no difficulty with her name and only a bit with "dressmaker," yet the phrase below it, "*modes elegantes*," confused him. He read them out right enough, but they did not seem right to him.

"Should be t'other way round—'elegant modes,' fancy fashions, like. Ain't that right?" Then I saw kindle in his eyes the fire of suspicion. "You bugger," said he. "That's Frenchy-talk! You thought to addle me with French!"

Then did I run from him, laughing, and then did he chase me, shouting that low epithet so loudly that heads turned—"Bugger! Bugger!"—as we ran through the crowd. Sour disapproval registered on every face. He caught me up in Half Moon Passage and we wrestled a bit in jest. Then, quickly satisfied, we walked on together arm in arm. Two lads out on the town. We went so into Bedford Street where I did see something—or rather, someone—that brought me to a halt, and perforce Bunkins, as well.

"What is it?" said he. "Why'd you stop?"

"That fellow on the other side of the way—the one loitering at the door of that dive talking to the other that has his back to us. Who is he?"

I had pointed out the one I called the bully-boy. As Bunkins looked, my eyes swept the street, but I saw no sign of Mariah.

"That one? You want nicks to do with him. He's a queer cull, if ever there was one, right nasty with a knife."

"Has he taken a stab at anyone? Who has he cut?"

"I ain't all that certain he's cut anyone. Still and all, he does dearly love to whip it out and scare people with it."

"Such as?"

"Such as? Whores mostly, and me once when I was a kid. I'd napped a ring he wanted. I tried to sell it to him. Out came the knife, and he made a lunge at me, prob'ly just as a scare. Well, it worked. I took to me heaters, and he kept the ring."

I was reminded of Yossel, whose way it was to threaten to cut off a nose or an ear and thus rob women of the streets of their earnings. He swore his were only threats; that he had never cut a one. Perhaps the bully-boy was just such a one—but perhaps not.

"Is he what you'd call a high-ripper?" I asked Bunkins.

"You can call him what you like, but he's a nasty cull. That much I'll give you."

"What's his name?"

"Jack something." Bunkins gave it a moment's thought. "Jackie Carver, he calls himself. But I think it's a made-up name, like 'Jack-the-carver'—he'll carve you up, see?"

As we discussed him, Jackie Carver concluded his conversation at the door of the dive, left his chum with a wave, and walked through it—lost from sight.

"Why'd you want to know about such as him?" asked Bunkins.

"We've had some dealings," I said, not wishing to tell him more just then.

The reason we went roundabout—from St. James Street to Little Russell Street by way of Covent Garden—was that Jimmie Bunkins was most eager to view the sites of the past two murders; the first two he had already seen. It was not mere morbid curiosity that prompted him, for I daresay, his years on the surrounding streets had given him a knowledge of the secret byways of the district superior to any other. He wished to be helpful, and as it happened, he was.

When I led him to the passage on Henrietta Street where the body of Nell Darby was discovered, he remarked that he knew the place well.

"On cold nights, or rainy ones, I used to dorse here," said he.

"Right here? Out in the open?"

"Do I look like an eejit? No, chum, there's a spot down here a bit. Let me show you."

He took me several steps down the way to a spot on the building which provided the east wall of the passage. It was a once-grand structure, built in the old style of wood and stucco. The lower portion was all of wood.

"See here?" said Bunkins. "There's a door here in the wood." He traced its outline, about three feet square, which was nearly invisible to the eye, even in daylight, so tightly fitted was it. "You got to know where to hit it."

He pounded thrice at different spots before hitting the right one. The door popped open no more than two inches. He swung it open to reveal the black space beneath.

"It's an old coal hole, see? The—what do you call them?—the hinges is on the inside so's you can't take it for a door from the outside. This was one of them big houses once where somebody rich lived. Now there's prob'ly a couple score living where four or five once did. And all who live here now must find their own coal, and there's no need for such as this. They store furniture and the like here."

"Where does this lead?" I asked. "Is there another door out?"

"Course there is. It leads to a hall and another door to Henrietta Street, which is kept bolted from the inside."

"That explains it then."

"Explains what?"

"How Mr. Tolliver heard footsteps behind him just before he found the corpus of that girl, Nell Darby. But he looked back and saw nothing."

"There's spots between here and the Garden where a body could step in and hide."

"I must tell Sir John of this."

We arrived at the stables at the foot of Little Russell Street to find Mr. Perkins "keepin' fit," taking great whacks and kicks at the sailcloth bag, sending it swinging this way and that. He was naked to the waist, and in a good lather on this cool autumn day. From the look of him, I estimated he'd been working so for near an hour.

Standing to one side, we looked on till such time as he chose to notice us.

Jimmie Bunkins was much impressed. He watched the constable's every forceful move and seemed most particularly impressed by the swiftness of his feet—the kicks, of course, but his feet seemed perpetually in motion, moving back and forth, in and out in an endless dance.

"I never seen such," Bunkins whispered to me. "And him with only one arm. He could take any man who's got two."

"He could indeed," said I.

The stump of the constable's left arm, just below the elbow, seemed florid by contrast to his pale trunk. Yet I noted that what there was of the arm above it had not withered. He must work it hard in some special manner to keep his strength up in that arm as well. The man quite amazed me.

At last his feet came to rest. He stood quite still for a long moment, breathing deeply. Then he stepped over to a low-hanging branch of that same tree from which the sailcloth bag was suspended and pulled from it a woolen undergarment. He threw it over him in a few swift movements and walked over to us.

"Right on time for your lesson, Jeremy, like the good scholar you are," said he. "And this must be the chum you said you'd bring by when the chance came."

"Yes, sir, Mr. Perkins. This is my friend, Jimmie Bunkins."

They shook hands quite solemnly.

"Well, if he's your friend, that's right enough for me, but it does seem to me I know him from many a chase in the Garden. If he turned round I might know him even better. It was always his back he showed me."

"And ain't I glad you never caught me!" cackled Bunkins. "I seen what you was doin' to that big bag."

"I hear you're a reformed individual now. Sir John himself gives you a good character. And you've grown a bit since your thievin' days, as well, it seems to me."

"And thank God for it. I feared I'd be tyke-sized all my life."

The two stood grinning at each other. I, for my part, sighed in relief. They would get on, as I had hoped they would.

Indeed, Bunkins and Mr. Perkins got on quite famously. After he had put me through my quarter-hour on the bag, which was then about my limit, the constable asked if he would have a go at it. Bunkins shed his coat and went eagerly to take my place. Perhaps a bit too eagerly, for Mr. Perkins thought it necessary to advise him in the proper method of delivering blows with his fists, just as he had done with me near a month before. Bunkins was eager to kick, yet Mr. Perkins kept him beating away with his fists upon the bag, urging him to put his body behind it, to keep moving about, et cetera. It was good for me to watch, for I realized I'd come some distance in my lessons.

It took only about five minutes to tire Bunkins, then was I brought back for another go at the bag. When I had done, Mr. Perkins brought us together for a bit of special instruction.

"Let us imagine a situation, Jeremy, of a sort that might happen to one on a dark street."

"What is that, sir?"

"Start walkin' at an ordinary pace, and I shall show you."

I did as he said, moving away from him until—having heard no sound behind me—I was stopped of a sudden by a vise thrown about my throat, and that vise proved to be Mr. Perkins's mutilated left arm. There was in it more strength than I could ever have imagined. The stump held me precisely at my throat. I could neither move, nor cry out.

"Now what can you do in such a situation as that?" asked Mr. Perkins, releasing me.

"Not much," I gasped.

"Ah, but something," said he. "You can always do something. Let us change places, and examine the possibilities.

And, with Bunkins looking on quite fascinated, that is what we did. The constable and I were near enough in height that I was able to throw my arm over his shoulder and give him a proper squeeze—but not upon his throat, for he had dropped his chin to protect it. Then he surprised me with a nip on the arm.

"Ow!" said I, more in surprise than hurt.

"Didn't really cause you pain, did I? Sorry if I did."

"No, sir, it was just that I didn't expect it."

"Well, neither will he. If you hear a sound behind you, or get any sort of hint that you may be attacked from the rear, then the first thing you do is cover your throat with your chin. Bite as hard as you can. If he puts his hand over your face, so much the better. Try to take his finger off—it can be done—or rip the skin right off his hand. He'll let go of you then. You can be sure of it. Then you'll be free to face him proper."

"Yes, sir."

"Now, throw your arm round me again, but leave it loose enough so's I can talk."

I did as he had directed.

"Now, let us say he has caught you by surprise—before you could get your chin down. He's got his arm round your throat, or p'rhaps his hand, and he's squeezing. You've still got weapons left. You've got your elbows—"

And with that he rubbed his left elbow into my ribs.

"He will then shift his position if he can, and you hit him hard with the other elbow. And when I say hard, I mean snap it back with your whole shoulder. Practice it at night. You can make it so you don't have to think about it. It'll just come, so it will."

"Yes, sir, I'll practice it."

"Good lad. Now, if that don't get you loose, you've got your heels. Try for his shins, and that can be very damagin', it can, but you've a better shot at his feet. Bring down your heel with all the force you can—not on his toes, for that gives less pain, but on the flat part of his foot. Try to break all them little bones in there, and if you do, he'll not be able to put weight on that foot. He'll be off balance, and you should be able to twist loose. You can let go now, Jeremy."

And so I did, glancing by chance at Bunkins. He was staring in awed concentration.

"Don't think because I've told you about these one at a time, that's how you should go at it. You must do them all at once—bite, elbows in the ribs, heel down on his foot. You must make him think he's got hold of the very devil hisself."

"Mr. Perkins, sir?"

"Yes, Jimmie Bunkins, what have you to say?"

"A question, sir: What if the cull's got a knife?"

"A very sensible question it is, for them who attack from behind often has them, for it is a coward's weapon. One thing I will say, first of all, about knives is that most who have them don't know how to use them. But to your question, if attacked from behind with a knife, you'll either be stabbed in the back, in which situation all you can do is hope it didn't hit your vitals, get turned around, and meet him head on. It ain't well known, but Constable Brede took a knife in the back, got loose, and subdued the villain with his club. With the knife still in his back, he marched him to Bow Street, then went to a surgeon to have the thing taken out."

Wide-eyed, Bunkins and I exchanged looks without comment.

"Then there's them who would cut your throat. But to do that your man's got to get at it. So the first rule: tuck in your chin. Next: bite like hell, hit with the elbows, and try to break his foot. Do whatever you can to get loose and face him."

"But he's still got his knife, ain't he?" put in Bunkins. "What can you do if you ain't got one, too?"

"The best defense against a knife ain't another knife but a good club and a pair of nimble feet. We'll go into that later, but just now I must wash up and dress for duty. Jimmie Bunkins, you're welcome to come along whenever you like at this hour."

On the day of the dinner planned for Mr. Goldsmith and Mr. Donnelly, we trudged a good way across London, Annie Oakum and I, to Smithfield Market to purchase meat for the occasion. We two, and Lady Fielding as well, had looked forward to the occasion as one sure to rouse Sir John from his lethargic silence. And so a great feast had been planned. A great feast demands a great piece of meat, and Mr. Tolliver being yet mysteriously absent from Covent Garden, we had no choice but to make the journey to Smithfield.

Annie and I had become great chums. Though she did not deign to discuss it, her heart belonged still to Lady Fielding's son by her earlier marriage, Tom Durham. For near a month after Tom sailed as a midshipman on the H.M.S. *Leviathan,* she moped about, neglecting all but her grand cooking. In that she did ever take pride. Gradually, her good spirits returned, in spite of the fact that in the year that he had been away there had been no letter to her. He wrote often to his mother, twice to Sir John, and once even to me. To give him the benefit of the doubt, since Annie was illiterate, he may have supposed there was no point in writing her a personal letter which would have to be read to her impersonally by another. He did include little personal messages to her in his letters to us—tell Annie this, tell Annie that—about the exotic foods he had eaten in Egypt or Greece, or some other distant land. Nevertheless, I knew that she longed for some direct communication from him she held so dear. Yet as he became more distant, she and I grew closer as chums and confidants. She became for me what I had never before had nor known: she became for me a sister.

So it was only natural that sometime on that long walk to the Smithfield Market I should open my heart to her and tell her of

Mariah. I told her all: how I had first glimpsed her as an acrobat when first I came to London; how, when her family returned to Italy, she had been seduced into staying and then sold into prostitution; how she had then been returned to Jackie Carver and turned out onto the streets; and finally, that he had offered to "sell" her to me for ten guineas.

Telling the tale complete took near a mile. Annie had listened carefully saying not a word, only throwing me a glance now and then on two occasions when, choking back a sob, I found that for a moment I could not continue. Finally, hearing no more from me, she rightly assumed I had concluded. Then did she face me square.

"Jeremy," said she, "tell me true. Do you love her?"

"I believe I feel for her exactly as you feel for Tom. Is that not love?"

She looked away; her face took on a most serious cast. After a moment's hesitation, she spoke: "I ain't sure of that."

Of a sudden, our nostrils were assaulted by the foul, bloody smell of the Smithfield Market, wherein animals of every size and description were slaughtered, butchered, and sold. There could be no doubt that we were close, and there, just ahead on Gilt-Spur Street, lay the entrance to the market.

"We've a job to do here," said she to me then. "Let me think on what you told me while we're about it. We'll talk on it more on our return. Will that suit you?"

"As you wish, Annie."

I took her to the stall where I had lately been buying for the household in Mr. Tolliver's absence. There I was recognized and greeted. But Annie made it clear to the butcher that it was she who had to be pleased that day. She asked to see what he had of beef for roasting. He showed her, and as he did, he extolled the tenderness and taste of the meat. Pouting out her lower lip, she examined it skeptically and asked the price of it. When he put it at five shillings, she pulled back and gave him a hard look.

"We'll search round a bit more," said she. "Come along, Jeremy."

As we left, the butcher threw me a hurt look. But in no wise did I attempt to contradict or persuade her. She was indeed the cook and was to be put to the test that night. The decision would be hers.

"That was quite a large piece," said I, thinking that incontestable.

"More than we need," said she, "nor was it fresh-butchered."

Annie proved hard to please. We spent the better part of an hour wandering through the market, looking at the offerings of one and another, until at last we came to a stall hard by one of the slaughtering tents from which a great stink arose. Because of the stink, there were not so many customers about; and when Annie inquired after beef for roasting, the butcher waved his hand at the sides of beef hanging behind him. He invited her back to take a look, just as Mr. Tolliver might have done. They came to an immediate agreement on the size and cut but haggled a bit on the price; both seemed to enjoy it. At last they agreed on a price, which was five shillings for a chunk about the same size as had been offered to her by the first butcher. I wondered at that. And when, as we were leaving (I, with a good ten pounds of wrapped meat and bone under my arm), I called it to her attention, she gave me the same sharp look I had seen her level at the butchers we had visited.

"Jeremy," said she, "that first chunk was too big because it wouldn't keep. There was green on it he was trying to cover with his hand. What we bought will keep for days after tonight. You're carrying fresh-slaughtered meat; still oozin' blood."

No doubt feeling she had acquitted herself well against the best that Smithfield had to offer, Annie set a lively pace on our return to Bow Street. She whistled a tune as she stretched her legs. In such a mood, she surprised me by immediately taking up again the matter I had painfully presented whilst we were on our way to market.

"I done what I said I'd do," said she most abrupt.

"Pardon?" said I, not really understanding what she meant. "You mean getting the meat for tonight?"

"No, Jeremy, as we was wandering about there in the market, I thought hard upon you and that Italian moll."

"Oh? And what did you think?"

"Well, first of all, you must give no money at all to her pimp."

"I have no money to give."

"Right so! Right you are! And there is but one place you could get such, and you must not even think of that—not for a minute."

"I agree," said I, though I had thought of it for just about that length of time.

"And don't I know Jackie's kind from my time on the streets! He'll never let go of her till she's wore out, sick with the pox, or dead."

Those possibilities had occurred to me, but to hear them stated so coldly did bring tears to my eyes.

"Oh now, Jeremy, get a hold on yourself," she scolded. "You must face what's real."

"But you're saying there's nothing I can do to help her."

"Yes, that's true. Only she can do to help herself. She's the one must save herself."

"But how?"

"Let her get a job in service, as I did. Those grand ladies and gents do think it fine to have French and Italian serving girls about."

"She would have no notion how to go about it."

"She dresses proper and goes knocking on doors in St. James Street, Bloomsbury, wherever there are grand houses. The butler will answer, and it's to him she would apply. Once hired, her pimp cannot then touch her."

Annie's mention of St. James Street set me thinking. Perhaps Mr. Bilbo might find a place for Mariah.

"And at the very least," she continued, "she can go into the Magdalene Home. Half the girls in there went in to escape one such as that Jackie fella. None who don't belong can get past that old shrew at the door."

But of course! There was a way out for her under my very nose. Yet what was it had been lately said about the Magdalene?

"But," I objected, "did not Lady Fielding say that the Home is fast filling up due to these monstrous murders?"

"She said the same to me. But if you can convince this little molly—what is her name again?"

"Mariah."

"Right enough—I'll fix it in my mind. If you can convince Mariah to go to the Magdalene, I'll tell Lady Fielding she's a friend of mine who wishes to change her ways. Room will be made for her then, I promise."

"Thank you, Annie," said I, most sincere.

"But, Jeremy, it's she must help herself. It's her who must decide. Bawds are lazy, most of them. They may not like the life, but they lack the will to leave it. Don't I know? I hated it, I did, and it took me near a year to change."

In the event, the festive dinner held that night to bring Mr. Goldsmith and Mr. Donnelly together proved both a stunning success and an awful failure.

Annie quite outdid herself with that piece of beef she had chosen so carefully at Smithfield. She cooked it in wine with slivers of garlic and plenty of pepper and salt—even tried a bit of that red spice, paprika, she'd been saving for the right occasion. There were four bottles of claret for the six of us, spiced vegetables to please all, and a tasty tart for dessert. After toasting host and hostess, Mr. Donnelly declared himself quite overcome by Annie's artistry and raised his glass to her. Mr. Goldsmith said he had never eaten better—and it was well known that he had been guest at many of the grandest houses in London. It was indeed a triumph for dear Annie.

And how the conversation at table did bubble that night; and the twin springs which fed it gushed joyfully and ceaselessly to their own amusement, yet most assuredly to ours. We were an audience to a magnificent entertainment staged in great Irish style. Two true-born Irishmen they were, one Catholic and one Protestant, yet both with the same wit and love of laughter. They sat across the table one from the other, telling story after story, each seeking to best the other. If in truth they did compete, I could not name the winner. Indeed we were the winners as they told outlandish tales of their medical education—one of them rather indelicate, to which Lady Fielding signaled her displeasure (after laughing heartily) by clearing her throat and raising her eyebrows. Taking note but undaunted, Mr. Donnelly launched into a series of less questionable but equally comic reminiscences of his several Viennese landlords (for it was in Vienna that he attended medical college); Mr. Goldsmith countered with stories of the French, for which he was well known (as I later learned); then did Mr. Donnelly return with further experiences from his stay in Lancashire (Annie later told me that not one of them had been repeated from his earlier recital in our kitchen). And so it went, moving from one topic to the next, on and on, through the dessert course, and, with the wine exhausted, into the brandy. We did all agree the next day that we had never laughed so long nor so hard at any other occasion in memory.

And Sir John with us all. He did chuckle and guffaw, and as a good master of ceremonies, prompt his performers with an occasional question or a jibe of his own. Yet after, in the beginning, praising Mr. Goldsmith's broadsheet and declining to answer his questions regarding the Covent Garden murders, he remained, for the most part, out of the swift swirl of conversation. He remained, to put it otherwise, as politely silent as was possible under the circumstances. In that way then did the dinner fail dismally, for we in his household had hoped that in such lively company he might be drawn in and participate in a more active manner. That he declined to do. He left the field to his guests. Next day he was as withdrawn and silent as ever before, which vexed Lady Fielding greatly, as she feared he was descending into melancholia. I, however, had seen him in such a state before, and it came to me that he might indeed be forming a plan of action.

One matter, however, does remain in my mind from that evening. Near midnight it was when our guests rose reluctantly from the table and gave their thanks to host, hostess, and cook. Lady Fielding then thanked them "for a most cheerful and spirited evening," which Sir John seconded. He then asked me to accompany the two gentlemen to the street, which of course I did most gladly.

On Bow Street, Mr. Donnelly and Mr. Goldsmith remained a bit in conversation, as they discovered they would be parting there. I remained attentively as they exchanged cards, and listened as Mr. Goldsmith broached the topic that Sir John had declined to discuss at table.

"Tell me, Mr. Donnelly," said he, in a tone more serious than he had sounded in the last hours, "was the corpus in King Street in the ghastly condition that I have heard bruited on the street?"

"Indescribable," said Mr. Donnelly, then of course proceeded to describe it: "The trunk was cut open and two great flaps of skin removed. Organs were taken out—the heart was in the fireplace and partly burnt, liver, womb, pancreas, and others had been cast about the room."

"It sounds to be the work of a butcher."

"Perhaps quite literally that, for one in Covent Garden is suspect. He has disappeared."

My heart fell. Sir John had never named Mr. Tolliver as such to me.

"Good God," said Mr. Goldsmith. "Disappeared, has he? Perhaps that will be the end of it."

"One can only hope. But by the bye, here's a matter you might be interested in as a physician. Do you know a fellow named Carr? Retired Army surgeon, I believe."

"Heard of him, never met him."

"He came to me again—the second time, mind you—urging me to examine the eyes of the victim under my microscope. He's convinced that the image of the murderer is etched upon the pupil."

"That old wives' tale—amazing! A physician!"

"I had to tell him that the eyes, too, had been removed and probably burnt in the fireplace. He seemed greatly disappointed to hear it." Mr. Donnelly hesitated, as if debating with himself for a moment what ought be said next. Then: "I notice signs in him of the onset of the late stages of the pox—the chancre. I fear his mind has been affected, too."

"No doubt it has. But . . ." Mr. Goldsmith offered his hand to Mr. Donnelly who grasped it in farewell. "I must be off, for I've work to do. Come see me, sir. My door is open to you, though I must tell you that late afternoon and early evening are my best times."

Then, with a wave, he departed. Mr. Donnelly turned to me and, in turn, offered me his hand.

"Sorry to have kept you here at the door, Jeremy. A goodnight to you, and my thanks to all above for a wonderful evening."

"But, sir," said I, "is it true that Sir John counts Mr. Tolliver suspect in these murders?"

"The butcher? I take it you know him? Ah well, I fear Sir John has said as much to me. A sad matter, eh? Well, I must be off."

And with that he stepped off sharply in the direction of Tavistock Street, swinging his stick and whistling as he went. I watched him to Russell Street, then did I return up the stairs and the mountain of dishes and pans that awaited me in the kitchen.

During the next few days, I carried about with me a slip of paper on which I had printed out in block letters the names of Mr. Bilbo and Jimmie Bunkins and their address on St. James Street. The day following my talk with Annie on the way back from market, I had talked with Bunkins after our lesson with Mr. Perkins. Telling him all, I asked if a place might be found for Mariah in their household, if only temporarily. He brought back word the next day from Mr. Bilbo that she could come ahead, but while she was with them she would have to earn her keep. I thought that fair enough, yet if for any reason she feared the name of Black Jack Bilbo (as some indeed did), I also wrote down Lady Fielding's name and the address of the Magdalene Home for Penitent Prostitutes.

With that slip of paper in my pocket I searched the Covent Garden district for Mariah. I had not seen her the better part of a month. She had disappeared, as had most of those who practiced her trade when news of the death of Libby Tribble spread through Covent Garden. Yet as the days passed without incident, necessity drove them out into the streets again. Some may have taken hope in the fact that for near three weeks there had been no murders and decided that there would be no more. Others were quite fatalistic. Annie told me of meeting an old bawd of her earlier acquaintance out once again on the stroll. When Annie asked her if she were not afraid that she would be the next victim, the woman replied, "Dearie, it's one or t'other with me. If him that does the hackin' don't get me, then the river will. In the meantime, I need money for gin."

Thus apathy or unfounded hope were the prevailing emotions out on the streets as I searched for Mariah. I looked most often where I had seen her often in the daylight and early evening hours. Yet time after time I came away disappointed from my walks up and down Drury Lane and New Broad Court. I walked the perimeter of Covent Garden at the twilight hour—to no avail. I searched Duke's Court, Martlet's Court, even Angel Court, and such places as it might be foolish to go alone and unarmed and in failing light. At last, I put my problem to Bunkins; and he, ever practical, pointed out that it was on Bedford Street we had seen Jackie Carver, and so it was more than likely I would find her somewhere nearby. "The pimps like to move their molls about, try out new patches, like," said he.

And so it was that on the way back to Bow Street from Mr. Perkins's place early that evening, I went out of my way a bit and walked Bedford Street up and down. It was on my way back that I glimpsed her and hastened to where she stood, near the entrance to the Dog and Duck.

"Mariah!" I called to her as I came closer—immediately fearful that I might frighten her off—yet it was a cry of joy at having found her at last.

Yet she saw me, recognized me, and did not start away. She seemed to force a smile as she waited my approach.

"Hello! What is your name? I forget."

"Jeremy," said I. "Jeremy Proctor."

She nodded a firm affirmation. "Is good—Jeremy. I remember it now. Did you bring the money? You give it me, and I bring it to him."

"No, Mariah. I did not bring the money for Jackie. I brought something better—for you."

"For *me?*" She turned away. Then, making no effort to disguise her exasperation, threw her hands up into the air and gave vent to her disappointment. "What could be better than I get away from this? He say if you don' have the money, you can steal it. Why don' you steal it?"

"I could not, I would not," said I. And seeking to explain: "Even if I could pay him what he asks, I would have no money to keep you."

"You could steal more."

Had the girl no sense of right and wrong? I could only suppose that in her trade it was swiftly lost. Now was the time to explain the plan to her—and quickly, lest Jackie Carver be near. I whipped out the slip of paper I had been carrying in my pocket. I explained that there were two houses that would take her in and feed her. In the first, said I, she would work as part of the household staff. In the second, she would be taught a suitable trade—as cook or seamstress, or some such.

"But the important thing," said I, "is that you will be off the streets in a place where Jackie Carver cannot get to you."

"How you know his name?" she asked, downright suspiciously.

"A friend told me."

"He don' like people at Bow Street know his name."

"That doesn't matter," said I. "All this will cost you is cab fare—no more than ten pence to the first, and no more than a shilling to the second. You have that much with you now, don't you?" I reached into my pocket again. "I can give you that."

"You give me twelve ned for him. That's all you give me."

"I thought it was ten."

"The price gone up." She faced me angrily. "You think I wash floor for people? You think I sew for people? Here, take your paper back."

With that I left her, her hand outstretched to me, the slip of paper in her hand. As I walked swiftly away down Bedford Street, I consoled myself that at least she had the paper with the two addresses in her possession. I prayed she might not cast it aside but keep it and perhaps later make use of it. I had done what I could, had I not?

That very night I sought out Sir John in the little room next his bedroom which served him as a study. As he had in the past when troubled or hatching a plan, he would sit there alone in the dark behind his heavy oaken desk for hours at a time. Lady Fielding had retired early on the night in question. Annie was in the kitchen below, amusing herself as she often did by singing ballads of the day she had picked up on her wanderings through Covent Garden. Thinking back upon my short visit that evening, I recall not only what was said, but also the little wisps of song that floated up from below during the frequent gaps and pauses in our communication.

I knocked upon the open door to the little room.

"Who is there?"

"It is I, Jeremy."

"Come in, lad, sit down."

Entering, I took my place in one of the two chairs opposite him.

"I do not mean to shut myself away so," said he. "It is only that lately, my thoughts have been so taken up with these fearful murders that I find myself unfit for ordinary human intercourse. Perhaps you can rouse me as you have so often in the past. In any case, let us talk."

I hesitated. "Perhaps what I have to say will be unwelcome, for it concerns Mr. Tolliver. From Mr. Donnelly I heard that you hold him suspect in those murders."

"He ought not discuss with you or any other what I have said about them. But—come, so long as what you have to say of him is material to the matter and not another endorsement of his sterling character, which I have had aplenty from Kate, I should be glad to hear what you have to say of him."

And so I did then tell him of the door to the coal hole which Bunkins had shown to me in that passage wherein Mr. Tolliver had discovered the body of Nell Darby; that there was a way through it to a hall and a door to Henrietta Street that was kept bolted from the inside.

"You are suggesting," said Sir John, "that the murderer could have made his escape in such a way?"

"Yes, sir," said I. "And such an escape would account for the footsteps in the direction of Covent Garden that he heard just before discovering the body."

The magistrate retreated into silence. There was little I could do but respect it, for I was sure he was weighing what I had told him against his suspicions of Mr. Tolliver. At last came the objections that I had foreseen.

"How then," said he, "do you account for what your man then did say of those footsteps? That he had turned about and looked and saw no one there. And what of the mysterious wagon that was suddenly there when it had not been there before—or perhaps it was, for he could not be sure."

"Bunkins told me there were places to hide there on Henrietta Street, and I confirmed it—two large beams to the house which would conceal a man; they are spaced along the way. As for the wagon, I cannot account for it any better than Mr. Tolliver did. But I have heard you say, Sir John, that there is always reason to distrust a story that is completely without inconsistencies."

"So you are suggesting that if his story can be defended in part, then it should be accepted in whole. Surely you can see the fallacy in that. But what about that disgusting homicide in King Street? Admittedly, there is nothing to place him there, but his sudden departure, you must admit, counts greatly against him."

"You did not specifically instruct him."

"Do *not* remind me of what I did or did not say. I am well aware of that."

He spoke to me as sharply as ever he had. I made ready with an apology before taking my leave. Yet he would hold me.

"I'm aware it was my oversight not to order him specifically to remain. I did tell him there would be an inquest. I did not tell him when it would be." He paused. Then: "If your Mr. Tolliver is held by me as suspect, it is by default, as it were—his failure to appear. If and when he does appear and can account for his absence, he will no longer be suspect. Then I shall have none.

"I had thought from something said by that silly fellow Ormond Neville that there might be further reason to suspect Thaddeus Millhouse. Do you recall? He said he had brought Mr. Millhouse a clean shirt for his appearance in court. Since I had been assured there were no stains on his shirt when he appeared before me, I thought perhaps there had been something incriminating on that dirty shirt. That did not prove to be so. I was told by Mr. Fuller that the dirty shirt was simply dirty. Nevertheless, I had him in for further questioning, for you and I both thought he was hiding something. There is something quite shifty about the man. You, I believe, were off on an errand, which was just as well. The secret he was hiding, which was easy to guess, was that he had indeed had sexual congress with Polly Tarkin. He felt greatly shamed by that, as well he should have, and that was the source of his guilt. He knew it was wrong; he knew what she was; yet that, perversely, was what drew him to her. He wept copious tears and wailed his sorrow to me, yet he also convinced me that so weak a man could never have committed these horrible crimes, particularly the last. In any case, he assured me that he has spent every night, but the one on which he was arrested, with his wife, to which I'm sure she would testify.

"In short, I am left without suspects, except for Mr. Tolliver, and wanting others, I must hold fast to him. Yet I am not so convinced of his guilt in this that I have not alerted the Runners to be cautious and watchful to an extraordinary degree. They are, and they shall continue to be. But in following this course I am guarding, merely, against his next attack—whoever he be. I prefer to make a plan whereby we may anticipate his next attack and catch him in the act. I noted that the last two murders occurred on the same night, and that was the night of the full moon—or so Mr. Donnelly has assured me. The full moon seems to affect the demented in perverse ways. I cannot say why this be so, but it is. We have not seen the murderer, whoever he be, strike since then. I suspect he will strike again at the next full moon, which comes again next week on All Hallows Eve. It is an occasion that may have a certain grim appeal to one such as him. It will take planning of details and much preparation, but with the Almighty's help, it could work."

He spoke not so much with certitude as with great hope. I waited to hear what more he would say, yet he said nothing. Finally, unable to contain myself, I asked, "What is the plan, Sir John?"

"You'll know soon enough, Jeremy. I'll tell you when it's time."

TEN

In Which I Am
Injured and A
Murderer Caught

A reward had been posted for the capture and conviction of the Covent Garden Killer, as he had been dubbed. This had a salutary effect upon Sir John Fielding's Bow Street constables who went about their searches into the dark corners of the district with renewed vigor. There were no more complaints of carrying cutlasses which rattled about in their scabbards, nor did the burden of lanterns seem to trouble them quite so much as before. Yet the twenty guineas promised by Parliament to him who brought the murderer to justice achieved also a negative result: It brought to Covent Garden a company of independent thief-takers, those rather rough individuals who sometimes operated within the law and more often without to accomplish their ends. I myself had been victim of one when first I came to London, and had little use for them; Sir John had even less; and the Bow Street Runners regarded them, in this instance, as poachers upon their territory. Yet they came and proceeded to thrash through the stews and dives, offering to split the reward with him or her who provided information of the sort that might lead to capture and conviction. The Runners had already sought out every reliable snitch in the district; they knew that whoever the murderer might be, he went about his dark deeds alone, nor did he afterwards boast of them or confide what he had done. What the outsiders lacked was organization and the intimate knowledge of Covent Garden which the Runners possessed. In the event, what they lacked most profoundly was Sir John's plan.

As the days passed and All Hallows Eve drew near, it became evident that Sir John had been correct in his prognostication that there would be no further attacks until that sinister night when it was believed until only a while ago that witches flew about on their way to meet with the Devil in their frightful Sabbath celebrations. If All Hallows Eve passed without incident, then Sir John would have been proven wrong; the constables would be back to their watchful patrols, and Mr. Tolliver's absence would weigh even more heavily against him. It was this latter contingency which no doubt stirred me to pray for the success of the plan and eventually to volunteer most insistently to be part of it.

It consisted of two elements. There would be, first of all, a great bonfire lit in the middle of Covent Garden once the stalls were shut, the carts removed, and dark had fallen. It would, said Sir John, attract all the rowdy and lawless, and bring the many prostitutes off the streets in celebration of the night. "They are at bottom simple people," said he when he announced the plan to his constables the night before its execution, "and will not be able to resist the opportunity to frolic before the flames. The last witch-burning took place early in this century. They have heard tales of such. We shall give them everything but a witch to burn—all, including chestnuts to roast. Mr. Marsden, make a note of that. There must be an abundance of chestnuts. A great many of you will be needed to keep order at this event. I have arranged for a fire brigade to be present to keep the fire properly under control. A windy night, unfortunately, must cancel our plans. But I expect a clear, still night."

A murmur of approval went round the group which crowded Sir John's chamber. However, the next part of his plan received no such approbation. It would require certain constables to go out armed, yet dressed as women, and another small force to follow them in stealth so that they may come swiftly should the decoys be attacked. "The idea, you see," said Sir John, "is to take the potential victims off the street, or significantly reduce their number, and put our own men there dressed as women, so that they may meet the murderer and subdue him."

Sir John was then met by absolute silence. It soon developed that none among them cared to volunteer to dress as women. When he made the call, not one stepped forward.

"Come now, gentlemen. This is no time to play shy. Decoys are called for, and decoys we must have."

Again, there was only silence. I felt embarrassed by the lack of response—whether for Sir John or on behalf of the constables I was uncertain, yet nevertheless embarrassed.

Mr. Benjamin Bailey, their captain, then spoke up. "Sir John," said he, "beggin' your pardon, but I don't think there's a one of us would properly deceive your man, no matter you dressed us up in silk and laces. We're all just too damned big."

I looked about me. In truth, he was right. The men in the room all seemed to stand six feet or more—with perhaps two exceptions, and I was one of them. I knew it to be true that Mr. Bailey took size into consideration in choosing his constables. Hardly thinking more upon it, I myself stepped out from my place against the wall.

"I will volunteer," said I, "for I am of the right size."

"That was you spoke up, Jeremy," said Sir John.

"Yes, sir."

"Then step back," said he. "This is no task for a lad."

"I will not withdraw, sir. I am as capable of handling myself in an attack as anyone here."

There was a bit of scoffing laughter at my boast. But one did come forth in my defense.

"Sir," said Mr. Perkins, "the lad has not been tried as yet, but he's learned well as any could. Take him, and you'll have two, for much as I hate the notion of going about in skirts, I would wear them to see that no harm came to him."

"And you would be Mr. Perkins, would you not?"

"I am, sir, and I am of a height might deceive an attacker. The Irish woman who was the first victim was no shorter than me."

Sir John sat quiet behind his desk. Then, of a sudden, did he slap the top of it with the flat of his hand.

"By God, I like it not, for I had hoped to put five or six out on separate streets. And most particularly do I not like the idea of using a boy of fourteen in such a way. Yet there are times when necessity forces us to make do with what is given us. I accept Mr. Perkins and Mr. Proctor as my decoys—though against my better judgment."

At that there were no ringing huzzahs and no applause. The only response from the constables was an uneasy shuffling of feet. Yet I chose that moment to speak forth.

"Sir John?"

"What is it, Jeremy?"

"I wish to correct you, sir. I am not fourteen years old. I am fifteen."

There comes a time when one may regret one's impulsive actions—or if not exactly regret, then to question them. That time came for me when, alone in my attic room, I donned the old frayed frock supplied by Lady Fielding from the store collected for the residents of the Magdalene Home for Penitent Prostitutes. It fit well enough, except in the shoulders, which had been altered to suit me better; the hem of the skirt had also been let down to cover my ankles and hide my feet. As I moved about the room, testing the shoulders which were still a bit tight, and noticing that the skirt impeded my stride somewhat, I truly had second thoughts about Sir John's plan and my part in it. Yet I knew such thoughts would change neither. Night was falling; the great bonfire in Covent Garden was about to be lit; the crowd would now be swiftly assembling. There was naught for me but to descend the stairs for the next step in my disguise—that which I dreaded most.

The length of the skirt proved a hazard on the stairs until I remembered the device by which women dealt with them and raised the skirt daintily to my ankles. Thus I arrived in the kitchen where I was met by Lady Fielding, Annie, and Constable Perkins.

I saw in him the fate that awaited me. Not only had his cheeks and lips been rouged, he had also been adorned with a cotton cap of the kind worn by women in that day, now a bit out of fashion. Yet what had been done to him had in no wise softened his strong, emphatic features. He looked, truth to tell, simply like Constable Perkins in rouge and a silly cap.

"Oh, Jeremy, sit down," said Lady Fielding. "I'm told we must hurry. Annie will apply the rouge."

"You'll not know yourself when I finish," said Annie. It sounded to me quite like a threat.

Mr. Perkins said nothing. He averted his face, pretending to look out the window, where there was naught to be seen but the rising orange moon.

As I seated myself uneasily, Annie dipped two fingers in the tinned rouge container and set to her task. After a moment she gave me an annoyed tap on the top of my head.

"Don't fidget so," said she. "I'll never get this on you proper."

I remained then obediently still. I wanted only to get this done as swift as might be.

"Constable Perkins presented quite a challenge," said Lady Fielding. "The poor man has hair all the way up to the hollow of his neck. We had to shave it off."

"And they cut me up proper doin' it," he grumbled.

"We couldn't let him out like he was," said Annie. "He'd fool no one."

One way or another, Annie completed her task. She offered me a mirror, but I declined.

"You look a proper bawd," said she to me. "A bit husky, like a farm girl, but many such are known on the street."

"Now this," said Lady Fielding, holding out a cotton cap like the one worn by Mr. Perkins, "should crown you properly."

She placed it on my head and tied it beneath my chin.

"I think we've done all that need be done, don't you, Annie?" said she.

"Yes, mum," said Annie, with a glance at Mr. Perkins, "or could be done."

Then did Mr. Perkins speak up rather gruffly: "All right, Jeremy, let's get on with it."

And so, with a nod to the women, I followed the constable down the stairs. There waited Sir John and the team of four Runners who were to follow us at a discreet distance.

Though I saw surprise and amusement in the faces of the four, not one word was said, and not so much as a giggle was heard. Silenced they were utterly by the furious, threatening look given them by Mr. Perkins.

"Are you ready?" asked Sir John.

"Ready as we'll be," said Mr. Perkins.

"But you must be armed in some way. Mr. Baker?" Sir John called to the night resident. "Give each a loaded pistol and a club—or you have your own club, do you not, Mr. Perkins?"

"Tucked in my belt under the skirt. Never without it, sir."

"Well and good," said the magistrate. "But I had thought it best if you were to carry the pistol in your hand, Constable, since we see your task primarily as guarding Jeremy."

"I ain't likely to attract any, not even one who wishes me murder. But I can't go about with a pistol in m'hand."

"You can if it is well covered. Constable Cowley? Do you have that shawl your lady friend lent us?"

Young Mr. Cowley came forward and offered an old blue shawl; it was tattered at the edges and raveling, yet large enough for the purpose Sir John had in mind.

"Mr. Baker, you have the pistols? Give one to Mr. Perkins. Now, Mr. Cowley, wrap the shawl around his hand and the pistol and cover as much as you can of the stump of his left arm."

I watched, fascinated, as the pistol disappeared in a roll of blue wool.

"Tuck in the end securely," said Sir John to Mr. Cowley. "We cannot have it come undone unless by the constable's choice. Can you get the pistol loose if necessary, Mr. Perkins?"

"Oh, I'll manage, sir."

"I'm sure you will, but, Mr. Perkins—you, too, Jeremy—please bear in mind that when I say *if necessary,* I mean precisely that. Think of the pistols primarily as signaling devices. We cannot have you shooting down the first drunken sailor who grabs at Jeremy. You men who will follow, when you hear a pistol shot or a shout from either Mr. Perkins or Jeremy, you will come as swiftly as ever you can, for you will know it is in earnest. Stay fifty yards behind—but no more than that. And try as best you can to keep unnoticed—though fitted out as you are, that may prove difficult."

Indeed they were fitted out in full gear; each wore a brace of pistols and had a cutlass in its scabbard by his side.

As Sir John made his concluding remarks, Mr. Baker gave to me both pistol and club. I hiked up the voluminous skirt and tucked them into the belt I wore round my breeches, then dropped the skirt again. They were well hidden, but I wondered that I would be able to reach them with ease. In any case, I reflected, I had five constables to protect me.

"So go now, all of you," said Sir John. "The fire is lit in Covent Garden. They will now be streaming in to dance and sing. The streets should be empty to you. May God grant us good fortune in this."

With that, we filed out to Bow Street.

The stream of humanity into the Garden which Sir John had predicted was more in the nature of a swarm. Turning towards Russell Street, we were buffeted and pushed by those eager to get on to the festivities. They paid us no mind at all. We saw no need to separate while the streets were yet so crowded, and so we moved on together, we six, and waited at Russell Street, one of the main entrances to Covent Garden, for the rushing tide of humanity to abate somewhat.

From our position at the cross street we could see the fire burning. It was a grand fire, but not near as grand as it would soon become. Wood was piled high, whole logs in the stack as yet untouched by the flames. And there was more wood to be tossed on to keep the fire blazing steadily. None that burned on Guy Fawkes Day in the coming week would be likely to surpass it, nor would any be able to attract such a crowd of people. They milled about; they stood staring; a few had begun to dance. How folk do love a fire!

Eventually did the rush cease. We crossed Russell Street together, but then, seeing Charles Street near empty before us, we spread out in the manner suggested by Sir John. Constable Perkins took the lead, and I followed some twenty yards behind. The four constables trailed not quite fifty yards to my rear, two on either side of Charles Street.

Our plan was to make a square about Covent Garden, and if nothing untoward occurred, we should then make another square, but again, if nothing were to have happened, we would concentrate our attention upon those places that were deemed most dangerous—tempting fate, as it were.

I looked ahead. Even at a distance, Mr. Perkins seemed nothing more nor less than a man in skirts. Not only had the rouge applied by Annie failed to disguise and soften his mannish features, he himself did nothing to alter his bearing. He moved along Charles Street in lengthy strides, turning watchfully right and left exactly as any constable might have done. Surely if the murderer saw him, close up or even from afar, he would know that something was amiss.

Behind me, the escort played their role a bit better. Their movement could be detected, and brief glints from their scabbards, but they went silently in the shadows, wholly visible only beneath the streetlamps; the light of the full moon had not yet touched Charles Street.

And I? I minced a bit as I walked, moving not too swiftly, seeking to appear in some sense available as I had observed such women to do.

In just such a manner did our strange procession turn down Tavistock Street, walk its length, cross Southampton, and proceed down Maiden Lane: The moonlight hit more direct in these quarters. The constables to my rear could no longer seclude themselves as they had, moving from shadow to shadow. Yet they managed to disguise their purpose by strolling, as one might say, in a way quite indifferent to me and Mr. Perkins. There were a few pedestrians on Maiden Lane; they seemed to take no notice of us, passing without suspicion, or even curiosity.

Then on to Bedford Street, which seemed to offer some threat, as it was off that wide way, with its stews and taverns of bad repute, that the mutilated body of Poll Tarkin had been found. Mr. Perkins seemed to be pulling away from me with his long strides and was now near as distant as the team of constables behind me.

I recall that I had gone no more than twenty paces down Bedford, having left my escort temporarily back on Maiden Lane, when a couple came blindly out of one of the gin dives and collided with me. I made to walk on, but of a sudden was jerked roughly back by a male hand.

"Here you! What kind of a blowen are you that you don't say you're sorry when you knock into a joe? I'll give you a proper kick in the arse, I will."

I knew that voice. Those words, delivered in a shower of spittle and a fog of gin breath, could have come only from Jackie Carver. I needed only to glance at his face to confirm that. I shook loose from his grip, but he grabbed at me again.

"Now, just where—" There he stopped and let out a sudden giggling laugh. "Just look, look who this is, Mariah! It's your joe from the Beak. He's all done up like a moll, he is—lispers and cheeks all painted in rouge like yours."

It was indeed Mariah who was with him. Having hung back, she came forward, staggering slightly under the weight of gin she had drunk. She thrust her head at me, with some difficulty focused her eyes, and laughed at me.

"*Dio mio, e vero!* Is true, is him!" And she laughed again.

She reached at my face, as if to smear the rouge away. I pulled back. He jerked at my arm, and I, moved to action at last, delivered a stout blow to his chest and sent him reeling back. He looked at me quite in disbelief.

"You know who I am, chum?" he shouted. "What I could do to you?"

And just as he was reaching behind him, ready to propel himself at me, he found himself in the grasp of stout arms, several of them, for my escort had caught up with me at last. And just as sudden was Mr. Perkins beside me, asking if I were all right. The pistol he carried was out from its wrapping.

Mariah looked round her in confusion, eyes wide, saying nothing.

Jackie Carver understood his situation 'most immediate. "Aw, now, gents, leave off, leave off. Just a bit of a misunderstanding, as you might say. I thought this here blowen was out on the stroll. If it's a Beak matter, I'll have no part. Just leave me be."

"Get along with you, Jeremy," said Constable Cowley. "We'll take care of this one."

"Come along, lad," said Mr. Perkins. "Perhaps we should walk together."

"I think not, sir. But let us stay closer."

"You walk too slow."

"No, sir, if I may say so, sir, you walk too fast—as a man would. Could you try to be more . . . more womanly in your walk?"

He looked at me angrily and seemed about to speak. But then, for a long moment, he held his tongue. "I'll try," said he at last.

Turning away, he went swiftly to a point fifteen or twenty yards down Bedford Street, stopped, and waved me forward. I followed, walking much as I had before, keenly aware that I was being watched by Mariah and her protector. I felt shamed at the thought, yet I continued, for this was, after all, a Beak matter.

Poor Mr. Perkins, he did his best. He could not mince, for I doubt he knew how, yet he did take shorter steps and not full man-sized strides. The gait that resulted was something in the nature of a shuffle—certainly an improvement. Yet he was impeded further by the shawl he had been given by Constable Cowley, for he sought to cover the pistol with it. He stopped and bent to it, seeking to use his stump to wrap it—quite impossible, of course. I hastened forward to help, but he waved me back. In the end, he simply allowed the shawl to dangle over the pistol. Covered it was, but it might not stay so for long. Yet we proceeded.

I wished powerfully that I had dealt swifter with that fellow Jackie. Why had I stood there dumbly and let him hold me? Why had I allowed Mariah to laugh at me? Why? Why? Why? I found myself trembling with frustration at the incident that was now minutes past. It was, I decided, best to put it out of my mind. Later, when I had the opportunity, I would think it through as best I could.

Looking about me as I passed the alley that led to St. Paul's churchyard, I saw the yellow-red glow of the great bonfire in Covent Garden, and I heard the roar of the crowd made greater there. And, as I looked, I was surprised to see a wagon stopped in the alley with no driver about—something not surprising in itself, but this wagon was unmistakably the Raker's own. Of that I was sure. Though I could not see the crude death's head painted upon the side of it, I would have recognized those skeletal, somnolent horses anywhere. Each was a spectral gray, and each stood, head bowed, on trembling legs. I wondered where the Raker himself might be, though of course I knew his errand. Perhaps he was in that very building where his wagon was halted. Perhaps some poor soul who had lived behind one of those windows had expired from sickness or poverty. Better that, thought I, than dying the victim of a murderer. And then did a shudder pass through me.

At the end of Bedford Street, Mr. Perkins crossed into King Street. I slowed, for I saw him stop directly in front of Number 6—Queen's Court, the site of the last and most inhuman homicide. I wondered if he intended to enter the court to search it through. Had he heard something? Seen something? No, again he was trying to wrap that shawl round the pistol—this time using his teeth. I came up closer behind him, intending to insist upon giving him my help.

I was just at the passageway leading to the adjoining court, which was known as Three Kings, when I was pulled bodily into the passage by an assailant who had been altogether invisible to me—as indeed he remained invisible to me as I was dragged back into the dark passage.

One hand was clapped over my mouth so that I could not cry out. My right arm was twisted behind my back. It was a foul-smelling hand, and it tasted even fouler when I bit down upon it. I bit hard on one finger. I grinded and chewed, never letting it loose from my teeth. And as I did so, I beat hard as I was able with my left elbow upon the ribs of my attacker. He was large, as I could tell from the strength of him, and he was near as wide as he was tall. My feet were of no use as he pulled me back and back towards the court, but I tasted his blood in my mouth, and I knew he could not keep his hand there much longer. We stopped, and I slammed the heel of my shoe down onto his foot. With that he let go all but my arm, and I squirmed round to face him.

By God, it was the Raker! I saw him plain in a patch of moonlight.

"*Perkins!*" I shouted out, loud as ever I could.

I heard footsteps from the street as he let go my arm, and a blade glinted in his right hand. He came lumbering at me, and I dodged him as we circled. He now had his back to King Street as Mr. Perkins appeared in the entrance to the passage, the pistol in his hand. I backed up.

The Raker must have sensed him there, for then did he come running at me down the narrow passage as fast as those bandy legs of his could move him. I saw he had no intention of stopping. I feinted left and jumped right—away from the knife. But as he passed, he threw me against the wall of the passage. Just as I heard Mr. Perkins fire his pistol, my head hit the brick wall, and I slipped into the black void of the unconscious state.

When next I came to myself I was quite alone, though no longer in the passageway. Of that I was sure, for I ran my hands over the space where I lay and found I was in a bed. My bed? With some effort I opened my eyes and found, casting them about, that yes, I was in my own bed in my own attic room. I made to rise, but the sudden pain at the back of my head sent me back 'most immediate to my pillow. I touched my aching head and found it wrapped round in a great bandage.

How long had I been here? How long unconscious? How even had I got here?

I concentrated upon the events just preceding my loss of consciousness. They were clear in my mind, and for that I was grateful for I had heard that a knock on the head can sometimes cause a loss of memory, sometimes complete. I remembered it all too well—being dragged into the passage, fighting back as best I could, the taste of blood in my mouth, then breaking away and finding, to my astonishment, that it was the Raker who was my assailant. I remembered also being thrown against the wall by him as Mr. Perkins fired his pistol. Could he have hit me? Was that what caused this awful pain at the back of my head? No, more likely my head had hit some sharp brick, a place where the mortar had crumbled away. Perhaps my poor head had been broken. It felt quite so.

So Mr. Perkins had shot the Raker. The murders were done. I was content in that, and thus content and glad to be in my own bed, I fell unconscious again. Yet it was sleep that came, and quite welcome it was. My dreams were most pleasant. I was on shipboard, a sturdy vessel with billowing sails which cut through the waves as smooth as a coach-and-four on a well-paved road. Mariah was beside me. We walked the decks together, fore and aft, feeling the wind in our faces. She did not laugh at me, but earnestly told me of her love for me. The seamen treated us with great respect, doffing their hats to us. And the captain of the ship, who was my near-brother, Tom Durham, invited us to the poop deck where he stood in his place of command. He opened a great, long telescope and took a view of what lay ahead. "Land ho!" said he. "I see the Massachusetts shore." Then did Annie Oakum appear.

Yet it was truly her and not a part in the dream. She had entered the room. My head was turned to her, and my eyes had opened; there was still moonlight enough for me to know her for who she was.

"You're awake," said she.

"Just now," said I.

"'Land ho,' you said. Was that in the dream?"

"Oh yes, but it was Tom said it."

"Tom Durham? I dream of him often, though my dreams are worth little."

I attempted to rise but again felt the pain at the back of my head, though not quite so severe as before. She pushed me gently back to my pillow.

"You must stay still," said she. "Mr. Donnelly said so. He was right firm in that."

"Was he here to see me?"

"Oh, indeed he was. He said you had a con . . . con . . ."

"Concussion?"

"So he said. And you was to stay in bed, and I was to keep a good eye on you. And here I am, you see." And then did she give a little curtsey, and I noticed she wore her nightgown. "My second visit of the night."

"What time is it, Annie?"

"That I cannot say, though it be late. The great fire in the Garden is all burned to naught." She sighed. "I declare that when that one-armed constable carried you in, I feared you might never wake, not in this life. Oh, Jeremy, I am so glad to see you alive!"

And then did she bend down to me and plant a kiss upon my cheek. With her face so close, I saw that Annie had tears in her eyes.

"No more than I."

"I must go and tell Sir John you are awake. He is so unhappy—you hurt so bad and all for naught."

"For naught?" Again, impulsively I rose, with the same bad result. "Didn't Mr. Perkins shoot him dead?"

"Oh no, all the constables was angry at themselves, for they let him get away. Didn't even get a proper look at him who hurt you."

"Annie, you must go and tell Sir John that I know the man. I know the murderer!"

Eyes wide and without another word, she fled. And in less than a minute there was a great thunder of footsteps upon the stairs. And of a sudden, my little room was crowded with visitors. Not only was Sir John present, but also Mr. Donnelly and Constable Perkins, now in proper attire—and Annie with them, as well.

"Ah, Jeremy," said Sir John, "words cannot express—that is, I . . . I blame myself for this terrible misadventure. You have my sincerest apology. But Annie said you . . . you . . ."

"Yes, sir," said I, "it was the Raker."

"The Raker! Good God, of course! He was always about, wasn't he? And I always thought him half-mad. But you're sure he was the one?"

"I saw him plain in clear moonlight, sir, and he had a knife—then he was as close as can be when he knocked me down. It was the Raker. I could not be more certain."

"And he with a knife. We're fortunate to have you alive."

"I would not be, save for Mr. Perkins's instructions."

"Good lad," piped Mr. Perkins, "you kept your wits about you."

"I heard you fire. I supposed you shot him dead."

"No, Jeremy, in my haste I missed. I feared I would hit you. Had I held off, I'd not have missed, I promise."

"Constable Perkins—" Sir John spoke in the tone of command.

"Yes, sir?"

"Go out and gather a party of Runners as swiftly as you can. Find Mr. Bailey if possible—but we cannot wait for him. I shall command the party, in any case." Sir John sputtered a moment as his mind raced. "Jeremy," said he then, "you saw the Raker, but did the Raker see you—well, of course he *saw* you but did he *recognize* you? Did he realize you had recognized *him?*"

I gave that a bit of thought. "I cannot say, sir," said I at last. "He must have known I was no woman the way I bellowed for Mr. Perkins. But he grabbed me from behind, and we were in the dark most of the time. And so he may indeed have supposed he left unknown to me."

"Very good," said Sir John. "We may then find him there in that ghastly house of the dead. Let us hope, in any case, he has not fled. Off with you then, Mr. Perkins—four or five Runners should do."

The constable left in a great rush and clattered down the stairs.

Mr. Donnelly, who had waited till these immediate matters were settled, then stepped forward and called for Annie to light a candle.

Then said he to me: "I can tell your brains aren't addled, but let me take a closer look at you, now that you're back among the living."

Though excited by my conversation with Sir John and eager to know the result, once all had left my little room I remained awake only a few minutes more. If dreams I had, they were lost to me when I wakened in the light of morning. Carefully I then tested my wound by rising once again from my pillow. Again the pain had lessened. I was able to bring myself to a sitting position, ease my feet to one side, and relieve myself in the chamber pot at bedside. As yet I dared not try to stand.

Down below, Annie and Lady Fielding stirred about in the kitchen, and hearing the sounds of breakfast in preparation, I became aware of the hunger in my own belly—or was it a certain queasy feeling? Or was it both? I was, in any case, glad to hear footsteps on the stairs, and happier still to see Lady Fielding bearing a bowl of what I took to be porridge. It was not.

"Annie has prepared a good, hearty broth for you, Jeremy," said she with a warm smile. "This is by command of Mr. Donnelly. He said you might not be able to hold down anything heavier."

I pushed up on my elbows and declared I could sit up without difficulty. Yet she arranged my pillow in such a way as to elevate my head. I leaned back on my shoulders. Then did she sit down on my bed and insist on spoon-feeding me like a baby. Though somewhat chagrined at this, I found the broth most hearty, just as she had promised, and it seemed to cause my stomach no distress. I had naught to do but open my mouth to have it filled, and listen as she told me what she knew of last night's events.

"You will want to know of the capture of that monstrous man," said she, "since 'twas you who made it possible."

"The Raker?" I paused at the offered spoonful. "Is he below?"

"He is indeed—locked up safely in that little gaol they keep behind the courtroom. He will go before Jack in an hour, then straight to Newgate. Jack says he confessed, and besides was caught in a . . . a compromising position—no need for me to go into that. Those hideous crimes, and to such hideous purpose! Dear God, Jeremy, London is such a frightening, lawless place. I've come to believe that Jack and his constables are all that stand between us and absolute anarchy."

"Yet they manage," said I.

"So they do, and you with them. You cannot know how proud we are of you. Jack himself said he knew of no constable in the Runners who could have conducted himself more bravely than you. He is greatly angered at himself for putting you in danger. I think he wishes your forgiveness."

I was somewhat taken aback at such a notion. "Why, there is naught to forgive. I would have done what I did a hundred times over for Sir John. I believe I would willingly die for him."

"He knows that, and he seems to feel he has misused your trust. Yet we none of us felt there could be such a threat to your safety. After all, with five constables to protect you, what could possibly go wrong? And if Annie and I treated it lightly when we prepared you for the street, it was because we, too, felt you would be safe. You must forgive us our frivolousness."

"There is naught to forgive," I repeated. "I was far more embarrassed than I was fearful."

"So we thought." She sighed and rattled the spoon in the empty bowl. "Well, you've taken it all. How do you feel with something inside you? Not stomach-sick, I hope."

"No, not a bit. Thank Annie for me. Tell her it was just what I needed."

"One good thing has come of this," said she. "That terrible man's confession should remove suspicion from Mr. Tolliver. You and I both knew he could not have committed such crimes."

"Indeed, it is true," said I.

"But here, let me fix your pillow, so you may lie comfortable."

She went about it as if her mind were elsewhere. When she had done, I lay back and looked up at her.

Then, after hesitating a moment, she spoke: "Jeremy, I shall tell you something I have never told Jack, so let it be a secret between us." Again she hesitated. "At the time Jack asked me to marry, Mr. Tolliver was also courting me with the intention of marriage. He made that plain. He was a widower, and in every way he appeared to me to be a fine, upstanding man. I would indeed have married him had not Jack asked me. I cannot believe that I am such a bad judge of character that a man I would have married would be guilty of crimes of any sort, least of all those of such horrendous nature. And so you see, I am especially grateful to you for your part in bringing that man they call the Raker to the rope. I thank you for it, and I thank you, too, for your words to Jack in support of Mr. Tolliver."

All that she told me I had guessed long before. Nevertheless, I said: "He will return and have a good reason for his absence. I'm sure of it."

"Let that be our secret," said she. And picking up the empty bowl she left me with the most serious of smiles.

Not long afterwards, Annie appeared at my door, stopping by prior to the buying trip to Covent Garden which, under ordinary circumstances, I might have made for her. She looked tired, and I told her so.

"And well I might be," said she, "with Sir John stompin' up and down the stairs, and me risin' to look in on you twice more durin' the night."

"But you needn't have, Annie. As you see, I'm in fine fettle."

"Oh, I see fair enough. I've no doubt you look better than me—feel better, too. Well, I'm glad for it, Jeremy, for indeed you earned it. Maybe you ain't heard, but it's Sir John's thought you should get that reward voted by Parliament—twenty guineas, and ain't that a fair fortune!"

"He said that?"

"He did. And wouldn't I take a knock on the head for twenty guineas?" Having said that, she looked down quickly to the floor. Then did she amend it: "Didn't mean it. I'm sure you earned the reward, as well." And, with a sigh: "Jeremy, old chum, I'm off to market. I'll buy some apples, should Mr. Donnelly say you can have them."

Within an hour of Annie's visit, Sir John came to see me. I had spent the time between dreaming of what I might do with twenty guineas. Annie was right: it was a fair fortune. With it I could buy Mariah's freedom still, and . . . and what? The bitterness I had taken away from our last two meetings had somehow been expunged by that remarkable dream I had had. Would what was left from her deliverance buy our passage to the colonies? I doubted it—though it might indeed see her back to Italy and her people there. Was that what I wanted? Of course not, though I should prefer that to seeing her remain in London with no trade, no proper work at all. Perhaps once she was free of that villain, I could persuade her to enter the Magdalene Home or accept the offer of employment Mr. Bilbo had made to her—yes, I was sure I could. In the latter situation, at least, she would be safe, live an ordered life, and best of all, I could see her often as I liked. My mind dwelt so on these possibilities that I gave no notice when I heard Sir John's step upon the stairs. Thus I was taken by surprise when he stood at my door in an attitude of uncertainty. He could, of course, not tell whether I waked or slept.

"Come in, Sir John," said I, "for I am eager to hear all you might have to tell."

"Ah, Jeremy, good lad. I heard from Kate you were much improved. Took nourishment, you did."

He stepped inside and stood, hands clasped behind him, beside my bed. For my part, I had rearranged my pillow and now sat up with no ill effect.

"I did eat," said I, "and glad I was, for I was most famished. I do believe I'll soon be ready to eat proper food again."

"Something stronger than broth, eh? Well, that will depend on what Mr. Donnelly has to say. He'll be by later to have a look at you."

He paused. I waited. Then did he launch into his account of the Raker's capture. There were, in all, six of them who arrived at the necropolis down by the river—four constables led by Mr. Perkins, and with them Mr. Donnelly and Sir John himself. They went quietly to the barn, from which a dim light shone. Yet there was little need for quiet, for when they arrived, they found him criminally engaged, oblivious of all but what he was at.

"*In flagrante delicto* we found him," thundered Sir John. "So sure of himself was he that once he had knocked you senseless and made his escape through the adjoining court, he had got himself one more victim, and done her in with that same single knife-thrust to the heart. He had practiced it for months on the bodies in his barn. Mr. Perkins put a pistol to the Raker's head, and the Raker left off what he was doing soon enough."

(All this, reader, was a bit vague to me.)

Found so, the fellow readily confessed and produced the thin, long-bladed stiletto with which he had done his villainous work. He allowed that there had been more victims than we knew. He had killed about one a month, for the better part of a year. It was only because Teresa O'Reilly's body was discovered before he could cart it off that his nefarious work came to light.

"I should have suspected him, stupid of me really," said Sir John, "for twice he was on the scene, unbidden, with his wagon. Yet he was so familiar, so much a part of the process, that I gave him no thought."

And, remembering, I then interrupted his narrative for the first time: "I recall, Sir John, that I saw his wagon in the alley off Bedford Street where Poll Tarkin was killed—and that just before his attack upon me."

"And you thought nothing of it?"

"Nothing at all. Only that he had come to collect one who had died of natural causes."

"Then I am perhaps not the dolt I supposed myself to be." Holding back but a moment, he then proceeded somewhat thoughtfully: "Something quite disappointing came out today in court. I held coroner's inquest on last night's murder and the Raker's hearing all in one. It may not have been proper procedure, yet that way I had done with it swiftly. In any case, it developed that while that madman quite willingly confessed to three of the murders, he quite hotly denied that he had had anything to do with the deaths of Poll Tarkin and Libby Tribble—that is, those in which the bodies were so brutally defiled. To quote him: 'I would not treat a woman so'—as if his method of murder were so much more merciful than that practiced upon those two women. I gave him a proper dressing-down on that point. I said—" He shrugged. "Well, it matters little what I said. The significant thing is, I had no choice but to believe him. And so, having apprehended one murderer, we must now seek a second."

"And Mr. Tolliver is still held suspect."

"For want of any other, yes."

"Lady Fielding will be sore disappointed."

"She has already expressed her disappointment. No doubt you are about to do the same."

"No, sir, you have heard all I have to say on that matter."

"For that I thank you. There is one other matter affected by this revelation, and it has to do with you, Jeremy. I had intended to put your name forward to Parliament to be the recipient of the reward that was offered for the apprehension of the murderer. But since we now know there are not one but two murderers, you will no doubt be given part, though not all, of the reward. I know not how it shall be divided, but you should be receiving a considerable amount."

Disguising my disappointment, I said most brightly, "But, Sir John, I am quite overwhelmed."

"Indeed it is you who deserve it," said he. "It was you risked your life. It was you recognized him. You did all but put the pistol to his head."

"Well, thank you, sir. I hardly know what to say."

"There is no more need be said—except perhaps from me, my repeated apology for putting you in danger as I did. Do forgive me please."

"I feel there is naught to forgive, but if it is my forgiveness you seek, you have it a thousand times over."

"Thank you, lad." He turned to go, then added just at the door: "Well, at least Hosea Willis is now in Newgate, assured of a swift trip to the gallows."

"Hosea Willis? Who . . . ?"

"That is the Raker's given name. I'd no idea of it. Even he had to think a bit before he could produce it. What a strange and unfortunate man he is—or was."

And so saying, he left me.

Indeed it was true. I recalled what I had heard of the Raker—Hosea Willis, if that be his name. He had inherited his strange calling from his father, who had it from his father before him, and now he would be the last in the line. The Raker had always seemed to me in my many meetings with him to be, as Sir John described him, half-mad. Had the work he did made him so? Who could say? Did he deserve Bedlam rather than the hangman's noose? Again, who could say?

Mr. Donnelly's call upon me began most professionally. He had found me sitting up in bed, which I think displeased him, though he said nothing of it. Instead, after a word or two of greeting, he set about unwinding that great turban of a bandage he had round my head so that he might inspect the wound. He touched the cut tentatively with a finger, and I flinched slightly.

"Does that hurt?" he asked.

"A bit," said I.

"I've no doubt that it does."

Then did he take a bottle of gin from his bag, soak a bit of cotton with it, and apply it to the cut. That produced a sharp, stinging pain. Taking another rolled bandage, he then wrapped me Mussulman-style as before.

"You're lucky you've a good thick skull, Jeremy. A fracture of your head would have put you in serious danger. What about pain inside your head? I take it that must have abated, or you wouldn't be sitting up as you are."

"I feel it only when I turn my head sharply."

"Well, don't. Let me now have a look at your eyes."

He lit the candle and, as he had the night before, he waved it back and forth before my face, asking me to follow it with my eyes. Then did he blow it out and peer into them.

"They seem right enough," said he. "Not seeing two where one should be? Or getting a blur anywhere, are you?"

"No, sir."

"Well and good."

"May I read?"

"I see no reason why you should not, so long as you do not strain your eyes. Not by candlelight, I should say."

"May I be up and about?"

"Not yet. A day or two more in bed should put you right, though."

"What about food?" said I. "I've had only a bowl of broth this day."

"You held it down? No nausea?"

"No, sir."

"Then you may eat what the rest eat. Perhaps Annie could make up a tray for you so that you could eat here in bed. I'll mention it to her." Then he nodded, apparently satisfied. "You've come through it well, Jeremy."

He began to pack up, rolling the soiled bandage and tucking away the gin bottle. As he did, I put a question to him.

"Mr. Donnelly," said I, "you have good Latin, have you not?"

"I should think so," said he. "Medical Latin, Church Latin, what have you. Why do you ask?"

"Sir John used a Latin phrase describing the capture of the Raker which quite baffled me. He said that he had been found '*in flagrante delicto.*' What did he mean, sir?"

Mr. Donnelly, who usually seemed ready to smile or break into a laugh, looked at me quite soberly. "That would translate roughly as 'caught in the act,'" he said.

"Caught in what act, sir?"

He cleared his throat. "Well, Jeremy, situated as you are here in Covent Garden, you must be aware of what is done between men and women, the commerce in prostitution and so on?"

"Oh yes, sir."

"Then I may tell you that that creature, the Raker, was caught in the act of sexual intercourse with the corpus of a woman."

"A *dead* woman? Is that possible? Can it be done?"

"It can be, and it was. Even I, who have seen a good deal more than I would wish to tell, was quite shocked by what I saw there in that barn. You see, Jeremy, the sex function is very powerful in men, a very great force indeed, and if it be thwarted, madness of a sort can result in some. In the case of the Raker, because of his gruesome reputation and the tales told of him, not to mention his hideous appearance, even the prostitutes of the street rejected him. The method he chose to satisfy his lust is not so very strange, considering his familiarity with the dead; they were his subjects; he was their master. With that little stiletto of his, he could change those who had rejected him, or might reject him, into his compliant partners. Sir John blames himself for not realizing the Raker's guilt earlier, since he was always about. I blame myself for not understanding the significance of the peculiar, virtually bloodless nature of the wounds he inflicted. For in death, his victims seemed always quite lifelike."

I listened most solemnly to all that Mr. Donnelly had to say. Inwardly, I was quite agog, amazed at the twisted logic he suggested. Yet my response to all this was a rather weak one.

"I had no idea."

"Nor, for that matter, did the rest of us," he said.

I sat there in bed, considering all this for a long space of time. Then, thinking to put my attention to practical matters, I said: "So as I understand it, he had a new victim—a new . . . partner?"

"That is correct."

"Would it be helpful for me to write out a new item for the *Public Advertiser* to call for those who knew her to come and give her proper name? I have little to fill my time here."

"That should not be necessary, Jeremy. The Raker himself knew her after a fashion, for she had so vociferously rejected him that he learned what he could of her and vowed that one day he would have her in his own way. She was an Italian girl known as Mariah—or Maria, more likely. No one on the street seems to know her family name."

Stunned, as I might have been from a great blow, I leaned back on the pillow with my eyes closed, striving to hold back the tears. Yet they came.

Mr. Donnelly grasped me by the shoulder. "Jeremy," said he, "I had no idea—Why, you must have known her."

ELEVEN

In Which Mr. Tolliver Appears and the Hue and Cry is Raised

Hosea Willis was brought before the Lord Chief Justice the next day at Old Bailey. The remarkable swiftness with which he went from capture to conviction came through the Earl of Mansfield's desire to have done with the matter as quickly as possible. There was nothing could be said in his defense, and nothing was what he said. He simply pled guilty to the three homicides with which he was charged, and allowed that there had been four previous which had gone undetected. With that, the Lord Chief Justice asked him if he felt remorse. I was told that the Raker did no more than look at him blankly and repeat the word as a question—"Remorse?"—as if to say he had no understanding of it. Then was the sentence of death by hanging pronounced upon him and the gavel brought down, effectively ending the Raker's life but for the formalities on Tyburn Hill.

With the Raker's brief appearance in court and the judgment passed upon him, I became the beneficiary of ten guineas in reward for his capture. The sum was brought me by Sir John in a leather pouch quite like the one in which Poll Tarkin had kept her treasure. He offered it to me with a warm smile, saying he wished it were more.

"In truth," said he, "I should have said twelve or thirteen guineas would have been a fairer division, but so it was decided."

"I am most grateful, sir," said I, weighing the bag in my hand.

"Do you wish to count them?"

"No, sir, I take the members of Parliament at their word."

"Then perhaps I ought take it downstairs to Mr. Marsden for safekeeping in the strong box. It is not wise having a large amount lying about, as you yourself have cautioned me."

"With your permission, I will keep it by me. I have need of it."

"Oh? Already have it spent, do you?"

"In a manner of speaking, I do, yes, sir."

"Hmmm." He mused for a moment. "Nothing frivolous, I hope?"

"No, indeed not."

"Well then, keep it, by all means." He went to my door, then turned back to me. "May I ask on what you have set your mind? Perhaps it is something with which we should supply you. Clothes . . . books—whatever is in our means, we try to give."

"I know that, Sir John, yet this is something quite apart. Trust me in this, please."

"Of course," said he, and with a firm nod he left me.

I sat in bed, a book and the bag of guineas before me. In fact I did open up the bag and look inside, though I did not count the coins. I closed it up and tossed it back on the bed, then did I pick up the book that lay open before me. It was a copy of Mr. Goldsmith's gentle romance, *The Vicar of Wakefield,* brought me as a gift by Lady Fielding that very morning; she had suggested he might autograph it for me when next I saw him. I delved into it immediately and found myself quite captivated by Dr. Primrose and his brood. Yet now, with the reward in hand so much earlier than I had expected, I found I was unable to concentrate upon the pages of the book, so impatient was I for Mr. Donnelly's arrival.

The day before, I had told him all of my relations with Mariah—from my first glimpse of her as an acrobat in Covent Garden to my last meeting when she laughed, seeing me in woman's garb. I left out nothing, not even my foolish fantasies of escape to the American colonies. Mr. Donnelly did not laugh at me, neither did he sneer. He told me that, years before, when he was a lad of about my age in Dublin, he had formed just such a fascination for a girl of the streets; that he had gone so far as to steal money for her from his father's shop in hopes of reforming her; that it had all ended badly when a shop assistant was blamed for the theft, and young Gabriel was forced to confess. His father, far from outraged, had taken him in hand and managed to convince him that the girl wanted only his money, for each time she asked for a sum, whatever the reason, it always was greater than the last.

"He was right," Mr. Donnelly had said to me, "for when I told her I could give her no more, she refused even to speak to me."

"I cannot say it was different with Mariah," said I then. "But to see a life wasted, then taken even before there be hope of change—where is the justice in that?"

"Life is not just, Jeremy. It is simply a space of time that is given us. We do with it what we can."

"Even so," said I, "I should like to do something for her."

That something I wished to do I left unstated, though I had formed a plan in my mind which was contingent upon the receipt of the reward I had been promised. Now that I had been given it by Sir John, I hoped that indeed it might be accomplished.

Mr. Donnelly did in fact arrive not long after Sir John's visit. And, after a cursory examination—nothing so thorough as he had given me the day before—he pronounced me "coming along nicely."

"May I leave my bed and walk about? I should like to dress and eat dinner with the rest."

"That perhaps, but no more for today."

There was silence between us. Then did I pick up the bag of guineas and give it a jingle.

"I have received my reward," said I, "ten guineas in all."

"Would that it had been more," said he. "Would that there were not another murderer to be caught."

"Mr. Donnelly, I should like you to take this money and arrange for Mariah to be buried properly."

"Are you sure you want to do this, Jeremy?"

"I am sure. Will it be sufficient?"

"Oh yes, if—There are some difficulties."

I had foreseen that. "She is from Italy and would be of the Roman faith?"

"Yes, there's that, but there are priests here in London. They have no church and are here more or less in disguise, you might say."

"There is no burial ground?"

"There is a field up above Clerkenwell whose purpose is kept in strict secret. There are no markers and no monuments, but it is hallowed ground."

"What, then, are the difficulties?"

"Well, first of all, she would have to be buried at night, unseen, and without much in the way of ceremony."

"Yes, but in a coffin and put where she would wish to be laid to rest."

"There is, however, the priest to be persuaded. I know none of them here, yet back in Dublin I would say one would have difficulty convincing a priest that a woman of her profession should be buried alongside those who had had a fair chance of dying in a state of grace."

All that was somewhat beyond me, yet I caught the sense of it. "Perhaps," I said, "if you were to say that her last act was to refuse one who would have her—might that not make a difference? Perhaps show she was on her way to bettering herself?"

"Oh, it might. Jeremy, I'll see what can be done. More than that I cannot promise."

Thus it came about that next evening I was in the back of an open wagon riding on my way to Clerkenwell. Mr. Donnelly had taken care of everything—rented the wagon and the team from a livery stable, hired an Irish teamster, and found a priest who would officiate at the burial. He had even engaged a woman to come into his surgery and wash and dress Mariah's body in a suitable way for interment. At my request, no rouge or paint was used upon her face. I was granted one last look before the coffin was shut. She looked quite as she had that first time I had seen her as a young acrobat in Covent Garden when she had smiled at me and kissed my shilling so prettily. So it was she would be buried. Bending down, I kissed her on the forehead, yet I had no tears as the lid was fitted over the simple oblong box and nailed down by the teamster. Then did he and Mr. Donnelly carry the coffin downstairs. It was of no great weight. The teamster claimed he could have managed it on his own.

The two of them sat upon the wagon box, and I, meaning no insult certainly, upon the coffin. I was dressed in my best and wore that bottle-green coat which she so admired. All that marred my appearance was the bandage wrapped round my head. I had thought my hat might cover it, yet it did not. I had expected questions when Mr. Donnelly called for me at nightfall, and I appeared as if dressed for a ball. But neither my appearance nor my unstated destination were remarked upon by any in the household. I strongly suspected that Mr. Donnelly had acquainted them with the purpose of our mysterious trip. In any case, all I received from Sir John and Lady Fielding, and even from Annie, were sympathetic looks and courteous wishes for a good evening. It was better so. I had no wish either to make explanations or evade them.

The teamster knew the way. He had been recommended to Mr. Donnelly by the priest as one who had made the trip many times before and could be trusted to keep the location of the cemetery secret. Through the thin evening traffic, he moved the horses swiftly at a light trot. Yet even so, we went a considerable distance. On St. John's Street, we passed through Clerkenwell and soon found ourselves alone on Islington Road, passing through open fields. Here there could be highwaymen out on the scamp, looking to rob us of whatever was left in that leather bag of guineas in Mr. Donnelly's pocket. Yet before we met any such challenge, the driver slowed the team and turned it to the left to take us down a country road like unto any one of a dozen I had seen us pass along the way by bright moonlight. How he could have told this one from the others was quite beyond me.

He had nevertheless chosen rightly. That became evident when, in the near distance, I spied the light from a lantern held still, then swung slowly in a signal of welcome. When we arrived, there was an open gate and a burly fellow in his shirtsleeves in the cool night air holding high the lantern. He, I supposed, was the gravedigger. Without a word, he went before the team of horses and led the way down a track towards another light not so very far away. When we were close, I spied the figure of a man standing by a considerable heap of dirt and an open hole.

At a gesture from the gravedigger, the driver reined in. He and Mr. Donnelly climbed down, and I hopped over the side. As the other two pulled the tailgate down and pulled out the coffin, Mr. Donnelly took me aside.

"Jeremy," said he, "there was something I forgot to mention to you. She should be given a family name for purposes of the service. I know you said you had no idea of it, but perhaps you could think of something appropriate?"

I had thought one might be needed and was ready with it.

"Perhaps 'Angelo' would do," said I. Even I knew a bit of Italian.

He smiled. "That should do very well."

And so we set out, the four of us, for the grave which was only yards distant—Mr. Donnelly bearing the lantern and lighting the path; the teamster and the gravedigger carrying the coffin, and I, the solitary mourner, bringing up the rear.

The priest was dressed in the way that a common laborer might be. A young man, not much over thirty, he looked big and strapping as one of Sir John's constables—yet he had the face of a scholar and wore a gentle expression. Mr. Donnelly went forward to him, and they talked in low tones. The coffin was brought to the graveside and placed on the supports above the hideous hole. I held back, not knowing what part I was to play in all this. So I remained for a minute or two until Mr. Donnelly beckoned me to him. The priest had asked to meet me.

"Father," said Mr. Donnelly to the priest, "this is Jeremy Proctor. He is responsible for this. I've simply implemented his wishes."

"Well, it's a very decent thing you're doing, Jeremy." He offered me his hand, which was rough with calluses, and I took it, removing my hat with my other hand.

The priest continued: "We'll just bury the poor girl, and let him who is without sin cast the first stone. That's as Our Lord would have it." He, too, was Irish by the sound of him.

Mr. Donnelly took a place close to the priest and held high the lantern. The priest opened a blackbound book, looked round him, and said in a most solemn tone, "Let us begin." Then, did he commence to read the Latin office for the dead. His voice droned on for many minutes. It is a language that fits ill to the tongue. I comprehended a fair part, though my knowledge of it was and remains meagre. Whole sections of it he seemed to have by heart, for he would raise his eyes from time to time and chant certain passages in a gruff voice made sweet for the occasion. At me he looked when he commended to God the soul of "Maria Maddalena di Angelo," adding a significant flourish to the name I had given her. There was business with a sort of wand which he produced and used to sprinkle the coffin with water. Then, finally, he gave a nod to the rest of us. Mr. Donnelly set aside his lantern and pointed to the straps beneath the coffin. I grasped the one nearest me, which was held the other side of the grave by the teamster. The priest himself pulled out the supports, and we began slowly lowering the coffin into the deep hole. As we did so, the priest tossed a handful of dirt upon the coffin, and intoned a few more words in Latin. It was only then, as Mariah reached her final resting place, that the tears came. I wiped at them with my coatsleeve, coughed and sniffled, and so brought them under control. The teamster and the gravedigger were winding in the straps, tugging roughly to pull them free.

The priest turned to me. "I regret, Jeremy," said he, "that she must be laid to rest in such circumstances as these—in the darkness, in this plain field, without a Mass to see her on her way. I assure you, though, that I shall say a Mass for the repose of her soul tomorrow morning, and I shall remember her in my prayers ever after."

"Thank you, Father." Mr. Donnelly had coached me in the proper address.

"You're a good lad. I wish we had you as one of ours." Then to Mr. Donnelly: "You may leave now. Mr. Dooley and I will take care of all the rest that needs doing."

And thus dismissed, Mr. Donnelly took me by the arm and we walked back together to the wagon.

So it had been accomplished. Though one more chapter in the story of my relation to Mariah remained to be written, I did not then know that, and I felt at that moment a sense of completion, of duty done, a peace with a kind of emptiness within.

Having left Mr. Donnelly at his door in Tavistock Street, I walked to Bow Street with five guineas jingling in the bag in my pocket. I had not expected there would be any amount left for me, and I urged Mr. Donnelly to take all, or at least part of it, for he had arranged everything. Yet he had declined.

"No, Jeremy," he had said, "it was my pleasure to aid you in this—and a very great pleasure it was."

"But what am I to do with such a sum?"

"Why, save it, of course. You may well have need of it in the future."

It was near ten o'clock when I entered Number 4. Inside I found an unexpected hum of excitement. There were loud voices from far within, perhaps from Sir John's chambers, and a buzz of talk in lower tones from much closer by. Then, as I advanced, I saw it was Mr. Langford and Mr. Baker who were talking near the strong room. Mr. Baker broke off his talk and came to me. The commotion from Sir John's chambers continued. Besides Sir John's voice, there was another—a familiar grumbling basso even deeper than his—and the two were raised together in contention.

"Jeremy, lad," said he, "you'll be glad to know that Mr. Langford spied that fellow, Tolliver, leavin' the coach house. He detained him and brought him here to Sir John."

Was I glad to hear that? I was not at all sure.

Constable Langford came sauntering over, the very picture of self-satisfaction.

"He gave me a bit of argument, he did—him and that woman with him, said she was his wife," said he. "But all I needed do was tap my club and tell him he could come quiet or not, it was all the same to me—but he *would* come. He takes a look at his little lady, who's saying, 'Oh dear, what does this mean? What can it be about?' and such like, and he decides to give me no more trouble. And I was just as glad of it, 'cause he's a strong one for fair. He hauled two big portmanteaus here from the coach house with no strain."

"Did he say where he had been?" I asked.

"Didn't he, though? Many times over, he did. Said he'd been the whole month in Bristol for to court this woman who'd answered an advert he'd posted there. A right pleasant-lookin' thing she is, as you might say, though not what you'd call young. She chimes in and says, 'You would not expect me to marry a man I did not know, would you?'"

"Well," said I, "it may be just as they said. Mr. Tolliver is a widower. I have reason to know he desired to marry."

"And she a widow. Don't mistake, Jeremy. I'd as soon he cleared himself of any doubts Sir John might have. Many's the time I've bought meat from him, and he seems right enough. But you must admit his sudden departure was right queer. And when Sir John says he wishes to detain a fellow for a bit of a talk, by God, I'll detain him!"

"I take it that is Mr. Tolliver in there with him now," said I.

"Oh, you may be sure of it. They been growlin' at each other right strong. The butcher won't back down. Says it was his right to go off when and where he liked—had no need to ask permission."

"They been at it half an hour at least," said Constable Baker.

"Is his wife in there with him?" I should not have wanted her to hear details of the murder of Elizabeth Tribble and of the brutality that had been inflicted upon her dead body. To hear the man she had just married was suspect in such a crime would surely be more than she could bear.

"No," said Constable Langford, "and ain't that strange? When I went upstairs to tell Sir John I'd detained his man for him to question, Lady Fielding come down with him and invited Mrs. Tolliver up for a cup of tea—all friendly like, she was. 'Call me Kate,' she says. I tell you, the butcher looked at her right grateful. The two women are up there in the kitchen right now, I reckon."

"It would probably be best then if I stay here," I ventured.

"Prob'ly would," Mr. Baker agreed.

I had not long to wait. As I listened to Mr. Langford's proud report, the voices from the rear had quietened considerably. While they could still be heard, they seemed no longer to be raised in strife. That I felt to be encouraging.

Eventually the two appeared. Neither spoke to the other as they approached us, and yet they gave the impression that all had been said. There was evidently naught of anger between them, nor for that matter did either of them smile.

"Constable Langford," said Sir John, "I have just had a frank exchange of views with Mr. Tolliver. I hold him at fault for failing to be available for further questioning and to testify at the inquest into the death of Nell Darby. He holds me at fault for failing to be specific in this and failing to emphasize the importance of this duty I placed upon him. In any case, he produced the letter that brought him to Bristol and read it to me. He has returned a married man, truly, so there can be no doubt of the nature and success of his mission. He has left the letter with me for further study. And so there is no need to detain him further. Therefore I ask you to accompany him and his good wife to their residence in Long Acre. And you might this time give him a hand with his baggage." Then, turning to Mr. Tolliver: "There. That should satisfy you."

"It does, completely. You are a gentleman, sir."

"Of course I am," said Sir John, a bit snappish. "That is what the 'Sir' before my name is meant to denote. Now, who will go up and fetch Mrs. Tolliver?"

"I will, Sir John," said I.

"Oh? Jeremy? You're back? Good. You should no doubt find her tête-à-tête with Lady Fielding in the kitchen."

With that, I marched up the stairs, reflecting that all I had got from Mr. Tolliver was a sullen nod of recognition. Surely he could have done better. Pausing at the door, I decided to knock out of respect to Lady Fielding's guest. I received from the other side the door a cheery invitation to enter.

After my introduction to Mrs. Tolliver, which I acknowledged with a polite bow, I announced that Sir John and Mr. Tolliver had concluded their conversation.

"You see?" said Lady Fielding to her as she rose. "It lasted no time at all. Jack simply wanted to talk to him. I do hope you can come sometime and visit the Magdalene Home soon. We're so proud of our work there."

Mrs. Tolliver, who in Constable Langford's just estimation was pleasant-looking, rather than pretty, smiled gratefully. "Perhaps a Sunday. I've said I would help in the stall during the week, at least for a little while."

"Perhaps a Sunday then."

There were further urgings and thanks until at last she made for the door. I volunteered to show her down, for the stairs were dark and steep.

She left on her husband's arm, twittering happily at Lady Fielding's kindness to her. Constable Langford followed, struggling under the weight of the larger of the two portmanteaus.

When he heard the door slam after them, Sir John turned to Constable Baker and me and said with obvious annoyance: "He is the most disputatious fellow ever I met. Should have been a lawyer, I daresay. Still, I could not lock him up in the strong room simply because of that, now, could I?"

Next day it was made plain that despite the fact that Sir John had sent Mr. Tolliver on his way, he had not completely surrendered his suspicions. In the morning, he invited me down to his chambers and asked me to reread to him the letter which had brought Mr. Tolliver to Bristol. It was a rather prim response to his advert ("object: marriage") which he had placed in the *Bristol Shipping News*, precisely the sort one might expect from a respectable widow in slightly straitened circumstances. She was frank to say she had not much to offer as a fortune but she did have something. Since the death of her husband, a shipping clerk, two years past, she had managed to support herself as dressmaker to some of the fashionable ladies of the town. She had no children, as both of hers had died in the smallpox which took her husband. She was not young but neither was she old and had no reason to believe she was barren. Although she, too, was interested in marrying again, she would not consider it without some period of acquaintance. If Mr. Tolliver were willing to come and stay a decent length of time, he might come ahead and present himself. There were many inns and lodging houses in the town of Bristol, it being a great seaport. She signed the letter, "Respectfully yours," rather than in some more ornate or personal manner.

"I see nothing wrong in this, Sir John."

"No, but just see when the letter is dated—a full ten days before the Tribble murder—no, eleven. It does not take so long for a letter to reach London—two days, three at the most. His explanation for this discrepancy is that his bride carried the letter about near a week before posting it, so unsure was she that she wished to engage in this venture. He claims to have found it under his door when he reached his dwelling after my interview with him at the scene of the Darby homicide. He said he was so eager to get on to Bristol that he gave no thought to his responsibilities to me but packed his portmanteau in a great hurry and caught the night coach to Bristol at ten."

"But I fail to see—"

"Don't you? If he had indeed caught the night coach, that would have put him on the road at the time of the Tribble murder. Note that his landlord said he left in the direction of Covent Garden. The coach house lies in the opposite direction—but King Street is on the way to Covent Garden, and King Street is where the Tribble woman was murdered and so horribly butchered. Now do you see?"

"Well, yes, but did Mr. Donnelly not put the time of her death hours later than ten o'clock?"

"Exactly! He must have left for Bristol next day in the morning."

I sighed. It seemed unusual for Sir John to build so ingenious a construction of supposition and contingency. Yet was his ingenuity perhaps born of desperation? I knew him to be in profound anxiety that the second murderer be apprehended before he could kill again.

"And so, sir, by your way of thinking, Mr. Tolliver's guilt or innocence hinges upon whether or not he took the night coach to Bristol or traveled next day."

"That may be putting it a bit strong, but if he did not take the night coach, as he says, then I would have good reason to suspect him instead of reaching as I am now. If I catch him in a lie, I will have the truth out of him."

"How do you propose to do that, Sir John?"

"I have thought of another likely flaw in his story. Tell me, have you been by his stall since his disappearance?"

"Yes sir, as you directed—though, I confess, not lately."

"But you market nearby at the other stalls for vegetables?"

"No, I buy generally from those closer by."

"Well, I wish you to go there to his stall and give it a good sniff. If he left in a great hurry, as he says, there would have been meat left inside, all locked up, and it would rot and raise a great stink. There would be complaints. If there is no bad odor, then I have found another discrepancy. I will have Mr. Fuller take him round to the coach house, and let Mr. Tolliver prove that he rode that night coach."

"But—"

"No, Jeremy, do as I say. I know your liking for the fellow, but it is just on seven. He is not likely to be about. He will be lolling in bed with his new wife. All you need do is go to his stall and take a good sniff."

I was off then to perform another task which I found disagreeable. It had been given me, and I would perform it, though not without misgivings. I hurried across Covent Garden, there being little in the way of a crowd to impede my way. The stalls and carts from which the fruits and vegetables would be sold that day were being prepared and arranged for the flood of buyers who would soon fill the immense empty space. There was a good deal of loud talk between competitors, most of it of the bantering sort. The street merchants filled their push-carts and barrows and argued with their suppliers. Thus did the Garden come alive in hoots and shouts.

Mr. Tolliver's stall was at the far end near Henrietta Street, where it was that he had hailed Mr. Bailey and me and informed us of the body he had found in the passage. I had visited it few times since his departure for Bristol and first on an errand I had also found disagreeable. It was as I had seen it then, shut tight and padlocked. I went round it carefully, using my nose freely, sniffing about like some hunting dog on a trail. And indeed I felt rather foolish doing so, particularly as I noticed I had caught the eye of the unpleasant woman who sold vegetables from the stall next his.

"Here, you," yelled she most rudely, "what're you about? If you're thinkin' of grabbin' that stall for your own, it ain't available. Him what rents it has gone off, but he'll be back. You can be sure."

Clearly, she had no memory of me from our earlier conversation. Just as clearly she took me for a possible competitor and wished to keep me away.

"You misunderstand," said I. "I come from the Beak on Bow Street. Have there been any unpleasant smells issuing from this stall?"

"Smells?" said she suspiciously. "What kind?"

Having cited the magistrate as my authority, I made to use it: "Just answer the question, madam."

"No smells," said she. "He's a butcher, he is, though why he ain't in Smithfield with the rest of them I don't know. The truth is, it smells better with him gone than it did when he was here."

That, of course, according to Sir John's reasoning, was disappointing news for me. I thanked her and turned away. Yet as I did, whom should I spy but Mr. Tolliver himself coming my way. He had also seen me; in fact, he gave a careless wave. There was no pretending I had not seen him. I went forward with a greeting, not knowing what else I might do—or more I could say.

"Lookin' for me, were you?" said he. "I s'pose His Majesty has summoned me for another talk. He said he'd not done with me."

"I thought you might be open for customers," said I, avoiding a more serious lie.

"Not today, but tomorrow. I shall have a job of washing up to do. Then I must buy my meat and fix delivery. It takes a day to start up again. But in truth, Jeremy, I'm glad I ran into you."

"Oh? Why is that?"

"I'm afraid I was a bit short with you last night. Short? I gave you no greeting at all! I was put out of sorts by the magistrate. Put plain, he seems not to believe me. Why, I don't know—unless it be something personal."

"Oh, I think not," said I. "It is just that having captured one killer, he came to discover there was another."

"He told me of that, said you were quite the hero in the matter—given a reward and all."

"Half a reward, for there is still one to be caught, and Sir John feels great urgency that he be apprehended before he kill again."

"Well, you can tell him for me that, beggin' his pardon, but I ain't his man."

He growled that out so loudly in his deep voice that the rude woman in the next stall turned to look.

"I believe you, Mr. Tolliver," said I stoutly. "I would not, could not, think ill of you. Nor could Lady Fielding. We have both spoken oft in your behalf."

He grunted a rumbling bass grunt. "I must say she treated my wife well. You may tell Kate for me that I'll not forget that, nor will Maude."

"Maude?" I asked a bit dully. My mind, reader, was at that moment on a much weightier matter. I was laboring to make a decision.

"My wife," said he, explaining the obvious. "Maude Whetsel she was, and Maude Tolliver she is now. I tell you, Jeremy, it's a sad thing to bring a woman you've just married back to a terrible muddle like this."

Then did he shake his great head as one would in a state of awful perplexity. What was to be done? What could be done? In that moment I felt that only I could help him.

"Mr. Tolliver," I burst out, at last giving in to the impulse with which I had been grappling these last moments, "is there any way that you can prove that you were on that night coach to Bristol? That you did not wait till the morrow to travel there?"

He looked at me queerly, as if a veil had been lifted from his eyes and he saw now clearly what he had before only dimly perceived.

"So," said he, "it all comes down to that, does it?"

"Tell me what you told Sir John, if you would, please. What did you do after you left us there on Henrietta Street?"

"Why, I went home."

"Back to your rooms in Long Acre. Continue—all the details, please."

"Well, coming in to my place, I found a letter'd been slipped under my door. It was from—"

"Stay a moment," said I, interrupting. "Do you know how the letter came to be there?"

"Not for certain, no, but I've an idea. I've a neighbor, Mr. Salter, who manages the backstage at the Theatre Royal. A man in a position like that, he gets a fair share of post from all over, so he stops by the letter office two or three times a week to pick up his packet. It's known that I live at the same address, and so the odd letter comes now and then for me they give to him for to pass on. He tucks them under my door."

"Good," said I. "Will you find out from Mr. Salter that he did in fact deliver that letter from Bristol so?"

"I can do that, yes, if he remembers. It was more than a month ago."

"Well and good, you found the letter, you opened and read it. Why did you decide so immediate to go off to Bristol to meet the woman who was to become your wife?"

"Sir John asked me that, too, and I told him polite that it was a personal matter, and I'd keep my own counsel on that. And we argued a bit, but since it's you askin', I'll tell you. I've had terrible luck tryin' to marry again. I came close once—" he gave me a look I would term significant—"yet that went for naught. Mostly it is that women who are respectable want nothing to do with a butcher. I don't know why, for they'll eat a good cut of meat ready enough. Yet I courted a few, and it all come down to that—bein' a butcher was somehow disgusting to them. So I'd put this advert in the *Shipping News* in Bristol where it was I grew up, and I made it plain in it butchering was my trade, and I swear to you, Jeremy, hers was the only letter I got back.

And it was a grand letter, so it was. I saw her as an intelligent woman who'd had terrible misfortune visited upon her, lost her husband and two children, yet managed to support herself and keep her self-respect. And so she is and so she has—she's a grand woman is my Maude. And . . . well . . ." He came to a full stop and looked away.

"And what? Tell me what you were about to say, Mr. Tolliver, please."

"It was what I just came from, finding that girl dead in the passage, that decided me to leave immediate. As I believe I said at the time, I'd seen the girl about—she'd bought from me on an occasion or two—and to see her so, a mere child she was, all crumpled up and murdered, people pawing over her to find her wound—well, it just made me heartsick. This is such a hard city, Jeremy, so little in it of hope and decency, especially for those of her kind. Well, I just wanted to get away from here as quick as ever I could. P'rhaps I should have given thought to Sir John's request that I be here for the inquest, but I'd told all I knew two times over. I just wanted to get away."

He had grown tense in the telling. His hands, both of them, were rolled into big fists; his head was bowed. I remembered his objections when Mr. Bailey had sought the death wound the Raker had inflicted just below her sternum. Indeed Lady Fielding was no bad judge of character, nor was I: Mr. Tolliver could not have murdered Libby Tribble and Poll Tarkin.

"You told Sir John none of this, I suppose?"

"No—just a bit about Maude, that I was eager to meet her."

"When he questions you again, as no doubt he will, you must tell him all of this exactly as you've told me." I saw resistance written in his face, and so I repeated: "Exactly so. But now, please continue. You packed your portmanteau in a great hurry and made ready to leave. Do you know the time you left your rooms to catch the night coach?"

"Well, as near as I can remember, I had a little less than an hour to get there. I've a clock I wind daily, so I can be right certain about that."

Something here was wrong. "But if you had near an hour to get to the coach house," I said, "why were you in such a great hurry? You could walk it easily in a quarter of an hour."

"But I had to get back to my stall here in the Garden. I'd meat inside, and it was all locked up. With no idea when I'd return, I knew the meat would rot. Couldn't have that."

"How did you dispose of it?"

"Why, I just hung it up on the hooks in front. I knew it would be gone by morning. A good two guineas' worth it was, over the counter. That's how eager I was to be away from London. Oh but, Jeremy, you must know that a butcher would never let his meat rot in the stall. God, the stink of it! I'd never be able to sell a piece of meat here in Covent Garden again. But with coming back here, hanging out what was left and all, it was getting on towards ten, though I didn't know the time exact, for I have no pocket timepiece. So I crossed the Garden, which is a risky thing to do at night, and caught a hackney at the Theatre Royal."

"Again," said I, "did you tell Sir John of this? All the details you've given me?"

"I may have told him I caught a hackney. But so far as the rest of it, no. We were mostly arguing about my responsibility to be at the inquest and so on. He rubbed me the wrong way, he did."

"That's as may be," I said, "but when next he interrogates you, you must tell him about your trip back here and how you hung out the meat. Those are very important details."

"They are?" He seemed doubtful.

"Yes, they are."

I said it with all the severity and authority a fifteen-year-old might muster, yet I wondered if I had convinced him. A man who is by nature not very observant, as Mr. Tolliver was not, had little respect even for the details he did remember. And so, continuing, I made every effort to maintain that same attitude of near-hostile severity.

"And so," said I, "you reached the coach house with little time to spare."

"So little," said he, "that I scarce had time to pay my fare and hop aboard."

"I've never ridden any but a hackney coach," said I. "Is a ticket sold to you? Something that might say 'Night Coach to Bristol,' or some such?"

"No, nothing of that kind. You pay your money; they give you a stub with a mark upon it; and you surrender it to the coachman—or as it happened to be, in this case, the driver."

I sensed something here, and so I moved in swiftly upon it: "Why did the driver take your stub, rather than the coachman?"

"The coachman had gone ill, and the driver said he must make the trip alone. I asked him would he like some company up there on the box, and he said indeed he would, a big fellow like me. He asked could I handle a fowling piece, should we run into any trouble on the road. And I said to him I had better in my portmanteau, and I produced my brace of pistols. I had them from the French War, used them, too, though I was a Sergeant Provisioner. We all fought when we were needed, Indians and the like. That's where I learned butchering—in the Army—slaughtering, butchering, I did—"

Again I interrupted: "Stay, stay. Am I to understand that you rode all the way to Bristol next the driver?"

"Indeed I did, and a good enough fellow he was—Ben something. Ben Calverton was his name. We had some talks during the stretches when he walked the horses."

I could scarce believe our good luck. "Why then, he will probably remember you."

"Oh, he'll remember me, right enough."

"Why? Did you meet highwaymen on the way?"

"No, and glad I am for it."

"Why then are you so sure?"

"Because I was unwise enough to tell him my Christian name."

"I don't believe I've ever heard it," said I.

"It's Oliver," said he. "The driver thought it a great joke."

"Oliver . . . Tolliver?" And at that, in spite of my intention to keep a solemn mien, I burst out laughing.

Leaving Mr. Tolliver for the coach house, I guiltily cautioned him to say nothing of our talk to Sir John, yet at the same time charged him to tell his story to the magistrate again exactly as he had told it to me. If my laughter had piqued him, as it seemed to have done, I was indeed sorry, and he had my apology for it. He told me that all seemed to react as I had; that the driver had gone so far as to make up a verse in jest upon his rhyming name—and that, of course, had pleased Oliver Tolliver not at all. "Nevertheless," said he, "he seemed a good sort, and no doubt they can tell you at the coach house when next you might find him about. He drives only at night, to and from Bristol."

And so I walked swiftly through streets now at flood tide with rushing waves of humanity. All that Mr. Tolliver said ill of London was true, of course, but to walk among the common people at such an hour did much to redeem my faith in the great city. It was and is still a place as no other. In fact, it was two cities: a London by day of honest clerks and toilers engaged in all manner of work; and another city at night, peopled by drunkards, thieves, whores, and pimps. Here and now in that sunny morning hour, I saw no sign of that dark London. I could but revel in my naive way that most of the faces I saw in the crowd seemed happy and guileless, and the rest at least resigned and docile.

So was it at the coach house when I went to him who sold the stubs and inquired after Ben Calverton. The fellow at the window did wear a smile and hummed a tune as I approached him.

"Ben Calverton?" said he in response to my query. "Ah yes indeed, young man, he is one of our best, he is—a hero of the road. He makes that long drive to Bristol every other night but one, man must have a backside of iron! None knows the road and its dangers as he does—thrice did highwaymen attempt to stop him, and he drove right through them, twice was gunfire exchanged. Ah yes, young sir, he is one of our best."

"When might he next be available to talk?" I asked. "It is a court matter. I am come from Bow Street."

At that there was the first hint of a frown from him. "You don't mean to say he's got himself into trouble, do you?"

"Oh no, nothing of the kind. It is a matter concerning one of his passengers some time ago."

"Ah—well, in that case, you're in luck. Ben Calverton should arrive from Bristol, God willing, in a quarter of an hour or so." He studied the clock on the wall behind me. "Yes, if nothing untoward has happened along the way, then he should be pulling in just about then."

A short line of passage-purchasers had formed behind me. The fellow at the window signaled to him behind me that he would be done with me in but a moment's time.

"Where might I wait for him?" I asked.

"The best for you," said he, "would be next door at the Coach House Inn. The drivers must give their report upon arrival. But it is Ben's custom to have a glass of ale first thing afterwards. I shall tell him you are there and waiting to talk."

"Tell him it concerns Oliver Tolliver."

"*Oliver Tolliver,* is it?" He laughed merrily. "Such a name! Oh, I'll not forget *that!* Good day to you, young man."

And so into the yard—coaches and horses and passengers waiting. There was a hum of excitement and expectation about the place, such as made me wish I were part of this congregation, portmanteau in hand, about to set off on some long journey to some distant place such as Bristol or Edinburgh, or even over the water to Dublin. The world was such a large place, and I was determined to see my share of it before I was done.

The Coach House Inn was but a modest place for eating and drinking, where travelers or those come to meet them might while away the minutes in a friendly setting. Though it was not near filled, the smoke of tobacco hung heavy in the place, darkening its ill-lit inside so that one might swear it were night outside rather than day. I took a place at the bar near the fireplace, and the barman approached, asking my pleasure.

"Coffee, sir, if you have it."

"We have it. You want that with or without?"

I was puzzled. "With or without what?"

"With or without a flash of lightning—in the cup or on the side."

"Oh, by all means without."

He returned with a steaming cup which cost but tuppence. Indeed it was strong but potable—yet would it be so with gin, as the barman had offered it? How could one drink the two together? It seemed a confusion of purpose.

Once settled I played a game that many play in such situations—looking about at the travelers and attempting to discern who and what they are and where they might be going. All the while I kept a sharp eye upon the door, looking close at those who entered, lest I miss Ben Calverton.

When he did enter, there was no mistaking him. A great wide man was he, though not so tall. He swaggered a bit as he walked and carried a long whip taller than himself, such as all coach drivers use to urge their horses on. Two steps in the door he planted his feet and looked around. Then did he bellow forth, "*Oliver Tolliver,*" and roared a laugh so great it near shook the timbers of the place.

Heads turned, talk halted, and in embarrassment I waved him over to me. There, as if by magic, a tall glass of ale had appeared before he arrived at the bar. Alas, when he did, there was disappointment written upon his round face. I, it seemed, was the cause of it.

"You ain't him," said he. It came from him near in the nature of an accusation.

"No, sir, I'm not," said I, speaking hastily. "It was *about* Mr. Tolliver I wished to talk to you. You see, I—"

He held up his hand, silencing me in the instant. Then, propping his whip against the bar, he took up the glass of ale and drained it in a single draught. He held it up to the barman and another was immediately forthcoming. He seemed about to speak—but no. Again he held up his hand for a long moment, then did he belch magnificently.

"Now," said he, "you wishes to talk to me about him. What is it you wishes to say?"

"First of all, do you remember him?"

"Course I remembers him. Great big strapping sort he is, taller than me by half. He rode up on the coach box all the way to Bristol one night about a month back. Oliver Tolliver! Who could forget a fellow with such a name?" He punctuated that with another laugh of a volume not quite so great. Then did his eyes narrow as he remembered: "That silly nit who sells tickets said it was a court matter. Is he in trouble?"

"Well, he could be, Mr. Calverton—that is, if he cannot prove he took the night coach to Bristol on a particular night and not on the next day."

"Which night? Which day?"

"That's as I hoped you could tell me. When did he ride with you?"

"Oh, now I must give that a bit of thought. I makes so many trips, I do." Then did he glance down at my cup and saw it near empty. "Barman," he called, "gives this lad another cup of what he's drinkin'—coffee, I s'pose it is."

"With or without?" called back the barman.

"With, of course," answered Ben Calverton, ignoring me as he stared off into space. "Now when was that?" he asked himself aloud.

The barman slammed down a full cup and pulled away my empty. I sipped it out of curiosity and found it seemed not so much different in taste as it did hotter in essence. It burned a bit—all the way down to my stomach. It wasn't near as bad as I expected it to be. I took another sip.

"I remembers," said Mr. Calverton, "he was traveling to Bristol to meet up with a lady he hoped to marry. You wouldn't happen to know how that come out, would you?"

"Oh, he married her, sir," I said. "Indeed he did."

"You don't say so! Have you seen her?"

"I have, yes. She seems . . . well, quite nice. She certainly pleases Mr. Tolliver."

"Well, that's the important thing, ain't it?"

He took a deep draught of his ale, this time emptying no more than a quarter of the tall glass.

"What's her name? Olivia?" He laughed again, something in the nature of a cackle. "But that wouldn't rhyme so good, would it? Maybe call her Olivia Tollivia." Again he cackled.

"Her name is Maude," said I, wishing we might be past this.

"That name of his," he persisted. "I teased him about it, I did. After he told me a little about hisself, I made up a little verse about him. I do often makes up verses in my head to pass the time on the road. I think I can call most of it to mind. Want to hear it?"

"Well, I . . ."

He took another gulp of ale, cleared his throat, and in a loud voice he began to recite:

"Oliver Tolliver
Rides on his way to Bristol,
And by his side he has him a pistol.
"Oliver Tolliver
By the light of the moon,
Off to Bristol to win him a boon.
"Oliver Tolliver
A butcher by trade,
He travels west to find him a maid.
"Oliver Tolliver
He don't give a damn
For—"

Then, of a sudden, he stopped and brought his fist down upon the bar.

"By God, that's it—'By the light of the *moon!*'"

"Sir?" He had me confused. "I don't quite understand."

"Why, I remembers it now like it was just the night past. There was a great big full moon that night. Oh, I remembers it well—what you call a 'highwayman's moon.' That's why I was right glad to have that big fellow Tolliver and his pistols up there beside me, with my coachman gone sick with the shits. Those out on the scamp do love a full moon, as you may know."

"So it was the night of the full moon? You're sure of that?"

"As sure as I can be. Not the last night of the full moon, mind. That was All Hallows Eve, as any fool knows. I don't know the number of the month. You could get it in any almanac, but it was the night of the full moon a little more than a month past."

"Would you be willing to swear to that in court?"

"Why not? It's so, ain't it?"

Finding an odd piece of paper in my pocket, I wrote on the back of it his name and the number of his dwelling place, which he gave me with directions to his room. Then, forgetting its potency, I took a great swig of coffee and made ready to leave.

"When you see Oliver Tolliver next," said Ben Calverton, "tell him I wishes him good fortune. He may ride beside me any time he likes, and I'll not tease him more about his name."

I thanked him. He clapped me hard upon my back and sent me on my way.

It was not until I stepped out into the coach yard that I felt the full impact of the gin I had imbibed so freely. I felt perspiration upon my brow at a time when the rest of me felt the nip of the November morning. My head was all at once both sluggish and light. It was indeed the strangest set of sensations ever I had felt—nothing at all like the time or two I had drunk a glass of wine too many. I set off for Bow Street, knowing the way perfectly well, only to discover, after walking half the length of a street, that I had set off in the wrong direction. I stood there befuddled, seeking my bearings, buffeted by the crowd which flowed round me, forward and back.

This would never do, of course! Giving some thought to the matter, I turned about and retraced my steps. I found the way back by the way I had come, though giving a wide berth to Mr. Tolliver's corner of the Garden. To my mind I'd spent enough time talking to him that morning and far too much with Ben Calverton—though with both it was time well spent. Sir John would have expected me back in minutes, and I was aware I had been gone well over an hour. Not only that, but I was returning in a state of less than complete sobriety. My feet were working better and took me where I wished to go. My brains had cleared sufficiently so that I realized that I had now testimony that would satisfy Sir John.

When I presented it to him, however, he seemed less than happy with it. I explained to him that I had gone to the butcher's stall and smelled nothing of rot or stink. But thinking to help things along, I took it upon myself to go to the coach house and inquire when the night drivers might be available for questioning—omitting my conversation with Mr. Tolliver, of course. By chance, said I, one Ben Calverton was available, and he did confirm that Mr. Tolliver had been beside him on the coach box all the way to Bristol on the night of the full moon in early October.

"Did you prompt him?" asked the magistrate.

"I did not, sir. No matter how I may have wished to do so, I did not."

"Ben Calverton, is it? I take it you got from him how he may be reached?"

"Yes, Sir John."

"Well," he said, "though you have exceeded your brief, you brought back information of some importance. For that I commend you." (It was said, reader, in a manner most half-hearted.) "That you return, however, smelling of gin I find less commendable."

"I can explain that, sir. When I—"

He raised his hand, silencing me. "Another time, perhaps. For now I think it best you go upstairs and ask Lady Fielding what needs be done there."

I learned that later in the day Sir John had sent Mr. Fuller to bring in Mr. Tolliver that he might be interrogated again. I, at the time, was occupied scrubbing up my attic room. Lady Fielding had noted on her nursing visits to me that conscientious as I might be in cleaning and scrubbing the rest of the house, I had let my own little dwelling place fall into a fearful state of neglect. And it was true enough: dust had collected in curls in the corners; there was a fine coat of it covering those books stacked against the wall which I had read; cobwebs had collected against the ceiling. I had never noticed until she called it to my attention. Thus my day was filled. I had no knowledge of Mr. Tolliver's visit until Sir John mentioned it at dinner.

As he chewed on a morsel of meat from Annie's well-spiced stew, he said without preamble: "Mr. Tolliver came in again today to be questioned."

Lady Fielding and I were suddenly frozen, spoons halted in mid-passage to our mouths.

"He was more forthcoming this time and not near so disputatious. In short, he was more cooperative."

We two looked one at the other.

Sir John continued chewing until, satisfied, he swallowed. "He is no longer suspect," said he, then dipped his spoon again.

As the days went by, tension mounted once again. The capture and swift trial of the Raker had provided a temporary release. Yet word got out on the streets that there were two homicides, and them the bloodiest, to which he had refused to admit. One by one, the whores took the shelter of the gin mills and dives and began again to be more careful about those whom they accepted as customers. Lady Fielding reported that even after a spate of defections, the Magdalene Home for Penitent Prostitutes was once more filled to its capacity.

The Bow Street Runners, too, had returned to the routine required earlier by Sir John. They carried lanterns about with which they were to look in all the dark corners. In addition to his club, each carried a brace of pistols. Only one accommodation was made: Mr. Bailey, speaking for the men, had registered a complaint to the magistrate that wearing a cutlass in its heavy scabbard impeded them so that they would be unable to run should they be forced to give chase; Sir John, giving due weight to the argument, allowed that the wearing of a cutlass might be considered optional. To a man they opted to turn them in to Mr. Baker.

Towards the end of the week, I was visited by Mr. Donnelly. I had glimpsed him below on his way to see Sir John sometime earlier, and so I knew that the two had had quite a lengthy conversation. With me, he had no need to spend so much time. He found me polishing silver with Annie—or, more accurately, polishing silver under her direction; indeed she could be as exacting as her mistress in matters pertaining to her kitchen. She greeted him right pertly with a curtsey and a smile. I, who was better acquainted with him, was a little less effusive in my greeting and certainly less flirtatious.

"I thought, Jeremy," said he, "that I might take another look at that cut at the back of your head. Perhaps we can make it the last."

"It would please me greatly to be rid of this great bandage," said I. "Should we go to my bedroom?"

"No, here in the kitchen should do well—that is, if you've no objection, Mistress Annie?"

Unused to being deferred to, she could only mumble something in the negative. She stepped back, blushing.

Carefully he unwound the great turban I had worn on my head for the last several days. Then just as carefully he examined the cut.

"Does it cause you pain, Jeremy?"

"Oh no, nothing at all."

"And what about the effects of the concussion? Any giddiness?"

"No, none. Well . . . there was gin poured into my coffee unbeknownst to me. That left me giddy for a bit."

"At your age? I daresay it would. You may tell me that story on some other occasion." Then did he add, "Soon."

Mr. Donnelly questioned me on all the other possible ill-effects I might feel following a concussion. And I truthfully answered in the negative to each one. Then, after washing the cut with gin, he asked for scissors, cut off a bit of my hair, and made a plaster which he applied to the cut. Through it all, Annie had watched, quite fascinated.

"There," said he, "that should do you. In no time at all, the plaster can be removed."

Packing up his bag, he frowned as if a moment in thought.

"Jeremy," said he, "I wonder if you might be my guest at dinner evening after next—I thought perhaps at the Cheshire Cheese where once we dined before. I've asked Sir John, and he has no objections. There are some things I'd like to discuss with you."

"With me? Why, yes, certainly, Mr. Donnelly."

"Good. I shall be by for you at about seven."

With that and no more he bade us both goodbye in taking his leave.

"Well," said Annie, quite consumed with envy, "dinner with the doctor. Ain't that a grand thing?"

"Yes, quite an astonishment," said I.

"What might he have to discuss with you?"

"I've no idea, none at all."

Although, because of the sordid nature of the Raker's crimes, every effort had been made by Sir John and the Lord Chief Justice to shield him from the public eye, the law called for his execution by hanging, and custom demanded that it be done publicly at Tyburn. They feared riot. He was, at least in legend, so well known and was so loathed by the populace, that when hanging day came (which followed the next after Mr. Donnelly's visit) all precautions were taken that he be given safe passage from Newgate to the triangular gallows. If the crowd were large and unmanageable, he could be pulled down from the cart and trampled to death or his body torn asunder. Therefore, in addition to the usual cavalry escort, who made their way with sabres drawn, there was a squad of foot immediately surrounding the cart, and they marched with muskets at port arms and bayonets fixed.

I, having long before promised Sir John I would attend no public hangings, was not present—nor indeed would I have wished to be. There is to my mind no amusement and little edification to be gained watching a man in the throes of strangulation at the end of a rope. However, my chum Jimmie Bunkins, who is not in the least squeamish, did attend the ceremony and brought back a report which he gave me following our instruction from Mr. Perkins, which I had that day resumed.

"Well," said Bunkins, "I went to Tuck 'em Fair this noonday to see the Raker get crapped, and first off there weren't no riot."

"I'm relieved to hear it," said I.

"There should've been, 'cause I never seen such a rum crowd with such queer intentions. They covered the whole hill, from the gallows back as far as you could see. There was some stones and shit-bits heaved at the cart, but as many hit the rum tom pat and the two others who were set to get crapped with him as hit the Raker. But each time there was a move at the cart to stop it or to pull the Raker down, those who tried would get a whack with the flat of a sabre or nudged with the point of a bayonet. So that way they brought him to the gallows. And the horse soldiers and the foot soldiers made a ring round him as they got him and the two others off the cart and marched him up the stairs.

"And when he shows, there's a great roar that went up from the crowd. I was up front, on'y I wished I wasn't, for first of all every drab and bawd in Covent Garden was up there with me, screamin' the foulest curses they knew. Oh, he heard 'em, he heard 'em fair. And you know what he does? He puts a great big smile on his ugly mug, like he's never had such a grand time before. He's standin' there, grinnin' away like an eejit, and the crap merchant is circlin' the noose round his head. And then he starts to do a little dance on the floor of the gallows, like he's tellin' them he'll soon be doin' a dance like that up in the air. So the rope was set, and he shouted out somethin' none could hear for the screamin' of the whores. Then, just before he went up, he lets fly this great gob of snotty spittle, and it hits the whore next me in the face. He got her with a rum shot, and she the loudest of all, I swear. So that was the other reason I wished I'd stood back in the crowd. I got a bit of the splatter on me coat."

"Did he take long to die?" I asked, having oft wondered if death for Mariah had been immediate.

"Not long," said Bunkins, as a connoisseur of such matters. "Yet he jumped around right queer on the rope. Though he was plain daft, I give him credit. He died damned hard and bold as brass."

I confess, reader, that I had wished his dying prolonged.

"What then are you two jawin' about?"

It was Constable Perkins spoke to us, descending the stairs from his rooms above the stable, dressed proper and wearing his red waistcoat, ready for his night's work. We three would walk together to Bow Street.

"About the Raker," said Bunkins. "He crapped today on Tyburn."

"He did, did he? And good riddance." Then, coming up to us, he fixed me with a look and asked: "You, Jeremy, how do you feel about it?"

"Good riddance," said I.

Thus is it so that when merciful principles are challenged by bitter personal experience, our principles must sometimes give way to the desire for vengeance.

Though Mr. Gabriel Donnelly and I had talked of many things along our way to the Cheshire Cheese, and many more once we were within and at our dinner, I was quite sure we had not touched upon those matters he had said he wished to discuss. I had indeed told him the story of how I had come to drink a cup of coffee with a "flash of lightning." And so was I able to tell him, too, how Mr. Tolliver's rhyming name had made him memorable to Ben Calverton and removed the cloud of suspicion that hung above the butcher's head.

And for his part, he told me further of his experiences in medical studies at the university of Vienna; amusing stories they were, as had been those he had told at table. It occurred to me that perhaps he wished to offer me an apprenticeship to him in medicine. If he were to do that, what should I say? I had not for some time talked with Sir John about my hope to read law with him. Perhaps he had forgotten—or worse still, hoped I had. Medicine I held to be a great calling, nor could I ask for a better master than Mr. Donnelly, but nevertheless I had a great longing for the law.

At last, midway through our meal, he began rather abruptly to explain.

"No doubt you wonder, Jeremy, why it is I've asked you to dine and what this great matter is that I said I wished to talk about."

"Well, yes, sir, I have."

"It is simply this: I shall be leaving London next week for Portsmouth to apply for a berth on a Navy ship as surgeon."

"Mr. Donnelly, you would give up your practice?"

At that, he smiled a sad smile. "What practice?" said he. "I have been here in London near three months and have had only the autopsy work that Sir John has generously given me. You have been my patient, as has Mr. Goldsmith. I regret to say, by the bye—and let it be in confidence—that he is not a well man. But that is neither here nor there. The bald truth is that I simply lack the funds to maintain a practice in this city until it becomes profitable; and indeed it may never become profitable. Perhaps there are simply too many medicos here, though indeed their quality is abominably low. Perhaps it is, as Mr. Goldsmith has suggested, that there is an inbred prejudice amongst the English against the Irish. He himself, during his years of struggle, applied for one paid position after another as surgeon or physician, and he said that all that was needful for prompt rejection was that he show them his unmistakably Irish face."

I knew not what to say. Having grown used to his presence these months, I was now sad to think he would no longer be about. I had confidence and trust in him of a particular nature that I had not in others. He was like a much older brother to me, or an uncle. Or so it had seemed to me when he so willingly obliged my wish to have Mariah properly buried.

All I could do in these immediate circumstances was lower my eyes and say: "I shall miss you greatly, sir." My sad tone of voice, I'm sure, conveyed far more than my inept words could do.

"Had I not gone larking off to Lancashire," he continued, "in pursuit of that widow, things might have been different. When first I came to London two years past, I had quite a sum laid aside from my years as a Navy surgeon. I might have managed then had I stuck it out in the city. Yet off I went and spent it all a-courting. I was not so much in love with her as in love with myself and my own ambition. Ah well, let my experience be a lesson to you, Jeremy. Vanity will always exact a price."

"But surely, sir, you've no reason to feel ashamed. The loss was Lady Goodhope's and not your own."

"Well," said he, "let's not dwell upon it, for my reason in taking you aside like this to tell you of my intended departure was to give you a few words of advice. Sir John already knows of my wish and approves it. We have discussed you between us.

"First of all, I took the liberty—and you may indeed feel it was a liberty on my part—of informing Sir John of how those five guineas of your reward were spent. He was quite touched by your action, as I of course also was. Yet he was concerned that you had involved yourself so deeply with a girl of the streets without telling him of it. He wanted to know if there were any possibility you had been infected with a disease of that sort, and I told him there was none, that your attachment to her had not been of that sort. He was relieved, of course, but said that all the same he wished that you had been more forthcoming. Then I made bold to tell him that I believed the difficulty in communication lay in your ambiguous state in his household. You are not a servant, but neither are you an adopted son. He told me then that he often felt towards you as a father, if indeed he knew how a father felt, that he could hardly want a better son, and that he had given serious consideration to adopting you formally. But he explained that he and Lady Fielding still hoped to have children and talk of a baronetcy for him had been floated about. That, of course, is an hereditary title, and I'm sure you can see the inherent difficulties there, Jeremy—if indeed they do have children."

"Of course," said I, with a serious nod.

"So my first bit of advice to you is that you consider yourself informally adopted. He would have it so, I'm sure. Talk between father and son at your age and older is never easy and, because of your situation, may no doubt be harder still."

"He is sometimes difficult to approach," said I, "often intimidating."

"I'm sure that's true, especially lately, for he has been near sick with worry over these murders in Covent Garden. But you must try to approach him on things that are important to you. When he opens a matter for discussion, if you have views or objections, then voice them—respectfully, of course. It should not always be 'Yes, Sir John.'"

"I have tried," said I. "It is not always so easy to get him to listen to what I have to say."

"Then keep trying."

"Did . . ." I hesitated. "Did he say anything in your talks with him of his intention to have me read law with him? He talked of it in the beginning, yet he has said nothing about it for over a year."

"Then you should open the matter with him. Discuss it. Ask if and when you may begin."

That silenced me for a bit. The thought of bringing such a matter up to Sir John was downright indigestible. I chewed hard upon it, harder even and longer than I chewed upon the chop that lay on my plate.

"But now," said Mr. Donnelly, "for my second, and I believe, last bit of advice. You'll recall, Jeremy, that when you told me of your relations with Mariah, I countered with a story of my own in which I was duped into giving money to a girl of the streets in Dublin, money which I ultimately stole from my father's shop to provide. It was painful for me to tell such a tale upon myself, and in blurting it out as I did, I may have left the wrong impression with you. I would not have you believe that because it was so that one time with me that it is always so with unfortunates who tell you similar sad tales. You allowed that it may have been Mariah's intent to use you so—but we cannot be sure certain of that. And certainly in her case, it is not for us to judge.

"There is so much misery in this world, Jeremy, and so little charity, that I would not have you harden your heart to anyone. As you grow to be a man, you will hear many tales of misfortune and injustice from individuals, and some may prove to be false, told simply to gain a shilling or some favor. But the next tale you hear may be true, and the innocence you perceive in the teller may be as real as real can be. So let us help as we can and not look too deeply into motives."

It struck me sad to think that I should be losing the companionship of this good man in a week, or perhaps even less.

When, having completed our meal, we rose to leave the Cheshire Cheese, I thought how much I liked this place and the life in this great city of London. I remembered my first meal here with Mr. Donnelly when we had been put upon by James Boswell, now the constant companion of Dr. Johnson. And I wondered when I, in my good bottle-green coat, would eat here next and in whose company. I glanced up at the ceiling timbers darkened by tobacco smoke and wood smoke, then around me at the company of men (not a woman amongst them) seated at the rough tables; and then did I look further ahead to a time when I, as a lawyer, might visit with my client to discuss the handling of some perplexing matter. I should be known here, have a favorite table, perhaps that one by the fireplace. Then would I truly take part in London life. Forgive me, reader, for deviating from the true course of my tale, but these dreams of my adolescence haunt me still and do sometimes ask expression.

As we left, Mr. Donnelly and I paused just outside the door—perhaps only to breathe deeply of the pleasant November night air. But as we stood, both of us at once became aware of a certain muffled roar which persisted and seemed to grow louder as we listened. We exchanged curious looks. What was that ominous sound?

Then did a single figure emerge from Butchers Row, moving as fast as his legs would carry him. He sped past us into Fleet Street, where two men confronted him and attempted to block his way; he lunged at them, swinging his arm in a wide arc as an object in his hand glinted; the men fell back, throwing themselves out of his way.

From Butchers Row came a great crowd of people, men and women, some just hobbling along, shouting as they went: "Stop! Stop him! Murderer! Murderer!" This, their voices commingled, was the great roar we had heard but moments before.

"The hue and cry is raised," said I to Mr. Donnelly, my own voice raised to a shout above their many. Then, realizing that what glinted in the light from the streetlamp must have been a knife, I shouted, "It must be the Covent Garden Killer!"

I began to pull away from Mr. Donnelly. He grasped at my sleeve. Then, as the crowd passed, I spied Mr. Benjamin Bailey, first of the Bow Street Runners, quite near the lead of the pursuit. I knew I must join him.

"It is Mr. Bailey!" I shouted, as if that were to explain all, and I jerked loose of the hold on my sleeve and ran as one might to catch the very Devil himself.

I, not having been so long at the chase, gained swiftly upon those in the lead, Mr. Bailey still among them. I noted that he had taken to the walkway, and following his example, I did the same. I soon saw why. The mass of people was confronted by a coach drawn by a team of two. The horses reared, their hooves flailing the air. The coach driver fought to master them and bring them under control; the footman could do little more than hold on tight, to keep from tumbling. Those in the street scattered, their cries of "Murder!" now screams of alarum. Thus was the number, though still considerable, depleted. I raced through this great hurly-burly, safe on the walkway, with not so many now between me and Mr. Bailey. Stretching my stride, I gained upon him. Farther away, though again not so far as before, I could see the shadowy figure of him we pursued.

Now, such a crowd as this is nothing more nor less than a swift-moving mob. I had seen in the instant why the constable had put himself at the forefront of the pursuit. When they had run the fugitive down, as surely they would, Mr. Bailey would have to protect him against the fury of the mob. I was determined to lend him my help in this, and so I pressed on, gaining step by step.

We ran the length of Fleet Street. I was close upon Mr. Bailey and a few others, when something altogether strange occurred. I had but for a moment taken my eyes from the object of the chase when, as I looked back, I found I had lost him completely. I was not the only one. Mr. Bailey slowed, as did the three or four others with him. I caught them up. More followed behind me.

We were just at the site of the old Fleet River Bridge. A proper bridge it had been until, but a few years past, the river had been arched and paved over all the way to the Thames; it was now not much more than a rise in the road. It was here the fugitive had disappeared. The men stood panting, looking in all directions. I went to Constable Bailey.

"Jeremy!" said he, startled, when I tapped him on the back. Fighting to catch his breath, he managed to tell that there could be no doubt that the man we had pursued was the Covent Garden murderer. "He was seen in the act in an alley off Catherine Street—" He took a gulp of air. "I left Constable Cowley with the body and joined the chase."

"Where could he be?"

"No idea . . . He . . . he was lost once on the way . . . then seen again. He cut him who tried to hold him and escaped . . . right down the Strand."

"Who is he? Do you know him?"

"Never got close enough to—" He broke off, having got his bearings at last. "Where are we?"

"The end of Fleet Street."

"At the old bridge, ain't that it?"

"Why, yes, sir."

"Then could there be only one place he had got to. Come along."

I followed him through what was now a growing crowd; they milled about, muttering, grumbling, and quite without direction. He led the way down Fleet Market, which ran the course of the old river as far as Holbourn, and as he went he kept his eyes cast down to the ground. There, among the shuttered stalls, he found what he sought—a trap door situated tight in the street with paving stones all about it. He looked up at me and nodded, having tried it just enough to know that it would open without resistance.

"Jeremy, you see that woman over there with the lantern? See if you can bring her over without causing much notice."

I went to her and recognized her from the Garden, a greengrocer from whom I'd bought in the past. She acknowledged me.

"Terrible thing, ain't it, young sir? He do seem to have got away."

"Well, we shall see," said I. "Perhaps you could step over this way? Constable Bailey would like to speak with you."

"With me?"

"Just for a moment."

She nodded and made no argument as I brought her to Mr. Bailey.

"Madam," said he with a polite bow, "I am Constable Benjamin Bailey of Bow Street."

"I reco'nize you," said she.

"I have need of your lantern."

"You'll not have it. It's my on'y one."

As if to make plain her refusal, she swung the lantern round and held it behind her back. Yet she did not walk away.

"Madam," said he, "it is only for to borrow, and if it is not returned, you may have a better one from Bow Street."

"A better one?"

"Larger, anyway. You have my promise on that."

"Well . . ." She hesitated. "Awright." And she handed it over.

He took it, a small hand-lantern that in truth shed little illumination, and handed it to me. Then he threw open the trap door and let the light shine below. I heard the flow of water.

"It ain't much," said he, "but I be damned if I'll go down there with no light at all. I left my lantern with Cowley. Now, Jeremy, I'm going to climb down there—it's the Fleet River is what it is—and when I reach the last rung on the ladder, you hand me down the lantern. Understood?"

"Yes, sir," said I.

He pulled out both pistols and handed me one. Then he took his club and clamped it between his teeth. Holding one pistol in his hand, he fitted himself carefully through the trap door, found the ladder with his feet, and began his descent. Then did I come to a most impulsive decision. Laying down pistol and lantern, I tore off my fine bottle-green coat and tossed it to the woman who watched all quite fascinated.

"Take this coat to Bow Street," said I to her, "for I am going down there, too."

Mr. Bailey shook his head emphatically, unable to speak for the club in his mouth, yet I followed him down. I hooked the lantern with the thumb of my left hand; only so was I able to proceed with the pistol in my right. I went down as careful as could be, yet when I descended below the level of the ground, and the mephitic odor of the river rose about me, I was near overcome. Whether my hand or my foot slipped, I know not, yet I landed with both feet and a splash into the water below. I held tight to the lantern, but in righting myself with my other arm, I wet the pistol.

It was quite like I had jumped into a chamber pot. Thank God, it was not over my head, but high enough. The water was well above my waist, nigh to my chest. To Mr. Bailey, who was much taller, it came only at waist level. He sloshed over to me, club and pistol now in each hand.

"Let's be thankful you didn't douse the lantern," he whispered. "You're down here, so let's proceed. Before you hit the water, I heard splashing up in the direction of Holbourn. Come along. You hold the lantern high."

There were now no sounds of splashing, no sounds of any sort except for the soft scurrying of rats. I looked about and detected movement on a kind of shelf that ran along the narrow course of the river on either side. We moved down its center where it was deepest. Though the Fleet was a sewer, it was also a river, and we struggled somewhat against its current.

Along the way, at intervals of about three rods, there were large columns on either side, abutments which supported the arches overhead. It became evident that it was behind one of these that Mr. Bailey expected to find our quarry. He slowed at each one, and was most especially watchful, directing me silently to swing the lantern left and right to illuminate the dark shadows at the far side of each of these columns.

So we had come to ten or perhaps a dozen of these but, more importantly, had just left one behind us, when close to our rear I heard a sound, though not a great one, and I whirled about. There, no more than six feet away, was the figure of a man, rising from the water. He stumbled towards me. I got my pistol up and fired point-blank. It flashed weakly, misfiring from its dip in the water. Yet he faltered before he lunged at me with his hand forward—though I cannot say I saw it, I knew somehow that it must hold a knife. I lept back and to my left, away from Mr. Bailey, and the blade did miss me, though by no more than the width of three fingers. At just that moment Mr. Bailey delivered him a great clout on the back of his neck; it should have laid him low, but it did not. He turned to the constable, and jabbed with the knife in his direction, which left his hand exposed. Mr. Bailey brought his club down upon his wrist, knocking the knife from his grasp down into the water. Still he came forward like the madman he was, seeking to overwhelm that much larger man with no more than his bare hands. His back was to me. I struggled forward against the current, thinking to bring down the pistol barrel upon him. Yet before I quite reached him, Mr. Bailey delivered one final, skull-crushing blow to his head. The man fell flat into the water and sank beneath it.

"Jeremy," cried the constable, "are you safe? Did he cut you?"

"No, I'm right enough. He missed close, though."

Mr. Bailey tucked away his club, still holding the unfired pistol; then did he reach down to retrieve the body of our assailant. He felt about.

"He ain't here," said he.

"The current," said I, "the current must have moved him."

I went splashing back, searching with my feet, and finally came in contact with the body about six feet or more from where he had fallen. I planted my foot firmly and held the body in place.

"Here he is," I called.

Together we lifted him from the water. I held the lantern to his face, yet the wet hair that obscured his features made it impossible to make them out. Mr. Bailey put his hand to the chest for a long moment, then shook his head. We had no choice but to drag him back between us the way we had come.

As we pulled him along, Mr. Bailey remarked: "I don't know was it my blow to his head, or drowning that killed him." After a bit, he added: "Think of drowning in all this piss and shit."

"He swam below in it to get behind us."

"Desperate men do desperate things. Or so Sir John says."

Some minutes later, I made out the dim shaft of light from the open trap door through which we had descended into this hellish place.

"He went at you first, Jeremy, because you had the lantern."

"The pistol misfired from the wetting I gave it falling off the ladder. All I could do was jump away from him."

"Aye, but you kept hold the lantern. In the dark he might have cut me proper. I couldn't have done without you, lad."

Somehow, pushing and pulling, we managed to get the inert form up the ladder to the surface. I, who had done the pushing, emerged last of all. To my surprise, a group had gathered in anticipation of our return, among them constables Cowley and Picker. They paid me little attention, for they had laid the body out upon the pavement and had pushed back the hair. Two good-sized Bow Street lanterns were held over him. Uneasily, I looked carefully at those peering down at the dead man and noted the absence of the woman to whom I had entrusted my beautiful bottle-green coat. Yet before I could worry overmuch about it, I heard the constables exclaiming.

"By God, Mr. Bailey," said young Cowley, "look who you brought up. It's the medico, that one who was an Army surgeon!"

"Damn me if it ain't! See here, Jeremy, it's Amos Carr!"

I pushed forward and saw, to my amazement, that Mr. Bailey was right. It was indeed Amos Carr.

TWELVE

In Which I Find
and Recover My
Bottle-Green Coat

There was great surprise and no little consternation when it was bruited about Covent Garden that Dr. Amos Carr was the perpetrator of those bloodiest homicides. Sir John Fielding himself was shocked quite beyond belief until he did order a search of the doctor's apartment and surgery which resulted in grisly discoveries that incriminated the medico *ex post facto.* There were bloodied clothes discovered in his wardrobe, yet worse was found in a cabinet in his surgery: there in a glass of gin discolored slightly to a brown tint were found two eyeballs—the missing eyes of Libby Tribble, as Gabriel Donnelly attested.

Mr. Donnelly also helped Sir John gain some understanding of what had turned Amos Carr in such a devious direction. He explained that Dr. Carr had the pox, which Sir John had, of course, not known; and further, that in the last stages of that dreadful disease the brain is sometimes infected with results quite unpredictable. It could be, he suggested, that Dr. Carr, perhaps for good reason, believed himself to have been infected by a prostitute, and that his diseased brain urged him to take revenge upon this unfortunate class of women. Had he not been spied in the act of mutilating the corpus of his third victim, he would probably have continued upon his murderous course as long as he lived (which, considering the advanced state of his disease, might not have been so very long). As later quoted to me by Mr. Donnelly, Sir John's comment upon all this was that, absent any other explanation for those otherwise incomprehensible crimes, he would have to accept Mr. Donnelly's, for there could be no doubt that Amos Carr was the man hauled out of that sewer, nor of the incriminating nature of the gruesome evidence found in his place of dwelling.

As for me, save for the tribute paid me by Mr. Benjamin Bailey, I received little praise for accompanying him down into the Fleet. Mr. Donnelly, who was among that group gathered round the body of Amos Carr, chastised me for having put myself in environs so insalubrious. And once the constables had done marveling at the identity of the corpus, they stood well away from it and from Mr. Bailey and me, for the odor of the sewer offended them. They were greatly dismayed when their captain ordered them to carry the body away.

Lady Fielding would not allow me upstairs until I had bathed and changed my clothes. She sent the necessaries down with Annie who held her nose in appreciation of my befouled state. Yet I did as told, off in some dark corner, washing well with soap as I shivered in cold water. As I did so, Mr. Bailey gave his report to Sir John. When he had concluded and I was fit once more for human society, Sir John took me aside and told me that it was "a brave and foolish thing" I had done and suggested that next time I was tempted to act on impulse I was to take a moment to consider the potential dangers.

He mentioned, too, that I might be entitled to some share of the ten-guinea reward for the second murderer, but I told him I wanted no part of it. I said Mr. Bailey had done all; that I had merely held the lantern and kept out of his way. That seemed to satisfy him. In the end, however, the constable did share his reward with one Albert Mundy, carpenter by trade; Mr. Mundy it was who'd spied Amos Carr bending over his last victim and ripping at her body with his knife and then did raise the hue and cry. There was general agreement that he was entitled to something, though certainly no more than the three guineas he got.

The good woman who did our wash was summoned next day, and she did look most doubtfully at my best breeches and shirt which I had, the night before, tossed upon the back privy to dry. They were stained and stinking and gave little promise of ever coming clean. Thus much she said, but pledged herself to do what she could. I gave her what words of encouragement I could, saw her on her way, and then set off for Covent Garden to find what had become of my bottle-green coat.

I found the greengrocer where she had always been in the past, settled in her stall, lustily calling out the quality of her stock to all and sundry. As I approached, I saw no sign of the coat. Since I had brought with me her lantern, I had thought to make a fair trade of it. I could but wonder why, failing to bring my coat to Bow Street as I had asked her to do, she had also failed to bring it to her stall. Surely she did not suppose I could have forgotten about it.

I presented myself and said to her rather sternly: "I have come with your lantern."

She left off her shouting and regarded me somewhat in disappointment. "I thought I was to get another in its place—bigger."

"Only if this one was lost."

"Well . . ." She shrugged and took the lantern from me.

"Where is my coat?"

"Ain't it been brought to you?" She turned away in a manner a bit shamefaced, or so it seemed to me.

"No, it has not."

She sighed. "Here's the truth of it, young sir. Soon as you went down the hole, a young fella comes up to me, and he tells me he is your friend, and he will keep the coat for you. I tell him no, that I'm to take it to Bow Street, and what does he do then but grab at it and says that he will take it there. Well, I held on awright, and he gives me a great shove, and I lands on my arse and lets loose your fine coat. By the time I got to my feet, he had got away, quite disappeared into the crowd, he did. I went after him, lookin' for help, and who did I come upon but a constable. I started to tell him how that fella said he was your friend just took your coat and ran, but all he wanted to hear about was why I had it, how you and the other constable went down into the Fleet. He would have naught but I show him the hole. Then another constable come along, and I showed them both. They fell to arguin' amongst themselves as to whether they should follow you down and give help. That was when I walked away and went home to my bed."

There was little I could say. Her story had the ring of truth. And had I not wondered how Constable Cowley and Constable Picker happened to be there waiting for us when we emerged from that foul underworld?

The disappointment must have been plain in my face, for she did touch my arm consolingly and said: "I'm right sorry, young sir. My on'y hope was p'rhaps he truly was a friend of yours and would return it, though I could not imagine that such as you would have that sort for a friend."

"What sort was he? Could you describe him? Had you seen him before?"

"Oh, you sees so many here in the Garden, wanderin' about. He never bought from me, of that I'm sure, else I'd remember him. He was about your size, I'd say, but older 'n you, and he had a right nasty look on him—why, I was doubtful of him right from the start."

"Was he well-dressed?"

"Not a bit of it. Not shabby, mind, but the coat he wore weren't near so grand as that one you gave me for safe-keepin'."

I'd held some faint hope that Bunkins might have taken the coat, though I could in no wise imagine that he would treat a woman so rude. And since joining Mr. Bilbo, he was as finely dressed as any young gentleman you might meet in Vauxhall Gardens. Nor could any say that Bunkins had a nasty look. No, not Jimmie Bunkins.

"I am right sorry it happened so," said she.

"I believe you," said I. With a shrug, I thanked her and started off on my way to Bow Street.

It seemed my coat had been seized by a common thief who had first tried simply to cozen her with a lie. That evening I sought out the two constables in question, and they confirmed the greengrocer's story. I wrung an apology from each that they had considered the stolen coat to be of so little moment. Their apologies, of course, helped little to retrieve my coat.

At my next opportunity, I brought up the matter to Bunkins and Constable Perkins. That came as we walked together part of the distance from Mr. Perkins's stable-top dwelling off Little Russell Street before parting to our separate destinations. I told them what the woman in Covent Garden had said of the thief, and attempted to describe the coat to them.

"But," said I, remembering, "you've seen it, Mr. Perkins. Do you recall? I was wearing it that day we walked together and discovered the body of what we took to be the Raker's first victim."

"Ah, so you were," said he, "and a handsome coat it was. As I remembers it, 'twas green."

"Dark green," said I, "bottle green, they call it."

"Dark green, is it?" said Bunkins. "And does it have white trim?"

I looked at him in surprise. "Indeed it does—about the pockets and the buttonholes. Have you seen such a coat?"

"It might be that I have," said he, "and worn by a joe you know, old chum."

"Oh? And who might that be?"

"Why not see if we can find this partic'lar joe? We may then find your toggy, as well."

And so Bunkins, saying nothing more, remained with us past that point on our walk where by custom he would have left us for the grand house in St. James Street wherein he dwelt with Mr. Bilbo and his company. We had not gone far thus together when he suggested that perhaps he and I might go round about the regular route to Bow Street and take a turn for Bedford Street.

"But you, Mr. Perkins," said he to the constable, "I reckon you must be on your way. Duty calls, as they say."

"Duty don't call for near an hour," said Mr. Perkins, overmastering a wry smile. "But as a constable I'm ever obliged to see stolen property returned to its rightful owner. You wouldn't be trying to be rid of me, now would you, Jimmie B.?"

"Oh no, sir," said Bunkins, all offended innocence. "How could you think such?"

Thus together did we three go round about to Bedford Street. Though I had asked no questions of Bunkins, I had a good notion of who it was in Bedford Street might be wearing my good coat. And all that the greengrocer had told me of the thief supported my present suspicions.

When we reached our destination, Bunkins told us to wait as he entered the first dive we came to. The street was not near as filled as it soon would be; those leaving work for home tended to avoid it due to its bad repute. I noted that Mr. Perkins, keeping silent, was casually engaged in buttoning his coat; when he had done, the red waistcoat he wore (which marked him as one of the Bow Street Runners) was no longer visible. Bunkins emerged from the place, shaking his head, and we went on to the next, which advertised itself as a grog shop, and then on to the next, a tavern so-called. It was not until we found ourselves waiting before the fifth of these low places that Mr. Perkins chose to speak.

"I'll stay well back from things," said he. "But I want you to remember what I taught you, and you'll be fine."

I, who had grown more tense as we had moved from one dive to the next, took heart from what Mr. Perkins had said: I had been taught; I was ready.

Bunkins appeared at the door; he beckoned us inside.

Mr. Perkins held me back. He took his club and tucked it into my belt right at the small of my back.

"Don't use it unless you've a call to," said he to me.

And so we went inside. Mr. Perkins left me and went to stand at the bar. I went to Jimmie Bunkins, who had reentered the place. He said nothing but simply pointed. It was near as dark as it was outside in the first hour of night. An oil lantern burned at the bar, a fire blazed in the fireplace, and there were candles alit at the few tables where drinkers sat. Thus, with so little illumination, it was not altogether easy to locate him I sought. As it happened, I heard him—that silly, whinnying giggle—ere my eyes had penetrated the gloom to the rear of the room. For yes, there he was, sitting at a table with four of his fellows—Jackie Carver.

I could not make out at such a distance, and in poor light, if the coat he wore was mine, and so I moved towards him, threading a path through the tables. Bunkins followed. As I approached, Carver saw me, recognized me, and left off his chatter. By the time I reached his table, I had seen the coat well: bottle green it was, with white trim, and unmistakably my own. All eyes at the table were upon me as I took my place close before him and waited.

"What do *you* want?" asked he, with a most theatrical sneer.

"My coat," said I.

"Your coat?" He laughed his little giggle. "This here's a *man's* coat. Last time I saw you, you was wearin' women's duds, makin' out you was a bawd. You got no right to wear a *man's* coat."

This caused hilarity among his table-mates. While he sat smirking, the rest fell into great guffaws; one of them, a villainous-looking fellow of about thirty, pounded the table with glee. All the rest in the place had fallen silent. The barkeep moved towards us.

I waited until the laughter had subsided. "Nevertheless, I want it."

"Well, you'll not have it." He stared hatefully up at me from his place at the end of the oblong table.

And then, to break the contact with his eyes, I reached my right hand before him and snapped my fingers. His eyes shifted involuntarily to them, as I knew they would. And in one swift, planned movement, I grabbed his ear with my left hand, twisted it, and pulled up. He had no choice but to rise, or have his ear torn off. When he was halfway to his feet, I gave a great push to his head and released my grip. He fell back in a clutter against the chair and the wall but managed to keep upright. The others at the table were too shocked by this event to do more than look wide-eyed from him to me. Then did he reach behind him as if to draw his knife, yet allowed his hand to remain there as a threat.

"You know who I am?" he shouted. "What I can do to you?"

It seemed to me I had heard that before. "Yes," I shouted back, "you call yourself Jackie Carver, and you are a pimp and a fraud and a back-stabber, and you would rather face the Devil himself than any mortal man in a proper fight."

"*Take it outside!*"

It was the barkeep. He leaned forward over the bar, a pistol in each hand. Though he had not cocked them, it was plain from his face he was willing to shoot.

"Come along," I called, then I turned, brushed past Bunkins, and headed for the door.

There was a general scramble for the outside. The dive emptied of drinkers who were eager to be audience to the fracas. Yet space was given me as one of the principals, and I emerged into the evening, feeling Bunkins pummeling my back.

"Oh, you called him out proper, chum," he crowed. "I never seen it done better."

"But where can we go?"

"Over here—the alley."

Bunkins took me by the elbow and led me to the very alley wherein the body of Poll Tarkin was discovered. We led the crowd. I heard mutterings of wagers placed, odds given. It seemed that in spite of a creditable performance inside the dive, I was not much favored.

I took a position well inside the alley and waited as the crowd poured in, taking up the space round me. After taking my old coat from me, Bunkins made a circle of the group, pushing them back.

"Give them room—back, back—give them room," he chanted.

At last my opponent arrived, accompanied by his four seconds. They chortled, and talked encouragingly to him of the great blood-letting that was soon to follow. For his part, he seemed more somber here than in the gin shop; he nodded, accepting their heartening words, yet he did not smirk nor smile, and neither did he giggle. I reached back to Mr. Perkins's club to make sure that it was tight enough in my belt to stay in place yet loose enough to be available when it was needed. Satisfied, I advanced to show that I was ready.

He shed his coat—*my* coat—and muttered something to his fellows. Then, in one final bit of bravado, he shouted to the crowd: "Be it known to all, this ain't about no toggy. It's about a moll, one of my bawds he wanted for his own self. She wanted no part of him. She—"

Through this declamation, as he looked left and right to his audience, I had continued my advance upon him. Too late he realized how close to him I had come, and as he broke off his speechifying, he barely had time to raise his arms in his own defense, much less grab behind him for his knife.

I covered the three paces between us in two leaping bounds and delivered two blows to his face, one each with my left and right fist, then did I give him a stout kick in the kneecap. He collapsed, falling down upon the other knee.

Then did I what I should not have done. I stepped back, allowing him to recover himself. This was partly to give me opportunity to bring feeling back into my fingers, for toughened though my hands were by so many days of work upon the bag in the stable yard, they were not prepared to meet the bones of his face. Henceforward I would hit in the soft areas of the—

His knife was out. He made a slashing arc at my middle. He had a quick hand, and indeed would have cut me but for the leap back I took. Then was he up, knife in hand, lunging at me, and I could do naught but keep moving backwards. I had no chance to pull loose the club from my belt, for both hands were needed for balance.

The crowd seemed especially to enjoy this. I heard *oohs* and *ahhs* with each lunge he took, for with each they anticipated a stain of crimson. This was what they had come to see.

But then did I do me a little dance, feinting left and leaping right, away from the blade. He followed the feint and quite passed me by, yet before he did, I caught him with a kick in his hip which threw him off balance; he staggered clumsily to regain it.

This gave me the chance I needed to withdraw the club from my belt. I held it in my right hand and slapped my left palm with it. The sharp pang that I felt brought new confidence to me. I had drilled with it often.

He had driven me back with a series of lunges. Would he continue? Or would he come to me and slash, as he had first done? I must be prepared for either attack.

He lunged.

I lept right again, away from the blade, but he seemed to be prepared for this, for he pivoted in my direction and might have done me harm, had I not, as I lept, hit him hard across the ear with the club. I ducked behind him and delivered another blow to the crown of his head.

He turned to me, throwing out his blade in a wide slash. Yet I had anticipated it, was waiting for it even, and was out of range when the knife swept past, and when it had, I stepped forward and brought down the club on the hand that held it. It dropped from his grasp. He made a desperate dive to recover it. I clouted him again on the head and thought surely I had knocked him senseless. Yet as I dug at the knife with my foot and sent it skittering over the pavement, away from us both, he managed somehow to struggle to his feet.

Standing there, panting, sweating drops of gin, bleeding from his ear and scalp, he seemed little of a threat, yet I knew I must finish him. I tucked the club into my belt and beckoned him to me. He came lumbering forward, his hands extended as if he meant to throttle me, which no doubt he would have done had I given him the chance.

What followed could not have been good to watch. Yet memory of Mariah loosed a fury in me that powered the flurry of kicks and punches I gave to his vertical yet inert form. Finally, with him leaning upon me for support I delivered a butt to his head with my own. I stepped away, and he fell flat upon the bricks of the alley.

I waited. He did not move. I walked backwards, unwilling to turn my back upon him until I was a safe distance away. As I went, I glanced left and right at the crowd and saw money changing hands. For the most part they were silent, whether from boredom now that their amusement was ended, or disappointment at its outcome, I could not tell. I found the four I sought, muttering amongst themselves.

"I'll have that coat, if you please." I pulled out Mr. Perkins's club and slapped my palm.

The ugliest of Jackie Carver's table companions—and none was a beauty—held on still to my bottle-green coat. He threw it to me, shaking his head in disgust. Then did all four turn and walk away, leaving their champion where he lay.

"Here! Here! What is this disturbance has taken place here?"

It was Mr. Perkins, coat unbuttoned, red waistcoat revealed, presenting himself as a constable just now come upon the scene. He went straight to me.

"Was you part of this?" he asked, in a manner most severe. "I'll just take that weapon you have there in your hand, young sir."

I handed it over without argument. (It was, after all, his own.) He took me by the arm and led me by an indirect route to Jackie Carver. On the way, he made a "discovery."

"Why, what have we here? A knife?" He bent and scooped it up from the pavement. "Was you usin' this on that poor fella lyin' there?"

Before there was need for me to raise my voice in my own defense, three of the onlookers came forward to put things right.

"No, Constable, that ain't how it was."

" 'Twas the other fella had the knife. He's known for it."

"The lad didn't use the club till the knife came out."

"Well," said Mr. Perkins, walking to the form lying upon the bricks, "even so, he's done considerable damage to this one."

Carver, thank God, had begun to stir. My three defenders trailed along for a closer look at him. Mr. Perkins knelt down, supposedly to examine his wounds, yet at the same time he seemed to be whispering in the unbloodied ear.

Of a sudden, Bunkins appeared beside me. "You've made me a wealthy man, Jeremy old chum," said he. "The odds was against you, and I bet all I had in my pocket and a bit more."

"Didn't hedge your bets?"

He regarded me in consternation. "I would never do such!"

"I know you would not." I smiled and gave him a reassuring wink. And as I did so, it occurred to me that if indeed I could now smile, then this ordeal must surely have ended.

"Why, dear me," cried Mr. Perkins for all to hear, "all this while I have had my foot upon this poor fella's right hand. I may have done him further harm."

All the same, he did not remove his foot until he had risen and put the full weight of his body upon it. Carver was now attempting to rise, pushing up on his elbows. The others looked on, more in curiosity than concern.

"Here, you three. Help him to his feet. I charge you to take him to a surgeon to look to his wounds. There is a medico round the way on Tavistock Street, Donnelly by name."

The three leaped to obey the constable's order. Another came to join them. They managed to get him upright.

"And you, young sir," said Mr. Perkins, taking me roughly by the arm, "I'm takin' you straight to Bow Street. And I warn you that if you resist, you will regret it!"

I hung my head and, needless to say, offered no resistance.

Our mood, as we left them, was one of suppressed jubilance. As soon as we were out of sight and earshot, Bunkins let out a great howl of triumph. And Mr. Perkins allowed himself at last to smile.

"I thought I upheld the honor of the Bow Street Runners quite proper. Would you say so, lads? Can't have them thinkin' we approve of alley-fightin'."

We assured him he had played his part well. And as Bunkins crowed over his winnings, Mr. Perkins asked to be certain I had not been cut. He assured me that had I been, he would have stopped the combat immediate. Then did he launch into a critique of my performance.

"Now, your only mistake," said he, "was backin' off after you'd sent him down with that kick at his knee."

"But the way he dodged the blade—" put in Bunkins.

"Was dangerous and right frightening to watch," said Mr. Perkins gruffly.

And so it went until, approaching Bow Street by way of Great Hart, we parted with Bunkins who declared he must hurry home to count his riches. Mr. Perkins and I walked along in silence for a bit. But he halted me quite sudden and looked me over critically.

"Well," said he, "you've sweat that's dried on you, and a dirty face, and hair that needs combin', but you come out of it well, Jeremy. And I do say that's a handsome coat you got on, quite worth fightin' for."

I thanked him, then added: "That's one thing that Carver spoke true. The fight wasn't about the coat—or it was only partly so."

"I had a notion of that."

And then we resumed our walk.

"Tell me, Mr. Perkins," said I, "when you bent down to look at him, you seemed to be whispering in Carver's ear. What did you say?"

"Oh yes, that. I did indeed give him a message. I told him that if he had any ideas about getting back at you, he was to forget them. If harm came to you, I would search him out and kill him deader and swifter than any crap merchant could do him. I asked him did he understand, and he gave out a moan, which I took to mean yes."

Nothing more was said between us until we were about to enter Number 4 Bow Street. Then did he urge me to wash up a bit and comb my hair before I went upstairs.

"There will be no charges then?" I asked with an impudent grin.

"No charges," said he.

There were comings and goings in the next few days, and a couple of them did seem most mysterious. One that did not was the return of the woman who did our wash. Proudly she presented the shirt and breeches I had worn to go wading in the Fleet River. Somehow, by washing them thrice and hanging them to dry on three rare November days of sunshine, she had got them clean. More important still, she had got the stink out of them. I was ever so grateful to her, so much that I rewarded her with two shillings from the great store of money that Bunkins had passed on to me. (His conscience would not allow him to keep all to himself what he had won from my efforts, and so he divided his winnings and gave half to me.) The good woman was quite overcome by my generosity. So long as I used this heap of shillings for such purposes, I had no need to feel guilt that I had accepted them. Or so it seemed to me.

More curious was an unexplained visit from the Millhouse family. Thaddeus, Lucinda, and little Edward entered one Sunday morning dressed in their best. I met them just as I was leaving on a trip to the postbox to send off letters for Lady Fielding. Greeting them, I found all, even little Edward, to be most solemn in demeanor. No doubt they had been summoned, though I had carried no letter to them, and it was evidently a matter of some importance. Since my errand took me all the way to the coach yard, I was surprised to glimpse the Millhouse family in Covent Garden on my return—surprised not so much to see them as to note the remarkable change in their attitude. Even at a distance—for I viewed them across the wide though near-empty piazza—I could tell by the smiles on their faces and the happy way they chattered that their visit to Sir John had cheered them greatly. Perhaps, I thought, he had forgiven altogether the fine for drunkenness he had imposed upon Thaddeus Millhouse. It would be in Sir John's nature to do so.

Next day—or evening it was, for we had just finished dinner—Mr. Gabriel Donnelly paid us a visit. He had not his bag with him, nor were any of us in ill health, so this could not have been a professional visit. Indeed the only reason I could think of was that he had called to say his final farewell. Yet there was no hint of that when he entered. There was no time for speeches, no occasion for tears, for Sir John arose from the table and led him up to the little room he called his study. We below in the kitchen heard the door close behind them and thereafter the rumble of Sir John's deep voice—even once the sound of Mr. Donnelly's laughter.

He did not stay long, less than half an hour I should judge, and when he returned, he was alone; Sir John had remained above. I looked up from the pot I was washing to see a broad smile upon his face. Surely no goodbye had been said.

"You'll not be leaving *soon* for Portsmouth, will you, sir?" I ventured.

"No, Jeremy, you'll not be getting rid of me quite so easily. No indeed!" And with that he laughed again and danced out the door.

Annie, who had been told of his imminent departure, looked at me with a question in her eyes—one I could not answer. Unable to do more, I simply shrugged; she returned the gesture.

So here was I with two mysteries to be solved. Nor could I have been likely to solve them on my own, for there were no hints dropped, and no help offered from other sources. There was naught to do but wait until Sir John himself chose to offer some explanation. That he did two evenings later as we sat together at dinner. He had called for wine to be served, which was rare for an ordinary meal with just the four of us in the kitchen. It seemed likely to me that a toast was to be offered, as it soon was.

Before we had touched knife and fork to plate, he stood up from his chair and raised his glass high.

"My dear family," said he, generously including Annie and me, "I give you the health of Mr. Gabriel Donnelly, for though he be absent from our table at this moment, we may look forward to his return to us many times in the future during what we anticipate to be his long and continued residence here in London."

Then did we three rise and drink his health together with Sir John, saving our questions till we be seated. Then came they in abundance: Had he been persuaded to stay? Had the Navy rejected him? Had he found him a patron? Why was he not present? Sir John raised his hand, stilling us, and launched into his explanation.

"No amount of persuasion on my part could have kept him here," said he, "for it was simple economic necessity which prompted him in his plan to return to the Navy, which, by the bye, would have taken him gladly, for I have learned he had a very distinguished record during his years of service. In a sense, yes, he has found a patron, as I shall make clear, since the announcement will be made tomorrow in Parliament.

"At last, by my continued urging, a new coroner has been chosen. He is Thomas Trezavant, a friend of the prime minister's and, between us, no better qualified than his predecessor, though considerably younger. Yet he makes no pretense at competence, and in a meeting with him and the Lord Chief Justice, I managed to convince both that what was needed was a medical advisor to the coroner, one whose opinions could be relied upon absolutely. Naturally I put forward Mr. Donnelly for that position. There was, I admit, some opposition to my nomination because he is Irish and, they rightly assumed, Popish. I countered with his excellent record in His Majesty's Navy and pointed out that his religion had been no impediment to him there. As for his reliability, I told them of his help to me in these terrible homicides that now, thank God, are behind us. I confessed to them that long before I was willing to recognize the possibility, he had urged me that they were the work of two murderers and not one; and he had done so on purely medical evidence. They asked to meet him. Yesterday that meeting was accomplished. Mr. Donnelly, whom we all know to be a fine fellow, presented himself very well in a most unassuming gentlemanly manner, and he was accepted by them. Since he has the prime minister's ear, Mr. Trezavant was able to persuade him to provide an annual stipend for the medical advisor—not much, to be sure, but sufficient to subsidize Mr. Donnelly's continued practice in this city. This official recognition is sure to bring him patients aplenty." He smiled broadly and gave a nod of affirmation. "But come let us eat. Our mutton will grow cold."

And so eat we did—and fine mutton chops they were, made finer still by the claret we drank with them. Yet one question remained in my mind.

"Sir John," I asked, "why is Mr. Donnelly not with us? Why must we toast him in absentia?"

"Ah, Jeremy, well you may ask. He dines this evening with his new master, Mr. Trezavant. It is, of course, a social and professional obligation. Mr. Donnelly sends his regrets and his promise to join us to celebrate the rise in his fortunes at any time in the future."

Having had one mystery solved, I was quite determined to get to the solution of the other. And so, after I had finished with the washing up, I made up my mind to approach Sir John and ask him direct. After all, had not Mr. Donnelly advised me to seek opportunities to speak with him? And perhaps if a discussion were opened, there might be a chance to talk to him of matters even more important to me. I knew indeed I would find him in that room above where he sat so often in the dark. It was to it that I went and tapped upon the open door.

"It is Jeremy, sir," said I. "Perhaps you might answer a question for me."

"I shall if I can, lad. Come in, sit down. Light a candle if you like."

I entered and sat opposite him, yet allowed us to remain in the dark. It was his element.

Then did I explain how I had seen the Millhouse family enter all solemn on Sunday last and later did spy them larking across Covent Garden as jolly as could be. What, I asked, had raised their spirits so?

"Ah," said he, "I blush that I had not told you before, since the matter concerns you. The truth is, Jeremy, I am somewhat obsessive by nature. I seem only to be able to think upon one matter at a time, and since Sunday Mr. Donnelly's appointment has occupied me fully. But as you rightly perceived, Mr. and Mrs. Millhouse have also had a rise in their fortunes. And it is you, Jeremy, who are responsible."

"I, sir? How is that?"

"It was you found Poll Tarkin's treasure, the proceeds of her career as a pickpocket and sneak thief. When at last I had had the burden of these Covent Garden murders lifted from me, my mind turned to that little family in Half Moon Passage—the father a drinker and prey to temptations of the flesh, them condemned to life in a single room with a baby of the bawling, squalling age. And it seemed to me they deserved something better. I learned, too, that his position with Mr. Hoole necessitated Mr. Millhouse to rise early each morn and walk clear to Clerkenwell, for it is there the work of translating Ariosto is done. To make it short, I saw there was every reason to get them out of this unhealthy environment and into something better, so I summoned them to appear Sunday last. Since they had missed a payment on the fine I had put on Mr. Millhouse, they may have thought I had brought them in to chastise them—hence, their solemn faces. When they heard that, on the contrary, I had decided to award them the bag of money which you had discovered 'neath the floor of Poll Tarkin's room, they were quite overjoyed. Though it was ill-gotten, I said, it could be put to good use by them. Yet I put a proviso upon how it was to be spent. I told them they were to move out of Covent Garden and into Clerkenwell, or near it, to a bigger and more comfortable location. And that Mr. Millhouse was not to take a single shilling of it to celebrate their good fortune. He took an oath that he would not, before his wife. I believe she held him to it, for they have found a place already and will move to it on Saturday. What say you to that, Jeremy?"

"Were it not that I might disturb Lady Fielding, I should give out a loud huzzah."

"I thought you would be pleased."

"How much was there in the bag?"

"Near forty guineas. I had Mr. Marsden count it out—guineas, sovereigns, and shillings—and that was roughly the amount."

"It will change their lives.'

"For the better, certainly."

I waited. Since no more was immediately said, I started to rise and take my leave.

"Stay," said he then. "Now that you are here, perhaps we should speak further." He hesitated, then: "Because of my obsessive state in the past weeks, we have had little opportunity to talk as we once did. I want you to know, first of all, that your help was appreciated in the matter of the homicides, more than appreciated. I still blame myself for putting you in danger in that charade by which the Raker was finally apprehended, yet you carried it through admirably and rightly deserved the reward you got. Though I said to you that your tramp through the sewer was 'brave and foolish,' it was far more brave than it was foolish. And I give you credit, too, Jeremy, you proved me wrong about Mr. Tolliver. You may not believe this, but ultimately I like being proven wrong from time to time.

"Mr. Donnelly told me of how you spent your reward money, some of it, and that, too, I thought admirable. I confess, however, that I was concerned that you may have had carnal relations with that poor girl. He assured me you had not. Is that the case?'

"I had none, Sir John."

"Good. The pox is rampant in London. You have seen in Amos Carr the possible result. You may see other examples in the streets—cripples and drooling idiots. It is a dreadful disease. Yet I find it altogether too easy to forget most of the time how it was with me when I was your age and a little older. The same desires burned within me, the same passion for adventure and risk-taking. If I had been less eager to take risks, I might have my eyesight today, it's true, yet I would not have had the life I have led; and on the whole, I think it a good one. Fate does ever present us with these queer trades. Yet on the whole, too, I think it good for you to consider potential dangers, Jeremy. Look before you leap."

Now I did suppose he was truly done. We had gone so far, however, that I thought it might be possible to go a bit further.

"Sir John?"

"Yes, lad, what is it?"

How to say this? "Well, sir, I wanted only to renew my intention to read the law with you, if that be also your wish."

"Have I forgotten your intention or my promise? Is that the question? No, though we have not discussed it for quite some time, I have not forgotten. You are just now a bit too young to begin. But it is a long process, I warn you, and a rather tedious one, too. Let us wait a bit, perhaps a year. Let us wait until you are sixteen. You may hold me to that."

As Christmas approached in that year of 1770, I was avid to buy gifts for all. Since I had all but two shillings left from that store given me by Jimmie Bunkins, I at last had the wherewithal to indulge my good wishes to all who were close to me. To Bunkins himself I gave a copy of *Robinson Crusoe,* which I was sure he would be able to read in the coming year; to Mr. Perkins, a chain for his timepiece; to Annie, a cameo on a silk ribbon; to Lady Fielding, a brush for her hair; and to Sir John, a new razor (I, who was needful of one, inherited his old one). In truth, I also spent two guineas of the reward.

Though I need not here give a list of all that I received in return on Christmas Day, I must mention that which I received from Sir John and Lady Fielding. It was a package presented me by my Lady, large in size and heavy in weight. As I unwrapped it in front of all, I had no idea what it might contain, nor could I have guessed, save for the fact that it had the general configuration of a great pile of books. And books it was—four in number, which comprised that great work by Sir Edward Coke, the great jurist of the previous century, *Institutes of the Law of England.*

Quite overcome, I thanked them both.

"What we have given you," said Sir John, "is a great lot of work, Jeremy. For my instruction to you is to read this work through, all four volumes. It is well written, and that should not prove such a task. But then I wish you to read it through a second time and take notes of all the questions which come to you. If you do a good job of it, two readings together should take a year. Then the real work will begin, for we shall then read it through together, discuss it, and answer all your questions. After that, we shall get on to other things. Reading the law is, as I warned, a long and tedious process—but ultimately beneficial."